The Harris Connec

Christie &

The truth, the whole truth and nothing but the truth – well, that depends on who you are asking.

The Harris Connection is a series of novels continuing on from each other, but from a different character's point of view.

In book 1, **Christie & Co**, we see the world through Christie's eyes. We discover how she juggles the changes in her life after her mother is revealed to be a world-famous actress. In the rollercoaster of events which follow, every truth she reveals is the truth.

Well, it's Christie's truth – and I believe her.

In book 2, **Maddie's Men**, we see the world through her mother's eyes, the fame, the fortune, the failures. As the secrets from her past tumble into the tabloids, once again, Maddie risks losing all she holds dear. Every truth she reveals is the truth.

Well, it's Maddie's truth – and I believe her too.

In book 3, **Trudy's Tryst**, we see the world through the eyes of one blessed with beauty, poise, status and wealth. Trudy's life spirals into a new realm of reality with the unexpected bonus of a roommate. Every truth she reveals is the truth.

Well, again, it's Trudy's truth – and, honestly, I believe her too.

About the Author

Kathleen Clunan was raised on a farm in Lancashire. Being the middle child of six gave her lots of freedom and opportunity for mischief making. Helping out on the farm, climbing trees, ditch dodging and hanging from zip lines were a big part of her childhood. Piano lessons – not so much!

But then she had to grow up. Kathleen played a major role in running the family business whilst bringing up her own family in the same farmhouse she's been raised in. After a significant brush with illness, she decided to pursue her real passion, writing. Her first book was published in 2019, *The Evolution of Christie Harris* (now re-released under the title: *Christie & Co*), and she had intended it to be a stand-alone novel. However, due to the popularity of the characters, she was inundated with requests to continue the story, which she did. *Maddie's Men* was published in 2023.

Kathleen is currently extending the characters further in her third novel, *Trudy's Tryst*, whilst still continuing to run the family business.

Follow her on Facebook

 Kathleen Clunan

www.KathleenClunan.com

The Harris Connection
Book 1

Christie
& Co

Kathleen
Clunan

Christie & Co
Kathleen Clunan

Published in the UK by Eagle Eye Books

Revision 1 2 3 <u>4</u> 5 6 7 8 9 26.08

Printed and bound by Cloc Books Print, UK

ISBN: 978-0-9931860-7-3
A CIP catalogue record for this title is available from the
British Library

Dedicated to my family.

Developments

- **Double Trouble**
- **Home Truths**
- **Monty Mitten Presents**
- **Evolution**
- **Brunch**
- **Key Critics**
- **Busted or Not**
- **Designated Driver**
- **Pottering Tuesday**
- **Happy Families**
- **Close Encounter**
- **Out of the Frying Pan**
- **Escape?**
- **Commando**
- **Reviews**
- **Fraya-Froo**
- **Meet and Greet**
- **Not a Date**
- **Paint Away the Heartache**
- **Glow White Knickers**
- **Pluck Required**
- **Tied Up**
- **Shifting Grains of Sand**
- **Flowers**
- **Shadows**
- **Compromised**
- **All for One**
- **Deadly Serious**
- **Dawn**

Double Trouble

'Five-inch heels here, remember.'

Trudy swings her magnificently-toned legs out of the car. Suzi dutifully follows, though not quite so elegantly.

I stride off in the direction of *The Rose and Crown*. I want to get away from here pronto. I glance back at Trudy tottering behind me.

She points down towards her beautifully painted toenails. 'Five-inch heels here, remember.'

'Sorry, Trudy.' I nod towards Suzi in her combats and *Doc Martins* combo. 'Suzi is dressed for the challenge.'

'Yeah, yeah, dressed for a challenge, or just dressed challengingly.'

'Excuse me! I am here, you know. And we're only going for a chillout drink.'

'And this, girls, is why I aways dress the part,' stage whispers Trudy, almost levelling up to me. 'You never know when you're going to come across gorgeous scenery like that.' She nods to the right.

I let my eyes drift, and they instantly lock with those of mystery-man Miles. I was hoping I'd bump into him again. But not now! I should have parked at the pub instead of near Mum and Dad's new house! Heat sears through my body. A tell-tale prickle of a blush rises up from my chest. Please, please don't speak to me, just get in your car and drive away. Fast. Go on. Scram.

Yet again, my telepathy isn't working. Here he comes, wearing his hello smile. A quiver of anticipation shoots through me.

The thought of frivolous banter with Miles in front of these two is the last thing I need. Now, really? Come on! I try my best glare, purse my lips and shake my head slightly.

Nothing!

He's still sauntering towards us, oblivious! I put my head down as he draws closer. Risking a glance up I note his look of confusion. Not surprising, I usually act mildly interested.

His step slows.

Mine speeds.

He skilfully intercepts me by stepping between me and my friends. 'Well, hello.'

'Shh. Not now!' I hiss under my breath. 'Pretend you don't know me!'

He frowns momentarily. 'Thought you'd be popping in to see your parents tonight, so—'

'I'm going!' I hiss. 'Shh.'

Miles turns slightly as Trudy totters towards us. 'Good evening, ladies,' he says, eyes alight with mischief.

I close my eyes while my stomach does its usual flip.

Trudy angles her shoulder in front of mine and thrusts one hip forward, thus giving Miles the full benefit of her minimal outfit. 'Just got better for me,' she oozes, brazenly looking him up and down. 'Didn't know country boys look so fine.'

Miles laughs. 'They don't, I'm only visiting.'

Dragging my bottom lip between my teeth an involuntary groan escapes. I look directly into his eyes.

His easy smile has been replaced by a wolfish grin. I'm conscious every part of my body is fizzing with desire.

'What a coincidence, so are we.' Trudy eyes him like a lioness about to devour her prey. 'You do know you're going in the wrong direction, the pub is this way.' She points a well-manicured finger in the general direction we're heading.

'Bit pushed for time tonight, need to get back home.' He doesn't take his eyes off me.

Trudy angles her chin up and wags her finger playfully. 'You, have just missed a once in a lifetime opportunity. Come on, ladies, prosecco awaits.'

And we're off, without a backwards glance, but I know Miles has turned around to watch us. I can feel the heat of his eyes on me.

'Another time, perhaps.' he calls out.

I can hear the laughter in his tone. Honestly, I could just die!

Suzi starts her tutting. 'I wish you wouldn't do that, Trudy. It's really embarrassing.'

'How many times, Suzi? When an opportunity presents itself, go for it, especially when it looks like that!'

Suzi shakes her head. 'He could have been married!'

'Well, it won't last if he is. I'm sure even you noticed the way he was looking at Christie.'

'Leave me out of it, I just want to get to the pub.' I can feel my cheeks burning.

'I was only trying to do you a favour. Turning beetroot and muttering under your breath is no way to grab a guy. It must be months since your last date, and I can guess why.'

Six months, and I'm certain Nigel will get over it. 'I've given up on men. Thanks for reminding me.' Not entirely true.

Trudy sighs dramatically. 'When you fall off a horse, the best thing to do is get right back in the saddle.'

'Well, I'm sick of being bucked off! And let's be honest, Trudy, I'm not likely to get a look in, with all you've got to offer on display!'

'Whatevs.' Trudy flicks her hair over her shoulder, and juts her chin up. 'Nothing wrong with having a bit of fun!'

Suzi shrugs. 'Christie has all this upset over her mum and dad, the last thing she needs is a man in the mix. Any news?'

I shake my head. My parents did a moonlight flit after Dad jacked his job. The village is abuzz with speculation as to why and where.

Suzi tucks her hair behind her ears, the slight crinkling of her brow and tilt of her head, complete her concerned look. 'He could have cast off his cassock and cardigan, then started a mad passionate fling with one of the Women's Institute.'

'Suzi!' I scowl. 'This is my dad you're talking about, remember, the one who wears socks with his sandals.'

Trudy grins. 'And be honest, would any man in their right mind? They're not known as "The Little Upton Mafia" for nothing!'

'True. How about a midlife crisis?' offers Suzi.

'Give it a rest. I'm sure the Rev and Mrs H will turn up soon.'

I stride ahead as my two, so-called supportive friends continue chortling about the latest scandal to hit the village. Okay, so Dad's created a bit of a stir.

Nobody, least of all me, expected him to up and leave. I mean, abandoning his flock, it's just not the thing for a vicar to do. But I've had this ongoing interrogation for a week now.

A whole week! Suzi's like a kitty with catnip.

'And nobody knows where he's gone. Christie, your mum and dad could be anywhere. Anywhere! And my mum is beside herself.'

Trudy smiles. 'Your mum knows everyone's business before it even happens.'

'Well, she does usually know what's going on.'

'Slow down! Where is this pub? We must have been walking for ten minutes. These shoes, are not made for trekking down country lanes!'

I turn as Trudy stops and looks down at her Jimmy Choo's. 'Seriously, Christie, I should have worn *Doc's* like Suzi.'

'Not with that excuse for a skirt,' I say. 'Anyway, it's just round the next corner, and the thing is, it's only going to be the two of you, I'll pick you up later.'

'Really?' drawls Trudy. 'Planning on kidnapping that hunk after all?'

'Err, no, Trudy! Actually, I'm going back to Mum and Dad's. I parked outside their new home!'

'Nooo!' splutters Suzi. 'That big house! So… so, you know who that bloke is!'

'Ish.'

Suzi scowls. 'No wonder you went a funny colour. Well, come on, details.'

'I've only met him a few times.' And my heart nearly bounded out of my chest every time, not that I'll admit it to these two yet. He has the kind of face I could gaze at for hours. And his body, well. There are only so many times you can get away with being a born-again virgin, even if you are a vicar's daughter. Obviously, I'm not going to let Trudy linger anywhere near, she who has the attributes of a goddess.

Suzi looks ready to stamp her feet. 'And you've known where your parents have been all along!'

'Well, of course, I have. It's only actually five miles away from the bothered busybodies in Little Upton, but feels like a world away.'

'Very true, and nicely done.' Trudy smiles. 'And look, isn't that quaint?'

The Rose and Crown nestles between two giant oaks, hazy evening sunlight bathes the courtyard as patrons relax. A shriek of laughter rises above the low hum of conversation drifting on the breeze.

Trudy turns to look at me. 'Children. You know I don't do children, especially at the weekend. This is supposed to be a civilised grown-up weekend, just the three of us, chilling out. Remember, civilised? We've got that art exhibition in a couple of days, the one your Auntie Maddie sent us the tickets for?'

'Yes, yes, I remember. And sorry about the children, but it's the nearest pub. I might need rescuing later.'

'What's going on then?' asks Suzi, eyes wide, eager for any drama.

I sigh. 'I don't know, but Dad asked me to come round for a chat, could be anything.' I catch my bottom lip between my teeth. The thought of either of them being ill... 'Whatever it is, Suzi, you'll be the first to know.'

Suzi flushes. 'I didn't mean—'

'I know. It's probably nothing.'

Trudy examines her talons. 'Right then, come on, Suzi. You find a quiet table away from the brats, and

I'll get the drinks in.' She gives me a half salute over her shoulder as she stalks off, her caramelised body inviting the usual attention. 'See you later. Good luck.'

Suzi turns to me, and catches my hand. 'Just have a quick one, you look like you need it, after the week you've had.'

'I'm driving, remember, seeing as your car needs a new thingy what's it, again!'

'Yeah, sorry about that, can't help my car being poorly. I'm having a bloke round to look at it tomorrow. Come on, just have a coke.' Suzi pouts, and makes her puppy-dog eyes.

'Okay, one condition.'

'Anything.'

'Don't go on about Mum and Dad.'

Suzi links her arm through mine. 'Okay, you've got a deal.'

At the bar, Trudy adds my coke to her order, then follows us out into the beer garden. 'Did Suzi twist your arm then?'

'She simply pointed out I've had a stressful week, and need a chillax.'

'Mine's not been much better.' Trudy brushes an imaginary speck of dust from her fingernail. 'One of the prehistoric rottweilers in accounts has been questioning my expenses. Apparently, prosecco isn't VAT deductible. Honestly! I was entertaining a potential client—'

'Good-looking?' I ask.

'Incredibly.' Trudy nods.

Suzi smirks. 'Rich?'

'Rolex says yes!' Trudy grins. 'Ha-ha... making a follow up next week.' Her eyes sparkle with mischief.

I shake my head. 'Only you can get away with charging a date to expenses. My only perk is my two-week half-term—'

'Ha!' barks Trudy. 'Knowing you, you'll be waffling on about how you're missing the brats by Tuesday, followed by ten days of prep for when you get back.'

Suzi pouts. 'All I've got to look forward to, is stool samples and swabs. Christie does get to influence all those young minds.'

'Yep, and I've got some very talented kids in my classes.'

'Okay, class, remember our first day.' I hold up a stick-man picture. 'Dexter's first attempt at impressing me.' I show the class Dexter's latest work, an intricate sketch of five bodies entwined on a sofa. 'Now, Dexter, this does impress… Not just me, look around the class… This level of detail allows each of us to connect with those tangled souls. Each face and body oozes individual personality, yet combined, they are family. A united collective. Well done, Dexter.'

'Thank you, Miss.'

The classroom fills with the sound of hands drumming on desks. Faces split by grinning mouths; eyes lit by the glow of achievement. I give them a moment to savour the feeling. They've earned it. We've earned it.

'Remember your hard work. Remember your failures and your successes, you can learn from both. But, mostly, remember the only limitations you have, are the ones you impose on yourselves.' I present both the pictures. 'Your choices are your future. Class dismissed.'

I place the two pieces of artwork back on my desk. Catch the high fives and fist bumps as the class file out of the room. From the corner of my eye, I spot Mr Sloan hovering in the doorway.

I finish my coke. 'I'm going to have to get going now, Suzi. Mum and Dad are going to think I'm not coming. And please, try and rescue that poor bloke from Trudy. He looks terrified.'

'Will do. See you later.'

I leave my friends and make my way back down the lane. Trudy's right, these are not lanes for Jimmy Choo's. The road gives way to lush grass verges, flanked by hawthorn hedges. The fields beyond, are green with neat rows of shoots, well on their way to providing a bumper harvest. From somewhere in the distance, I can hear the bleating of lambs. Perfect.

I'm sure Dad knows what chaos and rumour he's left behind.

In Little Upton, you can only actually be classed as a local in the village, if you are a third-generation resident. The exception to this rule, is if you are the local vicar, and have been for more than twenty years. Lucky for Dad, he's done twenty-three. Mum and I are therefore locals by default.

I'm not sure how deserters are punished.

Home Truths

Rolling down Buttercup Hill.

Well, their new house is like something out of *Hello* but without the fabulous celebrities. Every time I look at it, I get the urge to sketch.

Nobody could ever accuse my parents of being anything like stylish, yet here they are, living in the desirably chic village of Clover Beck. And honestly, this house and grounds are amazing. Eight tall elegant windows frame a huge solid oak door, and a portico adds grandeur to the already substantial Georgian house. The ageing red bricks add character, the clinging wisteria romance, and the symmetry assures confidence. The gardens boast generations of maturity, evidence of elaborate planning and years of meticulous tending.

If I didn't know better, I really would put it down to a lottery win. Whatever is going on, I think I'm about to find out. Taking a deep, steadying breath, I knock at the door and wait.

'Come in, don't loiter on the doorstep like a stranger.' Dad half drags me into the hallway, and envelops me in his usual bear hug. For a moment I relish his unique smell of shaving cream, fabric conditioner and Dad.

'Hi, Dad,' I muffle into his worn pullover. 'I was half expecting a butler to open the door!'

'Honestly, Christie, what are you talking about? It's our home, just walk in.'

'Okay, I will in future. It still feels a bit odd.'

'I'm sure you'll get used to it. Mum's in the sitting room.'

Sitting room!

I follow Dad into the beautifully decorated room. Propped up on the marble mantlepiece is a framed ink-sketch I did of them in my final year at uni.

'Really, Dad? Come on, this room's too elegant for any of my work.'

'Christie, we love it. Everyone who's seen it, loves it. And we are very proud of you, so, it's going up—'

'When your father remembers where he's hid the spirit level. Hello, Christie.' Mum gets up and gives me a little squeeze. 'I'll go and put the kettle on before we start.'

Dad sits down. 'How's school? Those pesky Year 7 children still trying to get under your skin?'

'Nope, they've settled down since spring half-term. Mr Sloan is being his usual self, trying to undermine me at every opportunity.'

'Then don't give him the opportunity.'

'I knew you'd say that.'

'And need I ask, how's your painting going?'

I smile, Dad knows I spend every spare minute up in the attic, painting, sketching or daydreaming. My own private world, away from the demands of teaching and reality. Suzi and Trudy are usually very understanding about me prowling about in the middle of the night. Though Suzi has an irritating habit of snooping round my makeshift studio... She calls it cleaning. I've started setting boobytraps as a deterrent.

'It's going well, I've just sent another to Auntie Maddie. I've called it *The Long Farewell*. It's how I last remember seeing her, all smartly dressed with a flowing red scarf. I hope she likes it, but I know as soon as she gets it, she'll be after the next!'

'Keeps you focused. Remind me, Christie, what's her motto?'

'Again, Dad? You ask me every time! "Effort and achievement go hand in hand".'

'So, it does.' He chuckles to himself, and years of chuckling, crinkles round his eyes.

'Anyway, Dad, get you, it's all a bit mysterious. First the three-minute retirement, and now "We've something you need to know".' I try to impersonate his gruff voice. 'So, what's it all about?'

His eyes lose their chuckle. 'I'll go and give your mother a hand in the kitchen.'

I try brushing aside another slither of worry.

And fail.

The house is beautiful, more beautiful than the rambling old rectory at Little Upton. I'm going to miss the old place, so many of my memories are entwined with the house and village. I suppose Mum and Dad are ready for some peace and quiet, after the demands of running a rural parish church. Everyone assumes it's quaint and cosy. Believe me, it's anything but. The Flower Ladies are as subtle as secateurs.

Mum brings in the tea tray, and Dad follows behind with a plate of evenly sliced Battenberg. They set them down on the table, and sit down together on the sofa opposite me. Always together, in everything. I resist the urge to roll my eyes.

'You're in your usual cup,' says Mum.

'Thanks.' I pick it up, it always makes me smile. "I'm a teacher, what's your superpower?" it asks. I take a sip of the familiar, sweet brew. I'm aware that neither of them has taken their eyes off me. I place the cup back down.

The last time they sat me down like this, was after I accidentally set the church on fire. It *was* an accident, and I *was* only six. Back then, all Dad said, after giving me a long hard look was, "Christie, we could have lost you". Mum had hugged me, and I cried. I didn't know why I cried, I just did, for what seemed like ages. Then I went to bed, and they never mentioned it again.

'So...' I swallow the lump down in my throat. 'What's going on?'

Dad steeples his fingers. 'There is something we need to tell you.' He draws his words out slowly. 'But before we do, we want you to know...' He looks at Mum, who pulls a hankie from up her sleeve. 'We want you to know, that you will always be our little Christie, and we love you very much. We couldn't love you more.'

Okay, here we go, I'm probably going to get a lecture on concentrating on my career, and stop pandering to Auntie Maddie's demands for more sketches and paintings. Or maybe I should reconsider dating Nigel again, "A polite young man with a ready smile and a healthy career ahead of him", Mum often said. Sadly, he's about as exciting as a Pot Noodle in the middle of a heatwave. Or, it could be because I keep moaning about Mr Sloan, because apart from him, my job is perfect. Whatever it is, it surely can't be that bad.

'As you know, your mother and I were married very young, we couldn't wait.'

So now I roll my eyes.

'As a curate, I was moved about rather a lot. Your mother was happy to follow me. Most of my postings were inner city parishes, and I became passionate about working with what were commonly referred to, as "down-and-outs". Eventually we got our own parish.'

'Dad, I already know all this.' They've told me the stories over and over again.

'Just listen, please,' says Mum.

'We set up help and self-help groups, and community-commitment programmes, and mother and toddler hubs, and all sorts of things. The response was almost unbelievable. The Bishop earmarked other struggling parishes. I became a sort of troubleshooting vicar, which was all very well, but it meant we moved about such a lot.'

Mum tilts her head to one side. 'We did a terrible thing, Christie.'

'Come on Mum, you're scaring me. You two are practically saints.'

'No.' Dad shakes his head, his voice is hushed, measured. 'You're wrong, just listen.'

'We had a daughter…' says Mum, her eyes heavy with unshed tears.

'I have a sister?'

'Hush, just listen, please.' Dad rests his hand on top of Mum's hand. She closes her eyes, tears escape, tracing paths down her cheeks, Dad brushes them away with his thumbs. Such a simple thing, but so intimate I have to look away.

I try swallowing back my own tears, as my throat tightens. I'm back to being six-years-old, needing to cry and not fully knowing why.

'We had a daughter.' Dad clears the frog from his throat. 'And she was beautiful and clever and she always had a smile on her face. One of those rare gems, who infect everyone with joy, by simply being who they are. She used to say the funniest things, she was the perfect daughter, just like you. You're so alike, in very many ways. When she was younger, she just followed us round. The moving about didn't seem to bother her, she made friends wherever we went, with anyone.'

'So, I do have a sister… Right?' I look from one, to the other of them. My mouth is dry, my heart pounding, and I'm in a haze. How could they keep her from me? I've never even seen a photo. She must be dead! An accident? What did they do that was so terrible? I look at my parents through eyes that no longer know them, not sure I want to hear what they have to say. 'Just tell me!'

Dad shakes his head. 'Just listen. Not only was she moved from school to school, and new house to new house, but she was exposed to the most desperate of people. We always ran an open house policy. Anyone who had a problem could just turn up, eat with us, join our family. We were too busy being Good Samaritans, we forgot that our family, was her family too. More importantly, she was our child. We let her sit with alcoholics, drug addicts, prostitutes, the desperate and those who had no shame. You name it. We exposed our lovely girl, to the most appalling, and potentially volatile situations, and expected her to smile through them… And she did…'

Mum nods. 'She always did.'

'I am ashamed…' Dad's voice is thick with emotion. '… Ashamed of what we put her through. We shouldn't have been surprised, when we had a full-on rebellion on our hands. She joined the ranks of troubled souls we left our door open for, except we saw more of them, than we did of her. How could we blame her? She'd seen the love and support we gave to others, and she'd been left with the scraps of our time and energy.'

'We are all equal in God's sight; I think she was testing the theory,' says Mum.

'We are all equal, but—'

'No.' Mum shakes her head. 'There is no but. We try our best, we do our best, and when we fail, hopefully we are wise enough to learn from our mistakes. We reap what we sow.'

'She pushed and pushed us, almost to breaking point. She needed to know if the unconditional love we preached, was true.'

'Your dad had been approached, short listed for a new appointment. It would have fast tracked him to become a bishop.'

Dad tuts and shakes his head. 'It doesn't matter about that... She was out all night, sometimes missing for days on end, doing God only knows what. We had nobody to turn to. The two of us who'd thought we were the answer to everyone's prayers, found ourselves in need of rescuing. All we could do was pray for a miracle.'

Mum's face looks haunted. 'Sometimes we don't recognise them, miracles. But they are miracles, life changing, and made just for us. It's only when we look back at the full picture, can we see all the different elements coming together.'

Dad sighs. 'One night she came in, chin in the air, hands on hips, and announced she was pregnant...

Despite her defiant stance, she was just a frightened kid, needing help. I just looked at your mother, saw the grief in her eyes, and knew that she was seeing all the possibilities for our little girl to get a good start in life, vanish. No matter what people say, once you have a baby, your choices have to be made around them. We wanted her to realise this baby was another life, not some point to score against us. We'd heard she'd been seeing a lad who'd been part of one of our programmes. He'd always seemed a bit of a loner, whether it was him…' Dad shrugs. 'We did try and talk to her about who she was involved with, she wouldn't tell. And we were very conscious of not wanting her to run away again, to push too hard.'

I swallow back the tears, do the maths. I look from one to another, these people I call Mum and Dad. I can see the hurt in their eyes.

They lost their daughter, but got me. It must have broken their hearts. 'I'm not your little girl, I'm hers, aren't I?'

Together they nod.

'What was her name?' The difficulty saying the words out loud, causes a spasm of grief to twist in my gut. Grief for a mother I lost before I knew her. I draw a sharp breath and hold it, as if I can make time stand still so they can't tell me what I already know.

'Madeline,' says Dad.

'I don't remember her at all.' Madeline, like Auntie Maddie. Must be a family name, so pretty. Madeline, it swirls through my brain like a multi-coloured cloud, touching every memory I have. I feel a tear uncurl down my face. I try to picture a younger looking version of Mum, maybe at the park twirling the roundabout for me, or pushing me on the swings. Or in jeans and a T-shirt, instead of the skirts and blouses Mum always wore. Rolling down Buttercup Hill with flowers in her hair, instead of striding purposefully down. Paddling in the brook at Fairy Meadow with me, instead of urging me to be careful. Climbing up trees to rescue me, instead of talking me down. Until ten minutes ago, I could never have even thought of imagining a better Mum, than the one I have.

Madeline, my mum.

Mum tilts her head; she looks so sad. 'It took a little baby called Christina Anne, to set her free.'

'I must have been very young when she died,' I rasp.

'Oh no!' gasps Mum, covering her mouth with her hand. 'No, Christie, Madeline isn't... No, she didn't die. She is very much alive!'

'So?' A brief burst of joy, is instantly swamped by a stab of realisation. This Madeline can't possibly love me, or she'd be here, now. 'Where is she? Where has she been for the last twenty-four years?' The taint of anger I hear in my voice, takes me by surprise.

'Christie, listen before you judge,' says Dad. He fixes me with serious eyes. Reluctantly, I nod. 'After you were born, we sat her down, just like we have with you, now. We asked her what she wanted to do. She was a frightened kid, honestly, only sixteen. She was beginning to understand how tough being a mum is. What the rest of her life was going to be like. She thought we wanted to have you adopted, but we promised her that would never happen. By that time of course, we'd realised God was giving us a second chance, with you, and with Madeline too.'

'Where is she?' I looked straight at Dad, demanding answers with my eyes.

'We'll get to that soon enough... More than anything, Madeline wanted to go to drama school, become a famous actress, the whole fairy-tale dream. So, we came to an understanding, if she could get into drama school, we would take care of you while she was away in London. She went to quite a few auditions, and eventually a school accepted her.'

Dad covers his ashen face with his hand for a moment before continuing. 'Before she left, she made us promise no more urban parishes. She made us promise to find a village church, with lots of fields for you to explore. She made us promise to stay in one place, and give you the stability she'd missed out on. She wanted you to make friends, who would last a lifetime. She wanted you to belong, and to know you belonged. It hit home how much she had missed out... How she'd craved to belong somewhere.'

'She could have belonged to me!' I splutter.

Dad raises his eyebrows. 'We did as she asked, expecting her to come back home during holidays, and to be back permanently in a couple of years. We thought she'd be older and wiser, and with our support, ready to take on the responsibility of being a mum to you. Maybe go to college and university, she could still catch up. Most of all, we wanted to give her time to grow up. But as well as that, we wanted her to have the freedom to make her own choices. By our moving around, she'd missed out on a stable upbringing, we'd spoilt her childhood.'

Dad sighs deeply, and glances at Mum. 'By the time we'd found Little Upton for our home, everything had changed. Madeline had been so sure of her future success, that she, with our permission changed her surname. To protect you, she said. Off she went to

London, and within five weeks...' Dad shakes his head. 'Within five weeks she'd landed the lead role in the TV drama *The Fallen*. Madeline played her role as a child prostitute, with such sensitivity and insight that the country wept at her plight. She was so believable; it was as if she'd lived it herself.'

He shakes his head. 'The critics could hardly believe she was only sixteen, tried to pry into her past. She went from the restrictions of being a clergy child, to the restrictions of guarding her privacy and public image. Ironically, her upbringing was a good preparation for her new lifestyle. She managed to keep herself to herself much of the time. She thrived and blossomed into a confident young woman. She had, still has, a certain mystique. She soaked up the attention, and was adored by everyone. She didn't put a foot wrong, and the camera loved her. Her work ethic and charm made it inevitable she'd become successful. She was spotted by an American talent scout; she just couldn't miss a chance at Hollywood fame. Our daughter is very famous.'

I look from one of them to the other. 'Well, who is she then? This woman who chose to leave me.'

Mum shrugs. 'Our little Madeline, is Madeline De-Muir.'

'Come on! You must be joking!'

'It's the truth, Christie,' says Dad

The truth?

I keep swallowing back the bitter taste in my mouth. How will I ever believe their version on the truth again? The knot in my stomach tightens. I look away from my parents. My hands clasped together on my knees are still shaking. I'm suddenly cold. I swallow again. The faint smell of cut grass drifts in through an open window. I don't want to throw up in this elegant room, with everything just so, after years of making do in a draughty old-fashioned rectory.

I manage to raise my chin, look across at the two people who've devoted their lives to others. Sometimes it made me so angry. It made me angry how much they did for all those villagers, who often didn't appreciate the work my parents put in to make everything happen. They made it look so easy you see, but I knew. I know.

And still they always had time for me, another imposter, it seems.

The only time Dad ever shut the study door, was when he wrote his sermons, even then, he'd let me creep in. Once I built a *Jenga Tower*, as tall as myself out of Dad's theology books while he scribbled away at his desk. When he'd finished, we played the game, tumbling his precious books in all directions. While we were sorting all the books back into the bookcase, he'd given me a mini sermon about how it doesn't matter how messy things get, we can always sort them out.

Oh, the irony!

And, no matter who was at the house, whenever I came home, Mum always said, "Excuse me a moment, this is really important, I want to see how my daughter is." I was always first, first before everything and everyone. I always knew I was special. Probably why I sometimes resented other people taking up their time.

So, how can it be? How can I be someone else's child? How can I be anything to do with the elusive Madeline De-Muir?

'I can't be, she's just so…' What is she? Perfect? I shake my head, almost snort out loud. 'So together. The whole movie star package.'

'She's a very good actress, she plays the part well.' Dad sits with his hands clasped, elbows resting on his knees, half out of the sofa leaning towards me. He looks suddenly older, less sure of himself than he did minutes ago.

'We're sorry it's like this, Christie.' Mum's eyes betray the myriad of contrasting emotions assaulting her, as her words seep out, barely a whisper.

I try to swallow down the knot of anguish in my throat. Covering my mouth with my hand, I turn away from them. It's not the end of the world, just a new one for me. 'So, why now?' I force the question. 'Why are you telling me all this now?'

Dad nods. 'Madeline wants to get to know you properly… It's time to—'

'So, she wants to swan back into my life after twenty-four years.' Every nerve in my body prickles, screams with resentment. 'I don't think so.'

I can't even look at them. How can they even think I would want anything to do with her? She left me behind, like an unwanted gift.

'It's our fault,' whispers Mum. She's beside me, her hand on my arm. 'It's our fault. She'd been gone too long, you were settled, had started school. We were happy in Little Upton, after all the moving about, it was nice to be settled, not looking to the next challenge. She wanted to be your Mum, but I,' she smiles, 'I already was… I couldn't let you go.'

Dad shakes his head. 'When she came back, she'd changed. And while the rest of the world clamoured for news of Madeline De-Muir's next blockbuster, we saw a fragile young woman close to breaking point. Photographers followed her every move, her agent phoned practically daily with offers of work. Madeline discovered the fame and celebrity she'd craved, was brittle, hollow and demanding. The people around her only saw the veneer of Madeline De-Muir, none of them saw the shadows of sadness threatening to engulf her. Until it was too late.'

'She shut herself away from everyone, we thought we were going to lose her again...' Mum purses her lips. A gesture marking her stubborn resilience I know only too well. '...We couldn't let that happen. We came up with a plan, it worked, of a fashion, until now.'

Dad nods. 'As I've already said, she is a very good actress. Your mum came up with an idea which would allow Madeline to meet up with you, and get to know you, without exposing her, or exposing you.'

Mum fiddles with the edge of her hankie. 'I thought, if Madeline dressed up, and made-up as someone much older, played the part, she could meet you without anyone suspecting. Not even you. It worked for three wonderful years—'

'But, Mum, the only person who used to visit was Auntie Maddie...'

'She came to see you whenever she could; but as you got older, you started to ask her too many questions. She said she couldn't keep pretending, it wasn't fair to risk exposing you to the media. So, she decided to stay away to protect you, but first she made you promise to send her pictures and write to her.'

'So, Auntie Maddie, really, is actually my mum?'

Mum nods. 'She is.'

I remember that last time she visited. The smell of cut grass hung in the air then too. We were outside in the garden. She cupped my face in her hands, and planted a kiss on the top of my head. She told me she was going away for a while. She told me to follow my dreams and work hard to make them happen. I remember a solemn pinkie promise to send her sketches, and paintings and doodles. She told me I was the most special girl she had ever met, and it made me feel like a secret princess.

Whenever I've felt sad about anything, I've always remembered that moment, the look in her eyes promising it was the truth. Then she gave me a tight hug and left, her scarlet headscarf slung over her arm, dancing behind her as she strode away; it almost begged me to follow.

I went to play on the climbing frame instead. I'd shouted "Bye" as I dangled upside down, swinging by my knees from the monkey bars.

She hadn't turned around.

And I hadn't followed.

I know Auntie Maddie. I've known her, loved her all my life. I've told her all my secrets, poured my heart out to her in my art. Always clamoured for her praise. Always got it. Always been encouraged to challenge myself, step out of my comfort zone.

I shake my head, try to wake up from this nightmare. 'Auntie Maddie,' I say, not sure if I can believe it still.

Dad rubs his hands over his face, and then clasps them again. 'I know it must seem like a terrible betrayal, but we were all trying to protect you.'

'And now? What's going to happen now? I presume one of you has come up with a plan.'

Dad lowers his gaze from mine. 'It's up to Maddie now. She's been watching from a distance as you've grown up. She thinks it's now or never; she chose now…' – I would have chosen never – 'And I think…' He looks at Mum. 'We think, the time is right.'

'Really? Well right now, I have no idea if I will *ever* want to meet her. Again. I need time to sort this all out in my own mind. I hope *she'll* understand that.' I try to keep my tone level; pretend I'm talking to an errant Year 7. My cheeks hurt, and my eyes. This must be tearing their hearts out, and I know I'm going to spill tears as soon as I say the words out loud. But still, I need to know. 'Are you still my mum and dad?'

They are one, either side of me on the sofa, hugging me as tears flood down my face. Mum dabs a hankie under my eyes. She's stroking my hair, her forehead is resting on my temple, muttering God only knows what. Dad's arms bind the three of us together, his chin rests on top of my head. I'm surrounded with love, pure and simple. I always have been.

But now I know the truth of how precious it is.

Monty Mitten Presents

'... that skirt is now officially a belt!'

Back at home, Trudy eases off her skyscraper sandals. 'So, you drag us out of a pub, on a Friday night at eight o'clock, because?'

I look at Trudy, not one to miss out on a night out for just any old reason. Yet here she is, putting her social life on hold for me. Wringing my hands, I fiddle with my stack rings. 'The thing is, I need you both to watch something with me. It's an interview Madeline De-Muir did a while ago. Mum gave it to me.' I bite the inside of my lip, and offer a wonky smile.

Suzi grins. 'My mum loves her!'

'Mine too,' I mutter.

'Why would you want...' starts Trudy, then scrunches her forehead. She flicks her hand dismissively. 'Forget it, forget it.' Wedging herself on the sofa between me and Suzi as usual, she hauls her legs up, and sits cross-legged, her otherwise dainty toes jabbing into each of us.

Suzi tuts. 'Honestly, Trudy, your toes get bonier by the day, and that skirt is now officially a belt!'

Trudy shrugs and grins, she stretches her arms back and slings one over each of our shoulders. 'I know you guys love me anyway. Come on, Christie, let's get this over with.'

I press play on the remote. My stomach churning.

Monty Mitten beams from our screen. 'Thank you, everyone, and welcome to the show. Tonight's gorgeous special guest, is a lady, who really needs no introduction at all. She shot to fame at the tender age of sixteen in *The Fallen*. Later, Hollywood success in a string of films including, *An English Rose* and *Here and Now*, has marked her as one of our best loved actresses of all time. More recently, she is known for her work with young people. Ladies and gentlemen, please welcome, Madeline De-Muir.'

I can feel Suzi grinning, I don't even need to look. I cross my arms and push myself further back into the sofa. With any luck it'll eat me.

Monty swings out his arm towards the sweeping staircase, the band strike up the theme tune to *An English Rose.* Madeline De-Muir gracefully steps into the limelight. She is wearing a shimmering silver jumpsuit, tall strappy sandals and a Mona Lisa smile. Her skin appears translucent beneath the studio lighting, and her frame, as fragile as a sparrow.

Suzi rests forward. 'She looks fabulous.'

'Probably Botox,' says Trudy.

'Don't be so cynical,' says Suzi. 'She has such a natural grace, your mum is like that too, Christie. Come to think of it, she looks a bit like your mum.'

'Oh,' is all I manage. I swallow back bile, and pray I'm not going to throw up.

Madeline glides towards Monty Mitten, and leans forward to accept the air kisses he offers. She smiles, and settles gracefully on the offered chair.

'Thank you for joining us this evening.'

Madeline inclines her head a little. 'My pleasure, Monty.'

'Now, d-harling, I know you are eager to talk about your charity work. But first though, I'd like to go back in time, because not many people rise to fame so meteorically. It must have been quite an adventure.'

'Oh, absolutely! I was nineteen, and being told I was the next Grace Kelly. I loved almost every second.'

Trudy tuts and shakes her head. 'Not in the same league, darling.'

Suzi pokes her in the ribs and gives her a death stare.

Trudy shrugs. 'What? I'm just saying, Grace Kelly married a prince.'

Monty leans forward in his chair. 'Tell us, what was it like, the parties and the jetting around the world?'

'At nineteen it was fun. Hectic. Tiring. But fun. I met people I never thought I'd ever get chance to meet, it was an exciting time. But what the public don't see, is this huge publicity machine. Everything, for me anyway, was so well organised and planned out, that I didn't need to think. All I did, was either turn up and act, or turn up and party.'

Whoa! Back then, while she was partying, I would have just been starting nursery school. Meeting these two. I glance at Suzi, my first ever friend. She'd led me by the hand into the playhouse, and cooked me a pretend meal of apples, eggs and cauliflower. And Trudy, she was always aloof with newbies, not keen on sharing the limelight… Or her toys. Our friendship was cemented when one of the boys tipped sand over my head. She walloped him with his bucket, and has continued to look out for me ever since.

'Well, your films were successful, and the partying always in all the tabloids. But amazingly, d-harling, never any scandal. So why did you give it all up?'

Madeline clasps her hands, looks down, then back up at Monty. 'Because, it wasn't the real me.' She flutters her hand dismissively. 'Sure, it was who I'd wanted to be. But I missed my family. I missed them very much. One day it just dawned on me… I'd traded who I was, for what I thought I wanted to be. And it wasn't worth the trade.'

A stabbing pain in my chest curbs my breathing. I'm trying to take deep steadying breaths, but every gulp of fresh air is like a sword to my soul. I rest my hand on my chest.

Trudy leans forward, and angles her head to look at me, frowning. 'Are you okay?'

'Indigestion.' I grimace. That's what having a heart attack is often mistaken for. It feels like my heart is actually imploding.

Madeline's honeyed voice oozes from the television. 'Even while I was having this wonderful time…' She touches her rib cage. 'Inside, I felt something was missing—' – Oh, could it possibly have been me? – 'What was missing was my purpose in life.'

Really, Madeline? I think it was actually me! Remember!

'So, you gave up the acting, and did what?'

'I did nothing, almost became a hermit I suppose.' She shrugs. 'I got back to basics. Down to the bare bones of existence. I stripped out all the frivolity. And yes, I was very low, as down as I've ever been. I couldn't go back and be the girl I was at nineteen or sixteen. The only way out, was to take responsibility, and become the woman I was always intended to be.' Her wide eyes search for Monty's reassurance.

He nods for her to go on.

'My parents were always out there helping people, and I discovered that I'd inherited this, I don't know what you'd call it, desire, vocation, need to help others. If anyone, had ever asked me, if I had anything in common with my parents, I would always have answered "No". So, it was a revelation, because, in a way, I'd always thought they were foolish to waste their time.'

Trudy untangles her legs and stretches them out in front of her, wiggling her toes. 'Pins and needles.'

Suzi shuffles. 'Well you shouldn't sit like that then, should you! You always get them, and I've missed what he's said now!'

'… is what your charity does. Would you like to tell us a bit about it?'

'Sounds like there's a plug,' says Trudy.

'Shh!'

'I started the *Keep-a-Key* campaign a couple of years ago. Basically, we ask people if they are willing to trust a young person to share their home, or even garden shed. Maybe give them the option to just turn up when they need a bed, or a meal, or both. A lot of the young adults we help have been in care, some are having problems at home, and others have perhaps been in trouble with the police, or are struggling with mental health problems.'

'And people what? Foster them?'

'People trust them. Obviously, all the carers have been police vetted. But they just say "Here you are, this is my door key. If you need a chat, somewhere to stay, or something to eat, help yourself". And it seems to work.'

'Well, Madeline, I wish you and your key sharers good luck. It certainly is a novel endeavour.'

'Thank you, Monty.'

'Now just before you go, I know you won't like this, but I must ask about your PA. There have been rumours about the two of you for years.'

'My Personal Assistant is my very best friend. Nothing more, nothing less.'

'He is your only companion. People are bound to jump to their own conclusions.'

'Monty! Well, of course he is a very attractive, young man, why wouldn't I want to be seen out with him.' Madeline laughs. 'But seriously, I'm forty-years-old, he's much younger, and let's face it, a hunk. Our relationship is purely platonic.' A coy smile plays on her lips, as she dips her gaze.

'Well, thank you. Ladies and gentlemen, the resplendent, Madeline De-Muir.'

I press stop on the remote control. Agitation spikes through me. She was so absolutely composed throughout, while galloping panic is still coursing through me. Surely, she must know what she's doing to me. I look down at my shaking hands. How can she be my mother? I don't even know if I'm brave enough to tell my best friends, never mind face the world. I turn to Suzi. 'So, what do you think of her, Suzi?'

'She's just lovely,' gushes Suzi.

Trudy leans forward. 'Too good to be true, if you ask me.'

'No, Trudy, you're just a cynic,' replies Suzi. 'She always comes across as honest and fresh. Just the perfect English rose, like in the film.'

Trudy looks heavenwards. 'Suzi, you're such a pushover! I'll admit she's a good actress, okay, but I think she's got her own agenda. Why thrust yourself into the limelight, after fifteen or twenty years? I think this is all a big PR stunt. She's either going to relaunch her abandoned career, or, this is a smoke screen, and she's trying to hide something. I can't really see your mum being starstruck by her, Christie. Why on earth did she bother downloading this?'

Suzi grins. 'Madeline De-Muir isn't her long-lost daughter, is she?'

I can feel the blood draining from my face.

Suzi laughs at her own joke, then stops short when she looks at me.

'Close, Suzi,' I mutter. 'Madeline De-Muir is my parent's only daughter… my birth mother.' I clamp my hands over my mouth, trapping the howl of despair. Closing my eyes, I squeeze back the tears.

'Nooo! She's your mum?' splutters Suzi. 'Is it some kind of joke?'

'If only.'

Trudy looks as shaken as I feel. 'Oh, Christie, how awful for you. I mean, what I've been saying about her. Obviously, I didn't mean to upset you.'

'It's only a fraction of what I've been thinking,' I say honestly.

Trudy sits back close beside me, and pulls me into an embrace, my head resting on her shoulder. The salt of my tears on my lips proves I'm still alive.

Suzi tuts. 'I knew something was behind your parent's retirement.'

'Give it a rest, Suzi!' Trudy strokes my hair out of my soggy face.

Suzi makes it a group hug. 'I knew it had been more than a chat about old times with your mum and dad. You poor thing.'

'The elusive Auntie Maddie, by any chance?'

Typical Trudy, nobody's fool. 'The one and only.' I shudder. 'She used to dress up as an old lady to visit me; it was the only way she could avoid being followed by the paparazzi apparently. I should have known something wasn't right, she was always wearing pretty clothes, stylish. According to Mum and Dad, Madeline has wanted to go public for years, but they made her wait. They said they'd wanted me to have a secure childhood,' I croak.

'Well, I don't suppose childhoods come much more secure than yours,' says Suzi.

Trudy stands and folds her arms over her chest. 'Well, I managed to survive childhood unscathed by the high-profile antics of my parents. And let's face it, Mummy's still a bit of a goer.'

'Trudy!' Suzi splutters. 'You used to hate it! I remember when your daddy dearest, used a family holiday pic to promote some gadget or other, you wouldn't show your face at school for days and—'

'That was different, Suzi!' Trudy plants her hands firmly on her waist, and raises her chin. 'Daddy should have asked us first. And Mummy's dress was practically transparent... anyway, when I realised being Lord Drummond's daughter had benefits, I fully embraced it!'

'I'll say!' Suzi snorts.

I feel the energy drain from my body. 'But I'm not like that, I just want to get on with my life. No fuss.'

'Christie, this is a fab excuse for letting your hair down, and having some full-on adventures. Grab it by the throat and enjoy!'

'Trudy, this is me. Seriously, what about my teaching? I'm not risking losing my career over this.'

Suzi's eyes widen. 'I know! People always love to gossip—' – And she should know with her mother! – '… but if you play it cool, and shrug it off as if it's really boring, and you've known for years—'

'But, Suzi, how can I walk back into school with everybody knowing I'm the daughter of the famous Madeline De-Muir?'

Suzi shrugs. 'You could sneak in early—'

'But I've still got to stand up at the front of my class and teach.'

Trudy flicks her head tossing her hair over her shoulders, legs astride, hands on hips and pout in place. 'Well, if it were me, I'd own it. Slimy Sloan might cut you a break if he's got the hots for Madeline.'

My stomach turns. 'Thanks for that, Trudy! Now I really do feel sick.'

'Christie! There's nothing wrong with taking advantage of the situation any way you can. I'm just trying to point out the potential positives.'

'Oh, having him… I can't even say the words!' I close my eyes. 'I just want to teach the kids. I want to go to work, come home, maybe go out for a drink with you guys… I want to be normal.'

Trudy moves directly in front of me, and sits on the floor. She has a thing about looking directly at people while she speaks to them. 'So, if that's what you want, call a meeting, take control of the situation. That's absolutely what I'd do.'

'You know I'm no good at taking control. And that's another thing, what am I supposed to call her? I can hardly call her Mum.'

Trudy curls her lips. 'I can think of a few names.' Disgust drips from every word.

'Call her Maddie. That's what you've always called her,' says Suzi.

'It doesn't exactly go with her image, does it?' I say.

'Not your problem,' dismisses Trudy, waving her arm. 'She's the one who's been pretending to live like a saint, for how long? Going by the interview we've just seen I'd say Madeline De-Muir is one tough cookie.'

'She's not as tough as she makes out. She's had a difficult childhood,' I say.

Trudy looks heavenward. 'Yeah, right. With your mum and dad!'

I explain about Dad being a sort of roving troubleshooting vicar. The moving about, and the unsavoury characters. As I'm telling the story of Madeline's childhood, I find myself trying to imagine how it must have been for her. Mum and Dad too busy with everyone else, to make time for her. Too busy opening their home to strangers, to make a safe environment for the little Madeline. Too busy making everyone else feel loved and precious, to make Madeline feel loved and precious. Too busy searching for their next mission, to see the mission right in front of them. Madeline. Maddie. A lost little girl. I wonder how I would have turned out, if I'd had that kind of childhood. I don't want to know. 'So, you see, things are not always as they seem.'

Trudy frowns. 'You feel sorry for her, don't you?'

'Wouldn't you, Trudy?' I ask.

'I don't know. I know I'd be furious she left me to go and play at being a film star.'

'Well, I can't seem to separate the little girl Madeline, from Madeline De-Muir, from Auntie Maddie. That woman on TV is terrifyingly confident. Not at all how I think of Auntie Maddie. So, if it was just Madeline who was my mother, I would be furious. But it's not, it's Auntie Maddie, and she's been a really big influence in my life.'

Suzi splutters, 'Excuse me, you haven't seen her for years.'

'Okay, but I wrote to her all the time while I was growing up. Trudy, you have brothers, and, Suzi, you have a sister...' Suzi screws up her face. '... I know you don't get on with Chloe, but she's still your sister. And I'm sure you've confided in her over the years. Am I right?'

'Suppose.'

'Well, I don't have brothers or a sister. I have always confided in Auntie Maddie. She has a wicked sense of humour, lots of down to earth advice, and she has always lifted my expectations of me. Built my confidence, and coaxed away my insecurities. She knows things about me, that I haven't even told you two. That's how close I've always felt to her.'

'Like what?' I can see Suzi is clearly miffed she doesn't know all my secrets.

'Okay, let me think...'

Obviously, I'm not going to tell them things that'll hurt them, like the fact that I've been sending them both Valentines cards for the past ten years. Dad always sends me one, and the first time I got one, Trudy and Suzi got none; at thirteen that's almost as bad as discovering your mum's growing facial hair.

'Number one. Dad sends me a Valentine card every year, and that means, on average, I've never had any admirers. Number two. The reason I was sent home that day in our last year at primary school, was *not* because I had suspected small pox, but because I sneezed and wet my knickers. Number three. The revision cards I wrote out for private study at school before our GCSEs, didn't have any useful data on them, I just used them to write out nasty things about the teachers. Actually, I still do that one in my head. When Mr Sloan has a go at me, I just imagine him in a chicken outfit doing the Birdie Song, you know. "With a little bit of this, and a little bit of that, now shake your ass. Na na na na". Oh, and this one is really embarrassing—'

'Like the others weren't?' Trudy wiggles her fingers while examining her talons.

Not sure I'm brave enough to admit my crush on Trudy's brother, Simon. A couple of years older than us, he's always possessed natural leadership skills, and enough confidence to strip to his waist through the summer months. As a serious artist, I had to study how muscles moved under the taut bronzing skin, of a potentially perfect male form. I close my eyes briefly to summon the image. Yep, that'll do it for me, any day of the week. I continue, 'Number four. I had a crush on your brother Simon for years.' There, I've said it, sometimes confession can be liberating…

Trudy sits bolt upright. 'What! Spotty Simon!'

And sometimes not. 'He was hardly spotty! And he can be quite charming.' I try to defend my teenage plus crush.

'And he can be a complete pain in the ass,' says Trudy.

Suzi tuts. 'That's two "asses" in the last two minutes!'

Trudy sighs. 'Well honestly, having a crush on Simon. He's not even human. More a cross between ET and Tin Tin.'

'ET is quite cute.' says Suzi.

'And Tin Tin has high morals,' I add.

'And they're both fictional characters, devised to appeal to eight-year-olds,' scoffs Trudy.

'Anyway, let's forget about Simon, pretend I never told you,' I say, wishing I hadn't.

'How can I?' asks Trudy. 'I'm probably going to have nightmares.' She raises her hands in mock surrender. 'Okay, I'll try, but no promises.'

'Thank you.' Like I've not got enough problems. Give a girl a break!

'So, Auntie Maddie knows all your secrets?' says Suzi.

Trudy wags her immaculate forefinger. 'Ah, ah, ah, just call her Maddie now!'

'Yes, *Maddie* knows all about me. It's making me feel exposed. I mean, she knows everything about me, and all I know about her are the bits Mum and Dad told me, and what she said in the interview.'

And I can admit, at least to myself, she's got Mum's easy grace.

I got Dad's hairy legs…

He's not my dad.

Fresh tears well up in my eyes.

Trudy taps her lips with her finger. 'You don't think she'll turn up at the art exhibition, do you? She does come across as liking to hold all the cards. Maybe she's planning to bump into you casually.'

Suzi frowns. 'That's only a couple of days away.'

Trudy leaps to her feet. 'I'll go and get the tickets.' Marching out of the room, she returns seconds later clutching an envelope. She reads aloud, 'You are invited to the opening of *Evolution*. An exhibition with a difference. Champagne reception at 2pm.' Trudy waves the accompanying note from Auntie Maddie, and continues, 'There is an informal brunch at 11am to meet the exhibition organisers to which you are also requested to attend.'

Suzi raises her eyebrows. *'Requested to attend,'* she repeats.

'Sounds more like an order,' says Trudy.

Looking at their expectant faces makes the decision for me. I'd been looking forward to a relaxing stroll round a gallery. I like to study how other artists perceive things, and if I'm honest, I'm always in awe of their courage, allowing all and sundry to pass judgement on their work. 'Sounds like a request we can't refuse.' Why should I be the one to miss out because of *Maddie's* interference?

Trudy throws up a high five, which neither me or Suzi catch, she shakes her head wandering off muttering under her breath. Seconds later she's back with a bottle of prosecco and three glasses.

When nobody else speaks, I decide they must be waiting for me to utter some words of wisdom. Not very likely, but still, I feel I should fill the silence. 'You think she'll be there?'

Trudy tilts her head to one side. 'I honestly don't know.'

Suzi shrugs. 'She might go as Auntie Maddie, so the press don't recognise her.'

'Well,' I say, 'I don't think she'll be there. I think it's too open. After all, she doesn't know how I'll react to seeing her. I don't know how I'll react to seeing her.'

Trudy points at Suzi. 'Ah, but what if she goes as Auntie Maddie, like Suzi said?'

'I'd still know who she is, and it would be worse for her to be outed in that way. Madeline De-Muir, dressed as a granny, all the press would go wild.'

Suzi nods. 'So, it might just be what it looks like, a nice day out at an art gallery for three friends. Or it could be a test, to see if you're up to life mingling with celebs.'

Trudy grins. 'There are hardly likely to be celebs at a minor art exhibition in Chippington. Christie would be more likely to meet celebs while she's stalking Simon.'

'I have never stalked him!' Well, only a couple of times anyway 'And I don't have a crush on him now!'

Much!

Ha.

'Okay, keep your hair on.'

'So, Trudy,' I say, swiftly changing the subject. 'Do we take the invitation at face value, or do we expect the unexpected?'

'I think, when Maddie decides to meet you, she'll want the backing of your parents. Think about it, at any time she could have revealed the truth. But she hasn't. She hasn't because she wants their support.' Trudy closes her eyes, and rubs her temples. 'She's in a very tricky situation.'

'Go on,' I urge.

'For years she's been the darling of the British film industry. She has always appeared to be above reproach. Excellent career, no scandal, no affairs, no public slanging matches, no enemies. In fact, everyone loves her. So, to tell the world that, not only does she have a twenty-four-year-old daughter, but also that she abandoned her in favour of her acting career, might just kill her image.'

'And not just her image,' chirps in Suzi. 'Her charity too. There she's been, encouraging people to open their homes to teenagers, while she didn't even bother to keep her beautiful, adorable, helpless little baba. She'll be branded a fraud. Trudy, you tell her…'

'She is going to have to play this very carefully. I guarantee she won't be there. Cheers, girls.' Trudy raises her glass to us.

Suzi grins. 'So, we're definitely going then!'

Trudy nods. 'You bet, free brunch and a champagne reception. Wild horses couldn't keep me away, I want to know what she's up to.'

Suzi pats her tummy. 'I'm glad I've lost a bit of weight.'

'Girls, we look fan-bloody-tastic,' confirms Trudy.

'Well I do feel much healthier,' says Suzi.

Trudy winks. 'So, do you feel up to jogging into the kitchen and grabbing another bottle? Go on, you know you want to.'

'Okay, but no more after that one.'

'Guides honour,' says Trudy, holding up three fingers. 'Dib dib dib.'

I shake my head. 'You weren't in the Guides.'

'*Ahh*, but I've held many a Scouts woggle to ransom.'

'I bet you have,' snorts Suzi, and stalks off out the room.

Hopefully for more prosecco.

Evolution

... her legs in the air ...

I'm not sure what exactly I'd been expecting, but I know it wasn't this. I suppose I'd thought the art exhibition would be held in one of those new glass buildings, airy and bright, oozing sophistication. I did think Trudy's Satnav must be wrong, because rather than heading for a city centre gallery, we've ended up in an entirely less desirable part of town.

Trudy deemed to drive us to the gallery, I'll drive us home. So, here we are, sitting in Trudy's flash car, outside an apparently derelict mill. My eyes follow the huge brick funnel chimney reaching skyward, random greenery sprouting from between the bricks. I close my eyes briefly in disbelief.

I wonder if Madeline knew this place was such a dive when she got the tickets?

Trudy taps the screen of her Satnav. 'This is definitely the place.'

'I can see that,' I reply, pointing at a huge banner with *Evolution* sprawled down it.

Suzi unclips her rear seatbelt, and leans forward between me and Trudy. 'Do you think Madeline's made some kind of mistake?'

I shake my head. 'I don't think she would have gone to the trouble of involving you and me in this day out, to go and make a mistake.'

'I hope she's not planning to kidnap us!' squeaks Suzi.

Trudy pokes her arm. 'Su-zi!'

A gang of youths walk round from the back of the building. It doesn't take them long to spot us, they huddle in a group, heads in, clearly talking tactics.

'I don't like this,' says Trudy. 'Call me shallow, but they look like trouble to me. They don't look like they've a tenner between them, but they're all wearing brand-new trainers.'

She's right! Not only brand-new trainers, but the latest must haves. One of the gang ambles over to the car, hands stuffed deep in baggy jeans pockets.

Trudy runs her finger over the automatic door lock button on the dashboard. 'Safe.'

The youth peers into the car, and nods. Trudy opens her window about two inches.

'Are you 'ere for the art exhibition?' asks the lad. Close up he looks nearer fourteen than eighteen.

Trudy nods. 'Yes, that's right, but there doesn't appear to be anyone about.'

'They're all round the back. What do ya think of it?' he asks, gesturing towards the awning where *Evolution* is splattered in multi coloured letters. 'We did that.' He sounds rather proud of the fact. The awning sways defiantly in the breeze.

Unclipping my seatbelt, I lean my whole body across Trudy, open the window fully and stick my head out. 'It looks great. Whose idea was it to use those bold colours?'

Trudy squirms under me.

'That was Mickey. Mickey get over here.'

A beanpole kid stashes an E-cig in his pocket, and they all scuff their way over.

'She did most of it. But it was my idea to use mixed up big an' little letters all different sizes though.'

Mickey, who on closer inspection, really is a girl, grunts an acknowledgement.

'Hi,' I say, doing my best to ignore Trudy poking my ribs. 'What great use of colour, shape and sizes. You must be very proud of your work.'

Mickey shrugs. 'Suppose.'

I notice the barest inkling of pride. 'Well I think it's fantastic. If the work inside is anywhere near as bold as that, then we're in for a treat.' I sport my beamiest beam.

'We ain't seen it. It's supposed to be top secret. We just did that banner, and tidied up the mill,' says the lad.

Mickey shrugs. 'Somethin' to do.'

'Well, you've done a good job. Well done.' Both of them shrug again and flush. 'So, where do you think we should park the car?'

'All the others are round the back. It'll probably get nicked if you leave it here.'

'Very reassuring,' mutters Trudy.

'Shh…' I hiss at Trudy. But to the kids, I say, 'Hope to see you all later.'

'You'll have to ring the bell at the back door to be let in, cos they always keep it locked.'

I drag myself back into the passenger seat, and Trudy closes the window. 'Take a good look,' she mutters. 'We'll probably have to identify them all at the police station later.'

'I've been memorising their clothes…' says Suzi, after being remarkably quiet for so long.

'I don't believe you two! They're just a bunch of kids, give them a break.'

'Which arm?' asks Trudy.

'Look, they've probably been involved in a youth programme or something. At least they aren't prowling the streets.'

Neither of them answers, but exchange looks. Trudy drives to the back of the mill. There are four cars parked along the back wall of the building, including a black sporty Porsche.

'I think it'll be safe here,' concedes Trudy.

We get out, and make our way over to the back door of the mill.

Suzi links her arm in mine. 'Are you okay?' she asks.

'Fine,' I say. 'It doesn't look like there are many people here for the informal brunch, does it?'

'Do you think it's a trick to get you to meet her?' says Suzi.

'Only one way to find out.' I reach to press the bell next to the door. My hand looks steady, but my whole body feels like electricity is buzzing through my veins, wouldn't be surprised if my hair is fizzed and standing on end. I can hear movement inside, the clink of a lock. A woman in a dated tweed suit and sensible flats opens the door. Relief floods through me. It isn't Madeline.

'Can I help you?' she asks.

I try for a confident stance, and take a steadying breath. 'I hope so, we've been invited to the opening of *Evolution*, and to an informal brunch at 11 o'clock.'

'Lovely. Names please.'

'Christie Harris, Tru—'

'Oh, I am sorry, Miss Harris, come in please.' The lady opens the door fully. 'I'm Annabel Price, do call me Annabel. Pleased to meet you. If you'll follow me?'

I exchange looks with Trudy and Suzi, as we are led through a bright reception lounge, then on into a large and surprisingly plush office.

'If you would like to make yourselves comfortable, Mr Hepworth will be with you shortly.'

I exchange a nervous smile with my friends before I sit down on the oversized leather sofa. Suzi plonks herself down next to me while Annabel Price closes the door as she leaves.

Trudy casts her sharp eyes over the immaculate expanse of office, as she perches on the edge of a desk. 'All very mysterious, even my office isn't this lush, and why, actually, are we in an office? Not quite the informal brunch we were led to believe.'

The door ebbs open, and Annabel's head appears. 'He's on his way. Don't let his brusque manner put you off, it's just his way, he can sometimes be a little—'

'Mrs Price, spare me the character assassination,' says an oddly familiar growl from outside the room.

An unexpected flutter builds in my stomach.

Surely not! It can't be…

Annabel grimaces, and mouths "sorry" to us.

I exchange looks first with Suzi, and next Trudy, who remains casually adorning the desk like a lavish accessory. What have I got them into? Mr Hepworth strides into the room.

It is him!

Miles, all six foot two of him in the flesh, and so much more…

Trudy raises an eyebrow, stretches her legs out and crosses one ankle over the other before looking speculatively in my direction. Suzi starts to examine her hands. I sit like an open-mouthed gawp. Surely there can't be this many coincidences in anyone's life.

The easy smile, and relaxed attitude he wears for my parents, has been replaced by a crisp business-like stance. A cool, confident smile has tamed the wolfish grin of Friday night. His angular face is softened only by the jet-black flop of hair that dares to fall forward over his broad forehead. Dark eyes give away not one clue as to what he's thinking. Those eyes, which rest steadfastly on me, strip away my shaky composure. A buzz of awareness flares through my body, disregarding the countless reasons my head is screaming to control my wayward reactions. I squirm at the realisation, that just one look can turn me to mush.

'Welcome, ladies. I hope you don't mind the unconventional circumstances of this meeting.' He reaches out to shake my hand. 'Christie, we meet again.'

Okay, now he smiles and leans forward, brushing a completely inappropriate kiss on my cheek. My heart practically leaps from my chest! I can feel Trudy and Suzi's eyes on me.

'And of course, Trudy and Suzi.' He shakes their hands in turn.

No kisses for them I note, Trudy looks slightly putout, hides it well with a head flick.

'I'm Miles Hepworth.'

'So, what's going on here, Miles?'

'I'm here on behalf of Madeline De-Muir. I'm her Personal Assistant—'

Unbelievable!

'… With help from some of her friends, Madeline has arranged a little surprise for you, Christie. But first, before I tell you about that, I'd like to explain why.'

I remember back to all my flirty little exchanges with him in the safety of Mum's kitchen. I feel like a complete fool. The heat in my chest is crawling upwards, and soon my ears will be glowing red with embarrassment. Once again, I feel outmanoeuvred. 'I've changed my mind. I don't want to be here. I do not want to be here!' I resist the urge to stamp my feet like a three-year-old, but I stand up ready to leave.

So do Trudy and Suzi.

'Please, Christie…' says Miles, placing his hand on my arm.

A jolt of awareness shoots though me. I just stare at him.

'Christie, give me five minutes. If you want to leave then, by all means do. Five minutes.'

I drag my eyes from him and look from Trudy to Suzi. United we stand, but still I raise my brows to silently question them.

Trudy tilts her head to look at me. 'If you leave now, you might regret it, Christie.'

'She's right,' says Suzi.

'But he works for Madeline!' I turn to him, clenching my teeth. 'You should have told me when we first met.' I'm impressed with myself for not actually hissing.

'We met by chance.'

'In my mum's kitchen!' Now I hiss.

'If she'd told me you were coming, I would have left before you arrived.'

'I just turned up, so she didn't know!'

'There you go then.' He shrugs, as if this excuses his omission.

'You could have told me who you were.'

'Your mum introduced me as a charity worker; she just neglected to say it was Madeline's charity. And of course, when we met, you knew nothing about Madeline.' His smile is infuriatingly self-righteous.

Irritation flits through my entire body. I'd look churlish to walk away without even hearing him out. He knows it, has used it to gain the edge.

'Five minutes,' I say.

'Thank you, Christie,' says Miles politely. He loses the smile, and glances at Trudy and Suzi. 'Should we be alone, perhaps?'

'Whatever you've got to say, just say it! These two know all about *Madeline*!'

'Okay. As you now know, I *do* work for Madeline. I spoke to your parents last night, so I know you are aware Madeline wants to go public with your identity. I also assume you know Madeline has wanted to do this for some time…'

I nod, can't speak, catch the fleshy bit inside my cheeks between my teeth.

'One of the reasons your parents have been against this, is because they felt it would interfere with your career as a teacher. Madeline agrees, but also feels your talent for art is very much overlooked. Madeline thinks, and I happen to agree with her—'

'You've seen my work!' I catch my breath; this is too much!

'… That you are talented enough to exhibit your art professionally,' continues Miles.

'I can't believe she showed you my work!'

'Please, just listen. If you are ever going to get the credit you are entitled to as a serious artist, it cannot be as Madeline De-Muir's illegitimate daughter. It has to be as Christie Harris.'

I can feel the blood pulsing round my brain and scrunch my eyes shut. How did I get to this?

'Is there a point to all this,' demands Trudy, stepping forward. 'Or are you just trying to upset Christie for the fun of it?'

'Yes, there is a point. As you know Madeline set up the *Keep-a-Key* charity, working with, let's say, challenging youths. You probably met a couple of them out there. Madeline bought this old mill to convert into small flats for some of the older teens, to have a warden or caretaker to oversee the complex. Then she had this crazy idea, to help you get the credibility your artwork deserves...' Miles' eyes rest solely on me.

The penny drops. She's displaying some of the paintings I've sent her. I feel the blood drain from my face, as panic grips me. 'So, some of my art is on display in *Evolution*?' I feel suddenly faint, nauseous, clammy. I flop back into the chair. How could she be so insensitive? Oh, that's right, she's Madeline De-Muir, she can do whatever she wants.

Suzi rests her hand on my shoulder, Trudy takes another hostile step towards Miles.

Miles raises his hands in a gesture of surrender. 'Okay, let's just stay calm. I need Christie to hear me out.' Trudy steps back, shrugs one shoulder, giving Miles minimal permission to continue. 'Christie, it's entirely all your work in there. So far, the only name anyone can the exhibition is Christie. It's up to you if you want to claim it as your own. The decision is yours. But think about it. The exhibition will open at 2pm today, with or without your approval. Remember, all those pictures *belong* to Madeline. If you want to put your name to them, it would serve you both well.'

I hug my arms tight around my body, holding myself together. I take in gasps of air to settle my stomach, shocked to the core, I want to throw up. How could she do this to me? How could she betray me so callously?

'I know this is a huge shock. Why don't you go and look at the exhibition with your friends before you decide? I think you'll be pleasantly surprised. Follow me.'

Suzi squeezes my shoulder.

Trudy gestures for me to get up. 'You can do this, Christie.'

Mindlessly I get up and follow Miles, Suzi to my left, Trudy to my right. He leads us back outside and round to the front of the mill. I notice the group of youths are still standing chatting together.

'Can you believe them?' Miles nods towards the group. 'They were each given a hundred and fifty pounds to get themselves kitted out for today's opening, and what did they do? They all bought trainers.' He shakes his head.

Trudy nods. 'We did notice the trainers.'

'Hey,' I shout. 'Sick trainers.' I give them an imaginary high five and fist bump. 'Bo-om.'

I'm rewarded with a "Deep" from Mickey, and a look of disgust from Miles. Good, I'm glad he doesn't approve. The need to contradict Miles, gives me a flicker of energy I desperately need.

My strength feels like it's been drained away, because? That's right, I've been betrayed.

Over and over again.

And Miles is part of that betrayal. The need to rebel gives me some relief from reality.

'We've been trying to encourage them to prioritise with their money,' explains Miles.

'I think they've done well,' I say. 'It's really important to wear comfortable shoes. It's hard to smile if your feet hurt.'

'But they could have bought a smart outfit for the same amount of money, including shoes,' counters Miles.

'And how often would they have worn their smart outfit, including shoes? Today? Once? They'll wear those trainers until they drop off their feet. Looks to me like they've got their heads screwed on the right way.'

Miles unlocks the main entrance to the mill. Sunlight streams in through tall windows, flooding the open foyer with light. Trestles laden with empty wine glasses and canapés stand to attention, waiting for the expected guests.

'I'm bringing you in this way, so you'll see the exhibition as the public will.'

Suzi points at the tables. 'Those canapés should be refrigerated.'

'Actually, they've been frozen; they're supposed to be defrosted at room temperature for four hours.' Miles looks at his watch. 'Two and a half to go.'

There is something about this man, actually making me want to scream.

'Like I said, we could have entered via the back of the mill, but I want you to see it the first time as the public will see it. The staircase to your left, leads to the main viewing area, although you may have noticed the odd sketching in the cabinet to your right. Madeline has had the vast majority of your work framed or re-framed, but some of your earlier pieces she felt were too naive to burden with frames.'

'Naive?' I question.

'Some of your very early pictures are so innocent and simple, a frame would look ridiculous. I'll leave you to it.' Miles turns to leave. 'By the way, Mrs Price has organised an informal brunch. Please join us when you've finished your viewing.'

I watch him walk up the stairs and through a door, presumably back to where we came from.

Suzi practically strains her neck watching him leave the gallery. 'No wonder you are off men if you've had him to drool over.'

'I've only met him a few times at Mum's!' I hiss.

'Okay, okay!' says Trudy. 'So, what do you think?'

'Arrogant, self-centred, totally un—'

'Not about him, Christie! About this?'

'I don't know; he's got me rattled!'

'So I see.'

'He is a little unnerving,' says Suzi. 'He nearly bit my head off when I said those canapés should be refrigerated.'

'Madeline's personal assistant, jumped-up lackey more like,' I say.

'Christie, it's not like you to be so judgmental. What happened to live and let live?'

'Oh, you know, too innocent, simple and naive, I guess.'

Trudy gestures towards the cabinets. 'He wasn't talking about you. He was talking about some of your early artwork.'

'Trudy, don't you get it. My artwork *is* me. It's the me, I don't let anyone see.'

'Until now,' says Suzi.

'Thanks.'

Trudy heads off towards the main viewing area. 'Come on, we might as well have a look. After all, it'll be open in a couple of hours.'

Suzi looks longingly at the trestle of food. 'I could just eat one of those, I'm starving. I only had toast for breakfast.'

'Suzi! How can you think about food at a time like this? All my emotions poured out on canvas, exposed to the world, and all you can think about is food.'

'They're still frozen,' says Trudy. 'You'd give yourself food poisoning. Anyway, let's look round the gallery, and then we can go and join the others for brunch.'

'Call yourselves friends.'

Trudy inclines her head. 'Christie, either way, people are going to be looking round in a couple of hours. We may as well look at the exhibition first.'

I follow them up the stairs. The distressed red brick walls are lit by natural light from huge skylights, and complimented by subtle up-lighting from the uneven wooden floorboards.

Each of my pictures, has a beautifully handwritten explanation of the scene or event on a small chalk board beneath it. Madeline's handwriting.

The first picture, *Suzi on Skates*, is a picture of, you guessed it, Suzi on skates. By Christie, age eight and three quarters. She looks rather cute, I think. With her long black pigtails flying in the breeze, her arms akimbo, a look of horror on her face, as she heads for the school's industrial-size dustbins. It could have been worse; I could have painted her after the collision.

'Christie, why have you painted me in such a ridiculous situation? You know I hated those roller skates.'

'It was your face. I just remember seeing the look of horror on your face, it looked so comical… Sorry.'

'You have captured her expression. How old were you?'

'Eight and three quarters, see, it says so there,' I say proudly.

Trudy grins. 'Don't be so miffed Suzi, you're going to be famous.'

'What as?'

'The very first portrait by Christie Harris,' replies Trudy.

But not the last.

The second painting is *Trudy takes a Tumble*. Quite. Which is, you guessed it. Typically, Trudy, even back then, managed to make falling off a horse look stylish! With her arms swinging franticly, riding hat slightly skewwhiff and her legs in the air – somethings never change. The horse doesn't look bad either.

'Okay, Christie, why does the horse look better than me?' she demands.

'Probably because he's the right way up. See, this is what I mean! You two are my best friends, and you hate me already.'

Trudy shakes her head. 'We don't hate you; it's just a shock recognising ourselves in an art gallery.'

'So how do you think I feel. All my work. What did you think I painted all these years? Buttercups? Mountains? Bowls of fruit?'

'Fine, we get the idea,' says Suzi. 'But how many more are there of us two?'

'Not many,' I say, crossing my fingers behind my back.

'Good!' says Trudy. 'Can we move along now?'

Next up is *Last Again*. A painting showing the backs of all the kids in front of me, in the one hundred metre sprint on sports day. Again, this features Trudy and Suzi, Trudy way out front, Suzi much closer. Neither of them looks their best from behind. Neither of them comments. There are a few natural world sketches next, including a classic called *Trees in the Breeze*. I went through a kitten stage at eleven; *Sooky on a Skateboard*, is my finest kitty in motion painting.

Suzi hauls me over to *Summer Sun*. 'Hey, Christie, now this one is lovely.'

It's a portrait of Mum and Dad sat on a bench in the back garden of the rectory. Just looking at it makes me smile. I remember making them sit there all afternoon. If it hadn't been for the partial shade of the apple tree, I'm sure they would both have had sunstroke. I, being the grand artist, had the advantage of a huge parasol. Poor Mum and Dad.

Trudy gasps. 'Oh Christie, how could you sink so low?'

'What?'

'Does *Score* ring any bells?'

Oh dear! 'I was only fourteen!'

'And that would put Simon at, what? Sixteen. You hussy!' says Trudy.

Score is a superb – okay I'm biased – action painting of an impromptu football match on the village green. The main subject of the painting is Trudy's brother, Simon, who just happens to be stripped to the waist, and wearing skin-tight Levi's. Bless him. What can I say? Hormones are a terrible thing, especially at fourteen. I manage to drag the pair of them past the most embarrassing of the paintings, without too much comment. Though, there is an avalanche of eye fluttering going on.

The Long Farewell, is greeted with knowing looks. It seems even more poignant now I know she's my mother. 'Life just gets better and better,' I groan.

Suzi places her hand on my arm, and tilting her head to one side offers a sad smile.

We continue to weave our way through images of my childhood in silence. Occasionally we exchange knowing glances. Between true friends, sometimes words are simply not needed.

Finally, Trudy reverently breaks the tranquillity. 'For what it's worth, I think they've done a splendid job.'

Her hushed tone caresses my soul.

She places her hand on my arm, and waits for me to raise my eyes to hers. 'All your work is in order, the lighting is just right, and the rustic feel of this mill is hauntingly evocative. It seems they've involved some of those teenager creatures in the preparation of this event, so, that should please you, Christie. And, they have organised an entire event without you, the artist, suffering a single doubt or headache.'

'But I am suffering doubts! Every time I look at any one of these pictures. And just walking around this place, it's like re-living my entire childhood, except worse, because in about an hour's time, a whole bunch of art critics, are going to prowl round this beautiful exhibition with their little notepads, scribbling horrid comments to print in the local papers.'

Trudy grins. 'Ah, you said beautiful.'

'Sorry?'

'You said, "Beautiful exhibition", that means you like it.'

'Trudy's right,' says Suzi smugly.

'Girls, let me explain. *Any* exhibition would look beautiful in this building.'

'Disagree,' says Trudy raising a pointed finger. 'A whole load of that blobby art would look stupid.'

'Why?'

'Because, it would, it looks stupid at the best of times, but here, in this old mill, the atmosphere is so mellow and achingly serene, it would look doubly stupid.'

Suzi groans dramatically. 'Really, now? Let's not get into this argument again, please.' She is well aware that it could go on for hours, if not days.

I tut. 'Okay, truce.'

'So, are you pleased with it?' asks Trudy.

Am I pleased with it? How should I answer that? I am not pleased that the all-knowing Madeline, has taken it upon herself to exhibit *my* work. Granted work that I've given her. But that was when I thought she was a lonely old lady. And, if I'd been asked last week if I thought any of my work was good enough to be exhibited, the answer would have been an emphatic no.

But here, it does seem in keeping with the environment. Okay, the building looks like a wreck from the outside… Inside, the floors aren't exactly level, the bricks haven't been pointed in years, and some of the skirting boards have buckled away from the walls, but it has real charm and character.

It feels comfortable, like a pair of old slippers. It doesn't feel like some of those modern art galleries, harsh and uninviting. It feels friendly and warm, almost as if the building is hugging you. Maybe it's just me, mellowed by all these reminders from my childhood.

Suzi runs her fingers along the brickwork. 'I've never understood people when they've said buildings have personalities. I've always preferred new, clean, easy to maintain buildings. But this place is awesome. I love it.'

'So, Christie, are you pleased with it?' asks Trudy again.

'Yes. Yes I am.'

'Good. Can we go and get that brunch now?' says Suzi. 'I'm starving!'

Brunch

'Go strut your stuff.'

We wander round to the back of the building, and Mrs Price leads us into a small conference room. Miles doesn't notice us coming in, he's too engrossed in his telephone conversation. 'Well there's nothing I can do about it... Not at the moment. I'm all tied up here. Yes, Maddie, it's going as well as you'd expect. You're just going to have to manage Terry as best you can, and you know what Pixy is like, she'll be out on the streets terrorising the other neighbourhood cats. If you're that worried, I'll look for her when I get back. That cat will outlive both of us, Maddie, she's tough as old boots... Okay, I'll speak to you later. And don't worry.'

Annabel makes a small sound, so as to draw attention to us.

Miles turns. 'Sorry about that. Mrs Price, would you let the caterers know we're ready to eat?' She turns to leave the room. 'Oh, hold on, you'd better round up all the Key kids, they've been invited to join us.' Miles gestures for us to sit down. 'Christie, I hope you like your exhibition, it has a certain charm, don't you think?'

'I think this building adds to its appeal. I'm not sure I'm going to enjoy it being metaphorically ripped to shreds by the critics,' I say.

'It won't be,' he says. His mouth curls into a smile, which again doesn't reach his eyes.

I suppose it's meant to reassure me. It doesn't, in fact, I find it rather patronising. The toad, wheedling his way into my affections, and then this. 'How do you know?' I say, trying to keep the irritation out of my voice. 'Are you an art critic as well as a PA?'

Trudy stands up, and waits for Miles to look at her, knowing no man can resist. She taps her foot impatiently as he takes a heartbeat too long. 'What Christie is trying to say, is, do you have any assurances you can offer her. You understand, most artists have months, years, to psych up for their work to be exhibited. Christie has come here today, completely unaware of all of this, and she's slightly unnerved.'

'I am *not* unnerved,' I snap. 'I am just *very* concerned about how this exhibition is going to affect *me*. If it's a complete flop, how am I going to live it down?'

'It won't be a flop,' says Miles.

'I'd lose the respect of the kids I teach... Be a laughing stock with the other teachers... Worse still, *Mr Sloan* would have another reason to undermine my abilities, such as they are. I'm a good teacher!'

Miles guides me back to a chair. 'Christie, come and sit down. Listen to me. Forget about school, for now. The appeal of this exhibition is unique. Think about it, a selection of an artist's work, starting from the age of eight. It has never been done before. Not consistent work of an entire development. Even the name of the exhibition, *Evolution*, requests patience.'

'I don't want patience, I want acceptance.' And if I'm honest, respect.

'You'll get it.'

'How can you be sure?'

'Do you think Madeline would have organised this exhibition, without asking a couple of her arty friends their opinion of your work?'

'I don't know! Remember, I don't know her.'

'Well, let me assure you, she has connections with some of the top experts in the art world. And, there aren't many artists, who'd have the nerve to exhibit their earlier efforts—'

Like I do have the nerve?

'… *Nobody* is going to rubbish your work.'

'Why?'

'Just because,' he says, with forced patience. His brow crumples into a frown. 'Can't you see? It's just too good, Christie.'

The complement takes me by surprise. 'Fine,' I say flatly.

The Key kids form an inquisitive circle round us. The caterers lay out the food. Trudy secures us a table. And Suzi starts queuing at the end of the serving table. What a team.

Mickey edges forward. 'So, are you the artist?'

'I haven't decided yet. It's a secret. I don't want everyone gawping at me. I know I can trust you, and your friends to keep a secret,' I say, smiling, hoping the gamble pays off.

The one who acts like the head honcho, pats his heart with his hand, and thrusts it forward to shake mine. I mimic his actions, and shake his hand.

The lad smiles, and is transformed from a scowling teenager, into a sweet-faced cherub. Remarkable.

'I'm Frank, but my crew calls me "Baby Face". Don't know why.'

Oh, I do. 'So, what would you like *me* to call you, then?' I ask.

He thinks about it, clearly not used to being asked the question. 'Dunno.' He shrugs. 'Authorities all call me Frank, mates call me Baby Face.' He leans in close to me, and whispers, 'It's a bit childish init?'

'How about I call you Frankie?' I whisper. 'It's kind of in-between.'

'Done.'

We move apart.

'Okay, Frankie, how about you and your crew joining me for a light brunch?'

'Yeah, Frank-ie,' one of his friends says. 'Come on, man! We're starvin'.'

Frankie grins his baby face grin, and leads the way. The others follow.

I ask Annabel to point me in the direction of the loos, and make a discreet exit. The toilets are rather swanky. No expense spared. I examine my face in the lavish baroque style mirror. I look flustered and flushed, not at all like a successful artist.

After a few minutes I amble back into the conference room. People are in groups, chatting away; plates balanced in one hand, glasses in the other. How they manage to eat anything is beyond me. Trudy, Suzi and the Key kids are the sensible exception. Remarkably, they are sitting at a table together, all making short work of the contents of their plates. Trudy beckons me to join them. I select a couple of topped bagels from the buffet, a glass of orange juice, and join them.

Trudy points about the room. 'Everyone here already knows who you are. I don't think you're going to be able to keep your identity secret.'

'Oh, I think I will, just for today. I don't mind people knowing my name, but I don't want people coming up to me asking me all sorts of personal questions.'

Suzi eyes the Key kids, then whispers in my ear, 'What if one of these kids tells?'

'They won't. They promised,' I say. I'm sure they won't, I'm one of them now. 'So, as long as you two keep quiet about my ID, I'll be fine.'

Suzi nods towards the kids. 'If you can trust them… You can trust us.'

Trudy nods.

'Mind if I join you?' asks Miles. He sits down without waiting for an answer. 'There are one or two things we need to sort out before the exhibition opens. First, are you going to acknowledge this work as belonging to you, as in Christie Harris?'

'Yes, I am.' Phew, how brave am I?

'Good. Secondly, are you going to meet and greet?'

'No.' Not very brave, then!

'Okay, will you meet and greet later in the week? When you've got used to the idea of being an exhibiting artist.'

'That would depend on whether or not I've had good reviews.'

'Right, so what day is best for you?'

'It depends on the reviews.'

'Yes, but as I've already explained, *you will* have good reviews. So what day is best? I need to organise press presence. It would have been easier today of course, since they are already going to be here.'

'Any day. If the reviews are good.'

'Great, I'll get on to the press office,' says Miles, giving us the benefit of his first genuine smile of the day. 'There are a couple of posters that could do with your endorsement, would you mind signing them?'

'Lead the way,' I say, abandoning my untouched bagels. They don't look very appetising anyway.

'Mrs Price,' says Miles, gesturing for the long-suffering Annabel to join us. 'Would you take Christie through to the workroom to sign those posters? You could get a couple of the kids to give you a lift taking them out to the front of the building.'

'Yes, Mr Hepworth,' she says turning towards me. 'Would you like to follow me?' She leads the way to a medium-sized workroom.

Tools are stacked neatly in storage trolleys, and paints sit to attention on shelving. Sturdy work surfaces look out over a small walled garden, and stretch the length of one wall. The room has been well planned.

'This was going to be the caretaker's work and store room, but the Key kids have been using it to do projects for Madeline,' reveals Annabel. 'Miles insists they keep the room immaculate, as you can see... If the council wants to be awkward, they could say that this is still a working mill, and then there would be no chance of getting the place converted into flats.'

'I assumed they'd already been given planning permission.'

'They had, but that was before Madeline started your exhibition, and Miles has a feeling the council would prefer it to remain an art gallery. Possibly with an attached working craft centre—'

Really?

'... I'm sure you've noticed the rundown state of this area?'

'We did think we'd taken a wrong turning, until we saw the *Evolution* sign outside the mill.'

Kathleen Clunan

'If this were to remain a gallery, with the added attraction of a craft centre, it would bring in much needed investment to the area. Push up the prices of the other derelict buildings and wasteland about. It would be a good thing for the people round here.'

'Am I right in thinking, Miles doesn't want that?'

Annabel glances towards the open door. 'I couldn't say... Are you going to sign these posters? Here's a permanent marker.'

'Oh, right.' Quick change of subject; methinks Annabel has said too much. Very interesting. The posters are the same design as the large *Evolution* sign outside.

'The idea is, we clip these up in the reception area, so people don't forget the name of the exhibition.'

I sign several posters. There's a knock on the door, and Frankie's head appears. 'Do you need a hand?'

'Yes please, Frank,' says Annabel.

'It's Frankie now, Mrs Price.'

'Okay, Frank-ie, come in.' Mickey, like a shadow, follows Frankie into the room.

Frankie gathers up the posters. 'Do you want us to take them round the front?'

'Please.'

We all traipse round again. Annabel unlocks the doors at the front of the building, and Frankie and Mickey clip the posters up around the reception area. Mickey walks over to the cabinet which holds some of my sketching, and looks in.

Frankie does a 360-degree turn, and lets out a low whistle. 'We've not been in here since they put your pictures up. It's been like *Fort Knox*.'

'Would you like to have a look at my other work?' I ask. Annabel takes a sharp intake of breath.

'Yeah, can we?' says Mickey, spinning round to face us.

Annabel looks at her watch. 'I'm not sure if there'll be time, it's quarter past one already.'

Mickey turns back round, and carries on looking at the sketches in the cabinet. Frankie scuffs one of his new trainers on the floor and looks down at his feet.

'Okay then...' I say, clapping my hands together in a, let's make a deal kind of way. 'It does seem very unfair that you've not had a chance to have a good nosy round. How about I give you, say, ten minutes to look? The deal is, you give me your honest opinion of the pictures. And I mean *honest*.'

'Done!' says Frankie.

'Even if we don't like them?' asks Mickey.

'Especially if you don't like them. That's the whole point, if they're rubbish, I'd rather hear it from my friends.'

Mickey nods, and they both bound up the open staircase to the exhibition.

'I really don't think it was a good idea to let those two loose up there,' says Annabel.

'Why not?'

'Why not? Because you don't know what they'll do.'

'They'll give me their honest opinion of my pictures, that's what they'll do.'

Annabel gives me a look implying I'm rather simple. 'Mr Hepworth isn't going to like this.'

'Well, we'll just have to make sure *Mr Hepworth* doesn't find out then, won't we?' My eyes are drawn back towards the entrance. Miles is resting on the doorframe.

Great! Just what I need!

'Make sure I don't find out about what?'

Really? What is this man? And where did he come from?

'Oh, Mr Hepworth,' simpers Annabel. 'Christie has let Mickey and Frank go and take a look at the exhibition, *on their own*. I told her it wasn't a good idea.'

'It's Mickey and Frankie, actually,' I say.

Miles raises his eyebrows, and is clearly not amused. 'That will be all, Mrs Price.' Annabel's shoes shuffle on the wooden flooring as she leaves the reception area. 'We'd better go and see what they're up to then, hadn't we?'

'I told them they could have ten minutes.'

'How long have they had?'

'About two.'

'I suppose we might as well wait then.'

Ahh, so he does trust them. 'I think I'll just have a look in the cabinet over there. I didn't get a proper chance earlier,' I say.

Anything to get away from him.

It doesn't work.

He follows me.

'Madeline is keen for this exhibition to be a success. We've put a lot of work into it,' says Miles.

I continue staring into the cabinet.

What does he expect me to say?

'You do know she has been wanting to meet with you for some time?'

I nod, not prepared to even turn to glance at him.

'She wants this to be a success for *you*. She wants you to have your own identity.'

I clench my fists by my side. 'How lovely, an identity of my own. Guess what? I already have my own identity, had it for years, thank you very much. I have family, friends and even a career. Wow! In fact, I was very happy with my life, until Madeline decided to interfere.'

'Madeline has waited years—'

'Well I wish she'd waited a few more!' I snap.

Miles steps between me and the cabinet, completely blocking my view; and entirely too close for comfort. His subtle aftershave fills my nostrils. His presence fills my space. I step back, his closeness making me uneasy.

He leans forward, so his eyes are level with mine. 'Listen, Christie, and listen well, I don't like this any more than you do. But this is what Madeline wants, and I will do anything in my power, to get Madeline what she wants. Anything; I'd walk over hot coals for her—'

'Madeline's little lap dog, are you?' As soon as the words are out of my mouth, I regret them.

Miles stands to his full height, his face unreadable. 'Hardly! But believe me when I say I'd do anything for her, I mean it. Just be careful.'

He starts to walk away from me.

'Sounds like a threat.' It's like my mouth just won't stop! Usually when these barbed little comments flirt into my head, I manage to keep them to myself. Not with Miles, it's like he deserves to know my inner thoughts.

'Whatever.' Miles unlocks an internal door at the far end of the reception area. 'You can get back to the conference room this way, when Frank-ie and Mickey have completed their viewing.'

Okay, the man's a complete control freak. And scary. And I don't like him. He obviously doesn't like me. And what is this with Madeline? What has she got over him? I'm still standing staring at the cabinet when Frankie and Mickey return.

Mickey's face is glowing. 'It's wicked. I wish I could paint like that.'

'Yeah, an' those two women who come with you today, they're the kids on the pictures, aren't they?'

'Yes, Trudy and Suzi, though I'd rather you didn't mention to either of them that you recognised them in the paintings. They're a bit sensitive.' The trouble is; if these two can recognise Trudy and Suzi, so will everyone else who visits the gallery.

'Who's that lad in *Score*?' asks Mickey casually.

'She's only askin', cos she fancies 'im.'

'Do not!'

'He's a family friend.'

'Told me he looked hot,' Frankie persists. 'Can't see it mysel'. Looks a bit of a wimp.'

'No, he doesn't,' I say, defending the object of my adolescent crush perhaps a little too forcefully.

'So, you've got the hots for 'im too,' says Frankie, rubbing salt in the wound.

'Don't be ridiculous, he's just a friend. Trudy's brother actually. And considering he's only sixteen in that picture, I think his muscle definition is rather good.' There I go, digging my own grave. 'He just happened to be playing football on the village green.' Without his shirt on. 'And I just happened to be watching.' Stalking.

'So, he's sixteen then, is he?' asks Mickey hopefully.

'Nooo, he'll be about... I'd say twenty-seven-ish.'

'Oh.'

'Out of your league anyway, Mickey. If he's her brother. She's dead stuck up.'

'Frankie, she's not stuck up at all. She's just not very good with anyone under the age of twenty. You'd be surprised at what she gets up to.'

'Go on, tell us then,' says Frankie.

'I could, but then I'd have to kill you.'

'So, she's a spy then?' He half-heartedly rolls his eyes.

'Something like that,' I say.

'What is she really?' asks Frankie.

'She's a senior technical sales executive.' I try to sound upbeat, but really, even I struggle. I suppose if you're naturally sassy, and smart with it, a fab job. How all those intricate thingy whatsits work, is a complete mystery, and I've always been short on sassy.

'Bor-ring,' says Frankie.

'She seems to like it, and she earns more than me and Suzi put together.'

'So, what do you do, beside painting I mean?' Mickey asks the question I've been dreading, and I pretty much talked myself into it.

'Can't you tell?' I ask, playing for time. They both shrug and shake their heads. Oh well, here goes. 'I teach art.'

'I hate teachers,' says Frankie. 'They're only interested in rules 'n stuff.'

'To be honest, I'm a bit of a rebel,' I say, trying to win back their confidence. 'I'm always in trouble with the deputy head, and spend most of my break times hiding from him.' Well it's the truth.

'Why's that then?' asks Mickey.

'Mainly because I don't stick to all the ridiculous rules, or, I just bend them to suit my situation.' They don't seem impressed. 'And also, because some of my Year 10 and 11 students are like you and your crew. They've got personality and spark, and a need to be recognised as wholly unique. I encourage my kids to embrace their individuality... Unfortunately, schools and most teachers like conformity. It makes life easy.'

'I've never fit in. Nobody ever listened,' says Frankie. 'Not until I got involved with the Key project.'

'I can see you're a valued member of this team, Frankie.' Ah yes, back to safe ground.

'I know. Doin' stuff like this makes me feel like I've done somethin' good for a change.'

'And you've both got a talent for it. In fact, I'd call you ambassadors for the project.'

'That's what Miles says,' mutters Mickey. ''Cept he says it more like a threat—'

I bet he does, trumped-up toad.

'... He's not that bad when you get to know 'im though.'

I raise an eyebrow. 'Really?'

Frankie shrugs. 'He just puts on that tough guy image to impress people—'

It doesn't impress me.

'... An' Madeline's got him wrapped round 'er little finger.'

'You've met Madeline?' I say, trying to keep the surprise from sounding in my voice.

'Ye-ah, loads of times. She's dead famous you know. She always makes cakes when any of us go round. Really good cakes an' all. An' she's always tellin' us 'bout things she used to get up to when she was a film star. Not in a showy off way, just kind of mischief, an' people she's met, an' what they're like 'n stuff.'

'Sounds like fun.' Please stop! You're breaking my heart!

'Yeah, mostly. But even she gives us a load of crap about not lettin' ourselves down,' says Frankie.

'Crap?' I raise an eyebrow again; it's taken me years of practice to perfect it.

'Sorry, I mean pressure 'n stuff. Real bad.'

'It's only because she wants us to do well,' says Mickey.

'Yeah, I know.'

I tap an imaginary watch on my wrist. 'Oh well, suppose we'd better make our way back to the others,' I say. As much as I like chatting with the two of them, I'd rather not hear too much about the wonders of Madeline. I lead the way back to the conference room, and make a beeline for Trudy and Suzi. From the look of them they've been having a good time with the complimentary champagne.

Unfortunately, I'm intercepted by Miles, who skilfully leads me to a quiet corner of the room. 'We open in fifteen minutes. I've already spoken to Trudy and Suzi, and they agree with me. So, to keep your identity under wraps, you're going to have to be my partner for the day.'

I nearly choke. 'Can't I just be on my own? You know, like a freelance art critic or something.'

'Not a chance. You'd soon be rumbled; they all know each other. Anyway, this way I can at least keep an eye on what you're up to.'

'Exactly what does that mean?'

'I've been having a little chat with your friends over there, and they've been telling me some more of the things you've got up to—'

Oh, I can do much worse.

'…So, I think you'd be better with me as your chaperone—'

'Chaperone!'

'Escort, then—'

'Escort! I have no idea what those two have been saying—'

'You know, just in case.'

'Just in case what?' I hiss.

'Just in case you talk yourself into trouble. Oh, don't worry, I'll not introduce you as my date… I'll say you're a family friend. After all, that's what you are.'

I turn on my heel and walk away. The man is a complete… arrrrg, words fail me. I can't wait to get my hands on Trudy and Suzi! They should have known better than to tell Miles anything about me. Now it's looking like me having to spend all afternoon with*him*.

My so-called best buddies are sat with their heads together, sniggering away about something when I get to the table. 'Having a good time, girls?' I mutter.

They both have the grace to look bashful. Not easy I suppose, when you've consumed the quantity of champagne, the two of them look like they've guzzled.

'We're not drunk,' says Suzi, shaking her head vigorously.

'Had a couple to help loosen up,' confirms Trudy with a nod.

'The champagne is very nice, have you tried some?' Suzi asks.

'I'm driving us home, remember! As per usual. And besides that, I just happen to be at the opening of my own art exhibition.'

'Oh yes,' says Trudy. 'How's it going? We've been chatting to Miles, he's keen to keep you close, you lucky, lucky girl!'

'You think, Trudy? Really?' I huff.

'I wouldn't say no—'

Well, that wouldn't surprise anybody!

'... But, anyway, he seems to think that you'd be better sticking with him today. Away from us two, in case we are recognised from your paintings.'

'Not very likely,' slurs Suzi. 'We have changed since we were kids.'

'What would you say if someone *did* recognise you?' I ask.

Trudy grins. 'I'd just say, you're a bit of hot totty, and you couldn't make it today because you've had a better offer!'

'Trudy!'

'Jo-king... Don't worry, kiddo. I'd think of something.'

'That, Trudy, is exactly what I'm worried about!'

She offers a beauteous smile, and blows me a kiss. Is it any wonder it feels like an Argentine Tango competition is taking place inside my stomach?

Miles is luring people towards the gallery.

'Looks like this is it, Christie,' says Trudy. 'Go strut your stuff.'

'Yeah, Christie. Go strut your stuff,' echoes Suzi.

'Thanks for your support!'

'Nooo prob-lem-o,' says Suzi, making the "okay" sign with her fingers.

Unbelievable.

She is so embarrassing when she's drunk *and* happy.

'Right then, ladies, show time,' says Miles. 'I think it would be a good idea if Trudy and Suzi make a late entrance to the opening. All the critics will be eyeing up who's there while I'm doing my introductory speech, so it'll be best for you to stay out of sight.'

'I think I'd be better out of sight too,' I say hopefully.

Miles smiles his tight little smile. 'I don't think so.'

'I'll stand out like a sore thumb,' I say.

'I thought, since you're getting along so well with Frank and Mickey—'

'Frankie,' I correct.

'I thought you could stand with the Key kids. Frankie is going to say a few words about how the project has changed his life. Madeline thought it was a good opportunity. The programme needs positive publicity and community support—'

She doesn't miss a trick.

'… So, you'll be able to blend in with the group.'

Suzi hiccups. 'Not without a pair of new trainers, she won't.'

'I'm sure she'll cope. I've arranged for Mrs Price to bring the two of you a drink while you're waiting to come through to the exhibition.'

'Ah… Lovely… More champagne,' says Suzi.

'Coffee, actually,' says Miles. 'We need to keep our wits about us. I'm sure we all want this to be a successful venture.'

'Perhaps it would be better if they stayed in here all afternoon,' I say.

'When, have I, *ever* missed a party?' says Trudy indignantly.

'Today!' If you don't sober up!'

'I'm not drunk! It's "Little Miss Environmental Health" here, who's necked all the bubbly, not me.'

'Well why didn't you stop her?'

'Because, I thought we'd come out for a nice, relaxing day out, not a sit up straight, knees together tea party.'

'Well, just try to keep an eye on her, will you?'

'Obviously… I'm going to pour three litres of black coffee down her throat, before I let her anywhere near the gallery. I am a responsible adult, you know.'

'Thanks for reminding me, never would have guessed.'

Miles turns towards me and tilts his head to one side. 'So, Christie, are you ready?'

Key Critics

'... her first lover.'

Miles holds out his arm for me to link.

I hope he's joking.

Unfortunately, not. Raising a brow, he waits, until I oblige. The fabric of his jacket feels reassuringly soft beneath my hand, and my fingers betray me by curling around the crook of his arm.

Miles opens the connecting door. As we enter the foyer, a hush settles over the room. All eyes turn toward us. Frankie and his crew stand uneasily on the dais by the side of the main entrance. Wide-eyed and twitchy, they look ready to bolt at any moment. I feel, rather than see Miles tilting his head to gesture them over to us. In the hushed room, five pairs of new trainers squeak across the wooden floor. Miles releases my hand. I escape and stand behind Frankie and his friends.

'Ladies and gentlemen,' begins Miles. 'It is such a pleasure to welcome you to *Evolution*.' A shimmer of applause ripples around the foyer. Miles bows his head slightly in acceptance. 'I know most of you have been bristling for a preview since you heard about *Evolution* several weeks ago, but once you've seen it, you'll understand the need for secrecy. Madeline has been privileged to view from a distance, the development of a fine young artist, Christie Harris. And I'm sure, Christie herself would be the first to admit, that without the intervention of Madeline De-Muir, this collection of art would never have been seen by the public—'

Too right!

'... Unfortunately, Christie is unable to be with us today, but I do believe she will be available soon—'

Pending good reviews.

'... Now just before you all go into the main gallery; I'd like to introduce you to Frankie. Frankie is one of the young people, who have been involved in getting this exhibition set up. For example, the *Evolution* poster design was developed by Frankie and his team... Frankie.' Miles extends his arm in Frankie's direction.

There's another ripple of applause as Frankie shuffles his way forward, chin slumped to his chest. He rolls his head up, and stands up straight, leaving his head on a slight angle as he looks round the room. 'Hi, my name is Frankie. I don't think any of ya will remember me tomorrow, but that don't matter. What matters is that I'm here today, 'n' without Madeline, I'd probably 'ave been locked up. Ya see, I'm one of the people Madeline 'as helped through the *Keep-a-Key* project. I'm not very old, but I'm old enough to know that I've seen 'n' done things that *nobody* should 'ave to see, or do...'

The foyer is still, every eye fixed on Frankie, every ear, eager to hear more.

'...My mam was sick of me. The 'thorities was sick of me. The police was sick of me. The neighbours was well sick of me. Probably even the man in the moon was sick of me an' all.'

A collective nervous laugh titters between his spellbound audience. 'Then one night, I met this woman. She was walkin' her dog, 'n' it was chuckin' it down. It was late, 'n' I was wet through cos my mam' ad locked me out, again. This woman, she asked me if I wanted a coffee. I thought she was takin' the pi… Thought she was jokin'. But she weren't.

She took me to 'er 'ouse, she made me a brew, 'n' a bacon butty, the best bacon butty I've ever 'ad, with all butter drippin' through my fingers…'

Every face smiles at Frankie's memory.

'…Then she asked me if I'd anywhere to stay, 'n' when I said my mam 'ad locked me out, she got me a sleepin' bag, 'n' told me to sleep on her sofa. I didn't want to, cos it looked dead posh. But then I thought there might be somethin' worth nickin'. So, I stopped. But I couldn't do it, this woman 'ad been dead kind to me. Most people didn't bother to look at me anymore, not even me, I wasn't even worth lookin' at, not even in a mirror or a shop window. I was just rubbish. But this woman, she'd made me a drink, 'n' a bacon butty, 'n' let me stop in her posh 'ouse. It was like, *Are you crazy woman?*' Frankie swirls his hands round his head. 'But she wasn't, cos I didn't nick anythin', see.'

Frankie stuffs his hands into his jean's pockets. 'Next day, she fed me some more. She likes feedin' people. Then she give me a key, 'n' said if my mam locks me out again I can stop at hers. That's the first time I've ever been given a key.'

Frankie reaches down the neck of his sweatshirt, and pulls out a key on a chain. 'This is it, the key what changed my life. Without this key, without this project, my life was worth nothin'. *Nothin'*. But now I know that I am worth somethin', 'n' I just want you all to know what Madeline did for me.'

Frankie shrugs and shuffles back to his place. I clap my hands together so hard they hurt. Pretty much everyone else settles for polite applause.

'Well, thank you, Frankie,' says Miles. 'I don't think I can add anything more to that, to support the *Keep-a-Key* project. Frankie and his friends are proof that trust breeds trust. I'm sure you have all had a look in the cabinet over there, and have had a taster for what lies ahead. So, I declare *Evolution* open, and trust you'll be fair with your reviews. Enjoy.'

People make their way up the gallery steps, chatting to each other along the way. As the foyer empties, Miles turns to face Frankie, he places a hand on his shoulder. 'Well done, Frankie. I think they'll remember your name, so just be careful if any of them become too friendly.'

'What do ya mean?'

'It's like this, they may be art critics, but any one of them would love a tasty scandal to fill their coffers. It's all very well when they write nice things, but more often than not, they'd rather dish the dirt.'

Reassuring for me then.

Mickey shuffles her feet. 'Like when they say you're Madeline's toy boy?' Everyone sniggers bar Miles and myself.

'Exactly,' says Miles, and silences them with a glare. 'So be careful what you say, and to whom. Better to keep quiet and look cool in your new trainers.'

Nobody moves.

'Go on, Frankie, you lead the way. Christie, you stay with me for now, until we've got your identity established.' Frankie, Mickey and the others leave me alone with Miles. 'I thought I'd introduce you as Anne, since it's your middle name.'

Is there any point objecting? 'Whatever.'

'If we go up into the gallery together, and chat with some of the more influential critics together, then maybe you could mingle alone. Get a feel for what they are saying about *Evolution*. They might be a little more honest about what they think with you. After all, they're not likely to confide in me, being Madeline's toy boy!'

'Quite.'

'People can believe what they want, but just for the record, Madeline and I are just good friends.'

'Whatever. It makes no difference to me either way… Unless of course, you're planning to become my stepdad.'

'What a charming thought, although I'd rather have a different kind of relationship with you—'

Not a chance!

His eyes twinkle as they did the first time we met. '… A far pleasanter thought, don't you think?'

'Errrr… No! 'I squeak sarcastically.

'Oh, you think!' He grins. Grins! 'Come on, like I said "showtime".' Again, he offers his arm, reluctantly I link my hand through. He smiles a wolfish smile and my heart bounces in my chest.

Oh, why him!

'Atta girl.'

I actually feel like strangling him, but offer a tight smile instead. He rewards me with a chuckle. We join the small throng of people in the upper gallery. He guides me in his desired direction.

'Just smile, Anne. Look like you're enjoying yourself.'

'How can I not enjoy myself, with such a charming companion?' I mutter.

Again, he chuckles. 'Well I'm enjoying it enough for both of us! Okay, first, I'd like you to meet Timothy Grey. He's the one over there wearing the Dr Who scarf. Don't let his quiet voice and gentle manner fool you, he's probably the most savage critic here, so let's try and put him in a good mood, shall we?'

Miles leads me to where Timothy is stood. He's looking at *Score* – the painting of sexy Simon at sixteen.

'Well, Miles, I'll say this for your mystery artist, she certainly knows her way around the male anatomy.'

'You're probably right,' says Miles. 'Most artists do. May I introduce you to Anne?'

'Mr Grey.' I smile. 'I've heard such a lot about you. What a pleasure it is to meet you.'

'Anne, my dear, the pleasure is all mine.' He lifts both my hands, turns them over and honours the insides of my wrists with a kiss. Very forward!

What a creep.

'What, pray tell, are you doing with this old rogue?' Timothy asks in a sly manner.

'Anne's a family friend.'

'Really?' says Timothy. 'I didn't know you had family. Or friends.'

'You'd be surprised,' says Miles.

I notice a flare of red creeping up his neck. Obviously, Timothy's comment has hit a nerve.

'He's only a very distant family friend. I don't want you to get the wrong idea, Mr Grey. And I'm sure I wouldn't be here today but for my great aunt. Bit of a matchmaker, she's been trying to marry me off since I was eight.'

Timothy and Miles laugh indulgently.

'Never mind, my dear, you'll meet lots of new people here, you should be able to give Miles the push before the afternoon is over.'

'What a lovely idea!' I enthuse with as much charm as I can muster.

'Here's my card, next time you want to preview an exhibition, call. Nothing is worth having to endure an afternoon with Miles. Ciao.'

Oh dear, poor Miles is not amused. We leave Timothy to continue his way round the gallery.

'You are supposed to be keeping a low profile, not flirting with the most notorious womaniser in the art world.'

'You told me he was the most savage art critic, not the most notorious womaniser.'

'It doesn't take a degree to work it out. He is called Mr Grey…'

'I was trying to put him in a good mood, not an easy task when he clearly dislikes you intensely.'

'He doesn't dislike me. He was just playing, and I'm an easy target. He knew I wouldn't cause a scene, not today. Right, next I think Sarah McBride. Sarah you'll get on with.'

Sarah is looking at one of my earlier paintings, *Trudy takes a Tumble*.

'Sarah.'

'Miles, sweetie, haven't seen you in donkeys'. I do know Madeline keeps you on a short rein, even so, what have you been doing? And who is this adorable creature? Something you've been keeping from me, you naughty boy.'

'Let me introduce Anne, she's a friend of the family.'

'And you expect me to believe that?' Sarah sighs, and takes me to one side. 'Now, don't be shy, tell me everything you know about Miles. He's never even taken me out for lunch, let alone to an exhibition.'

'That's not true, I took you out the other week,' says Miles.

'Doesn't count sweetie, not when you've got your chaperone.' Sarah winks at me. 'Of course, Madeline doesn't let him out of her sight, unless he's working, that is.'

Interesting, very interesting.

Now how can I describe Sarah kindly? Clearly, she's developed her large personality to disguise her size, though underneath the layers of caftans, she's probably not as huge as she looks to be. But multi-layers of lilacs, pinks and purples don't do much for anyone. And what is it with Dr Who scarves? Granted, Sarah's are probably silk, but still, the way they're draped over her ample bosom, it only serves as a colourful frame for her double chins.

Okay, I'm being bitchy, but if anyone is in need of one of Trudy's makeovers, it's Sarah. In fact, I'm tempted to introduce them to each other.

Sarah formally shakes my hand. 'You look like you're in a world of your own. You don't need to be shy with me. Goodness, I'm one of the nicest people here, aren't I Miles?'

'Sarah, you are the nicest lady I know, at least until you pick up a pen.'

'But, Miles, sweetie, it's my job. I'm an art critic I've got to be critical,' purrs Sarah.

'Well I hope you're not going to be too critical of *Evolution*,' says Miles.

Sarah shrugs. 'You'll have to wait and see, sweetie.'

'Mr Hepworth,' interrupts Frankie. 'Mrs Price would like a word with you in the conference room. Bit of a problem with—'

'Yes, yes, Frankie, I'm on my way. Excuse me please, ladies. Sarah, you will take care of Anne won't you, she's new to all this?'

'She's safe with me. Now then, Anne, what shall we look at next? I've heard a whisper about a topless schoolboy, shall we look him?' Sarah edges her way past the sketches and paintings until she reaches *Score*. There are already others stood round the painting, making notes and passing comments.

'So, I think this would have been her first lover—' Really?

'But don't you think he's rather too perfect?'

Oh yes, definitely.

'What do you mean?' says the first.

'If he'd already been her lover, surely, she'd have been tempted to show his vulnerability, and this boy is resplendent, so confident and completely unaffected by her presence. It's almost as if he's unaware she's painting him.'

Well, I was up a tree at the time.

'True, but teenage boys are an arrogant breed.'

'What do you think, Anne?' whispers Sarah. 'Do you think they were lovers?'

Simon is going to kill me!

'I don't know. It just looks like a lad playing football to me. But you're the expert, what do you think?'

'I think she fancied the pants off him, and he didn't even know she existed.' Sarah chuckles. 'I think this young man is in for a bit of a surprise, don't you?'

I just nod.

It's safer not to speak.

Or cry.

And it's too late to run away.

'See that skinny woman over there?' asks Sarah.

I nod.

'Well that's Bunty Hargreaves. She's never lived up to her jolly hockey sticks name. The woman's a witch. If she takes a disliking to someone, they may as well hang themselves, and be done with it.'

'Miles said you were lovely, until you picked up a pen,' I remind Sarah.

'Bunty Hargreaves has never been lovely in her life! I may make the odd barbed comment in my column, but it is generally well placed, and done with no malice. Bunty does a hatchet job if she doesn't like someone, or their work.'

'Where are you taking me?'

'To meet the wicked witch, of course. May as well have a listen to what she thinks of this Christie Harris gal.'

'Bunty, nice to see you. Have you met Anne, she's a friend of Miles Hepworth?'

Bunty looks me up and down, sucks in her thin lips, and narrows her eyes. 'Can't say that I have.' She holds out her hand, I obligingly shake her cold fingers. 'Young lady,' is her only greeting.

'What do you make of *Evolution*, Bunty? Quite something to have the early efforts of an artist on display like this. Must have taken some pluck don't you think?'

Bunty sniffs. 'Sarah, don't you think it's a little too naive? A little too sentimental and cute?'

'I suppose…' Sarah's eyes twinkle.

'It's like this, everything is too well stage-managed. The age of the artist neatly written beneath each picture, the speed at which this exhibition has *allegedly* been set up. I think someone is playing with us. I think it's fake.'

'Fake!' I gasp.

'It's not unknown for an established artist to try and pull the wool over our eyes, and make us critics out to be bumbling fools. Especially one who has been recently rebuked.' Bunty taps the side of her nose with her forefinger. 'I think there might be tears before bedtime.'

I think she's probably right.

Mine.

Sarah leads me away. 'Oh dear, it sounds like Christie Harris is in for a rough ride with Bunty. I do hope the gal's got her head screwed on.'

Strange, something I've never been described as having. 'But what if Bunty's wrong? What if Christie Harris is just a normal kind of—'

Sarah shakes her head and her bosom; though that was probably just a natural progression. 'Dear me, no. There's nothing normal about Christie Harris.'

You don't say? 'Nothing normal?'

'Nothing at all, sweetie. First of all, Bunty does have a point about the meticulous detail to age. "Christie, age eight and three quarters", it's almost like a doting mother proudly announcing her baby's cut its first tooth. And of course, again, the speed this exhibition got off the ground. Most young artists tout their work around for ages before they're spotted, so to speak.'

'So, you think she's a fake too.' Just rip my heart out and throw it to the lions. Go on, we Christie Anne's know all about lions.

'No, she's not a fake. Don't worry, we've not been bamboozled. My guess is…' Sarah looks about herself. 'You won't pass it on, will you? Don't like being upstaged.'

'Not a word. Promise.'

'Not even to Miles?'

'Not even to Miles.'

JUST TELL ME.

NOW!

'That's my gal. Liked you as soon as we met. My guess is, this Christie Harris is either someone already famous for some other reason, and doesn't want to be accused of exploiting her real name. Or, she could be the sibling or child of someone famous. Whoever she is, what I can say with certainty, is, she is one mighty fine artist.'

'Wow, really?'

'Oh yes, my dear, she's got talent by the spadesful.'

Oh, Thank You Thank You Thank You Thank You.

'Of course, the poor thing has probably been pushed by her overbearing parents. She's probably a complete basket case; that would explain her not being here.'

That's the way to do it, build 'em up to knock 'em down, the higher you build, the farther they'll fall.

But still, I, Christie Harris, have got talent by the spadesful.

I, Christie Harris, *am* one mighty fine artist.

As we wander silently round the gallery, I inwardly fluff my own feathers, preening myself, because, let's face it, I'm the next big thing.

Until I fall.

No, no, no, I shan't think of that.

Sarah takes out a small notebook from her oversized carpet bag, and begins to jot down notes as we stop at each picture. Her pencil is chewed from the top, and worn from the bottom. The three and a half inches which remain, have clearly seen some action. She holds her head to one side while looking at each picture, then her head rocks from side to side, as if she's summing up her opinion of the picture, then she writes.

The speed of her pencil causes a ripple effect all through her body. Especially her bosom. I haven't a fetish for big bosoms, but honestly, they've a whole life of their own. Throughout she doesn't utter a word; she saves those for her notebook. We reach *The Long Farewell.*

'What do you think of this?' asks Sarah. She taps her lips with the stubby pencil.

It'd been Suzi's idea, to paint my snapshot memory of my last meeting with Auntie Maddie. Looking at the painting now, leaves a hole in my stomach. A hole in my life. Auntie Maddie only remains in my mind's eye, and this painting. The pain of her deception is too raw to hide. I can feel Sarah watching me. I was the little girl, with years ahead of her, trying to please a woman who doesn't exist.

'It makes me profoundly sad,' I manage to say at last.

'Really? I think the old lady wants the little girl to follow her. She's tempting her with the gay red scarf, and tall heels. A promise of excitement.'

'Maybe the little girl is too young to understand.'

'Or maybe she doesn't want to follow, guess we'll never know. Unless Christie Harris cares to enlighten us.' Sarah starts making more notes.

'Excuse me, I think I'll go and find out what Miles is up to,' I say.

Sarah hardly seems to notice me leave, so intent are her scribblings.

I do hope she is kind.

Busted or Not

... her right boob threatening to liberate itself ...

'Right, I've a few things to tie up here, but I'll be with you as soon as I can.' Back in the conference room, Miles is on his mobile. 'No, there's nothing here that Mrs Price can't handle, so don't worry, Christie's fine. It's her two friends who need babysitting. I'm going now, and I'll be with you soon.' Miles turns to me, his expression grim.

'Problems?' I ask, trying to keep the gleam of hope from clearly shining through.

'Complications we could have done without, but it could have been much worse. Very much worse.' Miles rubs both hands over his face. 'I'm sorry, I'm afraid I'll have to leave.'

Yay!!! Free at last! 'I suppose I'd better leave as well, since you're my escort,' I say solemnly.

'Probably would be wise. I'll speak to you later, just don't let those two friends of yours anywhere near the gallery... Or the critics. The only thing I want to read about is *Evolution*.'

The cheek of the man. Suzi and Trudy aren't that bad. Maybe a little high-spirited... Now I'm free to escape, I am feeling more magnanimous towards my best buddies...

'Coo-eee. Any chance of some...' Suzi staggers towards us. 'Christie? Is that you, Christie—'

Really?

'... Course it is. Sil-ly me. Silly-silly-silly-silly-silly meee. Do I usually wear glassseesss, cos everything's all swishy-wishy-wishy-wishy-wOOOO.' Suzi makes two peep holes with her forefingers and thumbs, and holds pretend binoculars to her eyes.

Miles raises his eyebrows.

I cringe.

Suzi pouts. 'Christie-wisty, I really-really don't feel very-very-very well. I think I'm gonna be sick.'

'Come on, let's get you to the loos.' I put my arm round her and lead her back out of the room.

Why me? What did I do to deserve this? I mean, it's not as if Suzi's an out and out drunk, so why did she choose today, of all days. Oh yes, that's right, free champers. The main culprit for Suzi's alcohol induced illness, is muttering his excuses and making his escape. The toad.

That's right, leave me to sort out poor Suzi. I mentally give Miles a kick in the shin. It makes me feel better for about ten seconds, then I remember Dad saying that it's as bad to think of doing something, as to actually do it. The glow of satisfaction doesn't last long. Still, it's a shame Miles doesn't feel the pain in his shin I mentally inflicted.

We make it just in time. Suzi starts heaving her guts up. I, being a true friend, hold her hair out of the line of fire, and make suitably soothing sounds and gestures. The door creaks open.

'Having fun girls?' asks Trudy.

'Not really. I thought you were supposed to be looking after this one,' I say, nodding towards a dishevelled Suzi.

'She gave me the slip. I've been looking all over for her.'

'Well, I think she went in search of more alcohol, and found it, by the looks of her.'

Suzi gives us a soulful glance. 'It was lovely bubbly…'

Trudy shakes her head. 'Surely you've not been drinking again! She's already thrown up once.'

'I don't get out much,' says Suzi, from her half slumped, half kneeling position over the toilet. 'Anyway, it was free, and Annadel, Annadu, Mrs Price said I could.'

'Mrs Price should have known better,' says Trudy in disgust. 'Wait until I see her. She doesn't have to get you cleaned up and home. You'd better not be sick in my car! I'm serious! Come on. Christie, we'll have to get her home before she starts again. We can't stay here with her like this, if that Bunty Hargreaves gets her hands on her, all our names will be in the papers tomorrow.'

'Have you been in the gallery?' Please don't say yes. Please say you just peeped through a crack in the door. Please say Bunty Hargreaves is a family friend, a dear sweet lady despite what others say.

'I had to! Suzi was on the loose, and the last time I'd seen her she was singing *I've got a lovely bunch of coconuts*. Can you imagine what that lot in there would have made of her—'

Unfortunately, yes.

I nod.

'Hard-nuts Hargreaves, made a beeline for me.'

'Does she know who you are?'

Trudy shrugs. 'Ish'

'Ish. ISH. What do you mean, ISH. She either knows you, or she doesn't,' I hiss. My innards quiver, and tell-tale heat starts it's crawl up towards my ears.

'We've met at a few charity events. Always creeping up to Mum and Dad. Loves to schmooze with the crowd.' Trudy holds her arms out at full length, and examines her talons; a sure sign of hostility.

'Great. That's all I need. Did she pummel you for information?'

'She tried, but I didn't tell her anything about you. When I walked into the gallery, she looked at me, and a very smug expression came over her, as if she'd just worked something out. Not very likely, in my opinion.'

'That's it, my cover's blown!' I huff. How will I be able to show my face in school again?

'I don't think so, she seems to think I'm Christie Harris, and since I'm Lord Drummond's daughter...'

'You wouldn't want to be accused of using your connection,' I finish for her.

'Exactly.'

Okay, that makes sense.

'I think I'm going to be sick again,' whines Suzi.

I hold Suzi's hair out of her face, again, and Trudy rubs her back. I need to go back into the gallery and find out what Bunty Hargreaves thinks she knows. I also want to make sure Sarah hasn't made the same assumption. I don't want Sarah to think I've been deliberately dishonest with her. Although, I suppose I have.

Suzi staggers to her feet, and looks at her gaunt reflection in the mirror. She turns on the cold tap and starts splashing her face. She turns the tap off, bends double and holds her face under the hand dryer. This helps, now she's red of face, and green of gills. Her hands are white and her feet unsteady, but somehow, with the help of her two nearest and dearest, she makes it to the car, and promptly falls asleep on the back seat.

Friends, who'd have them?

'Trudy, I've just got to pop back inside for a couple of minutes. You'll be okay with the sleeping beauty, won't you?'

'Sure, but don't be long, or I might join her.'

I make my way back into the gallery, and go over to Sarah. She's chatting to Dr Who. As soon as she spots me, she excuses herself, and takes me to one side.

'Bunty has left. She told me she'd just been talking to Christie Harris, and is going to let the rest of us keep guessing until we read her review.' Sarah smiles.

'Oh.'

'Yes, "Oh" indeed. Now Anne, or should I call you Christie—'

'Shh! Don't let anybody hear you. How do you know it's me?'

'Just an inkling at first, my dear. And then your reaction to *The Long Farewell*. But what really clinched it was when Trudy came in. *Trudy takes a tumble*. Bunty is convinced that Trudy is you... Now Trudy wouldn't have painted herself, now would she? Silly Bunty, sometimes she can't see past the end of her own nose. I'm afraid it's going to be *Bunty makes a blunder* next.'

I smile, it has a nice ring to it. 'What are you going to do?' Even though Sarah seems to like me, I know that she'd be a fool not to exploit the situation. And Sarah is nobody's fool.

She tilts her head to one side. 'We need to talk, but not here with everyone about.'

'You could meet me at the back of the building, and we could go into the conference room.' I need to make this right before it gets anymore out of control. Madeline and Miles have a lot to answer for, leaving me to mop up the mess.

'Lovely, I'll meet you in five minutes, my dear. Off you go.'

'Poor dear,' Sarah booms to Dr Who, and anybody else in the room who cares. 'Miles, the cad, has gone off and left her. She's been looking for him all over the place. He's probably been summoned by Madeline.'

Everyone laughs. I don't know why, it's probably true.

Dashing outside, I briefly explain to Trudy what's going on. She decides she might as well try and get some sleep in the car with Suzi. I wait at the back of the mill for Sarah. When she arrives, she's breathing heavily.

'Didn't want to give the game up,' she huffs. 'I waited a few minutes before I left. I'm out of puff; I didn't want anyone seeing me come around here, so I ran. I can't remember the last time I did that. Come on, let's get inside.'

The place seems deserted. We sit down at a table in the corner of the conference room. Sarah takes out her notepad and three-inch pencil, and looks at me expectantly.

'Now then, my dear, where would you like to start?'

The truth, the whole truth, up until mother Madeline interrupted my life. I'm just plain old Christie Harris, spinster of this parish. It's only in the last few days I've developed a mysterious past.

'What would you like to know?' I ask.

'Well, first off, who did you paint your pictures for, and why?'

Good question. Here goes. 'When I was a little girl, an Aunt of my mother's visited us. She asked me what I wanted to be when I grew up. I told her I wanted to be an artist, so she set me the task of sending her my pictures. It was supposed to make me disciplined.'

'Did it make you disciplined?'

'Yes, I think it probably did. I didn't want to let her down. She'd made it sound very important for me to chase my dream.'

'I like that, a dream chaser. What about your family, any brothers or sisters?'

'No, it was just me and my parents, though I have two close friends.'

'Trudy and Suzi?'

'Yes, they're still my best friends. We share a house.' Maybe that's too much information.

'Oh, what fun, so all night parties, and boyfriends galore.'

'Hardly.' I laugh. 'It's more cleaning rotas, who ate the last Snicker, and which bin needs to go out this week.'

'No boyfriends then?'

'Not that I've noticed. Trudy tends to get the most, Suzi and I don't do too badly, but no one special for any of us, yet.'

'Never mind, plenty of fish in the sea.'

'Sharks too!' Now why did I say that? And why am I thinking of Miles? And why am I *still* thinking of Miles?

And still!

'So, Christie, what do you do when you're not eavesdropping at the opening of your own exhibition?'

'You mean in the real world? I'm an art teacher. And I love it, but I'd rather not mention the name of the school. I'm always getting into trouble with the deputy head, and I don't want to give him any more reasons to pick on me than he already has.'

'You intend to carry on teaching?' Sarah raises an eyebrow.

'Of course, it's what I do. I'm a teacher. I have the best kids, the ones who try the hardest. Some of them have hardly ever been praised before in their lives, so with a bit of encouragement, and a lot of hard work, their portfolios are just as good, if not better than the "A" sets. I love watching the kids grow in confidence. It just kind of bubbles inside them, under the surface, then all of a sudden, it explodes! With a bit of luck, the explosion is impressive enough to affect their whole outlook on life.'

'Wow, you really do love teaching; I can tell you're driven.'

'Oh, Sarah, I love teaching. It's what I was born for, and but for my love of art, I may never have realised it. I suppose I've a lot to thank Auntie…'

'Auntie?'

'Sorry.' I bow my head. 'She's no longer with us.'

'I'm sorry to hear that. Were you *very* close?'

'Always, we wrote often.' And then she betrayed me.

'And you kept all the letters?'

'As it happens, yes.'

'Any chance of sharing them?'

'Not in a million years.' Spot remedies, yuk. First disco, arrrh. My crush on Simon, too embarrassing for words. 'No, not ever.'

'Shame. Now, Christie, if there was one thing you could change about your life, what would it be?'

Oh, you know, just the last few days. 'What I'd really like is double glazing. The house is really draughty.'

Sarah looks crestfallen, I think she expected me to say money, fame or happily ever after. Oh well, never mind.

'Last question, do you have any splendidly sensational secrets you'd like to share with me?'

'None…' Ha! 'That I'd like to share with you.'

'But you do have secrets?'

'Sarah, everyone has secrets.'

'Well, thank you very much for your time, Christie.' Sarah closes her notebook. 'I'm sure you're going to be very successful in the future. Just promise me one thing.'

'What?'

'When you want people to know your secrets, tell them to me first!' Sarah winks and hands me her business card. Then off she glides like an oversized belly dancer. From behind, she looked disturbingly like the headmistress from the old St. Trinian's films; I'm sure she was played by a man. Oh well.

By the time I get back to the car, both Suzi and Trudy are asleep on the back seat. I rummage in the boot, find a picnic blanket and cover them both up. They look like two tired-out children after a day of excitement.

Suzi snores and dribbles, while Trudy truly does look like a sleeping beauty. There is no justice in the world. Sadly, I snore and dribble, so I can say this with conviction.

Key in the ignition and off we go. Oh no! Where did Bunty Hargreaves spring from? What's that she's pointing at the car? No, no, no, it's her mobile.

'I think that's your first brush with the paparazzi, a` la Bunty,' drawls Trudy – not dribbles.

'I'm well aware of that! But you do realise the mobile was pointing at you and Suzi in the back, and not me driving.'

'How very rude!' yelps Trudy.

'Indeed.'

Suzi belches. 'What's all the noise about? Trying to rest here.'

Trudy lunges forward, and makes a grab for the steering wheel. 'Stop the car!'

I start to break.

'NOW, Christie! I'm not going to let that sour-faced battle-axe get away with intruding in *our* privacy. Who does she think she is?'

The car scrunches to a halt, and Trudy launches herself out of the car, and marches across to where Bunty Hargreaves stands still happily tapping away. Trudy is barefoot, and the gravel must be cutting into her feet. Unbelievably, Bunty Hargreaves is *still* blatantly taking pictures. Clearly, she's never encountered anyone like Trudy before. Trudy does not take prisoners, "seek and destroy", is her motto.

'Hey, you, who do you think you are? How dare you take pictures of me, give me that mobile!'

Bunty staggers backwards as Trudy surges forward. Trudy snatches the phone and starts swiping her finger over the screen.

Bunty makes a grab for her mobile. 'How dare you! That is private property.'

Trudy continues swiping. 'So is my face and theirs.' She thrust the phone back towards Bunty. 'Have it! Put it away! Believe me, if you *dare* point it in our direction again, I'll crush the bloody thing!' Trudy stamps her unshod foot on the ground, and grinds it into the gravel.

I need to get to her before she really loses it. Getting out of the car, I snag my ankle on the trailing seatbelt, landing flat on my face in the gravel and a conveniently placed puddle. My hands, knees, elbows, chin and nose smart as tiny stones cut into then.

Muddy water gurgles into my mouth and nose. Gasping in pain and shock, I raise my head in time to avoid sucking up the yucky water. Suzi swings open her door, thwack. Pain sears the back of my head... I plunge right back into the muddy water...

Full frontal impact. Face fully submerged. Head throbbing. Hair dripping. Eyes stinging.

Fab.

Suzi plonks herself down in the wet gravel beside me, skirt up round her waist, cranberry knickers exposed for all to see, and her right boob threatening to liberate itself from the confines of her bustier. She yanks my head onto her lap, and starts RUBBING the gravel and mud from my face, whilst rocking forward and back, and humming *Is this the way to Amarillo*.

I try grappling Suzi's hands from my face... She's having none of it.

I can still hear Trudy and Bunty going at each other. A small group of onlookers appear, gawping from Trudy and Bunty's verbal assault on each other, to the two damsels in distress, or dis-dress, apparently mud wrestling. Finally, Trudy becomes aware of my plight, stalks across the car park and rescues me from Suzi's ministrations.

A woman on a mission.

'Oi, you! Frank or Frankie, whatever your name is. Get here now!' hollers Trudy, using exaggerated arm movements.

Frankie ambles towards us.

'Ever driven a car?' demands Trudy.

Eyes wide, Frankie nods.

'Then get your arse in that car, and park where it was parked before.'

Frankie gets in the car, and drives it ever so slowly away, clearly to not cause me any more upset. Speeding up dramatically, he does a handbrake turn at the end of the car park, slows back down to park the car, and gives a fuming Trudy a salute.

Cheeky moose.

'You lot, Mickey, Goofy, Donald…' shouts Trudy.

I cringe and shiver at the same time. One of my many talents, multitasking. Mickey and the other Key kids look at each other, and shuffle their way over to us.

'Is there anywhere we can take these two, to get cleaned up?'

'There's a posh bathroom 'n' shower next to the office. Mrs Price 'ill 'ave the key,' says Mickey.

'Okay, you help me with Christie. You three, see if you can manage Suzi. Good luck!'

Suzi sulks as she's hoisted to her feet, slithering back down again seconds later. 'Maybe, I just be a little teeny-weeny, itsy-bitsy, bitsy, bitsy bit, bit tipsy,' admits Suzi, her eyes squinting at the miniature gap she's conjured between her thumb and forefinger.

After three attempts, we're on our way back to the rear entrance of the mill.

Suzi makes a bid for freedom. 'Is this the way to Amarillo, ev'ry night I've bin huggin' my pillow. Come on you lot, join in. I'll be Peter Kay. Dreamin' dreams of Amarillo, and sweet Marie who waits for me. Sha la la la la la la la, come on clap. Sha la la la la la la la.'

The day, it seems, just gets better and better. Ah well.

A horrified looking Mrs Price leads the way to the bathroom; though I think she's secretly enjoying the spectacle. And because Trudy won't leave me on my own, I shower with my underwear on. Not that she hasn't seen it all before, but I doubt very much that I'd be able to bend my knees to get my knickers back on. And, I'd rather not stand butt naked in front of Trudy, whose body is sculpted to perfection.

I'll just have to go commando later.

'You're not going to like this,' announces Trudy, once I'm safely under the steaming water, wincing with pain. 'But I've arranged for Dr Pilkington to meet us back at the house in about an hour.'

'Gee, thanks,' I gurgle. Not sure if I manage to pull off the sarcasm. 'But I doubt I'm in a financial position to meet his professional fees.'

'It'll be covered by Daddy's expenses; Dr P. is always on hand for company emergencies.' Trudy flicks her hand. 'You know, you could have a concussion, and I refuse to sit in A&E for hours with Suzi in tow. Dr P is a real sweetie, it'll make his day! I'll call us a taxi when you get out of there, since none of us are in any fit state to drive.'

Trudy helps me out of the shower and dabs me with a pristine white towel which feels like sandpaper. Has nobody heard of Comfort?

Mrs Price has kindly found me some clean clothes "A spare set, just in case I have an accident while I'm here". The tweed skirt, smooth knit turtleneck and matching cardigan all threaten me from hangers. The colour, cow pat green, is not my shade to be honest. And really, would anyone believe that Mrs Price *hadn't* had an accident if she wore that ensemble? I think not. But beggars can't be choosers, so they say. Trudy helps me dress.

'Not really your colour,' states Trudy.

'Or shape, or size either,' I add, pulling at the gaping waistband of the itchy tweed skirt.

'It'll all come together when you put the headscarf on, dearie.' Trudy holds up her hands in self-defence. 'Joking, I'd better go and book the taxi now.'

'Couldn't Frankie drive us home?' I ask innocently.

'Only when pigs fly backwards through the valleys of Wales, but maybe Mrs Price could. Good thinking.'

Mrs Price jumps at the chance to drive us home. As we traipse to the car, I realise Suzi has been even less fortunate than I, in the clean dry clothing department.

The orange boiler suit, I surmise, wouldn't fit over her boobs, hence it's tied at the waist by its sleeves. The extra bulk caused by the boiler suit, under the "R U UP 4 IT?" black hoody, makes Suzi look like a delinquent *Teletubby*. Her scowl only adds to the effect.

Looking on the bright side, Frankie and crew are positively beaming. The sight of me and Suzi has cheered them up no end. Let's face it, it's not every day you get to see people at their behavioural and visual extremes.

AM (About Midday), absolutely stunning, well dressed, perfectly made-up, uptight, upstanding and sober.

PM (Post Mud-wrestle), completely uninhibited, battered, bruised, and suffering from severe, almost fatal, no dress sense syndrome.

So, you see, it's quite understandable why they all look so sodding cheerful.

Designated Driver

Trudy practically drags her out of the car ...

Mrs Price, once again, "call me Annabel", seems to have taken on the persona of an F1 Racing driver, as she gleefully revs Trudy's car.

'It's quite powerful,' says Trudy. 'It can be a little jumpy.'

'Oh, I'll soon get the hang of this baby!'

'Ahem, Mrs Price, Annabel. Are you sure you don't mind driving us home? It will mean you having to get a taxi back here, taking up your time, and I'm sure you're a very busy lady,' says Trudy nervously.

'Don't mind at all. I've always wanted to drive one of these beauties. I used to do a bit of off-road rally driving when I was younger. That's where I met my husband.'

'Oh.' Trudy's voice is uncharacteristically weak.

'So, you see, nothing to worry about. I'll have you home in a jiffy.'

Now, that's what worries me.

Trudy shrugs her shoulders, and mouths to me, 'How bad can she be?'

I wonder.

Mrs Price shuffles herself lower into the driving seat, rolls her shoulders, stretches her arms out before her, takes a firm grip on the steering wheel and revs the engine. Again. Slinging her arm over the back of the passenger seat, she swivels to look out of the back window. Swinging the car in a wide reversing arc sending a spray of gravel across the car park and splattering the Key kids who jump away in dismay. The car then jerks forward, scrunching to a shuddering halt at the road edge.

'Sit back, and relax, ladies. I'll have you home in no time.'

Mrs Price's promise to get us home in a jiffy, suddenly seems not such a good offer. As the car bumps off the pavement, it becomes clear Mrs Price has no concerns about the mental and physical state of us passengers.

At speed, we're off, the flash of a speed camera catches my eye as we swerve to the middle of the road.

'Watch out for that—' gasps Trudy.

'Cyclists!' hisses Mrs Price. 'They all think they're Bradley Wiggins! Shouldn't be on the road!'

It soon becomes clear Mrs Price has no concerns about other motorists – pedestrians either. She has no worries about mini roundabouts, or speed bumps as she calls them, traffic lights, or curbs. She certainly has no worries about speed limits, speed cameras, or any other aspect of the Highway Code.

And to be honest, none of that would matter if we were all inebriated, heavily sedated, or better still, completely unconscious.

But me and Trudy aren't, so we witness the shock and horror of other motorists and cyclists, see their hand gestures and mouthed verbal abuse. We see the wide-eyed fear of pedestrians, even hear some of them scream. Our stomachs lurch as the car mounts the series of mini roundabouts, and bounces over to the other side.

As we cruise towards the oncoming traffic after going through another red light, I can say quite honestly, I actually taste fear. The grind and jolt of *catching* the odd curb or two, sets my teeth on edge.

The *Mind your speed*, and *Please drive carefully through our village* signs are merely a blur at the roadside, while speed cameras flash happily at us as we rush over their fining white lines.

Trudy yanks out her mobile and phones for a taxi to meet us at home, ready to return the demon driver back to where she came from.

I don't know what she offered the taxi driver by way of an incentive, but bless his little heart, as we screech round the final bend, and I plunge for the last time into Trudy's lap, I see him ready and waiting at Rose Lodge.

'Just on the left here!' shouts Trudy.

The car skids to a halt, inches behind the taxi.

'Home sweet home, ladies. I enjoyed that.'

Trudy practically drags her out of the car and thrusts her into the back of the waiting taxi. The taxi is brisk to whisk the dice-with-our-life Mrs Price away. Gone. Vamoose. Vanished and banished, and never ever to be permitted to terrorize this trio again.

After Trudy explains the whole sorry story to him, dear old Dr Pilkington has the pleasure of examining three badly shaken young ladies. He jovially jabs my ass with a sedative, and tipples a handful of pink painkillers (two) into my shaking white hands.

'No concussion,' he decides, as he blinds me with a torch. 'Just a few bruises,' he announces as he prods my battered body. 'And abrasions,' he declares, as he swabs my face with an antiseptic wipe. 'A couple of days R&R and you'll be good as new,' he says, as he accepts a cup of tea rattling on a saucer from Trudy.

Suzi sits, silent. Her body slumps, eyes wide. Her dishevelled bob hangs about her face. The orange boiler suit creases around her middle, while the "R U UP 4 IT?" hoodie wisely disguises its challenge. Now it's more a statement, "UP IT", which in my drug induced state, I think rather appropriate.

'Somehow,' says Trudy, 'I don't think "Little Miss Environmental Health" is going to be up to stool samples and swabs tomorrow. I'll phone her department now and let them know she won't be in.'

'Bank holiday. Shut,' says Suzi without emotion.

'I'll talk to the answering machine,' says Trudy patiently.

I can tell she's at least trying to keep the sarcasm from her voice, in deference to Suzi's weakened state. Suzi nods oblivious.

'I'll tell them we've been in a road accident.'

I nod my head; a shooting pain makes me instantly regret it. 'We have. The accident was letting that woman drive, we might need counselling.'

'Don't worry, Christie, I've learned my lesson. The only person I will ever let drive my car from now on, is you. Anyway, I don't think I'll be up to going to work tomorrow either. So, I'll let them know. *And,* I'm going to get someone round to look at that poor car. I'm sure it must have suffered as much as we have.'

I'm not sure about that, but I nod anyway.

'Going to bed now,' says Suzi, but she makes no attempt to move.

'Come on, Suzi, I'll give you a hand.' Trudy leans towards her, and offers her two. She hoists Suzi up, puts her arm round her and guides her out of the room.

I hear their slow progress up the stairs. Some shuffling, voices, more shuffling, and then stomping down the stairs.

Trudy doesn't stomp, ever, at least not until today.

'Made an executive decision,' declares Trudy. 'I hope you don't mind. Can't put myself through all that again, so you'll have to sleep on the sofa. I've brought your quilt down.' Trudy tucks me in and makes me quite comfy. 'Okay, can I get you anything before I go and sort myself out?'

'I just want my mum,' I say, feeling like sobbing. 'And my dad.'

'It's been a long day, Christie. Sleep now, we'll get you home tomorrow.'

Pottering Tuesday

I was awestruck.

It has been years, since I've woken up uncomfortable and in pain on a sofa. In my youthful, early university days, it was like an initiation into the real world of an undergraduate. I'd stagger, sloshed and singing back to my digs, waking up bleary-eyed and uncomfortable in the morning. A small price to pay for a night of partying, or so I'd thought, foolishly, at first.

It hadn't taken me too long to figure out, that actually I was there for more than a good time. Hangovers, hallucinations and hedonism weren't for me. Hard work, honest friends and the occasional hot date were more my scene. I left the partying to Trudy.

So, why does my head feel like I've drunk a barrel of beer? Why do my eyes feel puffy and sore? And why is Trudy sat *in her silk kimono* watching me like I'm a scientific experiment gone wrong.

Trudy doesn't do in her kimono. Trudy does, dressed immaculately, at all times, and in all places, regardless. I'm trying to figure out why. I squint my eyes, turn my head, and wince.

Trudy nods at me. 'How are you feeling? Bit of an eventful day we had.'

It could have sounded patronising, but it didn't. Instead, slowly, dizzying images trickle into my head. The gallery, Miles, the *Keep-a-Key* kids, Mrs Price,

Miles, Bunty Hargreaves, Sarah McBride, the car, the gravel, Mrs Price, terror, Dr Pilkington, Miles.

'I feel—' How do I feel? Sore. Tired. Confused. 'Why are you not dressed?'

'Oh, I've just been pottering round, that's all'

'Trudy, you *never* potter around. And what about your poor feet?' I remember the gravel grinding.

'They're fine, years of ballet and surgical spirits has made them tough as old boots. But I think today we all need to do a bit of pottering. It can be pottering Tuesday.'

'Don't think I'm up to pottering.' I haul myself up into a semi sit. 'I might just be up to a coffee though.'

'Could you manage toast as well?' asks Trudy, shuffling herself into the kitchen.

'No thanks, just coffee would be great.'

'I'll take one up for Suzi too, I heard her pottering earlier.'

'Suzi always potters.'

The room hasn't changed. My head hurts. Rummaging, I find a Snickers wrapper stuffed down the side of the cushion. I smile. Everything is the same, but different. Not so long ago my only real problem was Mr Sloan. Now I have a head full.

I sit up as Trudy hands me my coffee, it tastes good. Just what I need to wake me up. After all, I could be a world-famous artist by now. I hear Trudy go up the stairs, probably taking Suzi her coffee. I wonder how she is this morning. Probably mortified by her behaviour yesterday. Probably suffering for it too. Suzi the saint, drunk as a skunk.

Balancing my cup on the arm of the sofa, I run my fingers down over my face. My skin feels tight and rough over the scratched skin. I feel round the back of my head to the painful lump under my tangled hair. I'm still trying to untangle my hair when Trudy comes back into the room.

She's still not dressed.

'How bad do I look?' I'm brave enough to ask.

Trudy tilts her head to one side, scrutinizes me. 'Do I compare thee to a—'

'No, seriously.'

'Dr P cleaned the cuts on your face thoroughly last night, there's no sign of infection, but they look quite raw. They're more like little scratches really, I'm sure they'll heal fine. All easily covered by the miracle of foundation.'

I nod, can't quite manage to speak, but attempt a smile. A tight smile. I can feel the pressure building as I hold my lips together valiantly. My chin begins to crumple, my nostrils flare and tears squeeze out of my swollen eyes.

'I'm not vain,' I profess, as Trudy dabs snot from my streaming nose. I know I'm not the prettiest, but I do try to keep myself looking okay-ish, most of the time. I go blotchy when I'm hot, so I try to stay cool. I burn in the sun, so I stay in the shade. My eyes are my best feature, so I always wear mascara. The last few days I've had panda eyes.

'I know you're not vain, you daft Muppet,' agrees Trudy. 'You just have a healthy interest in your appearance. Nothing wrong with that.'

'Nothing at all. I just don't want to frighten any children when I go out,' I add.

'Exactly.'

'So how bad do I look, really?'

'I'll go and bring a mirror.'

In the unforgiving sunlight, the mirror isn't as kind as I would have liked it to be. The grazes aren't too deep, just the odd one or two have started to scab over, but the skin around them is shiny and red raw, proof that Dr Pilkington has indeed done his job well. As Trudy promised, they aren't too bad. Suzi would be horrified if she ever found out she was responsible for some of them. But it's my eyes that give away my true state. Swollen and red.

Proof of my self-pity.

Sarah's words come back to me, "I do hope the gal's got some pluck". If she could see me now, she'd be heartily disappointed. Maybe it's time to find it. All I need to do is find my pluck.

Suzi ambles into the room. She doesn't look like she's borrowed my pluck, she looks like she could do with some too. 'My head is sore,' she says, and flops down into a chair without even looking at me. 'I can't remember much of yesterday, just being at that gallery. Was Tony Christie there?' She turns to look at me, her eyes widen. 'What happened to you?'

'Just a bit of a tumble. I'll be okay in a few days.'

'You look like you've been in a fight!' She stands up, and makes her way tentatively across the room, then starts to examine me like one of her specimens. 'You've got gravel in your hair. You've been attacked!'

'No, honestly, I just fell over, that's all.'

'Was it one of those unruly teenagers?'

'No!'

'I know you, pretending it didn't happen, just so they won't get in trouble with the police. Wake up, Christie, they're nothing but a bunch of hoodlums.'

Oh, the irony! 'Suzi, let it drop, it was nothing to do with them. If you don't believe me, then go and ask Trudy.'

I feel for Suzi. Her mum is such a busybody know-it-all, who judges *everybody*. Sometimes, in times of stress, Suzi's default button makes her just the same. She tries not to, I think.

'How would Trudy know? She was drunk!'

I shake my head in disbelief and immediately wish I hadn't. 'Not as drunk as you, do you remember your solo rendition of *Amarillo*?' A pained expression flashes over Suzi's face. 'Thought not. At least Trudy was in control of all her faculties, have you noticed what you're wearing?'

The way the crumpled hoody is now hanging, it reads "R U IT?", I doubt Suzi can figure that out at the moment though.

She half-heartedly pulls at the offending garment and shrugs. 'Whatever.'

"Whatever" isn't really a Suzi word, and Trudy just does not do pottering. And me, I don't do bumped and bruised on the sofa, not unless I have Mum looking after me.

'I need my mum,' I mumble and snuggle down under my duvet. I try to sleep. I hear Suzi shuffling slowly out of the room.

It's amazing how much can happen while we are sleeping.

Homemade broth, care of Trudy.

I know, totally amazing! She can cook!

Travel arrangements, are also care of Trudy, but why she had to ask Nigel I have no idea. Yes, he's good-looking in a geeky kind of way, is the perfect gentleman at all times, and so reliable he could be classed as boring except for his mischievously twinkling eyes. He is also sweet, kind and an incredibly humble genius. He's the head of the science faculty at St. Stephen's at only twenty-nine, and has a natural affinity with the kids. I first met him when I started at St. Stephen's. I was awestruck. It didn't take me long to figure out everybody loves Nigel. He's just great at making everyone feel great.

Didn't take long for the two of us to hook up, but, after only a handful of disastrous dates, he's now my ex.

I'm sure he'll be impressed with my new Quasimodo image.

Thanks, Trudy!

Happy Families

A truth.

Well this is awkward! Nigel marches up to the front door. He's insisted on carrying my proficiently packed, (care of Suzi), overnight bag.

'This looks very nice,' he says, twinkle in action. 'Clover Beck, how long have your parents been here, then?

'Not long.' I shrug. 'And yes, it is very nice. Thanks for the lift, I'm sure you've lots to do. So, thanks again. Enjoy the rest of the break.' I smile my big bright OTT smile and grab my bag.

Honestly! I could throttle Trudy.

This is excruciatingly embarrassing. Poor Nigel has been trying his best to impress me all the way here. I feel like I'm kicking a puppy. But really, it's kinder to be a bitch with him now, than to let him think there's any lingering chance.

I walk into Mum and Dad's new house without looking back. How rude. And without knocking. Again, how rude. I slump with my back against the door. Listen for the scrunch of Nigel's footsteps back to the car.

Phew, and relax. I can hear low voices coming from the kitchen. 'Hello, anybody home?' No reply, oh well. I shuffle through the hallway. The kitchen door is ajar.

'I know it's not ideal Anne, but I'm not sure what other options there are.'

Miles!

Suddenly I'm ultra-alert. What is he doing here? I edge closer to the door, can't quite catch what Mum's saying. I'm not eavesdropping, just listening in.

'She needs someone to look after her. I've got double the workload now,' reasons Miles.

'But... Christie?'

'But Christie what? Christie is a grown woman, Anne. Don't you think it's about time she started living in the real world? Madeline had been practically fending for herself for five years by the time she was twenty-four!'

'Madeline and Christie are two entirely different people, Miles! Maddie chose her own path.'

'That maybe so, but Madeline has taken a back seat for a long time now. Sometimes she needs her mum, too.' He speaks the words softly, not an accusation, just a truth...

A truth.

He loves Madeline. He really does love her! I slump against the wall as knot of resentment tightens in my chest.

'But what about the press? You know we can't cope with all that kind of carry-on. Not at our age, Miles.'

'I'll deal with it, I promise. So, can she come here, at least until she's more mobile?'

Mum sighs. 'Like you said, what other options are there.'

'Thank you.'

Giving the kitchen door a push, it swings silently open, just in time for me to see Miles stoop to kiss Mum on her cheek.

For a nanosecond I'm transfixed by their closeness. 'What's going on?' I hardly recognise my own voice.

They spring apart.

'Christie! What are you doing here?' Mum flushes. 'What's happened to your face?'

She steps forward, and reaches up, her fingers butterfly over my grazes.

'I'm okay.' I can feel tears forming. 'Just tripped up, that's all. You know how clumsy I am.' She holds me close. I squeeze the tears back and swallow. I will not cry in front of him. I can feel him watching me. 'Anyway, I didn't want to worry you by 'phoning, and you did say I could stay, if I ever needed a bolthole…' I loosen out of her embrace.

'Yes, of course,' says Mum.

'But it seems you have other… commitments.' I shrug her hand from my arm.

'Madeline has broken her ankle,' the words dripped from Miles. 'She needs somewhere out of the glare of publicity to rest.'

'Miles has just popped round to see if she can stay here.' Mum shuffles in her slippers on the tiled floor.

'I heard. How very thoughtful of him,' I try to keep the sarcasm from my tone.

Fail.

'Yes, Anne has very kindly offered to let Madeline stay,' says Miles pleasantly. 'Until she's able to get about herself.'

'I'd best start sorting out bedrooms, looks like we're going to have a full house. Will Maddie need to sleep downstairs?'

'That would be the easiest for her,' says Miles. 'Thank you, Anne. It really is appreciated.'

'Okay, Christie, you sit yourself down.' She leads me to the table and plants a kiss on my head as I sit. 'Miles will make you a nice cup of tea. She takes two sugars, and set a plate of biscuits out, there's a good boy.'

There's a good boy!

Am I hearing properly? Sure enough, as Mum leaves the kitchen, Miles clicks the kettle on, and starts rummaging for biscuits.

'It hasn't taken you long to cosy up to my mum,' I all but hiss.

'Which would you prefer, Hobnobs or Chocolate Digestives?' Miles turns to look at me. I can tell he's trying not to stare at my grazes, because his gaze burrows into mine, flint to flint.

'Neither,' I say, holding each of my hands in tight fists, so as not to wrap them round his conceited throat. I do not want to commit murder in my parent's home. Just who does he think he is?

'Okay, I think I'll have Hobnobs.'

'Just help yourself, why don't you?'

'It seems you have a problem with me being here, Christie,' he states reasonably.

Dah. 'You think?'

'I'm here on behalf of Madeline.'

'Like I said, I heard.'

'Who, unlike you, does not presume to just turn up, and expect to be taken care of.'

'Excuse me! Just who the *hell* do you think you are? This is *my* parent's home, but here you are, barging into our lives and passing judgement.'

'I've barged into no one's life. I've known your parents for over ten years—'

I snort, if he thinks I'll believe that!

121

'… Maddie and I have met up with your parents on holiday many times over the last few years. Believe it or not, we all get along very well.'

'I can't stay in here, with you, and listen to this tosh.'

I stalk out of the house. My whole body quivers with pent up anger waiting to explode. It's like a bad dream, except I don't wake up, and it keeps getting worse.

And I'm sure I could have found a more appropriate word than "tosh"! Let me see, bullshit, that would have been better. Please God, give me the patience to not kill this man, and not to say bullshit in front of my mother.

The grass is squidgy as I make my way across the lawn to the end of the garden. Daisies and dandelions make a colourful carpet at my feet. Weeds, very pretty, but still weeds. I've always liked weeds.

I need to put as much distance as I can between me and Miles. I pull out my mobile, I suppose I could phone Nigel to come back… but then I'd need an excuse for not staying… and I *was* rude when he dropped me off earlier… I'm sure he'd come back for me… if I ask… I'm not telling him about Madeline, or Miles, and I'm rubbish at telling lies.

Arrrh. I slip my mobile back into my pocket, carefully sit on the garden bench. I cover my face with my hands. When I was little, I used to cover my face up all the time. I'd thought, if I couldn't see anyone, then no one could see me. If only it were true, life would be so much easier.

I shiver as a shadow falls over me. I know it's Miles. Can feel his presence. The hairs on my arms bristle. I keep my face covered.

'You know, Christie,' his words are smooth, and sweet as honey. 'Lots of things happen in our lives over which we have no control. I've always found, in the long run, things turn out fine. You might not be able to see it yet, but only good will come of this. I'll put your cup of tea by the side of the bench.'

Get lost.

I drop my hands from my face in time to see him striding across the lawn towards the house. I resist, just, hurling the hot tea after him. *Things turn out fine.* How naïve does he think I am? How can anything good come out of this mess?

Oh, and here comes the cavalry. Mum in her beige pants, cream blouse and ditsy print apron with patchwork pockets. She always used to be the cavalry. I wonder whose side she's on now.

'Hi Mum. What's new?'

Thought I'd try for irony.

She smiles her placid smile, and sits down beside me on the bench. She picks up my hands, turns them over, and traces the scratches on my palms with her fingers.

'What's been going on, Christie?' she asks me.

She asks me!

My insides are a bubbling cauldron, fermenting a poisonous cocktail about to explode.

'You tell me, Mum.' I want to snatch my hands away, but don't. I'm trying to not cry. 'Tell me, Mum. What's been going on?'

'Where do I start?'

'Well, let's see? You've told me the beginning, then you told me the middle bit, so I suppose next comes the end.'

'Sarcasm doesn't suit you, Christie.' Her voice is soft, uncensored.

'What do you expect? All my life is a huge fat lie!'

Now I snatch my hands away.

'No, Christie. Your life is not a lie. We explained how it was, I thought you were okay with it?'

'Okay with it? What choice do I have? You and Dad brought me up as *your* child. The one and only Christie, how lucky I've always felt, the whole village marvelled at what wonderful parents you were! But all the time, you knew! You knew one day I'd have to deal with *this*!'

'We did our best.'

'Your best?' I hiss. 'You did your best? Well, okay, I was just about getting to grips with you *doing your best*, when all my childhood is put on display for the entire world to pour over!'

'Christie, please—'

'I presume you knew about *Evolution*?'

'Yes, but Madeline thought—'

'*Madeline thought*! Well yippity do!' I snarl.

She purses her lips. 'Madeline thought you needed to have your own identity, before she went public about you being her daughter.'

'I *have* my own identity! I'm me, Christina Anne Harris! Do you not think you gave me opportunities to explore myself over the years?'

'Yes, but…' sighs Mum.

'It's one of the many things you drummed into me. "Know your own mind, Christie, don't follow the crowd, think for yourself, set your own moral standards and stick to them"! Should I go on?'

'It was out of my control, out of our control, we had managed to pacify Maddie with your career. But she's ambitious; she didn't want you to settle for being a teacher.'

'Settle for being a teacher! I haven't settled for being a teacher, Mum. I was born to be a teacher.' I thump my chest. 'It's in here, being a teacher is who I am.'

'I know that, Christie, but Maddie doesn't.'

'Well, I hope she's a fast learner!'

'This is why, why I've tried to keep you two apart so long. Madeline is driven. She always has a new idea, a new project, she has to be doing something all the time. I knew she'd make your life into a new mission.'

'And she has. Congratulations, mother, on your insight! But then, she is your daughter!'

'Yes, she is—'

I snort.

'... And I love her very much—'

Again, I snort.

'... Despite all her failings. We all have failings, me more than most, as you're apt at pointing out today—'

And again, I snort.

'... Fundamentally, Maddie is a good person. She does good things—'

'Not for me!'

'How many years did she encourage you with your art? How many, Christie?'

'That's different; she did that to gain access to my life! My life!'

'She could have done that at any time. She did it to help you, to give you a purpose, structure, something to work towards.'

'To make me more like her; with her projects and glittering career,' I sneer.

'She walked away from her glittering career. It wasn't enough. She realised she'd lost more than she could ever gain.'

'Too late. She realised too late!'

'She was the same age you are now, when she left her glittering career. Do you think you could make that choice?'

'We are completely different people.'

'She was born to act. You were born to teach. Could you walk away from teaching?'

I glare at her. How dare she ask me that question?

'Well, could you?' she pushes.

'Never; I will never give up my teaching!'

'Good. I hope you never do. But you see, Maddie gave up the two most precious things in her life. First, she gave up you. Then she gave up her acting because of you.' The bench sighs as Mum stands up. 'Think about it,' she tosses over her shoulder as she makes her way back to the house.

'Think about it,' I mutter under my breath. Why should I? Seems to me like Madeline is quite shite at doing things right.

Close Encounter

The intimacy shocks me to my core.

And here comes Madeline's number one admirer now, virtually galloping towards me, with his practically, permanently-etched scowl on his forehead.

'Do you mind if I join you?' His tone indicates that he doesn't give a unicorn's fart if I mind or not. Sure enough, he settles himself down in the spot Mum minutes before left.

I edge away from him, not far enough to spare myself a whiff of his zesty aftershave.

'Do you know what your mother is doing now?'

'Rushing round, getting ready for the lovely Madeline, I guess.'

'You're right,' he says mildly. 'She rushed in, and started gabbling on about defrosting chicken fillets, peeling potatoes, cutting vegetables. She's a marvel, isn't she?'

He doesn't give me chance to answer.

'Yes, she just gets on with it. Whatever is thrown at her, she just gets on with it. It's called displacement activity, Christie. As long as you are keeping your mind busy with one thing, you don't have to deal with the other.'

'She always likes to be busy.' I shift uneasily away from him.

'I've noticed it often with Anne,' he carries on, as if I haven't spoken. 'But today there's an added urgency about it.'

'Well, that'll be because *Madeline* is coming to stay,' I hiss. 'Everything must be perfect for *her*!'

A hot, bubbling feeling surges up through my body, a feeling I'm struggling to put a name to. One I've never experienced before.

Jealousy!

'So, I asked her,' again he carries on as if I haven't said a word. 'I said "Anne, slow down, what's the matter?". And she said, "Christie and I have just had a full and frank exchange of opinions about how things are". By that, I assume you've had a row?'

He turns his body to face me, our knees touch. His jaw is tight, and the sinews in his neck protrude. His eyes challenge mine. 'Well, Christie? Care to enlighten me?' he asks softly, dangerously.

'It's none of your business.' I shrug, trying to ignore the goose bumps on my arms, and the rush of blood to my ears.

He smiles. 'Oh, Christie, you have much to learn about me!'

'Really? Do you suppose I have any desire, to learn anything about you? You flatter yourself Miles, you really do.' I can feel the heat of a flush creeping up my chest to my neck.

'Whether you have any *desire* to learn anything about me, is irrelevant, Christie. Like it or not, I'm here to stay.' Resting back, he folds his arms across his chest. 'So?'

'So, mind your own business,' I snap.

He stands up, arms still folded, and bends forward so his nose nearly touches mine. 'Listen, and listen good, I will explain this very simply, so that even you can understand. I have known Madeline and your parents for many years. All they have ever shown me, is kindness and respect, so, if anyone wishes them harm, let's just say, they'll have me to answer to.'

'Are you threatening me?' My eyes must be like saucers.

'I'm explaining how it is.'

'All I want, is to be left alone! My life has been turned upside down, through no fault of my own, and you, you come out here accusing me of wishing my mum harm!'

'You've upset her!'

'I'm upset!' Why doesn't he get it? A single tear slides from my eye. 'Is anyone jumping to my defence?' I shake my head. Turn away from him, before more tears escape.

The bench groans as he slumps back down. He peers round at my face, and passes me a hanky.

I snatch it from him.

No grace.

Blow my nose. 'Hay fever,' I lie.

'If I've added to that upset, then I'm sorry. We all want what's best for you; including me.'

'If that were true, why all this?'

'Your life has always been charmed, Christie. You have no idea what it's like for some people.'

I cross my arms, look into the distance. Right now, I don't care what life is like for other people, my own is enough. I can hear the distant hum of traffic from the main road, birds chirping merrily and trees sway elegantly in the breeze. Everything normal is going on about me.

But I feel arhhh. I want to explode, scream and shout. I want to hit out, and destroy. I want to rip off my skin, and give myself even more physical pain, to match the turmoil inside, so that everyone can see my pain exposed.

Miles sighs. 'Right now, Christie, you have an opportunity to find out who you really are.'

My cheeks hurt from clenching my jaw. 'I know who I am,' I say very slowly.

'You know who you are when you are surrounded by good things, good people. When it's easy to make good choices—'

My fingers dig into my arms, I keep my mouth tight shut because if I speak, I can't ever put the words back.

'… Like today. Do you care how much you've upset your mum? Are you going to leave her fretting about you? Does she deserve to suffer, just because you're suffering?'

My fingernails dig deeper into my arms, hurting me now.

'… So, who are you? Are you the caring, compassionate, cheerful Christie, everyone sees every day? Or, deep down, are you selfish, spoilt and spiteful? Who are you, Christie?'

'*She knew* I'd have to deal with all this! *She knew*, and never gave me a clue my life was so mixed up. Didn't prepare me!'

'She's spent twenty-four years preparing you.'

'Not for this charade!' I fling my arm up in the air.

'It's not a charade, *this is reality*. It's what the rest of us deal with every day.'

'Okay, so it's normal to find out your mum is your grandmother, and your real mum is a national treasure, who everyone seemingly adores?'

'It's normal to have to deal with everyday hassles.'

'Believe me, *Miles*, this is more than an everyday hassle!'

'Yes, yes, it is. This is you having to independently deal with your own dilemma, which incidentally, your mum, dad and Madeline have been dealing with for years.'

'They created it!'

Miles sighs and shakes his head. 'Can you imagine, what it must have been like, for each of them to make the choices they made? And stick with them.'

I don't want to think about any of them! This is about me. 'Well Madeline did very nicely out of it! Madeline De-Muir, the flawless charity worker, quintessential English rose, whose heart is as pure as driven snow, the darling of Hollywood.'

'Do not mistake Maddie Harris, for Madeline De-Muir! I work for Madeline De-Muir, but Maddie is my friend, the real deal.'

'They're the same person!'

'No.' He shakes his head; a flop of black hair falls forward; he scrapes it back into place and smiles. 'No. Maddie is the flawed Madeline, she's a rare English rose, she's the most passionate person I have ever met, and most certainly not, remotely the darling of Hollywood.'

'And I should care, because?'

'For you, Christie, she's prepared to expose her flaws and her mistakes. For you, she's prepared to risk losing the public's adoration. Because of you, she's passionate for young people to be given the chance to shine. Because of you, she left acting behind.'

'How very commendable. Maybe she should get a medal! How about, she could have been a single mum and surrounded me with love, and then maybe she'd have earned my respect.' The pain of her rejection spills spite into my heart.

'She can't change the past.'

'But she's trying to change my future. *My future*.' I shake my head. Dab at my drippy nose.

'You're a talented artist, Christie. She couldn't stand back and let you waste that talent.'

I'm exhausted with this argument, can scarcely raise my voice above a whisper. 'It isn't wasted, it's shared. I'm a teacher, and teachers share their talents.'

'Madeline wanted you to have the chance to become successful, a real artist.'

I shake my head; he doesn't get it. 'I am a real artist. I could have made the choice to submit work to galleries myself. She took that choice from me.'

'She knows you better than that. She knew you'd never risk being rejected.'

The grass tickles my ankles as I walk away from him. The garden promises to be beautiful through the summer; it's a relaxed mum and dad kind of garden. Just enough lawn to mow, not too much. Deep swaggering borders filled with perennials and shrubs, just enough to weed, not too much. A rickety bench and a bird table. A washing line with an old wooden prop. They probably love it already!

I assume Madeline bought this house for them. She chose well. It has charm.

I feel sick. With envy? Regret? I wonder if I'll get to spend much time here now. Already, I feel like an outsider.

Seems like Madeline has all the bases covered. Mum and Dad have the return of their prodigal child;

Miles is her dutiful and adoring PA, and to rank up the attention, she's got a sodding broken ankle!

Well they're all welcome to each other!

'Christie?' Miles has slunk up behind me. 'Do you think she was right?'

'What?'

'Was Madeline right? Would you ever have risked being turned down?'

'Well...' I offer a tight smile. 'I guess we'll never know now, will we?'

'I guess not, but for what it's worth, I think she knows you better than you'd like to admit.'

I turn and look at him fully. A pitying smile is pulling at his lips, his hands are casually hooked in his pockets, and his face is tilted to one side as he squints against the sun. And again, the urge to slap his arrogant face is unbearable. 'Do you think I care what you think? You don't even know me!'

He shuffles, and looks towards the kitchen where Mum is at the window, head down, probably peeling potatoes. 'Did you really trip up?'

His change of subject catches me off guard. He lifts my chin with the crook of his forefinger. I go to slap his hand away, and he catches my hand in his. 'Play nice, Christie, your mother's watching.'

I look up, and Mum waves on cue. Miles lifts my hands, palms up, and examines the grazes. I watch, as the pulse in my exposed wrist quickens.

'So, was it a trip, or did you decide to drown your sorrows with your two budding alcoholic friends, and end up having a drunken fall?' He begins to trace the scratches on my hand.

The intimacy shocks me to my core.

'They look quite deep,' he continues.

I snatch my hand away, but can still feel the traces of his fingertips. 'My friends are far from alcoholics; they only drink socially.'

'If that's what you like to think.'

'So, I take it you haven't spoken to the lovely Mrs Price today?'

'No?' He frowns.

'Perhaps you should.' I raise my brows, and catch the confusion in his eyes.

'Mrs Price knows only to contact me in cases of emergency.'

'Mustn't have been an emergency then!'

'What happened?' Again, he picks up my hand.

'Bunty Hargreaves happened!' I snatch my hand back.

'Bunty Hargreaves did this?'

'Bunty Hargreaves decided she'd figured out who Christie is. She got it wrong; she thought it was Trudy. As we were leaving, she started taking our photos.'

'I told everyone no pictures!' snaps Miles.

'Obviously, she didn't take any notice of you.'

Miles mutters something under his breath. 'And?'

'And Trudy objected to having her photo taken, physically, by snatching Bunty's phone. I tripped getting out of the car. Trudy was livid; I wanted to stop her from—'

'Getting herself into trouble.' Miles nods. 'I see. So, did Mrs Price sort it all out? She should have let me know.'

'She let us clean ourselves up, and sorted us some clean clothes out. And then she...' I feel the colour drain from my face as the memory of the car journey seeps back.

'Then she what? What did she do?' coaxes Miles.

'She drove us home.' My words are hushed, solemn.

'You let her drive you home? The woman's not safe!'

'I know.'

'She used to do rally driving!'

'I know.'

'She's a demon behind the wheel.'

'I know.'

'She doesn't understand the concept of traffic lights and roundabouts.'

'I know.'

'So why did you let her drive you home?'

'I didn't know.'

Miles drops his head into his hands. His shoulders start to shudder, and he shakes his head. He covers his eyes with one hand, then forces his other fist into his mouth. A howl escapes. He drops his hand down. Tears stream down his crumpled face. 'I'm… Sorry… I… Can't… Help… It…' he splutters between gasps. The air is filled with the most resounding belly laugh I have ever heard.

He's laughing at me!

I turn on my heel, and walk back towards the house, the sound of Miles roaring with laughter still echoing in my ears.

Out of the Frying Pan

Trust the Trolls to jolly things along!

Mum's not in the kitchen. Pans line up along the counter, sliced potatoes in the first, green beans in the second, carrots and turnip in the next, the last one has a Snicker and a note:

Christie, peace offering,
knew you'd peep in all the pans.
Mum x

It does look tempting, I've only had soup, but if I eat it, it's kind of like accepting what she's said to me makes sense. I don't want to eat it! I want to throw it at the wall, or stamp on it, or, even more nastily, hand it back to her.

I click the kettle on, make myself a coffee, sit down, peel the wrapper halfway down the bar and dunk it into my coffee, one, two, three, four, five, the bar melts into my mouth, sooo good! Chocolate dribbles down my chin.

'Looks like you're enjoying that!'

'Dad!'

'Don't sound so surprised, I do live here!' He drops a kiss on the top of my head and sits down opposite me. 'Now, what have you been up to? Your mum says you've been falling over, and I can see you've grazed your face. Have those two friends of yours been leading you astray again with some of that horrid vodka?'

'Sadly not, it wouldn't have hurt as much if I'd been drunk. I tripped getting out of Trudy's car, and landed fully face down.'

'Ouch.' Dad scrunches up his face.

'Then Suzi opened her car door, hit me on the back of my head, and knocked me back down again!' I moan.

'Double ouch,' says Dad. 'Was she by any chance tipsy?'

'As a toad, but racked with guilt today.'

'And rightly so! You young ones, I don't know.'

'Oh, I think you do.'

'And Mum says the two of you have had words.' Dad spears me with his piercing eyes.

'You could say that.' I force the last bit of Snicker into my mouth. It doesn't taste as good as the first bite, has lost its appeal. I gulp it down without savouring the taste, and swallow. I can feel its progress to my stomach.

All of a sudden, the fight has gone out of me. I know all of this isn't just Mum's fault, if any of it, but it's like I want to punish her for how I feel. And I know she's been the best Mum ever. I'll admit it to myself, I'm making her suffer because she isn't making this go away. Until now, I didn't think there was anything she couldn't sort out. Somehow – ridiculously, I know - it feels like she's let me down, even though deep down I know she never could.

'What would you say?' he asks.

I close my eyes. What would I say? Think, think, she deserves for me to snap and snarl after what I've been through. I rest my elbows on the table and cover my face with my hands – still not managing to be invisible. 'To be honest Dad, I don't know what to say.'

'She's very upset.'

'So am I.'

'And more than a little disappointed.'

'Me too.' Tears wet the palms of my hands. 'I'm disappointed.'

In both of us.

I hear Dad moving towards me, feel his embrace. I want to fall into his comfortable bear hug like I usually do, but my body won't relax, a shudder and a sob escapes.

'Oh, Christie.' His voice is hoarse. 'None of us wanted to cause you all this pain.'

'But you all have.' I wipe my nose on the already well-used hanky Miles gave me. 'You knew, Dad. You knew, and now all my life is a lie.'

'No, it's not a lie, all your memories are exactly the same. What has changed is the way you're cross-referencing them with what has happened.' He squeezes my shoulders. 'You'll always be my daugh—'

'Don't say it!' I pull away from him. 'I'm not! Am I?'

'You are, Christie! In my heart, I have never known you as anything else. I couldn't love you any more if…'

'If I were your own child?'

'Okay then! If that's what you want. Yes, if you were my *own* child. Does that make it better, Christie?' he demands quietly.

Looking at him, I can see the hurt carved on his face, somehow it feels more profound than with Mum. 'It makes it the truth!'

'We are all God's—'

'Don't! Don't start with God, don't start with God now my life is a lie! Start with the truth.'

'The truth, is, we did our best.'

'Really?' I find his simple truth hard to take.

'It was a difficult time for each of us.' Dad sits in the chair beside me, resting his arms on the table, as if still reaching to make a connection with me.

I turn, look him in the eyes. 'Was it the best for me? Did you do your best for *me*, or for *Madeline*?' That's the truth I need.

'We did our best for both of you. Maddie was sixteen, just a child, it would have been…' Dad wipes his hand across his face. 'She did love you; she does love you.'

'Well that's reassuring!'

'We just wanted to give her a chance at acting, we honestly didn't think she'd become the star she did. If she'd not been given that chance, well, she would have probably ended up resenting you. And that would have been no life, for either of you.'

'So, you'd no intention of keeping me?' Bile rises in my throat; I swallow it down. 'You thought she'd come back after—'

'We thought—'

'You thought she'd have her little adventure at drama school, then come back and…' I can't say it. I can't say "take me back".

'I couldn't understand.' Dad shakes his head.

'Why she didn't want me?' There, I'd said it. The words I'd dreaded hearing. She didn't want me. Both Dad's hands grip mine on the table. Tears sting my eyes. The comfort of those familiar strong hands around mine is hard to resist. I drop my head and rest it on my forearms. I can't bear for him to see my tears, but can't give up the comfort of his reassuring touch.

'Christie, I'm sorry, I couldn't understand her. Couldn't believe she'd just go off.'

'Leaving me with Mum and you.' I raise my head, and look at him now. Can see the pain of history imprinted on his face.

'I couldn't understand how she could leave you… Broke my heart that she could.' He shakes his head and looks away. 'Maddie got her part in *The Fallen*, and that was it.'

'The rest is history, I know.' I can't keep the bitterness from my voice. I just can't.

'We knew then, we knew she'd never put you first, we already couldn't have given you back even if she'd wanted us to. We had it all made legal. Maddie was more than willing to sign you over to us; we couldn't risk your life being made into a pantomime.'

'You mean, like it has been now?'

'Christie, you were so precious to us, *because* of how we'd been with Maddie. In a way she made us better parents for you. You don't know it, Christie, but you're strong.'

'Ha.' The hollow sound echoes round the kitchen. An echo of the emptiness inside of me.

'You've no idea, but you really are.' He grips my hands harder, gives them a shake. 'We made sure of it, like I keep saying, we did our best. *You* are *our best*.'

'I know I'm behaving like a spoilt brat, but I can't seem to stop being angry. I feel let down by all of you, and it's clawing away at me. I hate feeling this lost, out of control. Why am I being so pathetic? Dad?'

'Because for the first time, you're not sure what's going to happen next. Like you keep saying, we've all known for years. Until now, you've just been trundling along. Now, Christie, now is *your* time to shine, to let everyone see what an amazing person you are.'

'I hardly feel amazing. Look at me, Dad, I'm a crumbling wreck. She didn't want me, and you had no choice.'

'We had a choice. We made it. We chose you. If anything, you should feel more loved because of that.'

Even though he smiles his reassurance, I can see the strain on his face.

Even though I didn't start this whole chaotic charade, I know I'm adding to that strain.

Slowly, without warning, guilt begins to seep into my soul. I turn away from him, unable to witness the wounds I'm inflicting on this noble man. 'Dad, you should have told me the truth.'

'When?' He shrugs. 'When should we have told you? When you were seven, or twelve, or sixteen, eighteen or twenty-one? When do you think you'd have coped with it better than you are doing now?'

My throat is so tight I can hardly talk. 'I don't know. Anytime but now.' I look out of the window. Blue sky with fluffy white clouds slowly moving eastwards. The world just going on as normal. 'I wish things were different.'

He suddenly looks old, tired. 'It will get better, once you meet Maddie.'

'I don't want to meet her!' I yank my hands away from his, and clutch them to my chest.

'It's not just about what you want. Madeline could have forced it at any time.'

'And she would have been slated in the press.'

'I'm sure Miles would have packaged it, in such a compassionate way, as to have people sympathising over her lost years with you.'

'I can't believe I'm hearing this from you, Dad! She didn't want me!'

'But she does now. Look, Christie, I'm trying to help you, and if you won't meet her halfway, you'll end up being the one who is vilified in the press.'

'How, when I've done nothing wrong?'

'Maddie has put a lot of work into launching *Evolution*, and you're likely to become an in-demand artist because of that.'

'So, I'd be the ungrateful brat.'

'Something like that.' Dad nods.

Unbelievable. 'And you and Mum would let that happen?'

'We wouldn't be able to stop it.' He really does look old, defeated. She's done this to him, my dad, my rock, crumbling, just like me. His fingers are linked together resting on the table, he's probably praying, praying we sort this mess out.

The fight drains from me, my body feels limp. 'I have no choice, have I, Dad?'

His face softens. 'You do have some choices. You're smart and you're strong, Christie. This has all been sprung on you.'

'Everything is spinning out of control, out of my control.' Closing my eyes, I rest my head on the cool table. I'm talking to my dad, and it's hard to accept, that actually, he isn't my *real* dad. I know somewhere out there is probably Madeline's first love, maybe her only one. He obviously didn't hang about to meet me. Another rejection, but at least I don't have to meet that one face to face.

Only a few days ago I was happily looking forward to a relaxing break from school, not a care in the world, and here I am stuck in the middle of a family reshuffle. *The Jeremy Kyle Show* would have had a field day.

Dad stands and moves beside me, rests his hand on my shoulder, I lift my head to look at him. 'Well, Christie, *you* decide what outcome *you* want from this situation, then work your way back to where we are now.'

'And figure out what steps I need to take to make it happen.' This is a strategy Dad has talked me through many times over the years, to tackle situations I thought beyond my ability to deal with. None as complex as this.

Dad allows himself a half-smile. 'Good girl, Christie, you remember. What else should you aim for?'

'A win-win solution,' I reply.

'For all of us. Okay, so, what is the first step?'

'Ask myself what I want,' I parrot from the voice in my head.

'And then?'

'Consider what everyone else wants.'

'And then?' He raises his brows and tilts his head.

'Make it happen.'

'Simple!' He slaps the table.

'Maybe not that simple.'

'But definitely achievable. I feel better already, knew you'd sort it out, my girl! Right, I'm off to find your mother to tell her the good news.' And off he goes, probably to bring Mum up to speed.

From tears and tantrums to tactics in about two minutes. The way he turns things round is unbelievable. I could almost eat another Snicker; except my coffee is cold, and Mum only gave me one. I click the kettle on again and start rummaging through cupboards, now I've decided I want chocolate nothing else will do. I hear footsteps, probably Dad coming back.

'Dad, do you know if Mum's got any chocolate stashed?' I look up, feel the blood drain from my face as I see Miles. 'Oh, it's you.'

'Try behind the biscuit tin,' he says, and nods towards the cupboard he got the biscuits from earlier. 'I think I spotted a stockpile there.'

I manage to mutter, 'Thank you.' I find Mum's chocolate stash. Miles empties my cold coffee away and rinses the mug. He then takes over making my drink, adding his own mug to the counter, a tad too close to mine for comfort. 'Is this what you do for Madeline, make coffee all day.'

Oh, why does he make me such a bitch?

'Some days, yes, other times it's all work, work, and more work. Coffee two?' He sounds so upbeat. I feel like slapping him like Dad slapped the table.

I nod. He turns back towards the counter; he doesn't look bad from behind. Why I'm bothering to look, I have no idea, because his personality is abysmal. He turns back towards me, and catches me ogling his butt. A ghost of a smile flickers over his face. Why can one look from his smug face turn my insides to jelly? He puts both mugs onto the table.

'I don't mind if you dunk your Snicker, I know it's a habit of yours.'

I feel myself blush.

He casually pulls out a chair and sits down opposite me with a full-on smirk. 'There's not much I don't know about you.'

'You think?'

'And what I don't know, I'm sure I'll enjoy finding out.' He starts rapping a tuneless beat with his fingers on the table.

'Don't be too sure!' I snap.

Back in bitch mode. Again.

'I'm enjoying it already.' He leans back in his chair and folds his arms. 'Figuring out what makes you tick, what makes you blush.'

Two can play at that game. 'I wonder, Miles, how you'll feel when Madeline and I are reconciled?'

'I'll be pleased with a job well done.' He stretches his arms up, then casually links his fingers behind his head, resting back in his chair.

'Really? How long have you been working towards this reunion? How much time and effort have you put in? Are you not just a tiny bit worried, that when Madeline and I get together, you'll not be needed?'

'Good try, but you'll need to do better than that.'

Now his foot is randomly tapping away. He doesn't take his eyes off me as he sips his coffee, mine is left untouched and I'm itching to have my Snicker.

He nods toward my coffee. 'Go ahead, dunk it, I know you want to.'

'No, I'll save it for later. Actually, I think I'm going to go home, to my friends.'

He leans towards me. 'I thought you might like to make some plans about *Evolution*.'

'No, you and Madeline can do that. I want to go home and make some plans of my own.' I slip the Snicker bar into my pocket; I might like that later. I pour the coffee away, wash the mug, dry it and put it away. I do not want him accusing me of leaving a mess. 'Do you know what, Miles? A holiday sounds like a good idea to me.' I stalk out of the kitchen and walk slap bang into Dad.

'Whoa, where are you off to in such a hurry?' he asks.

'On holiday!' I wink at him to include him in the tease.

'Anywhere nice?'

'Don't know yet, but I'll send you a postcard.'

'Christie, you can't just go off. Not now!' says Miles from the kitchen doorway.

I turn, look at him and smile. 'I think you'll find I can do whatever I want.' It feels nice to have the upper hand for the very first time, and I'm going to savour it. I turn away, towards Dad. 'Is Mum still upstairs?'

'She is.'

'Mum!' I holler up to her. 'I'm going back home, you've enough to do looking after Madeline.'

'Wait! Wait!' Mum bounds down the stairs as fast as any lady in her sixties can. 'But I've sorted a room out for you now!'

'Another time, Mum, I'm sorry for—'

'Being a stroppy little madam?' Mum fills in.

'Well, yes… No.' Why am I sorry? 'I'm sorry for upsetting you, you're a good Mum. Actually, you're the best.' I lean forward, her cheek feels soft to my kiss. 'But I need to go, so bye for now. See you, Dad.'

I nod towards Miles, don't bother to waste words on him, pick up my bag and walk out the front door. I pull the door closed behind me, don't want spectators.

But still, how brave am I?

I pull out my mobile and phone Suzi as I walk down the drive. Come on, come on, answer!

'Hi, Suzi, are you fit to drive?'

'Possibly. Just about, why?'

'I'm desperate to get away from here.'

'You've only just got there, what's happened?' I can hear the impatience in her voice.

'Long story, short on time. Will you come, quickly?'

'On my way. But you'd better fill me in on all the details on the way home. Byeeee.'

'Bye.' The phone disconnects.

It's not a particularly busy road, but I feel slightly on show stood on the kerb with my overnight bag slung at my feet. I must look like I've been turfed out!

I peep back towards the house. No one is looking; I suppose I could wait inside the grounds, behind a shrub or something, hidden from the house and the road.

I sling my bag over my shoulder nonchalantly, and then tiptoe onto the gravel drive and dart behind a Flowering Blackcurrant bush, unseen, I think. I'm not sure how long it's going to take Suzi to get here, maybe fifteen minutes. I might as well make myself comfy. Patting down my bag on the ground, I sit on it.

Oh, and I've got my Snicker too!

It won't be the same without hot coffee to dunk it in, but still. I unwrap it, try to make it last, by sucking it. It's not as good as dunking obviously, but not too bad. The trouble is, the bit you're hold of starts to melt inside the wrapper. I stuff the last piece in my mouth, and let it ooze about. Yum, all gone, may as well lick the wrapper, as I'm all alone. I do hate waste, especially chocolate.

A car scrunches on the drive, it must be Suzi. She must have driven lickety-split. I don't want her knocking on the door; I'll just stick my head out and…

Oh no no no no no! It's not Suzi, unless she's nicked a Daimler. It must be, oh no can't be. A driver gets out. He opens the passenger door, leans in, helps the occupant out, and…Shit, steadies her on crutches!

Madeline.

My mouth goes dry, and my stomach feels hollow, despite the two Snickers I've eaten in the last half an hour. I'm so glad I got out of there when I did, or I'd be trapped now. The driver knocks on the front door, I peer through the bush as best as I can; it's a bit prickly this close. Miles appears and dashes forward to help Madeline.

'Where is she?' I hear Madeline ask.

'She's gone, you've missed her.'

'What do you mean gone!' she squeaks. 'I left as soon as you phoned, did she know I was on my way?'

He shakes his head. 'No, she thought you were coming later.'

'Oh, Miles, I just wanted to meet her.'

I'm shocked at how needy she sounds, almost the total opposite of her screen persona.

'You will,' soothes Miles. I'm transfixed by his clear devotion to her.

'But when? I've been waiting years…'

Her vulnerability is palpable, and the fear of being discovered is overtaken by my curiosity. I strain to hear them clearly.

'Soon, Maddie, be patient for a little while longer. She's skittish.'

'Skittish? She's not a bloody pony, Miles! Sorry, sorry, I just want her to like me.'

'And she will.' Again, the soothing tones. 'Everyone does. Come on, let's get you inside before anyone recognizes you.'

I've got sunshine in my pocket blasts from my phone, I snatch it up and disconnect Suzi's flashing name.

Trust the Trolls to jolly things along!

'Actually, Madeline, maybe you're in time after all.'

I close my eyes and groan.

'There you are, Christie. How fortunate, Madeline and I were just talking about you.'

'I heard.' I risk a peep. He looks just as smug as he sounds.

'I'm not sure what you've been doing behind this bush, but the sunshine in your pocket gave you away.' He reaches out, and plucks a twig from my hair. 'But perhaps now is a good time to come out.'

'Why, when I've been having a perfectly good time in here on my own?'

'I can see. You've managed to get chocolate all over your face.'

'Oh…'

'Quite.' He passes me another hanky.

I snatch it from him.

Level of grace… Zero.

'Do you know, finding you here, like this, has made my day?'

'*Regrettably, Miles*, I cannot say the same.' I hiss, rubbing at my face.

'Come on, might as well get it over with.' He pulls me up, and picks up my bag so I can't sit back down, then turns to walk back to the house.

'I'm not ready,' I scarcely whisper the words.

He turns back to me. Is that sympathy? 'She only wants to meet you, come on, how bad can it be?'

Does he really want to know? I'm dizzy with a million things spinning around my head. My hands are shaking, I feel sick. It feels like the ground is moving. I feel sick, and hot, and my feet will not move.

'Christie.' He reaches out and catches my hand; our eyes meet. 'Just say "hello", I'll help Madeline inside, by then your taxi should have arrived, and you can escape, okay?'

I nod, and swallow.

'Good.' He leads me out from behind the bush.

'Christie!' She's beaming like a beauty on prom night. Making her way awkwardly towards us, her lack of practice on crutches evident with every step, as she drags them through the gravel.

'Hello.' It sounds like a croak; my throat is so tight. I'd forgot Miles is holding my hand, until he squeezes it.

'I have waited so long! And look at you two, getting along so well already. It's like a dream.' Her voice sounds breathless. She lunges the short remaining distance, and clinches me in a bear hug; her full weight on me, crutches clanging to the ground at either side.

Miles steps forward. 'Steady, Maddie,' he says, half lifting her weight from me. 'Christie's had an accident too, don't want the two of you on the ground.'

I disentangle myself, stoop to pick up the crutches and pass them back to her. She takes them from me, and steadies herself. Her eyes never leave my face, it's like she's trying to read my mind. I feel heat rising up my chest.

'Your photos don't do you justice; you are so pretty.'

'And you are much younger than I remember, Auntie Maddie.'

'Touché, but I think, from now on, simply Maddie will do.'

'Maddie, okay.' I nod. I am strong. I am smart. I can do this… 'Maddie, I need to figure out how I feel about this situation before I get swept along with…' I scrunch up my face. 'You, actually.' *I've got sunshine in my pocket* blasts out again. 'Excuse me, but I need to get this… Hi Suzi.'

'Turn around,' she whispers. I turn and there she is, halfway out of her car, one foot in, one on the kerb. 'Is that Madeline?'

'Yes. Of course, I know you're in a hurry, I'm coming.'

'No, no! I want to meet her!'

'Honestly, one second, Suzi.' I hang up, and wave her back in the car. Thankfully she does get back in. I turn back to Madeline and Miles, cross my fingers behind my back, and force an overbright smile. 'Sorry, got to dash, Suzi's in a mega rush, hot date, I think. Bye.' Snatching up my bag, I turn and scurry towards my getaway car.

'Oh, right, bye then.' Madeline sounds deflated.

'See you later,' adds Miles.

I wave with my free hand without turning back or answering, and prepare to meet the wrath of Suzi.

Escape?

'I wonder if they share a room.'

I haul my bag and shaking self into the car and wait. Suzi starts the engine and sets off. The relief of escaping Madeline and Miles far outweighs the trauma of dealing with a seriously miffed Suzi.

After the fiasco of a drunken Suzi yesterday, I feel she ought to cut me some slack.

Not a word.

Silence stretches out between us. I knew she'd want to meet Madeline De-Muir at some point. She's been a fan for years, but I'm not ready. Not ready to let my best friend defect to the other side.

Maybe she will anyway. The sting of her silence feeds my self-doubt.

'Thank you for coming,' I mumble. I notice a slight acknowledgement. Vaguely encouraged, I flounder on. 'And I'm sorry, I know you want to meet her, but she'd only just arrived, and I've only just met her. I don't know how to deal with all this. And I don't want you to like her better than you like me, and now you're not talking to me, and it's not fair.' I end with a gulp, my throat tight, as once again tears threaten.

Suzi indicates, slows the car, mounts the kerb - in a very Mrs Price way, stops and switches on her hazard lights. Turning to me, she fixes me with one of her scary looks.

She says nothing.

Waits.

She is very good at this! A tactic she's learned from her mum, I think. Her theory is, if she waits long enough, she'll get a confession. So, wish me luck.

'I'm sorry, Suzi; I've had an awful day. When I got to Mum and Dad's, I found Mum and Miles having a cosy chat.' I pause for effect. I can tell Suzi wants to interrogate me, because she is still gripping the steering wheel.

I risk carrying on. 'Apparently, Maddie had some kind of accident, and has broken her ankle. Miles arranged for her to come to stay at Mum and Dad's house, until she can get about a bit better.' Again, I pause for effect. 'I had a sharp exchange of words with Mum.' I close my eyes to try and banish the memory.

'What about?' Suzi's curiosity gets the better of her. 'You two never argue.'

'About *darling Madeline*, and how she's ruined my life! Then Miles Hepworth, another blight in my life, took it upon himself to lecture me.'

Suzi releases her grip on the steering wheel, and turns towards me. 'What about?'

'About how I'd upset Mum. Apparently, he, Mum, Dad and Maddie are best buddies.'

'Nooo?' squeaks Suzi, eyes wide.

'They all go on holiday together! Can you believe it?' A knot begins to tighten in my stomach.

'No! Well… That explains why your Mum and Dad have encouraged you to come away with me and Trudy.'

'Doesn't it just!' That nasty feeling is bubbling inside me again. 'So that they can all play happy families without me!'

Suzi's eyes widen even more. 'I wonder if they share a room.'

'What are you on about?'

'Madeline and Miles! I wonder if they share a room, on holiday.'

'I don't know! I don't care!'

Oh, I think I do!

The knot tightens even more.

'But with your dad being a vicar, they aren't married.'

'Su-zi! Shut up!'

'Only saying.'

'Well don't!' I heave a great sigh. 'I'm trying to tell you what's happened *today*.'

'I know but…'

'Shh!' I carry on, while my patience lasts. 'Miles gives me a lecture about what kind of person I am. And makes me cry…' I remember.

'The pig.'

'Exactly. And then he *assumes* all these scratches came from me falling over drunk.'

'How rude!'

'Precisely, he even referred to you and Trudy as trainee alcoholics!'

'Well, he's gone right down in my estimation, that's for sure! The nerve of him,' says saint Suzi, who only likes the odd drink.

'So, I put him straight on that. Oh, and then I told him about that crazy woman driving us home.'

'Don't! She was something else.'

'And do you know what he said?'

'Go on.'

'Nothing! He just howled with laughter!' I huff. 'So, I just left him there, chewing on his fist. Next Dad had words with me,' I gabble on, eager to fully commit Suzi to camp Christie.

'What did he say?'

'Much the same as Miles, but with more tact. And he doesn't know about our near-death experience in the car with the mad Mrs Price… So, he didn't do the hysterical laughter thing.'

'It wasn't funny.'

'I know.'

'So, what about your dad, he usually comes up with practical advice?'

'He did, that's why I phoned for you.'

'He told you to leave!'

'No, he told me to think about what I really want out of this situation, work out what everyone else wants, then make it happen. And to do that, I need to have some space. I knew Madeline would be arriving at some point… I needed to leave before she arrived.'

'But you didn't quite make it!'

'Ohhh, I did. I was in the garden hiding behind a Flowering Blackcurrant bush when she arrived. I was at quite a safe distance… Close enough to see and hear what was going on, but not be seen and heard myself… Until, that is, you phoned the first time.'

'You didn't answer.'

'Funny that! I was too busy being escorted out from behind that bush by the ever-helpful Miles, with a very apt musical accompaniment, to go with my troll hair.' I point to my tufty hair.

'Oh, ha ha, sorry. Slightly embarrassing for you then.'

'You could say that. So, the first time I meet Madeline De-Muir, I'm being dragged from behind a bush, by Miles, with twigs in my hair and chocolate smeared over my face. And all you want is—'

'An intro. Sorry… But it did look like you were already relaxed with each other, Miles was holding your hand! What's all that about?'

I grit my teeth. 'He was making sure I didn't make a bid for freedom! So, when you phoned the second time…' I shrug.

'You escaped.'

'Bingo.'

Suzi's shoulders finally relax as she slumps back in her seat, all her indignation evaporates. She nods her head once, as if she's just made an important decision, clicks off the hazards, and off we go.

'It's time you start being the one making all the choices. If Madeline wants you to play happy families, she needs to play by your rules.'

'Just what I wanted to hear. On my side, then?'

'Only since we were three years old… you do know Trudy is going to want to kill someone?'

I look at Suzi, and smile. 'Oh well, never mind.' The thought of Trudy in a righteous rant is *very* satisfying. Maybe everything will turn out fine after all. 'We can always go and visit her in prison.'

Commando

On my hands and knees.

Back at home, with my feet tucked up on the sofa, and a mug of coffee clutched between my hands, I am happy to bask in the glow of Trudy's fury.

'That man is infuriating, and I'm none too pleased with your parents for letting him infiltrate their home and family.'

'It is their home,' I point out mildly. Now I'm in *my own home* I can afford to be a little magnanimous. 'So, it's up to them who they choose to let in.'

'But didn't you say, you thought Madeline bought it for them?' asks Trudy.

'Yes but...' I start, and then I remember! 'She bought this for me too! I'll have to move out! We'll all have to move out!' Panic seizes me as I clamber off my comfy sofa, trying not to slosh coffee everywhere.

'Sit down!' barks Trudy. She really is fearsome.

I do as I'm told without a second thought. 'I have no money! What am I going to do?'

Trudy manoeuvres herself to face me full-on. 'First of all, you're going to stop panicking! This house belongs to you. Your mum took you to the solicitors to have the deeds signed over to you, I remember you going. It was gifted to you from your Great Aunt Maddie, who we now know is Madeline.'

'I know it *actually* belongs to me, but *ethically* it belongs to her. I don't want her to have even more of a hold over me.'

'Christie, ethics don't come into it, and if they did, with what she's put you through, she wouldn't have a leg to stand on.'

'She has just broken her ankle,' chips in Suzi.

'She's probably done that on purpose to get sympathy!' snaps Trudy. 'It changes nothing.'

The doorbell rings, we all look at each other.

I frown. 'Are either of you two expecting anyone?'

'Nope,' says Trudy. 'We're both still in recovery mode.'

'Can we just pretend we're out?' I suggest hopefully.

'Worth a try,' says Suzi in a low voice.

We all keep quiet and still. 'Trouble is,' I whisper, 'the two cars on the drive are a bit of a giveaway.'

'We could have gone on a walk,' says Suzi. 'Or to the pub.'

The doorbell rings again, slightly longer than last time.

'Persistent, whoever they are,' says Trudy. 'I'll go; I'll say we're all suffering from the plague or something.'

'It could be Nigel though!' says Suzi. 'If it is, let him in!'

'No! He's only just dropped me off a couple of hours ago! I'll have to hide.'

Bang, bang, bang!

'I'm on my way!' barks Trudy. 'Honestly, the cheek of them.' I hear Trudy open the door with a brisk, 'Hello, and what do you think you're doing here?' I can't make out anything the other person is saying, just a low rumbling male voice.

'It could be Nigel,' Suzi whispers hopefully. She's too keen to be in with a chance.

'Well I'm out of here,' I say quietly. I roll off the sofa, and start making my way towards the kitchen on my hands and knees. Not quite commando style, but with a degree of stealth befitting my age and current recent physical limitations. I manage to nudge open the kitchen door with my elbow.

'Are you looking for something down there, or, let me guess, trying to make another daring escape?' croons Miles.

I can hear the laughter in his voice.

Now I have a couple of options here:

I can say, yes, I'm looking for something. Of course, he won't believe me. Or, I can say yes, I'm making another daring escape. And that, of course, he would believe. Or, I can simply ignore him, and carry on making my escape. Choice made, I continue on my hands and knees out of the room. Obviously now I've been seen, I no longer need to hunch down quite so painfully.

In the kitchen, I crawl up onto a chair, dust myself down, drop my head into my hands, and groan. I try my best to disregard the howls of male laughter coming from the other room. I slump, with the little dignity I can muster at the table, and wait. I know one of them will come in; I just hope it's not him!

And what is he doing here anyway? It's not as if anyone wants him here, both Trudy and Suzi are hacked off with him. He's got more layers than an onion, and the superpower to make me cry. I need to rise above my rancour and ignite my inner resolve. I'm just not sure if I can with that man, I'd probably explode.

Trudy comes in and sits down opposite me. 'He says he comes in peace. Doesn't want to talk about the family situation, because he knows it is all still very raw. But he says he does need to discuss *Evolution* with you. Can you manage that? I think he'd appreciate your cooperation.'

'I'd appreciate him leaving me *alone.*'

'Then the sooner you sort out what you are prepared to do, the better.'

She's "Miss Reasonable" all of a sudden! Two minutes ago, she wanted him to suffer a slow and painful death. He must've clicked on his charm button. 'I haven't had time to think yet, have I?'

Trudy places her hands flat on the table, her matt-mocha manicure at odds with the distressed pine. She leans forward. 'Look, Christie, you need to get up to speed, pronto! This is your chance to take advantage.'

'How do you work that out? He's in control of everything.'

'I assume Madeline has been pulling all the strings up until now. Miles has been following her plan of action. She's out of action, so you pull the strings.'

'I don't think—'

'Well start! He's Madeline's right-hand man, he is used to being told what to do by a woman. So how about you start telling him what to do, and see what happens.'

'He won't listen to me. He's too... I don't know?'

'Confident?'

'Bolshie, obstinate, pig-headed.'

'And you're being wholly reasonable? Come on, Christie, step up to the mark!'

'I don't know how!'

She flings her arms up in the air, and tosses her head back. 'Then wing it. I have to do it every day at work, surrounded by men who resent my status. Listen, if you act the part, they believe it… He'll believe it.'

'Trudy… He has just watched me crawl, *crawl* on my hands and knees out of the room.'

'So, you'll catch him off guard.' She plants her hands on her hips. 'He won't expect you to come out all composed and competent.'

'I'd need to get changed out of these clothes, they're too…'

'Casual, I agree. Perhaps you should wear your interview suit.'

'Isn't that a bit much?'

'You want him to sit up and take notice, pretend you're interviewing him. Actually, in a way you are. Now those two have done all the donkey work with the gallery, you could tout for an agent. That would irritate them!'

'You forget, Madeline owns all my art.'

'You've stacks of it in the attic.' Trudy waves her arm in the general direction of the stairs. 'Anyway, you can use this to springboard you to wherever you want to be.'

'Year 7C, I want to be with 7C, and work with them until they become 11C.'

'Then tell him, but please have a bit of fun talking about agents too, make him sweat.'

'I bet he's never sweat in his life.'

'Then it's time he started. Go out the back door, and back in through the front so he doesn't see you. Get changed and slap on some make-up. I'll bring you a coffee upstairs while you're getting ready. Take your time, make him wait. And think what you're going to say.'

Okay here goes. I'm changed into a pair of smart pants and plain white T-shirt. I've added some lippy, blusher and mascara, and brushed my hair into an *ish* style… Well, no twigs anyway.

'That bra will have to go!' Trudy ambushes me on the landing.

'What do you mean "have to go"! It's white.'

'Lose the bra! You need to start playing dirty… They have! Come on, Christie, live dangerously.'

Trudy lunges for me, shoves her hands up my back, unhooks my bra, snags it at one shoulder, pulls it down my arm, and then pulls it completely out the other side.

Clearly, she has hidden talents in the bra department. She's now spinning it round on her forefinger like a hula hoop. I look down at my tiny boobs, now only just making an appearance. Trudy is smirking.

'Give it back!' I hiss. 'I look about twelve without it.'

'No, you don't. You look confident, self-assured. You look like a woman who knows she's sexy.' She pouts, and blows me a kiss.

'And since I'm none of those, I'll have my bra back please.'

'He won't be able to concentrate on what you're saying. He'll promise you anything you ask for.'

I do my best glare. 'Or I'll just go and put another one on. Probably purple.'

'How about we meet halfway, leave the bra off, and drape one of your arty scarf things round your neck. It'll send him mad trying to tell if you've got a bra on or not.'

'Now you're making him sound about twelve.'

'The male of the species, rarely mature beyond the mental age of twelve when testosterone kicks in.' Trudy pings the bra in the general direction of my bedroom. 'And it's down to us females to take the advantage.'

'Okay, okay, I bow to your superior knowledge. I'll go and find a scarf. But if he laughs at me one more time today, I will probably kill him, and that will be your fault, so you'll be an accessory!'

'He won't laugh.'

I snatch up my bra on my way back to my room, sling it on the bed and grab the first scarf I see. Trudy follows me, and arranges the scarf in what I hope is an alluring fashion.

'And remember, he's used to doing as he's told. Must be, he's been with Madeline for years.'

'I hope you're right.'

'Send Suzi out to make drinks. Don't let her interfere; she is, after all, Madeline's number one fan.'

'So, Miles will rate highly in her estimations. Gotcha.'

'Go knock him dead!'

Tempted…

Reviews

Grappling round his ankles

Hobbling down the stairs, I try not to think about escaping out of the front door. In the lounge, Suzi and Miles are stood in front of the mantelpiece with their backs to me. They're looking at a caricature I did of us three girls.

'Yes, I know,' says Suzi, 'she did it as a memento of our detox week. Can you see we've all got revolting looking drinks, and bowls of brown rice?'

'It's very quirky; do you think she knows how good she is?'

'Probably not.'

'I predict she's going to become very collectable, very quickly. That charming caricature will be worth a small fortune in a couple of weeks.'

'We'd never sell it!'

'I didn't think you would, she's lucky to have such good friends. You know, she should really have a studio.'

'Oh, I know. She spends hours cooped up in that nasty little attic, it's a wonder she hasn't got rickets, lack of vitamin D, sunlight deficiency,' coos Suzi.

Miles nods.

I think now is a good time to interrupt their little tête-à-tête. 'Well thank you, Nurse Suzi.' I cross my arms and raise an eyebrow as they both swivel round to look at me. 'Nice to know how concerned you are for my health.'

Suzi flushes, not used to being caught out gossiping.

I tilt my head. 'Maybe you could dig out that smoothie maker; I'm sure Miles would love to sample one of your specials.'

'Didn't hear you come in,' mutters Suzi. 'Wouldn't you rather have some juice?'

'Yes please, juice would be lovely, but don't let Miles miss out on one of your health drinks just because I'm being boring.'

Suzi shuffles from the room, and I feel like a complete bitch, but I can't go after her, it would spoil the ploy.

'A little unkind... On both counts,' says Miles. He doesn't look happy.

What a shame. 'Whatever,' I say, and gesture towards the sofa. 'Care to sit down? I'm eager to get this over and done with.'

'You make it sound like a visit to the dentist.'

'No, much worse than that, my dentist is rather dishy.' I remain standing - I have picked up some tricks over the years. Miles pulls out some newspapers from his briefcase. Odd that he'd keep them there, they're all folded unevenly.

'Okay, to business. These papers carry the initial reviews for *Evolution*. As you can see, you've only managed a show in four.'

'Excuse me! What do you mean, *I've only managed a show in four!* Surely, you mean, *you've* only managed it! All I did was turn up!'

'That is precisely my point, all you did was turn up. Nobody felt a buzz about meeting you, because nobody knew you were there!'

'Sarah McBride figured it out.'

'Yes.' Miles shuffles the papers. 'Here we are, in the Independently Art. Seems she's taken a liking to you. Here, take a look.' He passes the folded paper to me. It has two short paragraphs boxed in red marker.

> Today I've had the pleasure of being one of a select few to be invited to a preview of a remarkable exhibition, Evolution, by Christie Harris. What an absolute treat! The name says it all; we are lured into being guests in the life of this young artist, as she evolves from the age of eight years, to the present time, a span of sixteen years.
>
> We witness innocence and charm, move on to teenage angst and unrequited love, and then again to wit and whimsical wisdom! Her work is funny, warm, poignant, self-deprecating, and wholly unaware of the remarkable flair it embodies. What's more, I happened to stumble upon the artist herself. Watch this space, a star is born, methinks - #Christie. Not to be missed.

I scan it a second time, and unravel the paper. Yes, it is the Independently Art! And it's a good, very good critique, except the bit about, oh here it is, unrequited love. Hope Trudy's brother doesn't figure that one out.

'Well, what do you think?' asks Miles.

'It's a good review, like you said, it seems Sarah McBride has taken a liking to me.'

'So, you did let her know who you are then.'

'She sussed me out while she was quizzing me about one of the pictures.'

'That's Sarah for you, she has an instinct when it comes to artists, can pick one out at fifty paces.' He shrugs. 'She was impressed by your work, and that bodes well.'

'And the rest?'

'Here, look at what Timothy Grey has to say.' He passes me another newspaper, again folded with red marker boxing off a review.

> From a clumsy start into a promising display, Evolution, by Christie Harris lives up to its name. The artist bravely shows off work that other less daring souls would hide away. None of us enjoy those first faltering steps into the limelight, especially when we know our imperfections are exposed for the public to devour. Bravo, Ms Harris, a masterclass in how to disarm the most venomous critics; I look forward to making your acquaintance.

'He says my work is clumsy!'

'No, he says a clumsy start, you were eight, what do you expect?'

'I expect to be judged as an eight-year-old should be, given encouragement and then pointed in the right direction.'

'Ah yes, but you aren't eight anymore, so, Mr Grey is quite right to treat you as an adult.'

'But it's cruel.'

'No, it's honest. Your work is, as Mr Grey points out, on public display, and therefore open to public scrutiny.'

'Not by my own choice!'

'Timothy Grey doesn't know that, and actually gives you the credit for bravery, which should belong to your backer.'

'You mean Madeline.'

'She has invested time, effort, and money. She's yanked a few influential strings to get some credible art critics to Chippington to view your work.'

'I didn't ask her to.'

'But she did it anyway.'

'I wish she hadn't.'

'We digress… Let's stick to what I'm here to do, and that is move forward with *Evolution*. So, the next review, here it is.' Miles hands me another folded newspaper. 'I don't think you met this one, James Butterworth?'

I shake my head, take the paper from Miles.

A beautifully executed display set in sympathetic surroundings. Evolution, by Christie Harris is about to take the mainstream art world by storm. Refreshingly honest, simple sketches build, to produce an exquisite display of childhood and beyond. Not known for its artistic talents, on this occasion Chippington is well worth a visit… Or wait a while, for I'm confident we shall soon see Christie Harris in a gallery near you.

'So, what do you think?' Miles raises his eyebrows.

'I hope my work lives up to the hype.'

'It does. So now you've seen these initial reviews, you should feel more confident swinging into full PR mode. I'm sure I don't need to tell you that art is its own ambassador, but a little schmoozing goes a long way in the popularity stakes.' Miles returns the papers to his briefcase.

'Hold on, I thought you said I had four shows, you've only shown me three.'

'Oh, the other is only a couple of lines, hardly worth looking at.' Miles clicks his briefcase shut.

'But, since it's here, I may as well read it.'

'I've put it away now.' Miles settles his briefcase down.

'You know, Miles, I get the feeling you don't want me to read the last review.' Maybe it's just too awful.

'Not at all, it just seems a waste of time, that's all; let's get on with planning.'

'Not until I've read that review.'

'Christie, it's not worth bothering about.'

'I'll be the judge of that! Now, hand it over.' I hold out my hand, like I do when confiscating an illicit item from a teenager. And wait.

Miles doesn't move a muscle. I lunge for the briefcase, and end up grappling round his ankles. Miles holds fast to the darned case, as if his life depends on it.

'Let go! This is private property!'

'It's a newspaper!'

'It's my newspaper!'

'Don't be so childish.'

'You're the one trying to wrestle a briefcase from me! Christie, please.'

'Here we are, refreshments. Christie! What are you doing down there? Get up! You're embarrassing yourself!' splutters Suzi.

'He won't show me one of the reviews… It must be really bad.'

'It's not in a reputable newspaper.'

'All the more reason to read it. That's the sort of paper most people read!'

Suzi nods. 'Christie does have a point there, Miles. It can't be that bad.'

'All I'm trying to do here, is be objective. Reading an ill-informed, factually incorrect review will do nothing to move *Evolution* forward. It may even make you decide not to be further involved with the entire project.'

That bad?

'Miles, Christie is much more resilient than you seem to think—'

Thank you, Suzi

'…She's had to deal with that teacher, the one the kids call Slimy Sloan. He's a real pain.'

'Ah, yes, I remember…'

'Always on her case over something or other; does it get her down? No, water off a duck's back—'

Well actually…

'But… Madeline told me—' starts Miles.

'Look!' I snap. 'Can I see the review, or do we call it a day?' I glare at him. I do not want Miles discussing with Suzi, my alleged "private correspondence" to Auntie Maddie. He shouldn't even know about it. It's not on!

'Fine, you win, but it just… Here.' He clicks open his briefcase and passes me the newspaper. 'It is rubbish, utter rubbish!' He reluctantly leaves go of it.

> Well, well, well, what have we here? Evolution, by the so-called Christie Harris, is an indulgence too far! Of course, parents want to see their offspring do well, but really, should they use their influence to launch the career of

a quite mediocre talent, (I use the word "talent" in its loosest form)? In the long run it can only lead to tears before bedtime!

I have met Lord and Lady X on many occasions. If they believe their dear daughter has any artistic skills, why, oh why did they not simply ask my opinion, before lavishing time and money on a purely futile venture.

Lucky for them, I am not so crass as to name them in a national newspaper, after all, their private embarrassment will surely be enough to bear. Then again, watch this space. Yours, as ever, Bunty H.

'Bunty Hargreaves,' I croak, as the now familiar knot tightens in my stomach.

Suzi thrusts two drinks at Miles, one of which contains a revolting slushy mixture about the same shade of green as my face. The other, the same shade as Suzi's face. Hope it's *Vimto*. She takes the newspaper from my hand, and begins to read.

'The cow,' mutters Suzi eventually, looking to me. 'Christie, it's just spiteful drivel because Trudy had a go at her.'

'She said it's mediocre.'

Miles shrugs dramatically. 'What can I say? She's delusional. Everyone else thinks it's brilliant. Bunty Hargreaves is the Slimy Sloan of the supplement section. Nobody takes her seriously.'

'Mediocre...' I repeat.

'I've already contacted the newspaper in question, and explained Bunty has made an error of judgement.'

'An error of judgement. About her critique, or about my identity?'

'Both,' says Miles. 'When you explained how you came about all your scratches, it all started to make sense. Bunty must have been mad as a wasp, having her phone snatched off her. The only way she could outdo her fellow columnists, was to sensationalise the situation.'

'But it's very close to the truth. Madeline has used her influence to get me recognition.'

'Maybe, but you weren't party to it. And, crucially, your work is remarkable.'

'Remarkable?'

'Yes, remarkable. Anyway, as she's made such an openly hostile attack on your work, others will clamour to see it.'

'You mean, she's done me a favour?'

'Exactly,' says Miles. 'Can we get on? Which of these two drinks is mine?' He holds up the two glasses.

'The green one!' Suzi and I say together.

Fraya-Froo

I am not getting changed!

Trudy preens. Suzi shuffles. I can barely look at myself in the bedroom mirror. 'I look like… What do I look like? I can't believe Miles talked me into this re-launch. And you were no help, simpering like a love-struck teen.'

Suzi shrugs, not the least bit concerned about my predicament.

Well thanks for that Suzi!

I glare at Trudy. 'And you were no better, "Little-Miss-Whip-Your-Bra-Off"! Trudy… what am I wearing? I can't bear to look in the mirror again… my eyes might start to bleed!' I risk a glance down, multicoloured silk wafts about my legs.

'It's a *Fraya-Froo*. She's an up-and-coming designer. Basically, it's a jigsaw jumpsuit, the *Jigjump*. There's a whole range, the *Fleurjump*, the *Skyjump*, the *Petaljump*—'

'I wish she'd go and take a running jump into the nearest river,' I say.

'Oh, there is a *Riverjump*!'

'Trudy! It's hideous! Suzi, back me up here! Please!'

'Well, it is quite loud—'

'Quite loud!' I squeal.

Suzi grimaces. 'And if I'm honest, I don't think I could ever bring myself to wear it.'

'Thank you.'

'Not even for a bet.'

'Girls,' says Trudy, 'you are both missing the point entirely! *Fraya-Froo* is a brand-new label, Christie is a brand-new artist. By wearing a *Fraya-Froo*, you, Christie, will, one, give her some great exposure, two, gain an instant cutting-edge image, and three…' Trudy screws up her nose.

'Show the world I have no style?'

'And three, have other designers clamouring over each other to give you freebies.'

'Trudy, I know you're probably right on all three points, but it's just not me. And if I'm standing in front of people, with my whole life exposed for their scrutiny, I need to be honest enough to be me. Let them actually judge the real me… Because once everyone finds out I'm Madeline's daughter… I'll never get that chance again.' My eyes smart as I hold in the tears. 'I'll be—'

'You'll always be Christie Harris,' says Trudy softly. 'Now get out of that gruesome pantomime outfit, and into something *Christiefied*. Come on, we haven't got all day!'

Relief floods through me. I shove them both out of my bedroom before Trudy changes her mind. I swing open my wardrobe doors and inspect the mayhem. I whip off the *Jigjump* and sling it onto the bed.

Skinny jeans, I think, I've got the bum for them, and… I let my hand trail over the sweep of random oversized jumpers. This baggy-necked cornflower blue one with, yep, my Elmo T-shirt underneath, just in case it gets overheated in the gallery. I dress as quickly as I can; a pair of white pumps finishes off my outfit.

Done.

Just being in my own comfy clothes, makes me feel slightly more relaxed. The thoughts of meeting all those critics again kept me awake half the night. Lucky for me, Trudy is a whiz with all thing's beauty, and has somehow hidden the sacks of potatoes hanging under my eyes.

'Okay, here I come,' I holler, and wander down to the lounge. Miles is sat on the sofa between Suzi and Trudy. 'Oh, I didn't hear you arrive.'

'I'd been outside for ten minutes. Doesn't anybody ever answer the door in this house?' Miles stands when I enter the room. 'You're looking very—'

'I am *not* getting changed!'

'No, no, you look lovely. Fresh, natural and chilled, you're going to blow them away!' He laughs. 'You know, I had an awful feeling you were going to come in like an overdressed peacock, but you're just you.'

Suzi and Trudy exchange glances.

'I'd rather people enjoy the gallery, than gawp at me. It's better if I just blend in.' *So* glad I managed to ditch the *Fraya-Froo*, I'd never have lived it down.

'Shall we get off then?' Miles gestures towards the door. 'We can all go together if you like, Suzi, Trudy?'

'Good idea,' simpers Suzi. 'I'll just get my bag.'

I notice the frosty look Trudy aims at Suzi. 'Actually, I've an early start tomorrow, so, I'll drive myself. You two get off, I can bring Suzi. Give you a chance to go over the last-minute details.'

'Good idea, come on then, Christie. There *are* a couple of things we need to discuss.'

Just what I need, more alone time with Miles. I follow him towards the door, turn and draw my forefinger across my neck giving Trudy my meanest glare. She returns it with a sweet smile, and blows me a kiss. One day, I will repay the favour.

I'm pleasantly surprised to see a classic Jag parked at the front. Not flash, just understated class. Miles unlocks the passenger door with an actual key and opens it for me.

'This is very classy,' I say, settling into the leather clad seat of his car. I love the smell of polished leather; not sure what that says about me.

'Nice isn't it? It's Madeline's; she lets me borrow it for special occasions.'

'Oh.' It would be hers, wouldn't it? The engine purrs, and we're off. Miles smoothly works his way up through the gears, and settles at a steady speed.

He starts tapping a random beat with his fingers on the steering wheel. 'Today, you are going to make them love you.'

'Most people usually just tolerate me, or humour me,' I say, and immediately think of Mr Sloan with his beady eyes and pulsing neck vein. I close my eyes and put him in his chicken suit so he can't intimidate me, fluffy yellow feathers, orange beak, overstuffed tail. That's better. I open my eyes and look ahead.

'Well today, all that is going to change.'

'Whatever.' I risk a sneaky glance at him, not sneaky enough because he smiles. His hands are slung casually on the steering wheel, and his fingers are still tapping an irregular beat. Very irritating, I doubt he even knows he's doing it.

'If I give you the formula, you have to promise to keep it a secret.'

'Pardon?'

'The formula! The formula for making people love you.' His smile spreads into a grin. I can't help but stare, his face is transformed.

A flutter starts in my chest. 'You are joking, right?'

We slow to a stop at traffic lights, and Miles turns to look at me with only the ghost of the smile remaining. 'It's no joke. It's not the truly, madly, deeply love. It's the superficial, wow, isn't she amazing, love. The sort celebrities clamour for.'

'I'm not a celebrity.'

'You will be.'

'Let's give the fortune telling a miss, shall we?' I say. 'And stop drumming your fingers!'

The finger drumming stops. 'Okay. Do you want the formula, or are you going to wing it?'

Probably best to humour him. I roll my eyes. 'So, what is it?' Anything to keep my mind off this re-launch will do. The lights change, and we're off again.

Miles glances at me. 'The first and hardest bit, you've already done, I'm impressed. That is, don't try to be someone you're not. Well done, you are wearing the kind of clothes you always wear, not too much make-up, casual pumps, and your hair is its usual fluffy self—'

'It's not fluffy! It's curly!'

'Fluffy, curly, same thing.' I can tell he's trying his best not to smirk. Failing.

'Strange you have this mystical formula to make people love you, and yet, still you manage to irritate me half to death.'

'Like I said, it's not the truly, madly, deeply - that takes a different route. Second, you need to be as absolutely honest as you can be, without, and this is important, not offending or upsetting people.'

'That's just good manners,' I say, everyone knows that.

'Without revealing too much about yourself. Which leads nicely to number three.' He nods, as if trying to secure this knowledge in his own well of wisdom.

'Have you always been so good at maths?' Starting to lose interest now.

'Hold back, make yourself an enigma; set people the puzzle. Let them glimpse only the edges of your secrets.'

Maybe I should have worn the *Jigjump* after all, now that is a puzzle. I fiddle with the edge of my jumper. I don't want people prying into my life, especially now. I'm struggling to come to terms with the whole Madeline De-Muir thing. I'm beginning to think becoming a recluse has its advantages, then I really would be an enigma. 'I'd rather, they didn't even assume I have any secrets.'

'Everyone has secrets… And four…' he carries on, clearly, either not picking up on my anxiety, or ignoring it. 'Eye contact and smile. Make the person you are talking to, think they are, to you, at that moment, the most important person in the room.'

'If I spend all day trying to remember all that, I'll probably end up with a nervous twitch.' Maybe they'll take pity on me.

Miles smiles, his fingers have started their random rhythm again. He must know how irritating it is. I stick my fingers in my ears. 'Will you stop drumming your fingers? The urge to sing la-la -la at the top of my lungs, to drown out that tuneless beat, is sending me batty!'

'Sorry, it's one of my many endearing habits.' Again, the smile, but he does stop drumming his fingers.

I gaze out of the window. Fields make way for rural villages, Wilton, Clover Beck and Brock Beck all pass by in a blur. The last of the open landscape disappears as we cross over the river into the large market town of Chippington. The tall spire of St. Mary's Church, and the backdrop of several old mill chimney stacks, dominate the skyline.

Miles negotiates the myriad of streets with ease, thankfully still no drumming fingers. After a maze of side streets, and lefts and rights we're back at the converted Mill. The *Evolution* banner, still proud and bold, sets my heart racing at what I'm about to face.

My critics.

If I'm honest, I suppose I've always wanted recognition for my work. I would never have chosen to show what is on display inside the mill right now. In my mind, I would have a complete body of work, which holds no tight emotional bonds to me. The work behind those walls is my life, or a huge chunk of it, and I'm terrified how I'm going to be judged.

'You okay?' asks Miles.

'Think so.' I lie so blatantly!

'Good, let's get to it then.'

We get out of the car, and Miles locks it manually, classics do have some disadvantage. As we walk across the gravel yard, the back door to the Mill swings open, and there stands Mrs Price.

The first hurdle of many.

'Oh, my dear girl,' she says, as she's squishing my face between her none too gentle hands, 'you're looking much better than I thought you would—'

Gee, thanks!

'… White as a sheet you were—'

Ummmm, I wonder why? Your driving, perhaps?

'… Let's get you safe inside. That Bunty Hargreaves has a lot to answer for, I'm surprised Miles invited her back today.'

'What!' I swing to face Miles. 'You didn't tell me you'd invited her!'

'Very good PR for us. Heaps of humble pie for her.'

'If Trudy sees her, the only kind of pie Bunty will manage, will be through a straw.'

'Trudy's cool with it.'

'You're sure about that, because?' I raise my well-practiced and manicured brow.

'Oh yes, we had a little chat while you were getting ready.'

'And?'

'And we all have reputations to maintain.'

'You blackmailed her!'

'I merely pointed out, that it was beneficial to all parties to preserve a veneer of mutual respect.'

'Mutual respect?'

'Yes.'

'Bullshit.'

'Exactly! That is why it is just a veneer; and I'm expecting you to go along with this mutual respect. In fact, I want you to make her feel so guilty about the way she's misrepresented you—'

'Lied about me.'

'Diplomacy, please… That she'll be on side when she discovers the actual truth, otherwise…'

'She'll dig up everything she can about me.'

'And Madeline. Don't forget, she was only sixteen when she had you.'

How can I forget that?

Once again, it's all about his precious Madeline. I'm sick of her name already. How am I ever going to manage to get along with her, knowing what she's done? And the way Miles is always on her side, is very unsettling. 'So, you want me to be sweetness and light?'

'I want you to be yourself, and pretend you are meeting Bunty Hargreaves for the first time. Give her a fresh start.'

'A fresh start? Like nothing's ever happened?'

'Exactly, you never know, a fresh start might be all she needs.'

'Whatever.'

'Christie, we all make mistakes sometimes.'

'Even you?'

His eyes crinkle at the sides, as a wide grin spreads across his face. 'I know! Hard to believe, but even me sometimes.'

'Well for all our sakes, I hope this isn't one of those times.'

'I don't make them very often, if that helps.' I nod towards Mrs Price, who is busy now stacking flyers. 'She isn't a mistake; she is in many ways awesome; even her driving when you're not a passenger…'

'Hmmm.'

'Mrs Price, could you remind me of the revised schedule for today?'

'There are only two revisions, firstly Frankie will not be talking about the *Keep*-a-Key charity, apparently a…' Mrs Price shuffles some papers. 'Where is it, oh yes, a Sarah McBride has his little speech on her Dictaphone. She's going to do something independently in one of the nationals about him and the charity. The other is you'll be introducing Christie as herself.'

'I don't have to say anything do I?' I ask.

'I'll just do a bit of background on you.' Miles looks at me as if I'm a terrified child. Very close.

'What will you say?'

'Local teacher from Little Upton, always loved art, always encouraged by a distant aunt to follow her artistic dream, vague. And then I will ask you to open the exhibition, all you need to say is something like, "I formally declare *Evolution* open". And then just mingle. Okay?'

'Sounds simple.'

'It is, so don't overthink it, you'll be fine.'

Meet and Greet

'Up a tree, actually!'

The hair on the back of my neck is prickling. Feels like I'm in a life-or-death situation. My hands are quivering, eyelids twitching, and my throat feels like I've just swallowed a brick. I'm not entirely convinced it's just because I'm stood in front of this hushed crowd.

Miles.

I can feel the heat radiating from his hand as it rests in the small of my back. His other hand is across the front of my body, and loosely clasping my fingers, "a casual, yet seemingly intimate poise", is how he blagged me into agreeing to this staged entrance.

A tad too intimate for my liking.

He keeps giving my trembling hand a gentle squeeze every now and then. It's his prompt for us to exchange smiles and eye contact, "Let's show them we're a great team". He's waffling on about the impact each new picture has had on him over the last few years. He's weaving in the background info about working with the *Keep-a-Key* team, to bring my art to the public's attention, blah-de-blah-de-blah, on and on.

'So now, here she is, my good friend, Christie Harris.'

Miles releases my hand, and gives me a gentle push forward. A ripple of applause fills the foyer. Whoops and whistles from Trudy and Suzi ease my tension slightly, making me smile. I feel a blush rush over my cheeks.

'Hi there, everyone.' My hand makes an involuntary wave. WHY??? 'So, thank you all for coming today. It's good to see my friends are here to support me, Trudy, Suzi. Some of you are here for a second time, so, thank you, Sarah, Bunty…' I scan the room. 'Oh, and Mr Grey, good of you, to all come back.' I rub my sweaty palms together, try to smile but my lips stick to my teeth. 'I'm not used to talking in public to grown-ups, so, sorry for being haphazard. I will be wandering about if anyone wants to talk to me later.' I try a smile again. 'So, feel free, but first I suppose I must open the exhibition.' I glance at the expectant faces. Deep breath. 'I declare *Evolution* officially open. Enjoy.'

Genteel applause, is accompanied by Trudy and Suzi's rock festival frolics, earning them both amused looks.

Can't take them anywhere.

'Well done,' whispers Miles. His warm breath on the nape of my neck sends goosebumps prickling down my spine. A wave of awareness ignites my senses. 'Just enough, not too much.'

Oh Miles… not enough, and way, way, way too much!

'Don't worry, I'll chaperone Tru 'n' Su. Off you go, mingle, and it might be a nice gesture if you mingle with the ever-charming Bunty Hargreaves first. Get it out of the way.'

I search the room for her frosty features. She's hovering over *Score* like a vulture about to pick at a carcass. Typical! I try to look casual as I saunter towards her, swallowing frantically behind my smile.

'How kind of you to give me a second chance,' I say, when I reach her side. My smile is glued on waiting for her response. She merely nods, so I continue, 'I've got to admit, I'm rather embarrassed by this one.'

'What's his name?' she demands.

'I'd rather not say, he's from my youth.'

'You're still a youth.' She looks me up and down, and I can feel my face burning. 'I guess he's your first lover.'

'Goodness me, no!' I splutter in horror. 'No; just, he was just someone I had a crush on, that's all, it was a long time ago.'

'By the colour of your face, I'd say you've still got a crush on him, can't say I blame you, he's a bit of a hunk.'

'Artistic licence, he's just a family friend, so it's going to be awkward when he finds out about this.' I point to the exquisitely defined torso of Simon in my painting.

Bunty lets out a low cackle, then examines Simon closely with her beady eyes. 'You know, he looks quite like the Drummond girl over there.' My eyes follow her line of vision to where Trudy is standing. 'So, I'm assuming it's one of her brothers. Let me see, which one?'

'It was just one of those teenage things years ago, long forgotten, he never knew.'

'So, the poor lad never found out then, I'm sure he'll be flattered, when he does.'

'Please don't!'

'What, dig and delve? Surely you know dear, it's what we do; we trawl through other people's lives and pick out a living for ourselves. But luckily for you, I've just had my wrists slapped for overstepping the mark, so I'll leave it for someone else to pick up on.'

'Thank you.' I bite my lip.

She turns to face me; steel eyes bore into mine. 'A piece of advice.'

I nod, transfixed, unable to break eye contact with her.

Her eyes scan the gallery. 'Do not trust them, any of them.'

'I'll try to remember that,' I say, trying to match her gravity. Not easy, when I'm eager to escape so I can go and lock Trudy in a cupboard until everyone has left.

'You're alright, despite being one of his pet projects.' Bunty gestures towards Miles. 'You've got courage, I'll give you that, after the roasting I gave you.' She twists her mouth into the semblance of a smile.

'You too.'

'I'll give you that,' says Bunty, narrowing her eyes. 'Now I suggest you trot along, and make pretend friends with the other scavengers.'

I scurry away and head directly for Trudy, who appropriately, is holding court in front of *Trudy Takes a Tumble.* A hand catches my sleeve.

'Well, well, well, if it's not the elusive Christie Harris.' Timothy Grey! Oh dear… 'Or should I call you Anne?' he purrs.

'Oh, hello again, Mr Grey.'

'Timothy, please.' He lifts my hand to his lips, and presses a kiss to the inside of my wrists.

YUK.

'Timothy.' I drag my hands away as gently as I can, look into his eyes and smile. 'How generous of you to come back for a second viewing.'

'Couldn't resist meeting the artist herself.'

'Here I am.' I shrug, with what I hope is a cute smile.

'So, now I've got you.' He secures his arm around my back, and starts steering me back towards *Score*. 'How about you tell me all about this young Adonis?'

'What is there to tell?' I say. 'Just a family friend.'

'You seem to have a lot of those.' He nods towards Miles. 'So, tell me, was he another of your lovers?'

'No! What is it with you all?' I gasp. 'And what do you mean, another?' My voice rises to a squeak.

'Come on now, it's obvious to everyone that you and Miles have a thing going on.'

'No! We haven't, we've only just, you know...' I nearly said met! Pull yourself together girl, or he's going to tie you in knots.

'Only just?' quizzes Timothy.

'Can I trust you?' I whisper.

Timothy's eyes widen. 'What a question! Of course, you can my dear. What's troubling you?'

You, you creep

'Miles is a friend of the family, of very close family actually, but, we don't always get on.' If I keep it as close to the truth as I can, he's more likely to support me after my exposé.

'And?'

'And just before *Evolution* got off the ground,' I whisper, 'we all had, let's call it a difference of opinion.'

'All?'

'Some family, and their close friend.' I glance across to Miles. He is going to kill me

'Miles being the close friend.'

'It's delicate,' I edge.

'I see.'

I hope not. 'So, please, not a word.'

'Your secret's safe with me, however, this young man here.' He points towards sexy, shirtless Simon. 'He was more than just a family friend?'

'I couldn't possibly say.'

Sarah McBride's bosom bounds into view, and heading towards it, I make my escape. 'Christie, dearest, how could you?' she says winking. 'Deceived us all with that innocent Anne act. Come and tell me what your game is.' Sarah links her arm in mine.

Relieved, I'm happy to relax a little in her presence. 'Oh, what a tangled web we weave, when first we practice to deceive,' I mutter.

'Yes indeed, my dear, so now we'll have the truth, the whole truth and nothing but the…' she says. 'Christie, my dear, what on earth is the matter?'

I feel the single tear snaking its way down the side of my nose.

'Come on, let's get you out of here.' Sarah manoeuvres me out of the gallery.

The cool air bites my damp face. Away from prying eyes I slump against the wall, and make no attempt to stop the waterfall of tears. Sarah makes no bid to comfort me, she just watches. A bungle of tissues are pressed into my hand, and I blow my nose noisily. I look at Sarah. Her jolly round face has lost its warmth; her face is stern, eyes harsh.

'Are you finished?' she asks; her tone flat. I nod. 'Okay. I don't know what all that was about, I do know there is a room full of people looking for you.' She picks up both my hands, and turns them over, palms up. 'These hands are talented, and at the moment, those people in there are interested in you, and your talent. Don't blow it.'

'It's all a bit much.'

'Sift through your insecurities another time girl! Today, now, you need to be in control.' I nod, goosebumps prickle my arms. 'I told you the first time we met, that you'd better have pluck, and you'd better!' I nod franticly, eager to appease her. 'I have seen too many destroyed by that lot, I'd rather not see it happen to you.' She closes her eyes. I'm half tempted to make a run for it, except she's still holding my hands. 'I am trying to protect you.' She sighs loudly.

'I'm sorry,' I mutter.

'Do not let any of us see any weakness.'

'I won't.' I draw my hands from Sarah's grip. All I want is to get away from her. 'You're frightening me.'

She steps away from me, embarrassed, shocked? I can't tell. My tears stop, and Sarah appears almost to be the jolly Sarah I first met. I can feel the emotional distance she's opened up between us; it's just a mask, she's back to being the reporter. The critic. 'I don't want you to waste this chance, I like you. But too many people blow it. And even more don't even get the chance in the first place. You need to shape your own future. Don't ever forget that. Right now, you have a choice. A biggie. You can either scurry off into obscurity, or get back in there, and make people remember your name.'

'I'm not going to waste this opportunity, honestly, everything's moving so fast.'

'How so?' She looks me over. I can see the speculation in her eyes. 'This has been months in the planning.'

If I'd have known about this months ago, I'd have emigrated.

She frowns. 'Surely you must have had time to adjust to all this, be excited about it?'

And so, how well can I trust Sarah? At this stage, probably not too much. 'I just got swept along with it.'

'Miles?' she asks.

I nod, if that's what she wants to think.

She nods. 'I've known Miles for eons, way back when he was first establishing himself as Madeline De-Muir's right-hand man. He was hardly a man to be honest, fresh out of university, but that's by the by. What I do know about Miles, is that he does nothing without Madeline's approval, or backing. And this reeks of Madeline.' She gestures towards the *Evolution* banner. Her words are left hanging in the space between us; I can almost taste her anticipation. 'You have met her, I take it?'

'Briefly.' At last, a shred of honestly. I'm beginning to think she has a built-in lie detector.

'Now, there's a woman who had it all.'

'To be honest,' – and I am – 'I don't know her. I've heard about her, but that's second-hand.'

'Most things are. I interviewed her once. Twice actually.'

'Oh…' Please don't love her too much.

'The first time she'd just landed the part of Rose, in *An English Rose*. She was so vibrant and full of promise. Then off she went to Hollywood, an innocent—'

Hardly innocent!

'… I know it sounds corny, but I described her as a golden rose in full bloom. She was the darling of the industry. But when she came home, she'd lost her sparkle. She was burnt out, still a beautiful creature, but without emotion.'

'It really is interesting, but I've got to get back.'

'It seems, we have Miles to thank for her edging back towards the limelight—'

Typical.

'… He made tentative contact with a select few charities, got her involved. She became patron of a couple. I did think she was going to try to make a comeback.'

'Look, I had better make a comeback myself, before someone comes looking for me.'

'Of course, she could be using you to haul herself back into the limelight.' Sarah nods for me to go, her lips curve into a sweet smile. I head towards the back entrance, so I can freshen up before going back into the gallery. I keep my head down. The gravel crunches under my feet, I can feel the stones through my pumps. I around the corner, and walk straight into Miles.

I can tell he's been waiting for me, listening. His stance is casual. One shoulder resting against the rough brick wall, his arms folded across his chest.

His face, not so casual.

Here we go then.

'Having a nice little chat with your new best friend?' he challenges.

'She's not my new best friend.'

'I know, I was being sarcastic.'

'And I know she's a critic, a journalist. We were just passing the time.'

'So why the blotchy eyes?'

'Overthinking. I needed to get out of there.'

'You should have come and found me.'

'Why?'

'Because it's my job to look after you.'

I shake my head. 'Well, you were busy, but luckily, Sarah came to the rescue.'

'Again, she's a journalist.'

'So, I should have stood there, in tears and waited for you to come running.'

'No, surely Suzi or Trudy would have been a better choice.'

'Probably, but they were both enjoying the exhibition.'

He lets out a deep breath, hoists himself away from the wall, and gestures towards the service entrance of the mill. 'Sorry I let you down, I'll keep closer in future.'

'No need. You didn't let me down; I wasn't depending on you.'

'Madeline requires me to look after you.'

'So, you let Madeline down.' I try to walk past him, but he catches my arm.

'I'm sure you don't need reminding, but you have Madeline to thank for this project.'

'Thank?' I pull my arm from his grasp. 'I don't think so.'

I head back inside, hear him follow. I go directly to the restroom and splash my face with cool water. I still look flushed, but no longer blotchy. I take a moment, open the door slowly, and check that Miles isn't waiting for me. Can't see him. I ease my way out into the corridor and make a dash for the exhibition.

As soon as I step back into the gallery, Miles falls into step beside me.

He smiles. 'So, shall we talk about the charming Sarah tonight, over dinner?'

'No. No need to talk about her at all.'

'Christie, I'm not a fool; but more importantly, neither is she. She can sniff out a story at fifty paces. And whether you like it or not, you are one hell of a story.'

'And whether you like it or not, I will be talking to her at some point. Don't worry, I'll run it by you first.'

Miles takes my hand and links it onto his arm. He leans in close. 'All our stories need to be more than airtight. They need to be pry tight and bombproof. So, I'll pick you up at eight, and we'll discuss this away from wagging ears.'

'Fine.' Just what I need, time alone with him. I remove my hand from his arm.

'Good, now that's settled, time for more mingling.'

The atmosphere feels relaxed. Sarah is back, and looks to be well established in conversation. Trudy and Suzi appear to be still basking in all of their newfound fame. Not missing me at all. So, all is well on planet *Evolution*.

Miles catches my hand, again, and links our fingers. My fingers curl of their own accord around his. My heart does a flippity flop, I wish he wouldn't touch me; I wish I didn't want him to. I'm trying to smile. I probably look more like one of David Attenborough's teeth-baring chimps off the telly.

'Relax, Christie, everything is going great today. Come on.' Miles leads me across the gallery, back to *Score*. A smart middle-aged man in a checked bow tie is scrutinizing it.

'Alan, I'd like to introduce you to Christie Harris.'

Alan's head thrusts forwards and nods as he pommels my hand. 'Well, hello there, Christie Harris, I'm Alan Devine. Great exhibition, well done.' He nods towards *Score*. 'This chappie here, does he have any idea how famous he's about to become?'

'Umm, no. As far as I know, he doesn't.'

'He's in for a big surprise then! Were you hiding behind a tree?'

'Up a tree, actually!' I laugh. 'Although I do hide behind bushes sometimes.' Why did I say that?

'Rather a lot,' says Miles.

'Sounds interesting,' says Alan.

'I like to rely on tried and tested methods. And, though I do say so myself, I am rather good at hiding in bushes.'

'Do you have any particular preference; in bushes I mean?' Alan Devine is very easy to like.

'Oh no, any bush will do, obviously the larger the better. On the last occasion it was a Flowering Blackcurrant bush, and it was rather spikey. If I'd had the choice... I would have chosen a Laurel. Sometimes you have to go with what you've got.'

'Indeed, and did you remain undetected?'

'Until her mobile rang, and then I found her.' Miles grins, as he lifts my hand and kisses the back of it. I can feel the heat of my immediate flush.

'You were hiding from Miles?'

'Sort of.'

'The plot thickens.' Alan and Miles exchange knowing looks. 'So, back to *Score*.'

'Yes, I had a crush on him, no he doesn't know, yet, and,' – oh, well – 'see that lady over there?' I point at Trudy, and he nods. 'It's her brother. So, shit, fan, hit. I've a feeling I'm going to need to find some bushes to hide in.'

Both Alan and Miles laugh.

'No. That isn't a joke. Really!'

Not a Date

'... my boobs will fall out.'

'It's not a date!'

Trudy raises her chin a notch. 'Okay, Christie. *You* keep telling yourself that.'

'Look, Miles just wants to go over what I'm intending to tell Sarah McBride. He's not interested in me, just Madeline's precious reputation.'

Trudy looks me over. As usual, she's dressed me up in a low-cut, skin-tight dress that just about shows every curve I haven't got.

I frown. 'If I lean forward in this, my boobs will fall out.'

She smirks. 'You haven't got any boobs!'

'Exactly! So how embarrassing will that be? No, Trudy. I'm just going to wear jeans and a top, maybe a dressy top. I don't want him getting the wrong idea.' Because if he ever finds out that I do find him slightly attractive, he'll get his own way with everything. And so will Madeline.

'Christie, you look great. And, so what if he thinks you fancy him? Use it to your advantage.'

I let out a deep sigh. I've got to tell her, here goes. 'Do you remember a couple of weeks ago, when I told you and Suzi about that bloke I really liked?'

'Oh yes, the mystery man? The one you said was a bit of a dish?'

'Yep, the mystery man.'

'And?'

'I told you I'd seen him a couple of times near Mum and Dad's. But then, just before school broke up last week, he was sat in his car across from school. He was on his mobile.'

'I see. You think it must be fate. You don't want to lead Miles on, because you're holding out for the mystery man to reappear.'

'Trudy, no.'

'He's probably married, with three kids and a mortgage. But if you want to let your imagination run wild, go ahead. Better still, I could track him down, and bring him to your door.'

'No need.'

'Good—'

'He'll be coming to my door tonight anyway.'

'You've got a date with him?'

'I keep telling you… It's not a date.'

I watch Trudy's face as the penny drops. Her eyes flash as she drags her teeth over her bottom lip to hide her delight at my embarrassment.

'It's not funny. If Miles finds out I've always fancied him, he'll get all his own way, use it to his advantage. Then I'll stand no chance with Madeline.'

Trudy plonks herself down on my bed, covers her face with her hands and starts to massage her temples. Her usual deep-thinking position. Good.

I sit down next to her, then flop back to lie on the bed with my arms dangling over the edge. 'What am I going to do? Come on, Trudy think. I get goosebumps every time he touches me, and I've got to stop myself from jumping away from him, in case he guesses what I'm thinking.'

'And what are you thinking?' Trudy uncovers her face, turns to look at me, her eyes scrutinizing mine.

'Do you remember those raunchy books we used to read when we were teenagers?'

She grins. 'I still read them, between trying to live them out! Go on.'

'Well, roll them all into one awesomely raunchy fantasy, and you'll be about halfway there.'

'But what about Miles? Not the fantasy Miles, the real one. The one whose job it is to reconcile you and Madeline.'

'Honestly?'

'Honestly.'

'Okay here goes…' I say, and hold up my hand to tick off pointers. 'First of all, he's loyal, he's proved that with Madeline. Second, he's protective, again, proved that with Madeline. Third, he has a wicked sense of humour, the Mrs Price incident? He had to almost eat his fist to stop himself from exploding into hysterics. Next, he's considerate; when I came face to face with Madeline for the first time, he let me escape. Then he's caring, he's lovely with my mum, now I've run out of fingers...' Trudy flops back and rolls towards me. 'What?' I roll over and prop my head on my hands. 'Just tell me.'

Trudy is looking at me, the same way she did when she found out I'd had a teenage crush on her brother. Horror and something else. 'Go on, Christie, what else is Miles?'

'I've run out of fingers, and you look a bit pale. Are you ill?' I bite my bottom lip. 'Trudy?'

'What else?'

'He looks at me. Properly at me. Like he can see inside, and knows my secrets. He probably does, if Madeline has let him read my letters.'

'And?'

'He's beautiful,' I admit.

'He has that scar under his eye.' Trudy's words are gentle, honest.

'I know. It makes him more beautiful to me. I've sketched him, from memory. Trudy, he is beautiful. He gets these tiny little crinkles at the side of his eyes when he's about to laugh, or trying not to, as if he can't wait to have fun. And his hair, I know you don't like Hugh Grant, but Miles' hair flops forward just like his. And when we met him together at the gallery, remember that first time, with Frankie and Mickey, I thought he was really horrible to the kids, but he's kind of like that strict teacher at school, that all the kids grumble about, but really love.'

'Enough!' Trudy points to the door. 'Go and make yourself a cup of tea, make mine a vodka and black. You've got a *date* tonight, and I need to think.'

There's no point arguing with her! I haul myself up off the bed, slip my dressing gown on over the skinny dress, and go down to the kitchen. It's almost seven now, Miles is picking me up at eight. I hope Trudy manages to do some fast thinking. I make my cup of tea automatically. No blackcurrant for Trudy's vodka, it'll have to be Vimto and vodka. Again.

Trudy stalks into the kitchen, and nods towards the table. 'Sit! I wish you'd told me sooner. This is serious.'

I sit and slide her tumbler of vodka across the table to her, like they do in westerns. She takes a gulp, and then sits down opposite me.

'Sorry, it's Vimto again,' I say.

'I know, never mind. Are you ready for this?'

'Just get on with it, Trudy, I'm in knots.'

'No, you're not in knots. You're in love.'

'I can't be! He's Madeline's.'

'Maybe it's infatuation, but probably not. And he isn't Madeline's. He only works for her. What you need to do, is find out about him, and why he's so loyal to Madeline. From my point of view, the only reason you haven't pounced on him yet, is because he's loyal to her. Find out why.'

'So, what should I do? Question him?'

'Flirt with him, get him to lower his guard, find out who he is.'

'And then what?'

Trudy picks up her drink, downs it, stands, leans over the table, ruffles my hair and winks. 'If it were me, I'd *devour* the man… But you, kiddo, you're on your own.' She walks out of the kitchen.

'But Trudy! Wait, what should I wear?' I shout after her.

'Whatever the hell you want! If he fancies you, you'll look good in anything… or nothing. I'm sure you'll figure it out without a diagram,' she shouts back.

'Trudy! Wait!'

Oh great, I'm on my own. I make my way back up to my bedroom, which still looks like a clothes bomb exploded. I pick through the discarded heap. Nothing. I'm almost temped to put my Elmo T-shirt back on, that would show him how uninterested I am. I look in the wardrobe and settle for skinny cropped jeans, yet again, but with a pink sleeveless top. Considering my artistic bent, I'm rubbish at picking outfits.

I slap on more make-up than usual, not hard really, and try to tame my messy mop of hair. All too soon I hear the door bell, and Trudy's cheery voice welcoming Miles in. They're in the hallway as I walk down the stairs. Trudy's smile is fixed. Miles looks smart in a suit, no tie. His shirt has the top two buttons open.

'You look lovely, as usual, Christie,' he says.

'Thanks,' I mutter.

'Well, you two enjoy yourselves.' Trudy practically pushes us out of the front door. 'I won't wait up.'

'She never does,' I say, and look over my shoulder to give Trudy my "help me" look. She blows me a kiss, and waves.

Well yes, that'll help!

Miles opens the car door for me. Like a proper date? I'm so confused!

He smiles as he gets in the car and starts the ignition. 'I've booked a table at *Santus*, I know you like Italian.'

'It's always good there, they do amazing sticky toffee puddings.'

'Your favourite.'

I nod, I'm sure I haven't told him that. Madeline. Or Mum, or Dad, or I'm paranoid. Why does it have to be him? I look out of the window as field after field of regimented green crops whiz by. If only my life were that ordered. In less than ten minutes we're at the restaurant, and neither of us has spoken a word since leaving the house.

'Are you okay?' asks Miles.

'Yes, just tired, it's been a busy week.'

'For both of us.' He smiles assuredly. 'I think the sooner we sort this out the better, don't you?'

I nod, and get out of the car. This isn't a date, it's an essential meeting. One where Miles is going to try and talk me out of letting Sarah McBride interview me.

I need to be on my guard, and make Miles lower his. Miles walks beside me; I turn and beam my brightest smile at him.

'Look, Miles, I know this is just work for you.' I walk my fingers up his chest – always works for Trudy – 'But, shall we at least try to enjoy each other's company?' Again, I offer a big smile.

'Sounds good to me. I always enjoy your company anyway.' He looks down at my hand now lying flat on his chest.

'Well played,' I say in a teasing way. I am so rubbish at this flirting malarkey! 'So, I take it Madeline is paying for tonight?'

'In a way, I'll claim it as expenses.'

'Then I'll eat lots.'

'You always do.'

'Cheeky!' I attempt to flutter my eyelashes.

'You don't need to try so hard, Christie. I prefer the real you.'

I let my hand drop away from him. 'This might be the real me.'

'I don't think so.'

I look at him, no sign of a crinkle at the sides of his eyes. All business tonight. I shrug and walk ahead of him, the burn of rejection flares through me.

Inside we are shown to our table, the waiter gives us our menus. I make out to read it, but I've already decided. Medium steak, fries, no starter. Not even Italian, shame on me. Let's get it over with. The waiter takes our order and hurries off to bring our drinks, hardly exotic, two sparkling spring waters. Clear heads, for clear thoughts.

'I've spoken to Madeline; she thinks it could be useful for you to go ahead with the Sarah McBride interview.'

'I'm going ahead with it anyway.'

'I know, I had already pointed that out to her. But what Madeline thinks… what she would like, if you are in agreement, is a double bill.'

'What do you mean?'

'What she's hoping for, is a double whammy. Your interview pre-recorded, explaining how Madeline's team have supported you. Obviously, at this point, it's important to keep your true identity under wraps. Madeline will gently release that within her own interview. However, just in case anybody gets an inkling of your relationship, your interview is to remain absolutely top secret, with the exception of Madeline's team.'

Ha! Does she really expect me to go along with that? 'By, Madeline's team, you mean you.'

'And her interviewer.'

'And who will that be?'

'Monty, Monty Mitten. She's known him for years, and he's the only one she'll trust to not destroy her. He'll be sympathetic.'

'To me, or to her?'

'To both of you. He's smart, and he's good at his job.'

'I watched their last interview, he seemed to treat Madeline gently.'

'He respects her right to privacy, and I suppose is flattered by the kudos the exclusivity gives him. He's clever enough to dance round the questions the public want him to ask, and wise enough to know when to back off.'

'Like when he questioned her about your relationship with each other?'

Miles offers a tight smile. 'Exactly. Madeline will reluctantly reveal her relationship with you—'

Oh, you might like to think so, but that bombshell is mine to drop!

'… So, Christie, does that sound reasonable?'

I sigh. 'I suppose, yes, that sounds reasonable.'

'So, we've cracked it before the main course.' Miles smiles properly now, his hair does its floppy thing, his eyes crinkle.

My stomach does a flip, but I can't let my traitorous flipping stomach control me. I close my eyes briefly, grappling for strength to take charge of this situation, before I make a complete fool of myself. Miles is resting back in his chair now; he takes a sip of his water. His hand curls around the glass reminding me of his hand being curled around mine… and the impromptu kiss he placed on the back of it. Again, my tummy flips. I need to get on with it, before I completely lose my nerve.

I lick my lips. 'So, Miles, what's in it for you?'

He shifts in his chair. His face loses its animated appeal, is void of expression and emotion. Hard. Unlike I've seen it before. 'What do you mean?'

'What do you get out of this, besides a free meal?' I say. I can't quite look him in the eye so start to straighten the cutlery.

'I get the satisfaction of knowing I've done my job well. I know that you will be, to the best of my ability, treated fairly in the press. I know Madeline's reputation will be held together. She'll take a knock in the popularity stakes, but ultimately, she'll be one step closer to getting what she wants.'

'And what is that?' I pick up my glass, and take a sip of the cold water, feel its icy progress to my stomach.

'Surely you know?'

I put my glass down. 'Tell me.' It sounds harsher than I intended it to.

'She wants you.'

'She'll never have me. I'm a grown woman, not the baby she abandoned.' I feel the tell-tale prickle of tears, look away briefly blinking rapidly to disperse them.

Miles sits forward, and looks around the restaurant, I presume to check if anyone's listening. 'She didn't abandon you.' His tone is low and measured. 'She did what she thought was right at the time. She knows she can't turn back the clock, she wants to get to know you.'

'She knows every little thing about me. *Ev-er-y-thing*. She's made sure of it.' And now the familiar bite of betrayal gnaws at me, chomping through my calm demeanour. The pain of my nails digging into my palms, offers scant distraction.

'She wants your forgiveness. She knows she has to earn it, give her the chance, Christie.'

I shake my head. 'Why, why should I?'

'Because you're a good person, and she's a good person, and you're both hurting. And I'm not saying it's going to be painless for both of you, but think of your parents stuck between the two of you…'

Now that's a low blow I wasn't expecting! 'That is not fair, Miles! It's not my doing.'

'But it could be your undoing. You could make it right—'

I could make it right? He sits there and puts that burden on me, like I haven't got enough to deal with at the moment.

'... Come on, agree, in principle at least to the double exposé, and let's enjoy our meal. The rest will probably pan out in time.'

The waiter sets our plates before us.

'Okay, Miles, one condition.' Our eyes lock.

Although he's still smiling, I didn't miss the unease, which, just for a split second flashed in his eyes. 'And what condition is that?'

'You. Why are you so loyal to Madeline? Why do you always defend her?'

'That's easy, it's my job.' He relaxes back in his seat.

I carefully remove the napkin from my lap, place it on the table beside my plate, and make to stand up and leave. With my hands resting on the table I lean very close to Miles, I do not want him to miss a word. 'There is no point in me being here, Miles. If you think you can pacify me with a throwaway line like that. I have spent a lifetime living, what is basically a lie. No more, Miles. From now on, I'm questioning everything and everybody. If you want to go back to Madeline with this sorted, I expect more than that.' I stand up. 'I deserve more than that.'

An unnatural hush settles around us.

'Wait!' He half stands and makes a grab for my hand still resting on the table. 'Sit down, please, I'll explain, but it's complicated.'

I ease back into my chair, and even though the only person I can see is Miles, I know everybody else's eyes are on us. The hush is replaced by an energetic buzz of conversation, and I'm sure we are central to most of that buzz. I replace the napkin on my lap, and try to rein in some calm by taking deep breaths. I'm not sure I really want to know what hold Madeline has over Miles. But I do know, that I need to know.

'Most things are complicated, Miles. But your loyalty toward Madeline, has nothing to do with working for her. One thing I know, is that loyalty is earned.'

He shuffles uneasily in his seat. All of a sudden, that usual confident, and totally in control man before me, appears vulnerable. 'I've never told anyone.'

'So, the choice is yours.' I can still feel the people around looking at us. My steak smells delicious, but I can sacrifice it. 'You can carry on the rest of your life, and tell no one, and I'll walk away, or you can tell me, and earn brownie points with Madeline for getting me to agree to this exposé. Look, Miles, I need to know if *I* can trust you, and why.'

'Okay.' Miles shakes his head. 'I'll explain it all to you. But please, tell no one else, not Trudy, not Suzi.'

I nod my agreement.

Miles lowers his gaze. 'It started with me. I was kind of the first *Keep-a-Key* kid.'

The conversation in the restaurant is back to normal. I'm sure one or two folk are still taking sneaky looks our way. I wonder if any of them have noticed Miles' ashen face. I don't think he'd risk lying to me now, but it sounds too farfetched to believe.

I narrow my eyes. 'What do you mean? The charity has only been going for a couple of years, and you must be at least late twenties.'

'I'm thirty… It's a tricky truth. Long, long ago, in the dark ages – they were dark ages for me anyway, my mum left us. By us, I mean me and my dad. She was unstable, unreliable, and she probably thought she was doing me a favour. She drank too much.' He shrugs.

'I'm sorry.'

'It happens. It's not your fault. I was fourteen, knew everything, so I thought. Smart ass at school, too smart to pay attention in class, not smart enough to keep my mouth shut at home. Dad did his best, but I was out of control, lashing out because I was hurting… He was handy, with his fists.' Miles touches the scar on his face. 'He didn't mean to, didn't want to be that person, he just couldn't cope with me without help.'

I let out the breath I didn't know I was holding. 'Sounds like hell, for both of you…'

'I know it was for me. I was always getting into bits of bother, with the police. This one night, I was almost seventeen and up to no good as usual. They took me home, laid it on thick, gave me a good talking to… Anyway, when they left, Dad just exploded. Told me to get out, he didn't want to ever see my face again. And he hasn't.'

Our meals sit between us, untouched.

'Harsh.'

Miles looks down, straightens his cutlery. 'He did me a favour. He would probably have ended up killing me, or me him. I'd grabbed some money, was okay for a couple of nights, slept on friend's sofas, that kind of thing. But I needed to get away. So, I started walking. Walked for weeks. I looked older than my years, did bits of jobs on farms for food, money, or a bed for the night. Eventually I ended up in Ashwood, the posh end of Chippington. Someone had taken a disliking to me, and I was nursing a few cuts and bruises.'

'I can't even imagine living like that.'

Miles looks me in the eyes, lets out a quiet mirthless laugh. 'I was surviving. It was still, kind of an adventure.' Miles rests his chin on his hand, glances away, then focuses on some distant vision. 'I was scrunched up in a church porch keeping warm, or hiding. It was late, after eleven. It was cold, I was hungry and sore. This woman came and sat in the porch. I don't think she even saw me at first. She was muttering away to herself. I thought she was probably a bit la-la. Then she started talking to me, and she seemed a bit posh, kind. I thought she might give me some money if I gave her a sob story. So, she got a potted history of what had happened to me.'

'Madeline?' I guess.

'Madeline, only she didn't give me any money, hasn't, ever, actually. She took me home, fed me. One of her famous dribbling bacon butties, gave me a bed for the night. Before I woke up the next morning, she'd bought me new clothes and lined up a job interview for me at one of the market gardeners.'

'Fast worker.'

'That's Madeline. I wouldn't tell her my name, and when she asked where I'd come from, I just said I'd travelled for miles. She called me Miles. And it's been my name ever since. Later on, when I trusted her, I told her my real name... I changed it to Miles Hepworth when I was eighteen.'

'So, your dad couldn't trace you?'

'I doubt he'd want to. No, just so I could have a real chance at being the person Madeline thought I could be. She said, "Miles, no one is on the scrap heap at sixteen." And she's right. She turned my life around; in the same way she's turning around the lives of the other *Keep-a-Key* kids.'

'So, she really is a saint.'

'Ha, if only. At first, she was like a woman possessed. Made me go to night school to do my GCSE's. Then browbeat me into going to college and university. Told me I owed it to her for harbouring a minor. Said that I'd be wasting my life, if I didn't make something of myself, after all the hard work she'd put in to reform me! So here I am, apparently reformed, and making something of myself. I hope.' His gaze returns to me.

I can read the vulnerability still lingering in his eyes; eyes which are usually assured and confident. I offer a small smile, resist the urge to reach out and touch his hand. 'I'm sure she's very proud of you.' Somehow the words don't ring true. And I can tell by the look on Miles' face that he thinks so too. 'Not proud, pleased with you, pleased for you. I don't know…'

'I think she still sees me as a work in progress.' He nods. 'And I always will be; we all are. She would give anything to be part of your life, Christie.'

'I've already worked that out for myself.' I look away.

'Can you not see, in a weird way, it's because of you, she goes so far out of her comfort zone to help kids?'

'Miles, honestly, I don't want to hear it. I get it now. I get why you are her most loyal supporter. But please, please don't expect me to play happy families. Madeline might know everything there is to know about me, but everything I know about her, is second hand. And she sounds wonderful, she does great work, helps lots of kids…' I shrug, raise my eyes to his.

'But?'

'I agree to do the interviews the way Madeline wants. I'm sure you'll be put in charge of organising that, so good luck. I'll keep your secret, Miles. And I respect your loyalty to Madeline. I hope we can be friends, you and I.'

'Me too.' Miles gestures to the untouched food between us. 'Lost your appetite?'

I nod. Miles gets the bill, and we leave. The silence in the car on the way back home is as deafening as it was on our way out. My stomach churns. I can't decide if it's with hunger, nerves, or both. I risk a glance at Miles. His eyes are fixed on the road, his face tense, emotional shutters closed. His fingers aren't drumming their usual random beat on the steering wheel.

For some reason I miss it.

I need to be away from him. Need time to process; time to weave the Miles I was getting to know, with the Miles, Madeline already knows.

The Miles she helped create.

This night hasn't been what either of us expected. I think he regrets revealing so much of himself. I'm glad he has. Glad at least to know why Madeline is so precious to him. I can't compete with her.

Won't.

She will always be the one he looks up to. I'm not going to set myself up for that fall. No matter how brave and vulnerable and beautiful he is. That particular fall would probably kill me.

The car stops outside my home, and Miles turns to me and offers a half-hearted smile. 'Good night, Christie. I'll start making the appropriate arrangements first thing tomorrow. I'll be in touch.' He starts to open his car door.

'Don't get out, I can manage myself, thank you.' My crisp words sound harsher than I intend, but I can't risk him seeing me fall apart.

I reach out and cup his scarred cheek with my hand, and look into his questioning eyes. Hope he can't see the longing in mine. Without thinking, I lean forward and brush a kiss on his lips, scarcely touching him at all, but enough to send a jolt of regret through my entire body. I get out of the car without uttering a word, and walk towards the front door. I don't look back. Silent tears escape.

Too late.

Trudy is right.

I love him.

Paint Away the Heartache

He looks amused.

I close my bedroom door quietly behind me. I don't want Trudy or Suzi to see me like this. Luckily, I think neither of them heard me come in. I can wallow peacefully here. Flopping onto the bed I hug my knee into my chest and force out tears. My stomach feels hollow as cramps and hunger pangs merge with grief.

I want to howl like a wounded wolf, instead silent sobs scream into my duvet. Thank God he doesn't know how I feel about him.

Will never know.

He will always belong to Madeline. But tonight, I will give myself permission to acknowledge the truth. Let myself mourn for losing him, before I've fully expressed my true feelings for him.

I love Miles.

Why couldn't it be someone like Nigel, with his easy smile and predictable nature? Someone easy to love, whose past isn't tangled with Madeline.

But Miles is easy to love.

Too easy.

So easy to love, I did it without even knowing. And now I do know, I've got to stop. I've got to pretend my only interest in him is professional.

I peel off my clothes, add them to the mound behind the door. There's only one thing to do to endorse my love. Dragging on my ragged painting garb

I head along the landing towards the little stairs to the attic, as quietly as I can.

I need to paint.

Suzi nudges her head out of her bedroom. 'Thought you'd gone out with the marvellous Miles… Christie! What's the matter?' Suzi darts from her room, catches my arm. 'What's happened?'

I close my eyes and shake my head. 'Nothing,' I mutter, I can't say the words. 'I'm okay.'

'Trudy, are you awake!' barks Suzi at full pitch. 'Miles has upset Christie. Again!'

Trudy joins us on the landing, her skinny silk kimono, a stark contrast to Suzi's *Me to You* fleecy dressing gown, and my paint-splattered T-shirt and joggers. I look up to meet Trudy's questioning eyes.

I shake my head. 'He's not who I thought he was.'

'Go and paint,' says Trudy.

Suzi scowls. 'What's happened?'

'I don't know,' says Trudy. 'I think Christie needs to work that out for herself, and she does that best by painting, alone. So, let's leave her to it, okay?'

Suzi touches my arm. 'Do you want me to sit with you?'

I shake my head and carry on up the stairs to the attic. I push open the door, close my eyes, and breathe in the magical mix of aromas, soothing and enticing, promising relief. I open my eyes and see if I can spot the booby traps I set last time I was in here. No idea, I squat down and crawl under my desk. Cobwebs and a pine cone. And a knitting needle, and what? Green, gloopy and smelly, it can only be *Swarfega*; Suzi hasn't been in, or she would have cleaned it up!

I select an A3 cold-press paper, secure it to my easel. Brushes, lint, pallet and water; I mix hues, colour. Closing my eyes, I bring the image of Miles sat across from me tonight. All the emotional elements of his personality drawn on his face. Each facet only hinting at revealing a hidden past. A past he wants to keep hidden. A past steeped in Madeline and misery.

His face is strong, solid jaw with a slight dimple, even and high cheek bones. Eyes of depth and emotion. Raven hair always threatening to tumble forward over his forehead. A scar. A face which conveys confidence. Expects respect. Is loved.

I open my eyes and look at the blank paper. My stomach rumbles, I pull out a Snicker from my desk drawer. Eat without tasting. All my senses centre towards the task ahead.

Okay, Christina Anne Harris, if you are an artist, make art.

I toss the chocolate wrapper in the general direction of the bin, stretch my arms above my head, roll my shoulders, and begin.

I paint in the background, next I block in the colour. I stand back, close my eyes and bring Miles into my mind's eye. Stepping back to my easel, selecting a broad brush I start marking out his outline. Stepping back often, checking detail and proportion. I start making tentative strokes with a fine brush… Soon they are bolder and more confident, almost taking on Miles' persona. I work all night like a woman possessed, constantly assessing, adding texture and depth. Each brush stroke, a symbol of my love for him.

Eventually, the essence of satisfaction begins to seep into me. I finish by dry brushing before the urge to alter any part of his image strikes. As the first light of morning streaks through the skylight illuminating the portrait, I see the face of the man I would happily see every morning for the rest of my life.

Miles.

There's a hint of amusement in his eyes. The slight tug of a smile on his lips. His hair is threatening to fall over his forehead. A scar, well healed, but not concealed, a stark reminder of what he has left behind, and who rescued him.

The urge to reach out and trace his face swamps me. I will when the paint is fully dry, I know I will.

I don't know at what point I decided it, but it was sometime during my frantic painting hours… This will be my final painting for Madeline. For Auntie Maddie. I can't torture myself by seeing him every day, out of reach. I might be the artist, but Miles is Madeline's masterpiece.

I rest back on my chair, close my eyes.

An insistent tapping on the door disturbs my peace. 'Christie, are you still in there?' says Trudy. 'I've brought you coffee, can I come in?'

I must have made some kind of positive sound, because the door swings open and she's in before I've even had the chance to cover my work.

'Don't cover it.' She settles the mug of coffee into my hands. Stands behind me, and places a hand on each of my shoulders, rolls her thumbs to unknot my muscles. After a couple of minutes, she stops and rests her chin on the top of my head. I know she's trying to see Miles through my eyes.

'You're right, Christie, he is beautiful.'

'I know.' I can feel a prickly tickle in my nose, the warning that tears are about to fall.

'So, do you want to talk about what happened?'

I reach for a piece of lint to dab my dripping nose. I nod, not sure what to say.

'If you'd rather not...' offers Trudy.

'No, I think I have to. I'm not sure where to start.'

'Something neutral, the interview, did you sort out a way forward?'

'Yes, me and Madeline, we're both doing our own interview; hers will be immediately after mine. Mine will be pre-recorded, and top secret until it is broadcast. Hers will be live, and I presume she'll respond to what I've said. She's going to tell the world.' My words sound flat.

'And you're happy with that?'

'Happy?' I shrug. 'I can't outmanoeuvre her, and she knows it. The best I can do, is play her at her own game, try to get some sympathy without sticking the knife in. I've not told Miles, but I'm going to let slip in my interview that Madeline's my birth mother... I need to be careful; I've got Mum and Dad to consider in all this.'

'She's a manipulative cow.'

'She's Madeline De-Muir, and my mother.'

'And a manipulative cow.'

'I think, honestly Trudy, she does regret what she did.'

'She didn't have to make it all so public,' says Trudy.

'It is, what it is.'

'And what of Miles?'

I swallow, and close my eyes.

And what of Miles?

I open my eyes to see him looking back at me.

And what about you Miles? 'I think it's best for me to forget about Miles.'

'But!' Trudy gestures towards the painting before us. 'It's plain to see what he means to you.'

'It's plain for *you* to see, because you know me. Anyway, it doesn't matter what I think of him, it's what he thinks of Madeline.'

'And what does he think of her?'

'It's complicated.'

'Try me.'

'He's in awe of all her charity work. Probably has some hero worship going on, I can't compete. I'm just me.'

'So, she does a bit of charity work. That doesn't make her a saint.'

'It does to Miles. He'd do anything for her. It's better for me to keep everything professional, and leave them to it.'

'And this will be what, a reminder of what could have been?'

'It's my final work for Auntie Maddie. He'll always belong to her.'

Trudy moves next to me, her hand finds mine, and she gives it a squeeze. It acts as a trigger to my tears, I put my untouched coffee down, shake my head. She puts her arms around me and holds me tight. 'Shh, come on, if it's meant to be, it will be.'

'No, there's too much happened between us.'

'The only thing standing between you, is Madeline, and I doubt Miles even knows it. Sometimes, Christie, it's worth the risk to get what you want.'

'I've never been one for risks.'

'Says the girl who set the church on fire.'

'That was an accident.' I half smile.

'I know, but you saw a way to heat up the church, and you made it happen.'

'I nearly burnt the entire church down!'

'No…well okay, there was a lot of smoke, and you caused significant damage to the boiler house.'

'And could have killed off half the congregation.'

'Ha! They're indestructible… the point is, the church got a new heating system. You achieved your goal.'

'Point taken, but this is different.'

'Why? Because it's something for yourself?'

'No.' I gulp. 'Because he might not want me. I might be nothing more than a project.'

Trudy steps back and looks at me. She passes me more lint for my nose, and runs each of her thumbs under my eyes to push away the tears. She smiles.

'What?'

'If Miles doesn't love every ounce of you, then he's the biggest fool this side of the Pennines. And as we both know, there's lots of worthy competition for that title.'

'Is it worth the risk of making a fool of myself, or making things even more complicated with Madeline?'

'Only you know the answer to that. But if it were me, then, hell yes!'

'Says the brave and the bold Lady Prudence Drummond!'

'I've only ever been Trudy, to the brave and the bold Christie Harris!' Trudy's face becomes serious again. 'Think about it.'

The flap-flap of Suzi's slippers on the stairs jolts me into action. I lunge forwards to drag a sheet over my painting.

Trudy catches my hand. 'Let her see. We've never had secrets, us three.'

'Cooeee…' Suzi's head pops through the open door. 'Is this a private party or can anyone…' She stops, mouth open, eyes agog. 'Oh… My… Word!' Trudy rolls in her lips to stop herself from laughing. I look heavenward. 'How long have you been—'

'I've been painting all night,' I say.

'No, how long…' Suzi wags her finger at me, narrows her eyes. 'Exactly how long, have you been in love with him, Christie?'

'All night.'

Suzi's face is like The London Eye on New Year's Eve. 'Oh, really?'

'She's only just realised.'

'Okay.'

'He's the mystery man I kept bumping into.'

Suzi nods. 'I see. He looks amused.'

'I'm sure he will be, if he ever finds out,' I say.

'Very wise, to play it cool, Christie, let him do all the running.'

Trudy shakes her head. 'He's a slow starter, on account of being handcuffed to the starting post by Madeline.'

'Madeline won't let him date you?' blusters Suzi. 'That's twisted, who does she think she is?'

'It's complicated,' I say. 'I'm sure she lets Miles date whoever he wants.'

'I'm going to *Google* him, what's his last name? Hepworth isn't it?' Suzi whips her mobile out of her dressing gown pocket. 'Let's see what—'

'Suzi, don't bother. It doesn't make any difference.'

'He might bat for the other side for all you know!' Suzi carries on tapping away.

'And I might not want the hassle of a boyfriend, with all my new-found fame,' I lie.

'I hadn't thought of that, but…' Suzi examines her screen. 'It's not coming up with anything anyway, other than Madeline De-Muir.'

Trudy grins. 'So, there we are, Madeline must keep him far too busy to fraternise with members of any sex, and I'm sure Christie can depend on us two to be discreet?'

'That goes without saying,' says Suzi.

Trudy suppresses a snort. 'Anyway, you haven't signed it yet. Do that, and once it's dried, I'll take it to your usual place to be framed.'

'No! I want it to go somewhere else, somewhere they don't know me. There's a picture framing shop on Vine Street in Driftwood Sands, take it there. I've heard they'll sometimes do it while you wait, if they're not busy; for a price. Please, if it's not too much trouble.'

'What's the hurry?'

'It marks the end. I want this charade with Madeline over, the sooner the better.'

'Get it signed,' says Trudy.

I select a fine brush and roll the bristles between my fingers, I dip it into the crimson paint on my pallet, and scrawl *Christie* under Miles' handsome face. I'm almost tempted to add "The end".

'All yours, Trudy. I'm off to bed.' I stand up, rinse my brushes, and do something I thought I'd never be able to do. I leave the two of them alone in my attic, no booby traps.

Glow White Knickers

... swooning like a Victorian lady.

Suzi is in mothering mode. My bedroom floor has been liberated from the mounds of washing. T-shirts, jeggings and jeans are on the line. My glow white knickers are lined up respectfully along the landing radiator.

Suzi no longer allows underwear to go on the downstairs radiators. What seems like a lifetime ago, when I was going out with Nigel, he called to pick me up, and rows of Suzi's knickers covered the lounge radiators. Suzi was mortified, and ever since, knickers only ever go upstairs. Suzi instigated an underwear embargo downstairs, so that no one ever needs to suffer that embarrassment again. I do love her, but I wish she'd loosen up a bit.

She's been busy in the kitchen too, there's a cottage pie in the oven, and peeping under a tea towel, I discover an apple crumble waiting to be reheated. I can hear the hum and occasional crash of the hoover, as she's making her way round the house. The whiff of Dettol surface cleaner present in every room, is proof of a sustained attack on germs and grime. Suzi's way of keeping the world at bay.

Bringing the washing in, I fold it as neatly as I can, and take it upstairs – it won't be up to Suzi's high standard. She's dragging the hoover out of my bedroom, has a healthy flush, and her usually perfect bob is skew-whiff.

'Thanks, Suzi, you didn't need to.'

'Oh, I think I did,' she says, holding up a carrier bag. 'The contents of this bag confirm you're back on your chocolate, Pepsi and occasional banana diet.'

'I have to eat when I can!' I try to defend myself. Suzi shakes her head in mock disgust. 'I'll make us both a cup of coffee,' I offer.

I dash downstairs as Trudy is coming in; she's carrying a large package wrapped in brown paper under her arm.

'You'd better make that three, I'm gasping. Why is it, that when I go to Driftwood Sands, the world and his mother goes too?'

'School holidays,' I say.

'Fine day,' shouts Suzi, bumping the hoover down the stairs. 'Is that what I think it is?'

'Yep.' Trudy puts the package down on the kitchen counter.

I try not to look at it. 'Thank you, Trudy, for taking it. How does it look in the frame?'

Trudy grins. 'It looks complete, and oh so obvious! I browbeat a man of about eighty-five into working at the speed of light to get it done. I had to bribe him with tickets to see Peter Kay at the Old Palace!'

'You had tickets to see Peter Kay?' asks Suzi.

'I went and bought him two tickets while he was framing Miles, you numpty!'

'He's awesome. Mum and Dad have seen him five times!' says Suzi.

Trudy's eyes twinkle. 'So, Christie, shall I unwrap Miles, or shall you?'

I pick up the package and lay it flat on the table. I can feel the frame beneath the thick brown paper. The course jute string tied in a double bow knot to keep Miles safe. I pull the outer knot loose, and slowly pull open the bow. Smoothing the string aside, I find the edge of the brown paper, take a deep breath and peel it back to reveal his image. A natural wooden frame complements his unnaturally beautiful face. He looks even more amused than I remember. I look away unable to speak.

'I think,' says Suzi, 'this is your best ever.' She gives me a quick squeeze.

I feel them both watching me. I pick up the portrait, hold it at arm's length. Remembering the frantic brush strokes of last night, I close my eyes and burn the image into my memory. I open my eyes, and lay the portrait back on top of the brown wrapping paper.

'I think you might be right,' says Trudy. 'Christie's poured her heart out.' She does what I long to, she traces her finger over Miles' face, from his brow to his chin, and then back up to his scar. 'I wonder how he got it.'

I shrug my shoulders, not sure if it was really a question aimed at me. My fingers flutter to my neck as I feel the familiar lump building in my throat, try to swallow it away. I don't want to remember his secrets, his past. They drag me closer to him. Bind him to my soul. I close my eyes, remember the scant kiss of last night. Wish for once, I'd been bold enough to drag him into my arms and—

'Boys will be boys, I suppose!' says Trudy. 'Both of my brothers spent half their school holidays in casualty. Mum used to say she needed a siren on the Range Rover!'

'I once stood on a nail,' says Suzi. 'It hurt too!'

'It would,' I say, thinking of Miles' hurt. My fingers instinctively following the same trail Trudy's had, over his brow, his cheek, his chin, and then back to that scar. It must remind him every day of what he's left behind. I can almost see the frightened boy scrunched up in that church porch, hiding and alone. I can't even imagine what it must feel like to be totally alone.

I swallow back tears again. I fold the brown paper back over his face; stroke it down like a blanket over a baby. I tie the string into a neat single bow, a double knot would be too final. Place it back on the counter. I can see their concern as I face my friends, my forced smile warning them to leave those questions unasked.

'Tea should be ready now,' says Suzi heading towards the oven.

Trudy dusts her hands. 'I'll just go and have a wash; I always feel grubby when I've been shopping.'

'And I'll set the table,' I mutter.

Suzi rummages in the cupboard, and pulls out a tin of mushy peas. 'Ta da!' she says. 'Got to have mushy peas with cottage pie.' She puts them in a bowl and into the microwave. 'And ta da!' she says whipping the tea towel from over the apple crumble.

'I'd already peeped, but cream or custard?'

'Whatever you fancy, we've got both.'

'Look who I found lurking on the doorstep,' says Trudy, leading Miles into the kitchen.

'Let me guess, just passing?' says Suzi.

'No, a peace offering,' he says, holding forward a foil container. 'It's sticky toffee pudding. You missed out last night, thought it would make up for...'

Instinctively I move towards Miles, trying for a casual smile. It's hard not to grin like a Cheshire cat, with all these butterflies flitting about my stomach. I feel hyperaware of every sensation gushing through my body. I need to savour these moments – I know, soon enough, they'll be replaced by the dull ache of emptiness. So, I'll enjoy them while I can, practise a bit of mindfulness and live in the moment.

Merely smiling, I say, 'Thanks, but you didn't need to.' Our eyes lock. I feel his scrutiny as keenly as I feel my own heart breaking. He makes to take back the pudding with a light-heartedness I can only pretend to match. 'On the other hand, it would be rude not to accept, since you've clearly made the effort.'

As I take the pudding from him our fingers touch, a spark of recognition triggers my blush. I put my head down and turn away from him to put the pudding in the fridge.

'What, you're not going to have it?' he splutters.

I turn back around and catch his eyes sparkling with jest. 'Suzi has made an apple crumble.'

He's wearing jeans and a rugby shirt. I've never seen him in casuals before, they suit his lean physique. I can't take my eyes off him; I'm just stood gawping, and he's grinning back. I can't help remembering the kiss of last night. I shouldn't have done it. Or, I should have done more…

Suzi claps her hands. 'Snap out of it you two! Miles, you're just in time to join us for tea; cottage pie,' the microwave pings, 'and mushy peas.'

'Sounds like an offer I can't refuse, if nobody minds?' His eyes still hold mine. 'I have made some progress in moving things forward with the interviews, I could fill you in with the details later, if you like?'

I shrug. 'Okay, but let's not talk about it until we've eaten.' I get out another knife, fork and spoon, and set his place between Suzi and Trudy, opposite me. Suzi places our meals onto the table as we all sit down.

'This is delicious,' says Miles. 'Christie's mum always says Christie would have starved to death if it weren't for you, Suzi.'

'Not true!' says Trudy. 'Christie always has a stash of chocolate, and if that does ever run out, she always has an emergency packet or two of chocolate digestives.'

'Says the vodka and Vimto queen,' I splutter, grabbing a chance to take the attention away from me.

'Can't say I've ever had that combination,' says Miles.

Suzi flashes him a smile. 'And since you're driving, you won't be having it tonight.'

And so, the banter continues, until four plates sit empty on the table. I rest back in my chair and pat my rounded tum, watching the three of them chatting easily with each other.

Like real friends.

Or family.

It could be like this. This natural. This easy. This perfect. Tears well up, I quickly collect up the plates and busy myself washing up. Their comfortable voices in the background, soaking into my reservoir of memories of Miles. Memories I'll be able to draw on later.

'You okay?' asks Suzi.

'Oh!' I drop a plate back into the sink.

'Sorry, didn't mean to startle you. Only you usually *don't* wash up,' she whispers. She picks up a tea towel and starts to dry the plates. 'And we do have a dishwasher.'

'Just putting some space between us. I'm fine.' I offer a half-hearted smile.

'I hope you two are talking about apple crumble,' says Trudy, 'because I have saved room for it.'

'Cream or custard?' Suzi lifts the steaming dessert from the oven.

Trudy raises a brow. 'What do you fancy, Miles?' she asks, her tone playful.

'Surprise me,' he says.

'Cream it is, ladies,' decides Trudy.

We eat our desserts accompanied by the same banter enjoyed during our meal. I feel like an observer almost. I join in the conversations when I need to, but feel like I'm hovering on the edge, not quite belonging. Stupid really, none of them would be here but for me. Both Trudy and Suzi seem completely at ease with him. I'm the one who is jittery. Can't let my guard down, even though last night, he did.

'Well, that was lovely, Suzi, thank you, and not at all expected,' says Miles. Suzi flushes at his complement. 'Christie?'

'Yes?'

'Sorry to spoil the fun, but can we have a word about the arrangements being made for the interviews?'

'Oh, yes.' I'd forgotten why he'd called round. It wasn't to see me. 'Are you okay if we go through into the other room, don't want to bore these two with the details?' They'd both notice how frazzled I am about the whole thing. Knowing Miles' history, is going to make it impossible to be totally candid with Sarah McBride.

Miles nods. 'Ladies.' He holds out my chair, and then opens the door to the lounge. Over my shoulder I see Trudy patting her hand on her heart, and Suzi fluttering her eyelashes dramatically and swooning like a Victorian lady. It almost makes me smile. If only, if only, it could be that way.

Miles sits in the same armchair he sat in when I grappled with him for Bunty's review. I try to banish the thought. This room is already laced with memories of Miles. Early evening sun bathes us in a soft golden hue. I sit at the farthest end of the sofa.

There will be no grappling tonight.

'Right then. I've had a very busy time of it, but I think I've just about gotten all of our ducks in a row. There are a few details you will need to decide on, but we'll sort those later.'

I nod for him to carry on.

'Because Madeline will only allow Monty to inter-view her, and she's adamant it will be a live broadcast, there is only one shot at it. Saturday twenty-fifth—'

'But that's this weekend!' I splutter. 'I go back to school on the twenty-seventh! No, it's too soon.'

He gets up and joins me on the sofa. 'Calm down, listen. I know you must feel like it's being sprung on you, but, and this is a big but, the sooner all this is out in the open, the sooner you can get back to normal. And it's not often any of the networks will clear a Saturday night schedule. This is going to be epic.'

My head spins at the thought of everyone knowing everything about me. 'Miles, I doubt my life will ever be normal again, thanks to—' I look away as a surge of energy rockets through my body as he places his hand on mine.

'I know that it must feel like that now, but trust me, it will settle back to a new kind of normal.'

I shake my head, try to drag my hand from under his.

He doesn't let go. Instead, he continues, 'Because of her broken ankle, Madeline has begged Monty to interview her at home. She argued, that since it would be a personally revealing interview, it would be more intimate to do it there. Thankfully, Monty has agreed.'

'I'm sure Madeline is used to getting her own way,' I mutter.

'So that opens up the same option to you.'

'What, you mean have Sarah come here?'

'Think about it… it'd give you the girl next door appeal, and, hopefully you'd be more at ease. I must say, Sarah is chomping at the bit, and is perfectly happy to go with whatever you decide. Don't worry, wherever it takes place, I will be there to support you.' He gives my hand a squeeze.

'Will all of the interview be shown, or will it be edited?' I ask. 'I mean, what if I'm a bumbling mess?'

'You won't be, like I said, I'll be here to support you. Sarah has got twenty-seven minutes to fill, and I would say, at least half of that will be the background information she's collecting right now. Over the next two days I am allowing her and her film crew one hundred percent access to the gallery, your artwork, and whoever happens to be viewing it. So, the comments she is making to camera over the next two days can't be changed, and her angle is of course, your work.'

'She's not going to be best pleased when she finds out you've tricked her!'

'I haven't tricked her, Christie. I have *freed* her to make an absolutely honest appraisal of your work, unbiased or tainted by her opinion of Madeline.'

'I'm not sure she'll see it like that.'

'Maybe not, but she's astute enough to know that she is in a unique position, and also, that her interview with you will be pivotal as to how the public sees you. As she already likes you, I'm sure she'll be eager to promote your profile, after all, it's going to elevate hers.'

'Okay.' I manage to prise my hand away from his. Stand up and walk over to the window, offering him the view of my back.

'Christie, she likes you. She sussed you out at the gallery the first time she met you. You chose her to do your first interview. She's going to be like the cat who got the cream after she sees Maddie's interview, and discovers Madeline is your mother. She'll be fluffing her feathers for months over her good fortune.'

Oh, dear! Sarah's going to find out much sooner than you think! 'But what if Madeline's reputation is ruined?'

'I think I know Monty well enough to say, he won't let that happen to her, or your parents. Also, Sarah has interviewed Maddie herself years ago, and I get the impression she's always liked to solve a mystery. Sarah will no doubt dig out her old interview, make another documentary by weaving a story through time. Get a second bite at the cherry, so to speak.'

'You think she'll be pragmatic over Madeline being my mother?'

'Absolutely. She's not that much older than Madeline, and I'm sure she can empathise. On the one hand, Sarah is as honest as anyone can be in her line of work, on the other, she'll not set anyone up for a fall. You chose well, Christie, but remember she is remarkable at seeing past the words you say.'

I nod, she won't need to, because I'm going to tell her who Madeline is!

Looking away from him now and out to the garden, I notice the how well the weeds are growing. Suzi usually galvanises me and Trudy into doing something out there. I've often thought dandelions with their bright-yellow burst of colour as pretty as any flower, and certainly tougher.

My thoughts drift back to Sarah. 'She should have been an artist; she sees people through their emotions.'

'Use that to your advantage.' I turn to look at him, as I rest back against the windowsill. 'Let her interview you in your studio.'

'Oh, I'm sure she'd love it there! Miles! It's crammed with all sorts, there'd be no room; and besides, it's private.'

'I'm sure Suzi would help tidy, and Sarah would love to be the first to see your studio. Like I said earlier, it would give you that girl next door appeal, if you were seen struggling away in a tatty attic.'

'Hold on, I didn't say it was tatty!'

'Sorry, Cinders.' Miles' laugh is deep and infectious. He puts his hands over his face, then takes them away, and looks at me seriously. 'I'm trying to make it as easy as possible for you, okay?'

I nod.

What else can I do? He's breaking my heart.

Pluck Required

... presenting him like a prize stallion.

Exhausted, I flop down on the sofa. Even though Suzi is still shuffling about upstairs in her bedroom, I refuse to feel guilty. I only had a handful of days to sort out three years of clutter in my attic studio.

It has taken all of them.

My two best buddies have been on hand in the evenings, helping heave a few boxes down the narrow stairs.

Ah, yes, and the supremely buff Simon has been on hand day and night to obey my every command. Trudy, honestly, is lucky to still be alive after presenting her sumptuous brother as a gift. I can feel the flutter of a blush creeping up my chest remembering how Trudy thrust him through the door, presenting him like a prize stallion. To say it was awkward, is something of an understatement! But, then, Simon being the consummate gentleman he is – apparently – proceeded dutifully helping his kid sister's best friend sorting out her attic.

Initially.

But, every time Miles came around to the house, Simon took on the persona of a lovestruck teen, following me about, and generally being a pain in the arse. This has made it near impossible to have any alone time with Miles. In theory a good thing.

In practice…

Very frustrating!

However, keeping me focused on the job in hand. All our bedrooms have been gifted boxes of all sorts of weird and wonderful things to keep safe until after Sarah's interview.

Suzi is mortified. Her Laura Ashley décor, has been tarnished by boxes of "junk". And now the dreaded day is here, all she is bothered about, is bedroom inspections.

In the world of Suzi, hygiene and order is of the highest priority. Her mother, a leading member of "The Little Upton Mafia" (WI), has done a sterling job of making Suzi examine every aspect of her life for signs of imperfection. Throughout Suzi's life, her mum has picked her to pieces, regardless of who was listening. At the age of twelve, Suzi made a pledge to be perfect, if only in her mother's eyes. So far, she's done a fantastic job. She only truly lets her guard down with me and Trudy, which is a shame, because she really can be very funny and mischievous. If her mother found out about the shenanigans at the gallery, Suzi's life would be hell.

Which brings us back to Suzi guarding her usually pristine bedroom from any media type, who might potentially expose it as a dump. I'm sure what those media types are going to learn about me is a tad more newsworthy than Suzi Stapleton's bombsite of a bedroom.

Trudy passes me a cup of coffee and joins me on the sofa. 'You okay?'

'Think so.' I shrug. 'Thanks for protecting my stuff. I know Suzi would have chucked it out if she could.' I've stashed some boxes in my car boot, to save them from a trip to the tip.

Trudy turns to face me. 'She can be a bit clinical, but…' She shrugs. 'Anyway, how are you feeling about the interview?'

I pull a face. I've tried not to think about it. 'I don't know, one minute I think I've got everything under control, the next I'm panicking about being sued by Madeline.'

'She can't do that; it was her idea. You'll be fine once you get into it. If you can manage a class of thirty teenage rebels, I'm sure you can manage one middle-aged dear, and a film crew.'

'Thanks for that.' I sigh.

That middle-aged dear, is supervising two cameramen, a lighting chappie, and a sound technician up in my attic as we speak. Last time I looked they were all stricken with fear. The producer, who looks to be about fourteen, is wandering about with a mobile pressed to his ear, a tablet clutched in his hand and a scowl on his brow.

I can hear Suzi pacing the landing. She's been guarding all the bedrooms since they first arrived. I can say with certainty, the attic is the only sterile and tidy room in the entire house. Even the bathroom has had some unorthodox additions. A family of Toby Jugs reside on the windowsill, housing a selection of toothbrushes, an unsuspecting Easter Island replica statue is now a spare toilet roll holder, and a mosaic plant pot hosts a half-dead cactus. No doubt, in the fullness of time, these could all become valuable collectables, Christie Harris originals.

And what of Miles?

No idea!

So much for guiding me through this!

Oh, I know I'm being oversensitive, on account of doing my best to not be in love with the man… but honestly! The level of neglect today is helping *too* much. I'd feel much better wallowing in self-pity with Miles pandering to my every whim. Simon really was beginning to grate, especially since, it became apparent he'd only put on his 100-watt devotion while Miles was about, almost as if someone – Trudy – had briefed him.

Men!

For the last three days, Miles has been texting and popping in to see how I'm getting on fifty times a day, (well 2 or 3, maybe 4). And now that Simon is safely away, Miles is nowhere to be found.

Typical.

Only the absolute fear of having strangers in my sacred attic, has pushed me into making it as impersonal as I dare. That dear old lady up there now, is as sharp as they come. The less she has to pick up on, the better I feel. I've done all I can to prepare for this interview.

And now, now I've about half an hour of free time to immerse myself in the anguish of my self-denial… Miles is nowhere to be seen.

'Sorry, sorry, sorry!'

Speak of the devil.

Trudy stands up. 'I'll leave you, to get on with…' She gives me a wink. 'Whatevs.' And off she goes.

Miles sits down in Trudy's place, and leans in close; the subtle aroma of his aftershave invades my senses. I can feel my heart slamming into my ribs, and my pulse quicken. For a split second I think he's going to kiss me. 'Mrs Price has had a run in with one of the kids, I had to do damage limitation, on both parts,' he whispers.

'Oh.' I manage. Maybe it would be better if he weren't here to scramble my senses.

He leans slightly away, fixes his gaze on my face. 'So, how's it going, everything under control?'

'I think so, I've been keeping out of everyone's way.' I do my best to sound relaxed, but my voice is all high-pitched and squeaky.

'No Simon, today?'

'Not today.'

Miles smiles, nods. 'I suppose Sarah has everyone jumping to attention.'

'She's very…' I turn, swivel towards the door, and put my finger over my lips. Miles frowns, I shake my head. I can hear her making her way down the stairs slowly, and quietly. I know it's her, the swish of her beads gives her away. Suzi says I've got ears like a bat. 'Oh yes, Miles, she's very efficient,' I say, loud enough for her to hear, while turning back towards Miles.

'That she is.' Miles grins, catching on. 'One of the best about. Lucky to get her.'

Sarah stomps down the last three steps and bounds into the lounge. 'Ah, there you are, thought you'd deserted the poor gal,' she declares. 'Look at her, she's like a rabbit caught in headlights.'

Miles is up on his feet, and giving Sarah air kisses. 'Couldn't be helped, but I'm sure you know I'm not the deserting kind of bloke. Certainly not if I have you to answer to.'

Sarah studies him, and snorts. She's obviously immune to his charm. 'I'm expecting you to be on your best behaviour, Miles Hepworth. Unlike the rest of the female population...' she gives me a pointed look, 'I'm unimpressed by mere lip service. I'll go back and wait in the studio while you give Christie her last-minute coaching.'

'She doesn't need any coaching,' he replies as she waddles out of the room. He shakes his head. 'Can you believe her? Just be yourself, Christie, and everyone will be enthralled.'

'I hope you're right. No last instructions?' I ask.

'Like I said, you'll be great. After all, I've already given you my fool-proof way to make people fall in love with you.'

'Ah yes, but I've forgotten.'

'Come on, Sarah's waiting, and I for one am already in her bad books.' Miles takes the stairs two at a time.

I don't.

Madeline is not going to be happy when she learns I've given away the secret she's kept for twenty-four years. Especially, after I'm sure Miles assured her, I'd be a good little puppet, and do as she request.

Not even sure I can go through with it now.

My legs are rooted like tree trunks, my belly is churning like a washing machine full of bolts and my heart is trying to beat its way out of my chest. I'm keeping my hands clasped together, stopping them from trembling. Suzi offers me a nervous smile as I pass her maintaining her bedroom guard.

'I take it we're going up there,' says Miles.

I nod. He's up there in no time, clanking about. I can hear him chatting to the others. Trudy's head appears in the attic doorway, grinning like the demented diva she is, and waving excitedly for me to join them.

Suzi continues resting on her doorframe.

She takes her guarding very seriously.

Tilting her head, she asks, 'Have you decided what you're going to say yet?'

'No, I'm just going to be as honest as I can.' My chin gives way to a wobble, I try to rein it back under control by clamping my lips together. Blinking rapidly, I banish the threatening tears. I cannot go up there like this!

Suzi steps forward, and envelops me in a wholesome hug. Her simple show of support bolsters my resolve, but triggers another threat of tears. I feel our synergy, try to absorb strength from her, knowing she's willing it to me. 'You'll be fine.'

'Thank you,' I whisper. 'I really needed that.'

'Well for what it's worth, I think you're the bravest person I know. Everything that's happened... well, it would have sent most people running for the hills.'

'Have I still got time?'

She shakes her head, and points to the attic. 'Afraid not, go!' She pulls her hair into two mini pigtails at the side of her head, and sticks her tongue out, making me laugh. 'Christie, just go and be you!'

I doubt I could love this girl any more than I do right now.

The third step groans under my weight, it always does, as if to say "not you again". I usually answer it back, "and what if it is?", but not today. Today it's a relief to have its protestation. I'm tempted to loiter and force another groan.

Sarah hurries me into the attic with arms, scarves and boobs waving. 'Ah, here you are. Everything has been set up. Trudy, bless her, has been acting as your body double for our lighting chappie—' Trudy takes a bow. 'And the cameras are fixed, one will be trained on you, the other I. As you can see, it's rather cosy, but I'm sure you knew it would be, since it's your studio. Anything else, anything else, anything else?' Sarah scratches her chin. 'Oh, Miles has stipulated no longer than twenty minutes of filming, rather stingy I think, but hay ho.'

Miles steps towards Sarah. 'I'm sure that will be plenty of time, after all you are excellent at seeking out the extraordinary in people. And Christie herself would not want this to drag on all day.'

Sarah gives him a scathing look. 'So, Christie, if you'll settle yourself on your stool, it *is* the one you use when you are painting, yes?'

'Usually, sometimes I stand up.'

'Well, as long as you keep sitting down today, dearie, that's it.'

Miles steps between me and the camera, bends down and crosses my ankles. He puts his hand in the small of my back, and gently pushes it forward. Next, he puts his forefinger under my chin, and lifts it about two inches. He nods, eyes dancing, he leans forward. 'Knees together, even in jeans.'

'Very familiar, Mr Hepworth,' notes Sarah.

'Good luck, Christie.' He leans in again, and his lips are brushing my ears, sending quivers through my body. 'Remember, don't reveal your true relationship with Maddie. Sarah is a canny one, she's bound to try and quiz you about it.' He leans out again and nods, his face no longer animated, has a haunted expression.

I can feel my face flush in readiness for the secret I'm about to spill. This is excruciating. A premeditated act to sabotage Madeline's plans, after an implied promise of silence.

'Places, everyone, step back, Mr Hepworth.' The producer claps his hands. 'Chop-chop.' His mobile and tablet are nowhere to be seen. Neither are his manners. 'I'm expecting this to be one take. If either of you *do* need a break, raise a hand and we'll cut.'

Sarah shuffles her ample behind into her chair, and smiles for the camera. Her bounteous breasts are buried behind layers of scarves, I do hope they don't become too animated. Her hands rest gracefully on her lap. She is poised, and oddly elegant in an ecliptic kind of way. The urge to grab a sketch pad and pencil overcomes me.

'Excuse me,' I say. 'Could I get out a pad, I think it might make for a more relaxed mood.'

'If you think it would help.' The producer snaps. 'Don't move. You can get it.' He points to Trudy. She raises a brow, but rummages in my desk drawer and finds an A5 pad and passes it to me.

'And a pencil, sharp please.' It takes her a moment, but she passes me one.

'Okay, step away, Miss,' the producer says. 'All ready? Good.' He whips out a clapboard. 'On my count, three, two, one, take one, action.'

Snap!

Arrhhh, nearly had my nose off! I didn't know they actually still did that.

'Hello, I'm Sarah McBride, and I feel very honoured to be invited here, to the attic studio of Christie Harris. Hello, Christie.'

'Hello.' I glance at my pad, and my hand starts guiding my pencil over the paper.

Sarah's eyes twinkle. 'I'm sure some of you are aware of Christie's explosion onto the art world scene. Although this is not remarkable in itself, Christie's work is. And that is because of the meticulous attention to detail, not only of her work, but of the evolution of her progress from an early age. So, Christie, how did it all start?'

'I have always loved to sketch and paint, and am lucky to have parents who have given me the freedom and support to do it.' My pencil is moving frantically over the paper.

'But I notice that your work is only chronicled from the age of eight. What changed when you were eight?'

I close my eyes for a second, and remember my dear old Auntie Maddie. I miss her. And that red sports car, which has for years – if I'd ever been honest with myself – bugged me for being so out of character for an old dear.

'You're smiling, Christie, want to share?'

'When I was young, my very old, and very dear Auntie, used to visit. She was for a while, always bobbing round, she took a great deal of time to delve into my soul.'

'How so?'

'She was always asking about my friends, what I did, what I liked, hated. I suppose she was just curious about how I spent my time. On the last time I remember her visiting, she asked me what I wanted to be when I grew up.'

'And you said?'

'More than anything in the world, I wanted to be an artist. So, she set me a challenge, to prove my determination, and that was to send her two pieces of artwork every half-term.'

'And I believe the artwork in the exhibition *Evolution,* is the sum of all that work.'

'Yes, yes, it is.'

Sarah nods her encouragement, and looks for all the world, a sweet old dear, herself. 'Had it not been for your Auntie, do you think you would have been so unwavering with your artwork?'

'Never!' I laugh. 'The thought of letting her down used to keep me awake at night. Still does.'

'You still send it to her?'

'Oh yes, in fact my latest piece is waiting downstairs. I'm going to deliver it later.'

'So why does it keep you awake at night?'

I bite my lip. Why does it? Why? 'I suppose when someone expects the best from you, you only ever try to give them your best. If she'd have said, send me a painting whenever you feel like it, I might have only sent her a couple, and then got bored.'

'So, you started sending her paintings, and then what?'

'She started writing back, encouraging me. She always made a point of asking for the story behind the work at first. And I remember her saying the work should tell her the story. I think that is when I started to push myself.' I glance down at the sketch my hand is creating, almost of its own will.

'So, had it not been for her, you might have even given up?'

My pencil stops. Looking down at my pad I try to process this question. Sarah is coming along nicely. Would I have given up? I look back at Sarah. 'I think I might have wavered, but being creative is part of who I am. The *Evolution* exhibition defines me as an individual. Every facet of my personality is etched out for anyone to see. It's personal. The shape of the person I am now, has been composed by who I've been while I've been growing up.' I shrug. 'But I suppose that's true of everyone.' I try to search out Miles, but the lighting is too strong for me to see beyond it.

'My, that's a profound statement from one so young! I can tell you are trying to see your friends who are here with us today. Have they also been supportive over the years?'

'Oh, yes, although they were both surprised to be on public display!'

'You didn't tell them?'

'They hadn't seen all of the pictures, and it didn't occur to me that they'd ever see them.' I tap my lips with my pencil. Shut up, Christie!

'But surely, when you started to put the exhibition together, you must have thought about it then.'

I look down at my pad. Sarah really is coming along nicely. I'll show her at the end of the interview. I tap my lips with the pencil again, and look directly at Sarah. I wonder if she can feel the vibes coming from me, if her intuition is that good. Wonder if she can see my heart pounding under my Elmo T-shirt. 'I didn't take any part in the planning of the exhibition... Actually, I didn't even know anything about it, until that first day I met you.'

There, I've made the first admission, the rest should be easier.

'Let me get this clear.' I can see Sarah mentally regrouping. 'You didn't even know about *Evolution*?'

'That's right. In fact, you, and the other art critics knew about it before me.' I'm gripped by the same feelings now as I was then. I shuffle on my stool. Try to shift the queasy tummy and internal quiver.

Sarah sits bolt upright in her seat, and her bosom swings to life. 'So, excuse me, but I'm having a problem piecing this together. You didn't know, or participate in *any* of the preparation for *Evolution*, beyond it being your art in the exhibition.'

'That is correct.'

I can almost see her mind scrambling for facts, and snippets from our previous encounters. An almost unperceivable smile tugs at the side of her lips. I think she's made some connections. Surprised it's taken her this long. Her eyes lock with mine briefly, then she talks directly to the camera. 'The *Evolution* exhibition is housed in an old mill which has been redeveloped with the *Keep-a-Key* charity.' Then back to me. 'Of course, you know that, Christie.'

'Yes, I do, that's right. You interviewed one of the teenagers helped by that charity, didn't you?' I try to stave off the more probing questions.

'I did. The charity's founder, is Madeline De-Muir. She's quite a philanthropist. I remember asking you last time we met, if you had ever met her yourself, and you said you had, briefly.'

'That's right.'

Here we go. My queasy tummy is gripped by an iron fist.

'Forgive me, but could it be possible, for your Auntie and Madeline De-Muir to be one and the same person?'

If I can capture the look of excitement on her face. Her eyes are positively electric, her jowl is quivering. She leans forwards in her chair. The various fabrics of her scarves clamour for attention; beneath them her bosom oscillates.

'Christie?'

'Yes.' I clear my throat, and my thoughts. 'They are one and the same.'

'Okay.' Sarah rests back in her chair. Her breasts back under control. She's studying me. 'Is this something you have always known, or is this too, something you have only recently found out?'

Cunning.

'It's something I have known for a little while,' I answer honestly, vaguely.

'And, how did you find out?' Sarah shakes her head. 'It must have been quite a shock.'

'It was, although when I look back, my Auntie… Auntie Maddie, was always cloaked in mystery. She appeared to be an old lady, but she drove a red sports car.' I shrug. 'My painting, *The Long Farewell*, was painted from memory, my final childhood meeting with her.'

'I remember the way you were looking at it in the gallery when we first met, with longing?'

'Yes, I suppose I was. We have an odd kind of relationship,' I muse. 'She used to send me hurried postcards from exotic parts of the world, then sometimes rambling five-page letters packed with all sorts of things. I always looked forward to hearing from her.'

'You must have felt like it was a very special relationship.'

'Yes. As we never actually saw each other, I felt able to tell her anything and everything about my life.' At last some of the anxiety is ebbing away.

'All your secrets?'

'All my secrets, yes. All my worries, and my hopes, and all the icky teenage stuff we've all stressed about.'

'Your relationship was that close?'

I nod, hold her gaze.

'So, I wonder, why she kept her identity a secret from you.'

'I don't know, honestly. I have it on good authority it was to protect me, and that is as much as I know.' I look away, try again to seek out Miles' face behind the lighting. I've got to hold on to the facts as long as I can. I hope no one can tell I'm shaking.

'So, when you discovered Madeline had organised an exhibition of all your artwork, how did you feel?'

My pencil stops scribbling, and I look at Sarah. I can tell she knows her question is distressing to me. Her expression is one of compassion not cruelty; that alone prompts me to answer. 'My work is, as I said earlier, an expression of who I am, and how I got to be me. And yes, initially I did feel like I personally was on display. I felt exposed, vulnerable. I felt like she'd taken advantage of me. Betrayed my trust. But Auntie Maddie was part of how I became who I am. Someone asked me a question, a question I would never have asked myself.'

'And that was?'

'Would I have ever been brave enough to risk exhibiting my work? Risk bad reviews, failure. And I know, deep down, I'm not brave at all. I'm not the kind of person who thrives on adventure, so I would never have fulfilled my ambition of becoming an artist. Not ever. I'm a happy trundler, I trundle along, and if I come up against a huge problem in my way, I go around it, rather than try to tackle it.'

So now the whole world knows I'm a coward. And still my hand is guiding the pencil across the paper.

'And now, how do you feel about Madeline taking the bold step to exhibit your work?'

I can tell Sarah is trying to gauge my current relationship with Madeline. 'I wish I'd had more time to get used to the idea of all this.' I wave my pencil in all directions, aiming to include all my intruders. 'And although I doubt that I could have improved on *Evolution* in any way, I still would have liked to have had the chance to work with the *Keep-a-Key* team; they're a great bunch.'

'So, would you say you've forgiven her?' Sarah tilts her head, searches my soul.

'For what?' I scrunch up my face, very attractive I'm sure. For a moment there, I forgot she doesn't know Madeline is my long-lost mother

'For taking things into her own hands.'

I offer what I hope is an indulgent smile, maybe folk will forget my scrunched-up face. 'In her own way, she feels like she's finished what she started. After all, had she not prompted me to put some effort and discipline into my art, who knows what I'd be doing now?'

I know I wouldn't be sat here trying to smile and look normal, that's for sure. I am smiling my best smile at Sarah, but I've a feeling she's unravelling the truth. Every time I've met her, it's like she can strip back my words, and sense what's going on behind them. She's like that old-fashioned TV detective, Columbo, who always has just one more question.

'I wonder, it does seem odd that someone of Madeline De-Muir's calibre, would select one little girl, and strive to mentor her over almost two decades.'

Here we go, so Sarah might just have put two and two together and made the magical four.

'As you said yourself, she is renowned for her philanthropist endeavours.' I wave my hand, and dart a look at the camera.

'Have you not wondered why, of all the little girls, in all the villages, in all of England, why you? And why the charade?'

My heart is pounding so hard in my chest, I'm sure it can be seen. My mouth feels like a dusty Havana street after midnight, and my finger like lumps of lead. I look at the set of Sarah's face.

She knows.

Her eyes are telling me she won't push me. I know this look well; it's the look Dad gives me. A look of expectation. There will be no cajoling, no pressure, just the expectation that I will make the right choice, because it's the right thing to do.

I look down at the almost completed sketch. Slowly, I close up my pad and clasp it with my pencil in my lap. Forcing myself not to raise my hand for a break is almost killing me. If I don't say it now, it will be up to Madeline to offer her story first.

I look up at Sarah. Her eyes are like pools of pure compassion, and I regret closing my pad. She reaches across and brushes my arm with her hand. The tender gesture is almost my undoing. I swallow back the tears as I feel them forming.

'Take your time, dear, we are all friends here,' she says.

'Madeline is my biological mother.' The hushed words seem to speak themselves. 'I never knew.'

'You've only just found out?' Sarah asks almost reverently.

'Only just.'

It feels like a lifetime ago.

'It must have been a shock.'

'It was.' I bite the inside of my cheek.

'Would you like to take a moment?'

'No.' I shake my head; I can feel a single tear trickle down the side of my nose.

'Okay.' She nods and looks to camera. 'I'm sure we can all see this is not easy for Christie to talk about.' She looks back at me. 'It seems, Christie, if you met with Madeline alias Auntie Maddie as a child, your parents must have known that she was your natural mother. Is that right?'

'Yes.'

'And I also assume they were aware of your correspondence.' The lilt in her voice is calming, spellbinding.

I nod. 'Yes, they encouraged it.'

'They must have had a great deal of confidence that Madeline wouldn't reveal her own identity to you.'

'I believe it was agreed my childhood would not be disrupted, so they each had faith in each other. My parents trusted Madeline to keep a respectful distance. And Madeline trusted my parents to give me a stable, loving upbringing.'

'And you've had a stable and loving upbringing?'

I dash away the trickle of tears with the back of my hand. I hope this waterproof mascara really is. I raise my chin. 'My parents are the best.' I attempt a smile. 'Mum and Dad are my heroes.'

'Go on.'

'Dad is a vicar, and without fail sees the best in people. He's shrewd, and funny and honest. He sees beyond people's imperfections, he acknowledges we all have them, but then looks past them. I could always get away with bits and pieces with Mum… But Dad, he always saw through my master plans. Put me right, even before I went wrong.'

'Sounds like you didn't get away with too much.'

'I got up to all sorts… but you're right, I got away with nothing. Almost every week his sermons included one of my many gaffes.'

'That must have been embarrassing.'

'He didn't do it to embarrass me. He did it to prepare me for the real world. For this, I was a vicar's daughter in a rural village. Everyone knew me, and I think, to some degree I was cushioned from the harshness that is everyday life for most kids. He wanted me to be an orange not a peach.'

'I've not heard that before, what does it mean, exactly?'

'Well, peaches bruise very easily, and then go rotten quickly. An orange has a tough skin; you've got to dig a bit to get under that skin, and it only goes rotten if the skin is broken, or if it rests next to something else rotten. Basically, peaches might look good, but they don't do as well as oranges in the long run.'

'I like that. So, your dad tried to toughen you up?'

'In his own unique way, yes.'

'And your mum?'

'Mum is just Mum. She is amazing, the one who is always there when I need her. She makes everybody else's life run smoothly. She doesn't make things happen, but she makes sure everything and everyone are in place, to make it happen.'

'So, she's never the one to get the credit or stand in the limelight?'

I shake my head. 'She'd never want it. Happy to take a back seat.' An image of Mum in one of her mumsy cardigans makes me smile, but it soon drops away as I remember the heartache I've caused her this last week.

'Do you think, that could be, because she knew one day, Madeline would step in to take the limelight from her?'

'No, she's just happy without the fuss.'

'All of this now must be difficult for her to cope with.'

'She doesn't like me being upset. I think she maybe regrets not telling me sooner about who my biological mother is. She says there never seemed to be a right time. When everything settles down, she'll be much happier. And so will I.'

'I'm sure she will. I'm sure it must be hard for her to let you go.'

I laugh as a fresh batch of tears swell in my eyes. 'She'll never let me go! She is my mum. How can a lifetime of memories change? I doubt I'll ever meet anyone who's as much on my side as she's always been. I love her to pieces, even though I can be a complete pain.' I look into the camera. 'Sorry, Mum.'

Sarah nods. 'So why now? Why has Madeline done this now?'

'Madeline wants to have a proper relationship with me, not just letters and paintings.'

'And she has used *Evolution*, as a way to entice you away from your parents?' Sarah frowns.

'Oh no; she's no intention of coming between me and my parents. Couldn't if she tried. She wants me to have a chance at being recognised as an artist in my own right, and not as Madeline De-Muir's daughter.'

'She wants you to have credibility,' says Sarah. 'That seems to be very noble.'

'Yes.'

'And refreshing, in the celebrity world of "me, me, me".'

'I know,' I say, I really hope my face looks like I'm grateful. Life would be so much simpler if Madeline were an out-and-out bitch. The more I find out about her, the more I have to admit to myself, the only mistake she made was to give me away. Only one mistake, but a huge one; and she's been trying to recover from it ever since.

'She must have been what? Just sixteen when she had you. A child herself in many ways.'

'Yes.'

'It must have been a terrible decision for a young girl to have to make, to give up a baby.'

'I'm sorry, Sarah.' I close my eyes. 'I'm not comfortable speculating about the emotions of someone else.' I open my eyes. Sarah looks relaxed, in control. My stomach feels gripped by an iron clamp.

'Yes, of course, but I'm sure people will be interested to know what your feelings are about that.'

'I'm sure they are, but I'm not prepared to risk damaging a new kind of relationship with Madeline, simply to satisfy other people's curiosity.'

Sarah smiles and her eyes twinkle. I re-open my sketch pad, my urge to capture her twinkle takes over as my pencil glides over the page.

'You are very wise,' Sarah allows. 'So, what do you think the future holds for you now?'

'Good question. Three weeks ago, I could have answered with absolute certainty. Now I only seem to be able to think short term.' I close my eyes, and instantly an image of Miles jumps into my mind; I scrunch my eyes to banish it. I try instead to think of 7C, remember having to blast their papier-mâché maracas with a hairdryer to get them dry. Chantelle,

Dexter and the rest of my GCSE group, Mr Sloan. I open my eyes.

'So how about short term?'

'I'm eager to get back to school, and to guiding my GCSE pupils through their upcoming exams.'

'Do you expect to be treated any differently, now that everyone knows you're Madeline De-Muir's daughter?'

'It'll probably be a one-day wonder. I'd like to think people will be pleased I have an art exhibition, especially my pupils. But no, I don't think I'll be treated any differently.'

'And you plan to continue teaching?'

'I think I'll always teach. I'm as much a teacher as I am an artist. Luckily, I can do both.'

'Well, you seem to be very confident of where your future lays, career-wise. What about your family, friends, relationships, boyfriends?'

'I can't see it making any difference to my friends. It hasn't so far, and I don't have a boyfriend.'

Sara nods, makes a slight shrug of her shoulders. 'It's surely bound to have an effect with your parents.'

'They have always had my best interests at heart. I can't imagine anything changing that. They will help Madeline and me ease into getting to know each other properly.'

'They must be very generous people, to help rebuild your ties with Madeline; I imagine most adoptive parents might feel threatened.'

'They are very generous. Also, they hold Madeline in very high regard.'

'Do you suspect that is because of her celebrity?'

Here goes…

One last blast of truth…

I take a deep breath. 'No. I think it is because she has kept her distance for all these years. But mostly, it's because she is *their* natural daughter.' I raise my hand to signal an end to my inquisition. I look down at the sketch of Sarah, and then pass it to her. 'I'd like you to keep this as a reminder of today. And thank you.'

'Christie, you are full of revelations! I thank you for your time.'

I incline my head in acceptance, and Sarah then looks to camera.

'And during this interview, Christie has been sketching me. May I show everyone?' I nod, and Sarah holds my pad up. 'Christie Harris truly is a gem.'

'Cut!' Shouts the director, and slams the clapboard.

'Christie Harris,' cackles Sarah, 'you're an absolute gem!'

Tied Up

Offering us both a nugget of hope.

The weight of this brown paper package tied up with string, is making my legs go numb. My decision to take Madeline this final piece of work immediately after my interview, holds me captive.

I can hear them up in the attic, bickering on at each other. Not the cameramen. Not the lighting chappie. No, they were smart enough to sign the confidentiality form, and leave quick sharp.

It sounds like Sarah's signed, but the weasel of a producer keeps barking on about ratings and media hype. Miles is having none of it. I keep hearing a rant from said producer, followed by the level tone of Miles' voice.

Given I've told all about dearest Madeline, I'm surprised at just how calm Miles is staying. I've stolen Madeline's chance of a coy confession to the world.

Not a lot she can do about it now.

And by spending more time here, Miles is putting off telling her. I don't blame him!

And here I am, trapped by my good manners. I want to go and give this painting to Madeline and get this over with, before Miles tells her about my revelation!

Yep…

One hundred percent coward!

But how can I leave without saying thank you to Sarah? She allowed me a swift escape, and was tactful with her questions. And what Sarah chooses to be included from the gallery, in the half-hour special, is up to her. Oh, and that producer!

I've been rolling this jute string between my fingers and thumb for so long, I've got friction burns. The temptation to untie the bow, and take a peek at Miles, is gnawing at my resolve. Knowing my luck, he'd walk in.

'I'm not happy about this!' shouts the producer, as he bounds down the stairs. 'This is my production, and you've gagged me.'

'You were well aware of the conditions before you came here,' says Miles. His progress down the stairs is more leisurely.

'But that was before I found out who she is!' He casts me a menacing glare as he reaches the lounge door.

'Exactly, so now you know *who* she is, I suggest you start thanking your lucky stars. You and Sarah have only a limited time to work on the final edit, and get a copy back to me before Friday lunch. A copy needs to get to Monty's production team ASAP. Tick-tock, time's a-wastin'.'

The house vibrates as the front door slams.

'Problems?' I ask.

'No, he's just rattled because he didn't get his own way.' Miles leans against the door frame, arms folded, a satisfied smirk settles on his face.

'You enjoyed that!'

'He deserved it. He should be rubbing his hands in glee, not complaining.' Miles frowns, rubs his hand over his mouth and chin. 'You've put me in an awkward position, Christie, with Madeline. Thought we had a deal.'

I hold out my hands palm down. 'Look, I'm still shaking. It needed to come from me, Miles. She's been controlling everything.'

'You could have given me the heads up. I could have prepared Maddie. She's going to be upset—'

'Upset! Really? I've had no control over any of this. I needed to do this one thing, have some input as to how this plays out. Not simply be a puppet. Can you blame me for—'

'No, Christie, I can't,' says Miles in a low voice. He lets out a long sigh, shrugs. 'It's done now.'

I look away from him. 'I'm going to see Madeline now, I'd appreciate it, if you'd wait until later to tell her about...'

He nods. 'Okay. It will give me time to figure out how to break it to her.' Again, he shrugs. 'Doing that sketch of Sarah was a masterstroke. Now everyone will be able to see what a fine artist you are. Maybe that will end up being the real talking point.'

'Hope so, Sarah has such character.'

'Somebody talking about me?' says Sarah. Miles backs out of the room to let Sarah through. 'Aha, Christie, so this is where you've been hiding, while our menfolk have been doing battle.'

'Yes, I'm a coward. But thank you Sarah, for not, for not tying me in knots. Even though I'm still shaking, I think you treated me gently.'

'Oh, you silly thing!' Sarah bustles over to me, and gives me an awkward hug over my brown paper package. 'Like I said, we're all friends together. And besides, you might just be the find of my career. Lucky me!'

'I hope you're right,' says Miles.

Sarah places her hand on Miles' arm. 'And, thank you, Miles.' She grins at me. 'He's getting your sketch of me, framed.'

'That's thoughtful,' I say.

'Is that by any chance a picture for Madeline?' asks Sarah, looking at the brown paper package.

'It is.'

'Any chance of a quick peep?'

'I painted it for Madeline, so I'll let her choose who she wants to see it. Sorry.'

'Oh well. I've got my own masterpiece, and much work to be done, thanks to you! So, I'll be on my way.'

Miles walks Sarah to the door. I tuck my precious package under my arm and follow them. Sarah is halfway down the drive by the time I've even reached the door.

'Not even going to let me have a look at it?'

'You'll have to ask Madeline.'

'I understand.' He nods. 'I might catch up with you later then.'

'Not sure how long I'll be stopping at Mum and Dad's, but maybe.'

'You did well today.' Miles touches my elbow with his hand, leans in and brushes a scarce kiss on my cheek, hardly making contact at all. A jolt of yearning surges through my body. I snap away from him as if I've had an electric shock. He looks surprised, offended.

'I need to go.' I look down at my feet, and shuffle past him. 'Tell Suzi and Trudy I won't be late back.'

'Alright, bye then.'

Thankfully he doesn't follow me to the car; I wrestle my precious package onto the back seat.

*

The pleasant spring weather has everyone out and about. The roads are busy with lots of day trippers to Driftwood Sands. The journey to see my parents seems to last forever. I try to appreciate the lovely countryside, it's not easy. I want to get this finished with.

I'm ready to say goodbye to Auntie Maddie.

Nowhere near ready to say hello to Madeline.

Mum is pottering in the front garden; the scrunch of gravel announces my arrival. She waves, trowel in one hand, weeds in the other. A smudge of dirt on her face, tells me she's been at it for ages, probably overdoing it. A displacement activity maybe?

'Oh, what a relief! I've been wanting to have a break for the last hour, but if either of those two sees me, I'll be roped into yet another game of scrabble!'

'It's lovely to see you too, Mum,' I say. Her tools patter to the ground and she rushes over and gives me a squeeze. She smells divine, she smells like Mum. Her hugs are the best Mum hugs in the world.

'How did it go, Christie?' She holds me at arm's length, her eyes searching.

'Okay.' I shrug. I'm not going to tell Mum about my revelation about Madeline in my interview, I'll leave that to the ever-resourceful Miles. 'I'm getting used to all the fuss. It's only going to get worse.' Oh, it really is.

'It'll pass, love. Things have a way of working out.' She offers a wistful smile.

'I know, that's why I'm here. I thought it would be better to at least have one proper conversation with Madeline, before the media stick their oar in.'

'Maddie thought so too, but she's anxious about what to expect from you, after you bolted from her the other day.'

I glance at the bush I hid behind, remembering Miles' amused expression as he found me. The same expression I've painted. A flutter of embarrassment feathers over me. I feel my cheeks flush and try to brush away the rush of goosebumps from my arms. 'It was too soon; I wasn't ready Mum. That's why I was trying to leave, remember. If Suzi had got here five minutes sooner, I would have escaped.'

Mum tilts her head, and clasps my hand. 'Are you sure you are up to it now? I can't imagine how you feel. I wish we could have found a better way.' I can hear the echoes of regret in her voice. Know I certainly haven't made it any easier.

'It's done. It can't be easy for you either. How are you and Dad?'

'Bored out of our minds! I know it sounds awful, but I'm almost glad Maddie's broken her ankle, because your dad has a captive scrabble opponent, and I can pretend to be too busy. He seems a bit lost, follows me round the house asking "What needs doing next?" every two minutes.'

'Poor Mum.' Poor Dad!

'So, I have to keep coming up with excuses to leave the house.'

'After all those years of complaining about him always being out.' I manage not to laugh. 'I suppose we could both escape; go to Driftwood Sands and walk along the prom.' I sound almost as desperate as Mum.

'After you've talked to Maddie, put you both out of your misery. She's in the back garden.'

'Playing scrabble?'

Mum nods then wanders over to her gardening things. 'I'll go and put the kettle on, send your dad in to give you and Maddie some time to talk in private.'

'Okay.' I reach into the car and get the package off the back seat; this at least should prompt our initial conversation. I focus on each step as I prepare to meet the woman who gave me away.

Dad and Madeline are sat across from each other. The table between them holds the scrabble board, two letter stacks and the mini sack for letters. Dad is leaning back. He looks smug, probably winning as usual. Madeline's looking at the board, her chin resting on neatly folded hands.

Their closeness is palpable. The urge to turn and walk away is strong. I have to crush the wave of jealousy threatening to engulf me. He's my dad, but I have to remind myself, he was hers first.

It's like she has first dibs on everyone I love.

I shake my head, shake that thought away too.

Taking slow, steady steps towards them, I fix a smile on my face. They both turn and see me at the same time.

Dad is up on his feet, and embracing me in a bear hug before I've time to say hello. 'Look who the sunshine's brought out, I said it was going to be a beautiful day, didn't I, Maddie?'

Madeline nods, awkwardly scrambling for her crutches.

'Don't get up,' I say. She looks alarmed. 'I'll join you, if you don't mind.'

'Pull up a pew,' says Dad, and laughs at his own little joke.

'Dad, I think Mum wanted you for something, inside.'

'But we're halfway through a game! Oh, oh yes, better go and see what she wants me for.' He picks up the paper with their scores written on. 'I'd better take this with me.'

I sit down in the seat Dad has just vacated, glance at the letters on his letter tray. Madeline doesn't stand a chance at winning. I rest the package awkwardly on my lap.

'I'm glad you've come, after the other day.'

'I wasn't ready.' She nods. Waits. All my thoughts seem to have evaporated. I hold out the package to her. 'It's for you.'

'Thank you.' Her face lights up as she takes it from me. She holds it to her nose and takes a deep breath in. 'It smells of you, they always do.' She smells it again, and then rests it down over the top of the scrabble board. Covering her defeat.

'It's the last one.'

'Then I shall savour opening it.' Her eyes softly crease at the corners, her smile curbed. Her skin is smooth peaches and cream, and she has not a single line on her forehead. She doesn't look forty, not even close-up, nearer thirty than thirty-five. Nearer my sister than my mother. Her expression is giving nothing away, other than caution.

'Madeline, I want us to talk properly, before all the media get involved.'

'Maddie, please, Madeline sounds—'

'Okay, Maddie it is.'

'So, what do you want to know?'

'I want to understand why, why you left me, in your own words.'

Madeline looks down at her hands, then back up to me. 'I was young. I didn't feel like I belonged anywhere. I met a lad who was on one of Dad's famous youth programmes. He was a bit of a loner, a rebel in a quiet reserved kind of way. He had an inner confidence. Super good-looking, he was to me, anyway, and we just clicked. He made me feel like I was the centre of his life. All of a sudden, I was pregnant. Dad's job always kept us moving about. We moved before I dared to tell him about you... I couldn't risk him not loving me. Didn't trust he loved me enough. Stupid really.'

'He wouldn't have wanted me, would he?'

'I don't know, Christie. I was young, so was he.'

'At least you had a choice,' I say it like a challenge. For a moment she looks hurt. I'm glad. I want to hurt her. I'm hurt.

'I had a choice, yes. I don't know if it was the right choice I made, but neither do I know it was the wrong choice.' She shrugs. 'That's life. I can't go back and change it, and see how it would have worked out any other way.'

'Everything has worked out quite well for you.' My words are hushed, the spark of spite slashed by her calm reasoning. But then, she's had twenty-four years to marinate in her own perspective.

She sighs. 'It certainly looks that way. I was sixteen. I'd never even lived in one place for more than eighteen months in my entire life. The thought of committing the rest of my life to looking after another human being, was beyond terrifying. I'd always accepted being wherever Dad's job demanded. I was given a chance for the first time in my life, to go and be what I wanted to be. I didn't for a single moment expect anything remarkable to come from it.'

'Then what did you expect?'

'An adventure of my very own. I expected some excitement away from Mum and Dad. That's the real reason I changed my name, so I'd not be embarrassed by being connected to them. You know, have some freedom without the embarrassment of being a vicar's daughter… You must know how that feels. I only ever expected the occasional bit part. But then, within a year I was being treated like a star. And then Hollywood, I was eighteen. How many eighteen-year-olds do you think could resist that opportunity?'

'Did you ever intend to come back for me?'

She looks at me. Her hands reach out, resting on the table. I keep mine resting on my knees, clutch my jeans to hold them down.

She shakes her head. 'Not then. I was too drawn into this new exciting world with everyone hanging onto my every word. They warned me, Mum and Dad, said I was living in a make-believe world of happily ever after. I promised I'd let them keep you.' Again, she shakes her head, and briefly closes her eyes. 'They told me time wouldn't stand still while I was off doing what I wanted. As usual, they were right…'

'Do you regret it?' The words tumble out without thought.

'I wish I'd been strong enough, when I first came back. They'd wanted me to come home to you then. They said we could be a family together; you could be brought up as my younger sister. I couldn't…' She looks down at her hands, then back up to me. 'I couldn't have seen you every day, and not been your Mum. I was too broken, drained. I would have clung to you like a leech. Maybe two or three years down the line, but by then, it was too late to introduce a big sister to you. So, between us, we invented Auntie Maddie.'

'It worked very well, up until a couple of weeks ago.'

'It was never enough.' The snag in her voice claws at my conscience. The noose around my feelings relaxes, as I sense the pain Madeline's honesty is causing her. And still somehow, I can't let go of the jabbering jumble of bitterness I'm nursing. Seeing her so close with my dad, taking my place, makes me rumble with resentment.

'You were good at Auntie Maddie, I loved you. Relied on you for good advice, craved your praise.' I surprise myself by resting one hand on the table, allowing our hands to touch for a moment, offering us both a nugget of hope.

Madeline nods. 'I so wanted to be close to you; to be part of your life.'

'You have been, probably more than you realise.'

'And now, are you going to let me be part of your life?'

'I have no choice really, have I? What kind of life have Mum and Dad had to live, keeping our lives apart? They will always be my mum and dad, just like they've always been yours.'

'But we can move forwards?'

I purse my lips. 'As long as you know, it's only for their sake. They've earned a rest from all these theatrics.'

Madeline nods. The meagre crumbs of reconciliation hardly appear to satisfy her hunger for total acceptance. What does she expect? I know for sure Mum and Dad would have wholeheartedly welcomed her back all those years ago, she's their child.

But the more I think about how they've had to shield me from the truth, year after year, and the strain it must have put them under, the less I feel like yielding to Madeline's charm.

'About your father…' she says, tapping her finger on the edge of the scrabble board.

'Dad?' I frown.

'No, your natural father—'

She can't be serious!

'… He's likely to put two and two together. He's always known who I am. He might want to acknowledge you.'

I close my eyes. Cascades of panic rip at my already rocky composure. Is there no end to this nightmare? My instinct for self-preservation demands I escape. I open my eyes, and can't help the withering glare I give her. 'He might want to acknowledge me? This isn't some period drama on the BBC! And I'm not some babe in swaddling who can be picked up or discarded at your whim. Whoever he is, I'm not prepared to go there Madeline.' All of my, until now, controlled bitterness is evident as I spit the words out. 'So, don't! He's your problem, not mine!'

I stand and walk away, my hands balled in tight fists. Electrical bolts feel to be thundering through my veins, every neuron in my brain is sparking at the same time firing my inner fury.

Cups rattle on a tea tray as Dad breaks into a trot to catch up to me. 'Christie, I've made us a nice cup of tea. Mum's got a Battenberg.'

Battenberg! Shove your Battenberg I want to scream. But it's not his fault. The bite of gravel through my thin pumps is a welcome discomfort, one I can live with. I yank open my car door with such force it swings open, and then crashes back into my legs. I hold in the shout of pain, embrace it as a welcome manifestation of my anger. 'Bloody car!' I hiss under my breath.

'Christie! Wait!'

The sight of Dad in his carpet slippers, desperately holding the tea tray before him like a peace offering, almost breaks my resolve.

'Please, Dad, I can't!' Angry tears spurt from my eyes, I swipe them away with the balls of my hands. Every negative emotion I've ever known, is alive, threatening to explode. I need to get away before my poisonous thoughts escape.

'I know.' He sets the tray down next to where Mum's abandoned gardening tools lie. He pushes my hair off my forehead and plants a kiss on the top of my head.

How come he's so good? Takes everything in his stride, absorbs the shockwaves. Surely, he feels as trapped as I do.

'Go. I'll say goodbye to Mum for you.'

Nodding a "thank you" biting back tears, unable to speak, I leave.

Shifting Grains of Sand

caught in an exotic dance ...

I'm gripping the steering wheel as if my life depends on it, it does, as the tears bubbling from my eyes blurs my vision but I find the salty taste a strange comfort. Out of the corner of my eye, I notice the sign for the backroad up to Driftwood Sands. Dropping my speed, I turn right, to take what is laughingly called the shore road, the sea only ever a distant dream. The road soon narrows to a single track, sweeping on towards the seaside town stuck firmly in the middle of the last century.

I pull over and park in one of the many lay-bys dotted along this stretch of road. Sand spilling from the dunes is forever shifting across the road, caught in an exotic dance with the ever-changing sea breeze. Resting my head back, I close my eyes.

I need to get all this Madeline mess into perspective. I look out across the lane to the marsh running down towards the sea. But for the barbed wire fence, and avid bird watchers, I'd be running across that marsh, allowing my screams to echo with those of the gulls.

Getting out of the car, I grab my trusty hoody, and head for the dunes gulping in the fresh sea air. As I clamber up the track, loose dry sand oozes into my pumps weighing them down, they slip off allowing the cool sand to caress my feet. I scoop up my pumps in one hand and grip the reedy grass with the other and hoist myself up the makeshift path.

Spotting an already flattened clump of grass, I smooth out my hoody and plonk myself down.

Now I can cry without being disturbed. Without prying eyes. Or concerned friends consoling. Or imposters judging. Without causing any more upset to Mum and Dad.

I rest back and look at the enormity of the sky, birds swirl and soar high, occasionally calling out to each other. The sky is where they belong, where they are free to be. Like me with a paint brush.

But thinking about it, even though it was Mum who first put a paint brush in my hand, it was Auntie Maddie who made me commit myself to art. She has always been a tenacious critic, and enduring champion.

I don't think I'd even be half sane if I couldn't paint. Every major junction of my life, including this one, has been accompanied by frantic painting or sketching. Even when I'm only mildly stressed, I doodle on whatever scrap of paper I can find.

Even now! I've snapped off a long stalk of grass and I'm tracing the outlines of the clouds, without it being a conscious decision. It's as much a part of me, as the air in my lungs. Each breath of air is different, but each refreshes my life. Just like all my doodles, sketches and paintings.

I wonder if Madeline regrets giving up acting. Mum said she gave it up for me, for my protection. Right now, it doesn't feel like it. If I was born to paint, then surely, I can try to be fair-minded enough to at least acknowledge Maddie was born to act. She was given a chance, and she took it. And then, she let it all go.

I doubt I could do that.

What about Dad? On his way to becoming a Bishop! Focused always on helping people, leading by example, gives up that path to tread a gentler one with me in rural Little Upton. Now that is a change of gear from urban troubleshooting. He must have felt smothered by the layers of tradition woven into the fabric of Little Upton life.

And Mum, always in the background making everything run smoothly. Sorting out problems, making sure everyone had what they needed, to do what they were doing. Feeding us with food, which frankly, Jamie Oliver would be proud of. She's never taken the limelight, but without her, the whole shebang would've come tumbling down about us.

I can't count the number of times she hasn't *told* me I'm wrong, just shown me an alternative viewpoint. She's like one of those tribal guides in the Amazon, hacking down all the major obstacles in my path, leaving me only the smaller, more manageable ones to deal with. I wonder how many she's tackled for me with Madeline over the years.

I know I've got to get to grips with all this. All of them have made sacrifices. All of them for me.

But I just start getting over one revelation, then along comes another.

How did Madeline think I'd react to the possibility of some random bloke stepping forward to, as she says, "acknowledge" me? Why doesn't she go the whole way, and search him out for me on *Long lost family*? I'm sure she'd get a hit.

I can't even think about that now. I just wish everything was back how it used to be, normal. Mum, Dad and me, with the occasional letter from Auntie Maddie. My phone vibrates in my pocket, pulling it out, I see a message from Miles.

But then without all this, I wouldn't have met Miles.

Flowers

'Somehow I doubt that, Miles.'

Once again Miles is in my front room. My eyes follow his every movement. The tilt of his head, the scant furrow of a frown that lasts only a moment, the way he drags his hand absently through his hair.

His thoughts, as always are with Madeline. 'Yes, I know it *is* short notice,' he says into his mobile. 'I know, sorry, should I try another florist? They're for Madeline De-Muir. After two-thirty, but before four, the message? If you just write, "believe in yourself", you don't need to say who's sent them, she'll know.'

At least he doesn't know how I feel about him. It's like knives are being juggled in my stomach. I don't know why he isn't with her, today of all days. I doubt she's as confident about her interview tonight, as she's used to being. "Miss cool, calm and collected", must at least be worried about what her adoring public are going to make of my revelation.

'So, Christie…' Miles slips his mobile into his jacket pocket, and focuses his attention back to me. 'I hope you've got a master plan for keeping yourself busy today, otherwise I'll have to resort to Plan B.'

'I was hoping to go over some lessons for next term, but I don't think I'm going to be able to concentrate. Has Madeline gone back to her own house now?'

'I took her first thing this morning, Mrs Price did offer…' He lets his words hang, as a glint of mischief dances in his eyes. My heart somersaults about my chest. 'I thought she'd be safer with me driving her home.'

Relief soars through me. The thought of seeing her again after my outburst, has kept me away from Mum and Dad's all week. 'I might go and see Mum and Dad then.'

'I take it, you don't want to bump into Maddie, then?'

I shake my head and a shiver snakes up through my body. I wipe my sweaty palms on my jeans.

'She's not that bad,' he says in a half-joking kind of way. Tilts his head to one side, and offers a smile. 'She's almost got over you telling all in your interview.'

Goosebumps cover my arms; I try to brush them away before he notices. All it takes is a smile from him, and I'm lost. It's not even as if that smile was fully for my benefit. It was, as usual, an appeal on Madeline's behalf. I bite the inside of my mouth to stop waspish words escaping and force a smile.

Miles continues, 'Try to see her through the words she's written to you over the years; because that's who she really is. You probably know her better than anyone.'

'Including you?' I challenge, annoyed by the knowledge it's jealousy prompting my words.

'Yes.'

He says it so casually, he could be saying yes to a coffee. And why can't he understand why I'm so… whatever I am? 'Somehow I doubt that, Miles.'

His expression changes to something more complex, anger tinged with hurt, smothering me in guilt.

He stalks away from me, turns and walks back. Standing too close, crowding my space. The spice of his aftershave, further stirs my awareness, like I even need that. I can feel his eyes scrutinizing me. I keep mine averted from him. Don't want him reading them. I feel the heat of my blush working its way up my body, feel the pounding of my heart high in my chest. Again, I wipe my sweaty palms on my jeans.

He raises my chin with his finger, and I swallow. My eyes drift to meet his, the pain in mine, mirrored in his. 'You know what she is to me. And I know, she's always held herself apart from everyone... including me... including your parents. The only person, the only one she has ever fully invested her emotions in, is you. So, don't, Christie. Do not drag my relationship with Maddie, between us. We've both got too much to lose.'

Without breaking eye contact, he slowly dips his head. I moisten my lips; know before his lips brush mine, he is going to kiss me. The tingle of anticipation heightens the sensations swirling through my body as we melt together. I close my eyes to hide the intensity of my feelings from him, but at the same time my traitorous body moulds to his. A myriad of sensations brought to life.

The longing for this to last forever, overtakes my rational thoughts as my fingers rove through his hair, pulling him closer, deeper. Suffocated by desire, I'm lost in the moment. Can feel the heat of his body, his heartbeat.

The vibration of his mobile phone brings me to my senses, and I pull away from him, before it makes a sound.

He looks at the screen, and disconnects the call. 'Look, I've got to go.'

'Summonsed?' I can't even savour his kiss, without her intruding.

'It was Mrs Price; she left a message earlier about the gallery. I need to check it out, okay?'

'Oh.' I bite my lip.

'She's probably being overcautious; she knows how much it means to Maddie for *Evolution* to be successful.'

Again, with Maddie.

Whether he knows it or not, we've both already lost. My throat tightens as I swallow back the hurt. Always her before me. 'It means a lot to me too. Most of my childhood is in that gallery. I don't think any of you understand, it's my life on display. My life. Those pictures are part of who I am.'

'I get it, Christie, honestly.' Miles drags his hand through his hair where moments ago, my own fingers roamed. He looks away, and then looks back at me. 'And that is why I'm going to see what the problem is. I understand. And believe me, you don't need to explain how each of those pictures holds a chunk of you. I can see it in them.'

My throat still feels tight, and I try to swallow the choking ache away. Miles looks so earnest; it's hard not to believe him. I nod my acceptance of his words, and he touches my elbow.

I sigh. 'Go on then, sort out whatever it is you need to.'

'I'll be back as soon as I can.'

'I might not be here.'

'Don't worry, I'll track you down! There's a favour I need to ask. But I need to sort this out first. Until later then.' He tucks my hair behind my ear, cups my cheek. His eyes search my face. He turns to leave.

'Bye,' I murmur, following him to the door to watch him. As soon as he's in his car, he's on his mobile.

I turn and go into the kitchen. I flick on the kettle to make myself a coffee. The house shudders as the front door slams with force.

'Sorry!' shouts Suzi. She waddles through into the kitchen, grappling with shopping bags, she dumps them in the middle of the table. 'Been shopping.'

'You don't say.' I try to laugh, but it comes out wrong. Suzi doesn't seem to notice, she's too busy riffling through her bags. 'I'll make you a coffee, give you chance to hide all the good stuff.'

'Thanks. I'm going to hide them in easy to find places anyway. I think I'm going to be having a chocolate week.' Suzi starts piling boxes on the counter next to the fridge-freezer.

'Good idea. Is that a cheesecake?' I spy an interesting array of desserts.

Suzi slaps another box on the counter. 'Yep! And another sticky toffee pudding, and a chocolate torte, oh and some éclairs.'

'I love a girl who thinks ahead. Are we celebrating something?'

'Yes, getting fat, but only for a week.'

'Okay, so how does a chippy dinner sound?' I ask.

'Sounds good, Trudy said she'd be back for half twelve, so we'd better make sure we get her some. And is Miles coming back?'

'Oh, perhaps. I'm not sure what his plans are; he just popped in on his way to the gallery.'

Suzi smirks. 'Hardly on his way then. I'd better text him later.'

'You've got his number?'

'Oh, yes! He gave me and Trudy his business card. Thought you knew.'

A familiar blush starts rising in my cheeks. 'I didn't know. You phone him then. You'll be able to report back—'

'Christie! It's not like that.'

I sigh. 'I know, I'm a bit confused about how I'm feeling. He did actually, come to ask a favour of me.'

'And what favour would that be?'

'Don't know.' I wrinkle my nose and grimace. 'He got called away.'

Suzi's laughter howls through the house, her face is so scrunched up it looks like she's ninety. She drops down on a chair dramatically clutching her sides.

I tut. 'He did get called away… It was Mrs Price.'

Suzi flaps her arms and draws a deep breath, and then starts laughing all over again.

'What?' I ask, the beginnings of a smile threatening to escape. 'He *was* called away!'

Suzi covers her mouth with her hand and pinches her nose. Her squeaks still sneak out. She rubs her eyes on her sleeve, digs in her pocket for a hanky and blows her nose elephant style. 'I'm sorry,' she says between giggles, 'but you're both so obvious, it's embarrassing.'

'I wish I'd never told you about him! It's not funny.'

'I'm sorry. But it's entertaining seeing you try to act all coy and uninterested, when you are more than interested. And Miles making up strings of excuses to keep calling here.'

'They aren't excuses!'

'He's been here four times in the last three days.'

'Talking about the interviews, or the gallery!'

'You do both have mobiles.' Suzi is loving this, likes to be with all the action, as long as she isn't the centre of it. Close enough to catch the vibes, but not get burnt. Safe in her self-contained security bubble. Right now, I wish I could be in there with her.

'It's all very complicated.' Plonking myself down on a chair at the table, I drop my head into my hands. 'My head is scrambled with all this stuff going on.'

'Oh well, by this time tomorrow all the worrying will be over. Trudy has put herself in charge of filtering through the social media networks tonight, to scupper any unpleasantness.'

'Stop!' I raise my hand. 'I can't even think about it.'

It hadn't even occurred to me that I might be target for trolls; the only trolls I know are those other cute little things called Poppy and Branch. The real ones, who hide behind their online persona and destroy people's lives, are a total mystery to me. I don't think I can handle being a # trend. I close my eyes and turn away from Suzi. I know she's only trying to help, but I think we both know I'm out of my depth.

'You don't need to think about it. Trudy has it all under control.'

'I really want to believe that, Suzi, but somehow, I think it's going to take more than Trudy and her trusty tablet, to turn the tide of public opinion.'

'Aha, but she's recruited a team of trusty technological taggers, bloggers, vloggers or whatever they're called.' Suzi scrunches her face up, the trauma of tech taking its toll.

'Really? Do we know them?'

'Ye-es,' says Suzi.

'Well, go on, who are they?' I've got a bad feeling about this.

'Just some whiz kids Trudy knows.'

'Trudy doesn't know any kids, whiz or otherwise.' Please no. I close my eyes as the realisation hits me. 'She's enlisted the kids from the gallery, hasn't she, Frankie and his crew?'

'It seemed like a good idea at the time.'

'But they're Madeline's kids! They'll be on her side! And if we're being completely honest, what chance has a group of disadvantaged teens got to influence the bullies in cyberspace?'

'Trudy made them advantaged.'

'She's bribed them!'

'No!' Suzi shakes her head. 'She's simply provided them with the proper equipment for the job.'

'And that is?'

'Whatever the latest in mobile thingy whatsit technology is, that is what she's got them. I don't know what they're called, but the kids were well impressed.'

'I bet they were. And how does she intend to make sure they're all going to be monitoring the various tweets and whatnots tonight?'

'Well, this is the clever bit. Do you know when they have elections in America, and it shows on telly all the young political wannabes locked in offices, madly phoning and texting and generally drumming up support? Their only relief, when they're sent boxes of pizza and Starbucks. Trudy has set up a "Campaign Headquarters". Mrs Price has volunteered her front room, and her husband is going to be the pizza delivery boy.'

Could it be any worse? 'And does this not sound like a recipe for disaster to you?' I shake my head. What was Trudy thinking? 'I thought Mrs Price and Frankie have issues.'

'Whatever they are, they seem to have been set aside for the greater good. Mrs Price has assured Trudy, that she'll watch both the interviews with the kids, to make sure they know what it is all about.'

'Does *she* know what it's all about?'

'She will do after she's watched your interview.'

'And, I presume Miles knows all about this?'

'Trudy talked to him about it, before she approached everyone.'

'And he's okay with it?'

'Trudy said he ran it by Madeline first, but yep, he approves.'

I glare at her.

'What?'

'This is why!' I grind my teeth. 'I cannot let anything happen between him and me. "He ran it by Madeline first", he didn't run it by me! What am I, chopped liver?'

'It wasn't like that,' says Suzi.

'Well, what was it like? Because from here, it looks like I'm the only one, out of the loop.'

'Trudy wanted to make sure you got some cyber backup for her #Christie campaign—'

'#Christie? So, I take it Trudy is all for this #explosion.'

'Oh yes, Trudy has it all under control now, don't worry. You're going to be everywhere for all the right reasons. She has all her work colleagues onboard too, even the dragon from accounts. And, like you said, she doesn't know any whiz kids. So, since you had such a good rapport with Frankie and co, she thought it was a good idea to get them in on it.'

'So why did Miles have to "okay it" with Madeline, then, if he thought it was a good idea, tell me that!' I cross my arms firmly across my chest, steam must be spurting from my ears.

'Because, Christie,' explains Suzi, with exaggerated patience, 'Madeline has duty of care for those kids, being a teacher, you know that.'

I let out the breath I didn't know I was holding. Of course, duty of care, her kids, her responsibility, what was I thinking? It's all about her.

Suzi shrugs. 'And, obviously, it's his job to report back to her.'

'He will always put her first.' All the anger seeps out of me, I need to accept it, nothing can ever properly start with me and Miles.

'He works for her, Christie. He's just doing his job.'

'And calling here, sorting things out for the gallery and interviews, is his job too. Look Suzi, I can't let anything develop with him. How can I know if he's being overly friendly with me, because he likes me, or for the benefit of his job?'

'Because he calls here every chance he gets.'

'Just doing his job,' I reply.

'He could phone or email, he comes here to see you; he watches you.' Her words fall over me like feathers from a burst pillow.

I tilt my head to one side, unfold my arms, and rest back in the chair. What would Suzi say, if I told her that less than twenty minutes ago, I was in his arms? I touch my fingers to my mouth; trace the line of his kiss. My lips are alive with sensations, and tingle with the memory of his. Only a kiss. I can feel Suzi studying me.

'You don't need to pretend with me, I already know how you feel about him.' She touches my arm and offers a lopsided smile.

'I'm scared.' I didn't intend the words to be spoken aloud.

'Me too, scared he's going to steal my best friend away.'

'No one could ever do that, you know all of my secrets, remember?'

'I think Miles could, whisk you away to a glamorous celebrity lifestyle, with proper dinner parties, no knickers lined up along radiators.'

'Don't.' I half smile. I've never wanted that lifestyle, I'm not a social climber, I'm just average.

'With proper posh puddings, champagne. And what about poor old me? I'd just be left here rambling around with only Trudy to boss, and there'd be no fun in that.'

'Suzi, you've been bossing me for twenty years, you're never going to stop!' It suddenly dawns on me, how true that is. Trudy might be the best friend who rides shotgun, striding in and taking control, but Suzi with her tweaks, and occasional unfettered remarks has steered my path many times. Probably totally unaware. Like right now.

'I could always apply to be your housekeeper.' Suzi puts on a forlorn face and sighs. 'Mother would be so disappointed.'

'Suzi, seriously, everything's changing, and I have no control over any of it.'

'Christie Harris, for once in your life, just go with it. What is it you say to me? "Loosen up", well, now it's your turn. Enjoy the adventure.'

'He kissed me. Just before he left...' I trace my finger along my lips, remember the sensation.

'Well, it's not as if you've never been kissed before.'

'I've never been kissed like that before. He said we've not to let Madeline come between us, we've got too much to lose, and then he kissed me.'

'So, don't. Don't let Madeline come between you.'

'How can I not? He's bound to her in ways you don't know.'

'Then tell me.'

'I can't.' I shake my head.

'Whether you tell me or not, whatever it is that binds them, it sounds to me like Miles is ready to risk the consequences of breaking those ties.' Suzi shrugs.

And she's right, maybe that's what frightens me more than anything else. 'I don't know, Suzi.' Can I take that risk? If it all goes haywire between us, I've still got Mum and Dad and the ever-zealous Madeline.

He'll have nothing.

I don't think I can do that to him. Don't think I can risk him doing it to himself. The thought of the Miles, Madeline rescued all those years ago flits through my mind. Alone and afraid. I can't risk him going back to a solitary life. He needs my family as much as I do. Maybe even more, after all, I'll always have Suzi and Trudy.

Suzi scurries her fingers across the table, and gently prods my arm. 'I think Miles has already made that decision for himself. And what's more, from what I've seen of him, what Miles wants, Miles gets. Maybe, my little friend, this is not your decision to make.'

I close my eyes. A curled-up image of the teenaged Miles in the church porch dominates my thoughts. Opening my eyes, the chair screeches as I stand. I need to do something, anything.

Paint!

'I'm going upstairs to paint; I might be some time.'

I'm halfway out of the door before Suzi replies, 'Whatever happens, you'll always have your paintbrushes.'

Shadows

But it seems I was wrong.

I'd been too impatient to paint. Now I'm glad of it. The fragile and broken pencil strokes add to the vulnerable spirit of the image on my pad.

His knees are drawn up to his chest, baggy jeans clasped by weary arms, laces hang forlorn from well-worn trainers. His face is framed by unkempt hair, eyes are wide and alert, fearful. There's shading under his eye, a bruise or perhaps blood. There's a tear, or just a hint of one threatening to fall.

He's in a church porch, coiled on an uneven wooden bench. His jeans look too long for his legs. A crumpled paper bag rests at his feet.

A shadow can be made out on the wall at the back of him. The shadow of a woman.

Madeline's shadow.

It almost wasn't there, but it crept in when my guard was down. Good, I must always remember, with Miles, there will always be Madeline's shadow.

I look away, watch the particles of dust highlighted by the sun streaming in from the skylight. I always thought that, when I fell in love, I'd be like an Amazonian, strong and able to fight off any challenge.

But it seems I was wrong.

I'm not saying I'm happy to walk away, but that's what I'm doing. I can't let Miles give up this life he's carved out for himself. He deserves to have a settled life after his unsettled childhood. Now I know what went before, what the future needs to be, becomes clear.

And it's not as if I'm never going to see him again. No doubt he'll still pop in to see Mum and Dad. He'll still be Madeline's PA. If I ever do get to popping round to see her, he'll be there too. Perhaps.

The intensity of the last couple of weeks has probably heightened our senses, thrust us together in a way that is overly charged with extreme emotions. Yes, that'll be it, extreme emotions. Don't know why I didn't realise sooner. I glance back at the hunched-up child in the church porch, and know I'll never stop loving him.

'Christie! Are you up there?' Trudy's voice cuts into my thoughts.

'Yes, what do you want?'

'I think you need a hearing test! I've shouted twice. Fish and chips,' she says slowly. 'Suzi's buttering some bread, how many slices?'

'Two, thanks.' I close my pad and put it in the top drawer of my desk underneath my official sketch pad, the one I let anyone see. Miles can rest there awhile, safe. I'll check on him later. I close the drawer, and look up towards the skylight. Bright sunlight streams in. Again, I watch tiny specks of dust floating in the air; they're at the mercy of their surroundings, just like me.

'It's going cold!' shouts Trudy.

I close the attic door and go down to the kitchen. Trudy, Suzi and Miles sit cosily at the table. A mountain of buttered bread waiting to be eaten sits in the middle. Open fish and chip wrappers sit eagerly on plates in front of each of them. Mine remains wrapped.

'Miles texted back…' says Suzi, mischief dancing in her eyes.

'Hello, again. Suzi did invite me.' Miles has the grace to look bashful, though he shoots the smirking Suzi a look.

'Tuck in,' I say, 'don't wait for me; I need to wash my hands.' By the time I sit down, the mountain of bread has been cut down to size.

Suzi has laid aside her knife and fork in favour of her fingers. 'Did you manage to get any painting done?' she asks, waving a chip in my general direction.

'No.' I shake my head. 'Just a bit of sketching.'

'Anything in particular?' she asks.

With a mouth full of chips, I nod, and then shrug.

'I like your sketches,' says Miles. 'They're full of character. The one of Sarah really catches her mischievous nature.'

'Thank you,' I mumble. 'Did you manage to sort out Mrs Price?'

'Oh, yes and no. There's been some graffiti at the back of the mill the other night. Mrs Price had *mistakenly* thought it could have been a couple of our kids. Anyway, we've looked at the CCTV together yesterday, and now she's satisfied it's none of ours.'

'It could have been Banksy,' says Trudy.

'Don't think so. There were three hooded people.'

'So, what's being done about it?' asks Suzi, all eyes.

'Well, Madeline pointed out it is an art gallery, so we've left the images; they're quite good. The police have been asked to keep an eye open for any trespassers. Not a lot we can do.'

Trudy shoots me a glance, then looks pointedly at Miles. 'Are they likely to try and get in?'

'Probably not; the mill is alarmed up to the hilt anyway.'

Suzi snorts, 'That wouldn't stop them if they wanted to damage Christie's exhibition. I don't know what she'd do if anything happened to her art.'

'No need to worry, Christie.' Miles reaches across the table and puts his hand on top of mine. 'I promise nothing is going to happen to any of it.'

'Miles, I know I gave them to Auntie Maddie to keep, but I didn't expect to feel as attached to them as I still do. And I know it sounds stupid, but seeing them all again brings all my memories alive. I remember every one.'

'Trust me. I won't let anything happen to them, okay?' His voice is soft and coaxing as if talking to a fearful child.

I'm not a child, still, I look away. Those pictures are a measure of my childhood. He probably thinks I'm oversensitive.

In my head, my pictures were only ever for Aunty Maddie. I imagined her sat waiting for them, warming gnarly hands by an open fire, and when they arrived, I thought of her having all the time in the world to pour over their every detail. Getting pleasure from me carving out time from my busy career to set aside simply for her.

I thought they'd be propped up on bookcases, balanced on sideboards, wedged behind heavy-cut glass vases, because, surely somebody of Auntie Maddie's age wouldn't be hammering in picture hooks. Or have the services of a local handyman.

Or have an enticing PA called Miles.

I didn't think of a woman in her prime, whose delicate demeanour commands the adoration of an entire nation. Who, just because it seemed like a good idea at the time, could transform an old mill into an art gallery, and organise an exhibition. Who could empathise so effortlessly with disadvantaged young people, make them bacon butties and fairy cakes… offer them hope.

Somebody who, in the midst of her own despair, had enough presence of mind, to recognise a kindred spirit. The courage to take on the challenge of turning the future of a young man's life around. Somebody who'd nurture him into the man he is today, strong, confident and competent.

So now, as Miles assures me my artwork is safe, I know I should trust him. There's just a niggle, Miles and Mrs Price seem to have invested a fair bit of time, trying to find out "who dunnit".

Trudy pats my arm. 'It was probably just kids short of something to do, they'll have forgotten about it by now.'

'Hope so,' I say. But I'm not convinced.

Suzi is nibbling her bottom lip. Always a sign of trouble pending. She looks at me, and offers only a weak smile. 'Miles, Christie said you wanted her to do you a favour.' There she goes, trying to change the subject.

'Ah, yes.' He takes his hand off mine, and coughs. 'It's a big one, but it will pay dividends.'

I raise an eyebrow. 'Sounds ominous.'

'I think.' Miles takes a deep breath. 'I think it would be very beneficial to both you and Madeline, if you could be involved in the interview with her tonight.'

'Absolutely not!' My chair crashing to the floor echoes my attitude. 'How can you ask that?'

'Christie, please…' Miles is on his feet too. 'I don't mean being interviewed with her.'

'I should think not!' I turn to leave the room; I do not need to hear this; can't even believe he's asking. I'm sure Madeline must have filled him in with what happened last time we met.

Oh no! She might have even shown him the portrait, no wonder he kissed me, probably thinks he can have me eating out of his hand.

He catches my arm. 'Listen, please.' His voice is quiet, imploring. I bite the inside of my mouth; swallow back the bile rising in my throat. Half-turning toward him, I raise my chin an inch. 'Thank you,' he says. 'Tonight, your mum and dad are going to be at Maddie's house while she is being interviewed. Your mum thought Maddie might need some moral support. Anyway, the conversation they had, led into "how about you three come into the room at the end of the interview?" And your mum and dad agreed.'

'So, you thought I would too?' My voice sounds alien even to me.

'I thought you might consider it.' He gently squeezes my arm.

Turning to face him, I catch the concerned expressions of my friends; friends who are wise enough to stay out of it, and loyal enough to back me whatever I decide. My moral supporters. I swallow again.

'Why?' I speak softly. Shrug. 'Why should I be there?'

The warmth of his breath caresses my cheek as he lets out a low sigh, I can already feel my resolve starting to crumble. He looks at my lips, for a moment I think he's going to kiss me again. He looks away, and then back, searching me out. Slips his hand into mine.

'Christie, this could be…' he falters. I can see him mentally selecting his words carefully. 'I think this time, right now, could be a healing time for your family. It's been a long time.'

'It wasn't my fault.' My voice is hushed.

'I know.' Again, he squeezes my hand. 'I know it wasn't your fault.' He looks back towards Suzi and Trudy – our spectators. 'Excuse us please.'

I let him lead me back through the kitchen and outside into the garden. The sun is still fairly high in the sky, throwing out her rays of light to the greedy garden, and me, and Miles. The rambling wild roses already threaten to overwhelm the picket fence, and dog daisies dominate the unruly borders. The bird feeder needs filling, again – if Trudy ever catches that squirrel, it'll be a kebab.

It really is a lovely little garden. Through the winter months it always looks kind of sad and unloved. The Buddleia dies leaving a desolate corpse, its bare branches taking on a sinister form from October to March. Only now, in spring does it start to offer a glimmer of life. The perennials creep out almost unnoticed, cramming the flowerbeds and keeping the weeds at bay. By mid-June the boarders become a riot of blooms all competing for their place in the sun, attracting all sorts of insects for Trudy to bat away while she's sunbathing.

Oh, and in a few weeks, no doubt there'll be rounds of debates about whose turn it is to cut the grass, and should we get someone in to trim the hawthorn hedge at the back, even though, really, it's the farmer's responsibility. And ought one of us think about giving the shed a coat of wood preserver, in the hope that it won't completely rot away.

Miles leads me to the bench, it groans as I sit down, reminding me, that it too could do with some TLC. I rest back against the warm brick of the house. He steps back, and sits down on the grass, runs his fingers through it. He plucks a daisy from the ground and passes it to me.

'Beautiful isn't it?' he says, looking around the garden. 'I like the outside, it's honest, no pretence. It is what it is.'

'Mum says that, "it is what it is".'

'I know. I stole it from her. She's a good mum, you're lucky.'

'I know.'

'And that's why, that's why it would be good if you could be there.'

I snort, and shake my head. 'For Mum? Bit of a low blow, Miles.'

'For all of you. I know Maddie, have known her for a long time, and your mum and dad. Your family has been apart for a long time.'

'Like I said, that isn't my fault.'

'I know, but believe it or not, you're the one who holds it together.'

'I don't think so.'

'Listen,' Miles speaks softly, 'I know each of you; and you are all warm and caring people, good people, the best I've ever met. Maddie and your parents are the closest thing to a proper family I've ever had.'

His expression is so intense, I have to look away. 'Sorry,' I mumble.

'Don't be, they've shown me what a family should be like. Not always happy with each other, and more often than not, disagreeing over the silliest things. Your dad and Maddie could bicker for England, your mum is like a referee. I can see how much you love your parents.'

'They should have told me sooner.'

'Maybe they should, that's something you are just going to have to talk to them about. That's something they all disagreed about. They all wanted to protect you, and that shows how much each of them loves you. And they love each other, even when they don't act like it. That's family, simple as.'

'My life was just fine until Madeline turned up.'

'Maddie didn't turn up... she's always been here. She has been waiting for you all those years. Does that sound like a selfish person to you? Because it sure as hell doesn't to me.' His voice is gentle, controlled.

I shake my head.

He drags his hand through his hair, and then leans forward. Crinkles appear at the corner of his eyes as he offers a weary smile. 'I don't know how you feel, can't know how you feel, but please, for all of you, meet Maddie halfway.'

I close my eyes. Please God help me.

Sunlight bathes my skin, and the warmth it brings seems to drain the fight from me. The seed of acceptance matures as I breathe in the fresh air, fragrant with the scents of spring flowers. I open my eyes. Miles is watching me. I don't know if the seed of acceptance will bloom into forgiveness, but I nod. 'Okay, I'll be there.'

'I promise, you won't regret it.'

I hope I don't.

Compromised

The remains of a once-white lacy bra ...

The wrought iron gates swing open automatically, as Miles presses his fob. He drives through, and the gates close. Mature rhododendrons well into their crimson spring bloom line the short driveway, offering added privacy to Madeline's home. I almost gasp as the driveway opens out to reveal a beautifully proportioned house. Impressive conical stone steps lead to a double front door.

To one side of the house, I notice Mum and Dad's car, dwarfed by two huge vans with satellite dishes on top. To the other, there's a ramshackle outhouse with a lean-to greenhouse.

Despite being minutes off the main road, it feels like we're in a country garden, a world away from all the hustle and bustle. I suppose if you've lived your life in the goldfish bowl of celebrity, an oasis of tranquillity is the best cure. And this certainly fits the bill.

The car rolls to a stop behind one of the vans. Miles turns off the engine, and he looks at his watch. 'You okay?' he asks.

Am I okay? He asks some stupid questions.

He isn't even looking at me, more concerned about the time. Clearly doesn't want to be late.

And no, I'm not okay!

He should be looking directly into my eyes, and at least pretend to be bothered. Now he's got his way, or rather, Madeline's way, about this interview, his charm has vanished like a Yeti in a snow storm. He hasn't even noticed I've not answered him yet.

His knuckles are white he's gripping the steering wheel so firmly, almost as if he's afraid to let go. And on the way here, there's been no random finger tapping. He must be more worried about Madeline's interview than mine, she is the main event, after all.

'Bit nervous. It looks very grand, imposing even.'

'It does, I remember how I felt the first time she brought me here. I'd thought houses like this only existed on TV. You'll soon feel at home.'

Somehow, I doubt that. But still I nod, and he smiles back, hopefully content with that. I open the car door.

He touches my arm. 'It's all going to be fine.'

Again, I smile. I must remember to do that when the camera is pointing at me.

'Coo-eeee,' sings Mum. 'We're all in the dining room. It's all very exciting, isn't it? Maddie's front room looks like a television studio, and I've had my make-up done by a proper make-up girl.'

'Mum, you look stunning as ever, give us a twirl.'

Mum does a slow 360. She looks fab. She's wearing a seaside print skirt, coupled with an aqua twin set. Very Mum. She's obviously had her hair done, and I notice she's wearing the pearl earrings I bought her for Christmas.

'Oh Christie, I'm so glad you've decided to come.' She envelops me in a Mum hug, and even though she's had a mini makeover, thankfully she still smells of Mum.

'You look amazing.'

'Oh, thank you. I'm so nervous I could explode, and I'm not even going to say anything. Monty said, you know it's Monty Mitten?'

I nod.

'Well Monty said if it's okay with you, he just wants a tableau of us all at the end of the interview. Anyway, I'm sure he'll tell you, come on.' She catches my hand and leads me towards the steps.

'Oh, Christie!' huffs Mum, and pulls me closer as Dad waits in the doorway. 'Tell him he can't go on the telly in that cardigan!'

'Yes, I can.' Dad plants his hands defiantly in his cardigan pockets. 'What's wrong with it, you're wearing a cardigan.'

'Yes, but mine's new.'

'New! Well, mine is just like me, comfortable and well worn.'

'It's almost worn out!'

'Exactly, just like me. Now that's sorted out, how are you, Christie? I do hope you're not going to succumb to the trappings of make-up and image.'

'Probably a little bit.'

'Well as long as it's just a little bit, I suppose I can cope with that.' He gives me a bear hug and leads me in. The hallway is bright and airy. Fresh flowers sit in a huge vase on a stone pedestal at the base of an elaborate staircase, their scent fills the air. Voices drift through, Monty and Madeline. 'Come and say hello, they're in the dining room. Chin up, Christie, you can do it.'

I can hear Mum and Miles behind, making no effort to join us. Mum is probably enlisting his help to get Dad to part with his cardigan.

I'm as nervous to meet Monty Mitten, as I am to meet Madeline again. He has that kind of reputation – he either loves you or hates you, and since Maddie is his favourite…

'Here she is,' says Dad.

'Well, aren't you the gorgeous one! How lovely to meet you.' Monty glides out of his chair. He's wearing a purple, snake-skin shirt with black skinny jeans, pointy boots and a perceptive smile. His eyes cruise over me as he bows elaborately. Taking both my hands, he leans forward and air kisses each of my cheeks. He smells amazing, and his grip much stronger than I expected. He tilts his head to one side, and looks into my eyes. 'Madeline has told me so much about you.'

I'm taken aback by his intensity. 'Hello, it's lovely to meet you too.' I glance over to Madeline; she's struggling to stand up with her crutches. 'Please don't get up.'

'Hello, Christie.' She perches on the edge of her chair, holding out both her hands to me.

For a hug?

I manage to extract my hands from Monty's, and offer him a shrug of apology. Walking over to Madeline I take hold of each of her hands in mine, lean forward and plant a brief kiss on her cheek. 'Hello, Maddie.'

'Thank you for coming this evening. It's all a bit nerve-racking, but I know Monty is going to do a great job, for both of us.' I glance back at Monty, not sure if I'm expected to say anything.

Monty inclines his head. 'Shall I run through what we've got organised, d-harling girl?'

'Sounds like a plan,' I answer.

'Shall we?' He gestures towards a window seat set in a large bay. He waits for me to sit, and then sits down, leaving a wholesome distance between us. 'So, Madeline and I will watch your interview together in the lounge immediately before our filming begins. We've obviously watched it through a few times already. I must say, sweetie, how well you handled Sarah – she's a wily one. Everything is set up in the lounge for the live filming. Everyone else will be able to watch your interview in the snug, is that right?' He looks to Madeline, who nods.

He taps his lips with his forefinger, then continues, 'And then the fun will begin! Obviously, d-harling, you'll be watching it with Madeline's wonderful mum and dad… your mum and dad too, ha ha.' He flushes at his faux pas and clears his throat. 'So, at twenty-three minutes in, I'll start to wind things up. Some historic images of Madeline will be cut in, and some of yours from the gallery. During that time, you and your parents will be ushered into place.' He claps his hands and clasps them to his chest. 'For an historic family tableau!'

Madeline nods. 'We thought it would look quite natural, if you and Mum perch on opposite chair arms with Dad stood at the back, his arm resting on Mum's shoulder. What do you think?'

'Okay, that sounds okay.' I watch as she visibly relaxes. I want to ask why Miles will not be included…

But then, he isn't *family*.

'And it will then cut back to moi,' says Monty, briefly placing his hand on his chest. 'I'll do the final round-up, and then it will cut to you all around Madeline. And fade…' He sweeps his tanned hand downwards, and rests it on his knee.

'I'm hoping our united front will deflect some of the negative backlash,' says Madeline, more to Monty than to me.

'Madeline, Madeline, your public adore you, clamour for your every word. People are far more open-minded than they used to be, sweetie. I wouldn't be surprised if you gain new devotees, most people admire honesty.'

A tatty terrier trundles into the room, his advance hampered by the remains of a once-white lacy bra hooked over his head and right paw. Despite this, he is holding his head high, and valiantly trying to look dignified. Madeline purses her lips and claps her hands, then points to the floor by her left foot. 'Terry! Heel!'

The dog continues to tootle over to me, sniffs my outstretched hand, gives Monty an insolent glare then ambles over to Madeline. He has at least the grace to bow his head in submission.

'Terry! Have you been stealing again?' The dog lies down with his legs in the air, exposing his pink belly, and black paws. Maddie unravels the bra from Terry and holds it up for inspection. 'That's another for the bin! He's probably done a dozen circuits of the garden with that.'

Monty strolls over and tickles Terry's tummy. 'Isn't he adorable?' Terry's back leg starts to sporadically shake, as if trying to scratch an itch. Monty stops and backs away.

'He's a common thief,' declares Maddie. 'I've lost count of the number of things he's stolen out of the washing basket, half of them buried in the garden, the other half ripped to shreds like this. And it's his fault

I've a broken ankle!' She reaches down and tickles behind his ear. 'It's a good job I love you, little rascal.'

Monty sits down close to Madeline. 'Well, I'm sure when the time is right, Miles will put that broken ankle to good PR use, d-harling.'

On cue, Miles and Mum meander in, arms linked. Everyone, it seems, is very cosy, and I feel like a spare part.

Miles nods towards the discarded bra. 'I see Terry's been up to his usual tricks.'

Madeline sighs, and drops the bra on the sofa arm. 'It's just his nature.'

Dad stands up. 'So, are we all ready?' He picks up the bra, and stuffs it in his cardigan pocket.

From nowhere, it seems, a young woman with a tray of make-up swoops in on me. 'You okay if I just take the shine off?' Before waiting for an answer, she clasps my chin in a vice-like grip. I close my eyes and suffer the assault. Thankfully it lasts only a few seconds, so, either I already look fab, or expectations aren't that high.

'I think we are,' Monty answers for us all. 'Madeline, sweetie, we need to go through now, not long.'

'I'll just hoist myself up,' says Madeline.

Monty, Miles and Dad all rush forwards to help, my eyes automatically roll heavenwards.

'Thank you, thank you, thank you.' She balances delicately on her crutches. 'Must make sure these are out of shot while we're filming, don't want people thinking I'm looking for sympathy.'

That would never do!

I cannot believe it! Even on bloody crutches she's elegant! Her flowing wide-leg pants cover her pink plaster cast. She's wearing a loose chiffon caftan. No doubt it'll be precisely draped around her once she's seated again.

I really must try harder not to be a bitch, but it's very difficult. 'Good luck,' I muster as she's pampered out of the room.

Everyone follows, except me. I relax back in the window seat, close my eyes. I let out a sigh; it's so good to be alone. It's still light outside; I tilt my chin towards the window. Slipping off my pumps, I tuck my feet under me on the seat, rotate my shoulders in an attempt to shift the tension that's been there since all this began.

I can't believe I'm even here. If Miles hadn't given me that speech about "time for healing", I'd be at home getting blotto on vino or vodka, with friends. I'd be healing myself, not— I open my eyes. 'Oh! You scared the life out of me! How long have you been stood there?'

'Only a minute or two,' says Miles. He's resting on the door frame. He seems to do a lot of that. 'I didn't want to come in and disturb you.'

'And, you think standing there watching me, doesn't disturb me?'

'Does it?'

'Errrr yes!' I say. 'Put "not normal", and "behaviour" together, and you've got it.'

'Oh well, never mind.'

I can't help noticing the unicorns frolicking about and plucking at my heartstrings.

He smiles, and walks towards me. 'But you looked like you were either dozing, or deep in thought.'

'I was thinking *I'm not a celebrity, get me out of here.*'

'It'll be over before you know it. It's almost eight o'clock, your mum and dad are in the snug waiting to watch your interview. I was sent to get you.' He holds out his hand to help me up.

'I think I'll give it a miss. It was embarrassing enough doing the interview with Sarah. I'm not sure I can watch myself on TV, Mum and Dad will probably be embarrassed enough on my behalf.'

'I'm sure they're very proud of you.'

'Sure, they are.' Sure, they must be prouder of Madeline. I glance out of the window. 'I love this time of evening, everything seems still.'

'Enjoy it a while longer, I'll go and tell them you'll be in in a few minutes.'

'No. Tell them I'm getting some fresh air.' I slip my feet off the seat and back into my pumps. 'They'll understand. It's not as if every second of that interview isn't seared into my brain.'

'It wasn't that bad.'

'Maybe not for you. Anyway, tell them I'll be in in time for our family huddle.'

'Okay, will do.' He waits for me to leave the dining room first. 'Quickest way out is through the boot room, there.'

I escape in the direction I've been pointed. The air feels cool, much cooler than when I arrived less than half an hour ago. A shiver sneaks up, and shimmies through my body, I rub my hands over my arms.

The garden is made up of deep borders filled with perennials and shrubs all bursting with promise. The tinkle of water draws me to the far end of the garden. A small waterfall trickles into a pond strewn with water lilies closing up for the night. The fading sun sparkles on the ripples of water ebbing over the pond. I crouch down to get a closer look. I squint my eyes to make it into a magical hazy moment, like I used to do with Suzi and Trudy all those childhood years ago.

Evening birdsong accompanies the faint rumble of traffic in the distance. I could be anywhere. I wish I were anywhere but here. Back in fairyland maybe.

I look at my reflection in the water, distorted, like in the funhouse at Driftwood Sands with its wiggly mirrors. Just how I feel, all over the place, belonging nowhere. I hear a twig snap, look up to see Miles strolling across the lawn.

'If you're planning on drowning yourself, may I suggest either off the pier at Driftwood Sands or the boating lake, that pond is only two feet deep.'

'I'm not, but if I were, even I know it only takes a couple of inches of water to drown in,' I return.

'Mind if I keep you company?'

'Not at all,' I lie. 'It really is a lovely garden.'

'It sure is.' Miles sits down on the grass, stretching his legs out before him. 'Maddie spends hours out here. She's been going mad to get out since she broke her ankle. When I called round earlier, she was shuffling round on her bum pulling out weeds.'

'Not an image Madeline De-Muir's adoring public would expect.'

'She's Maddie here, not Madeline.'

'Ah, but Maddie manages to keep her hands beautifully manicured for Madeline's image,' I say.

'Gloves, she always wears gardening gloves. I've noticed your mum always does too.'

Touché. 'Any idea how Mr Mitten is going to maintain her reputation?'

'Mr Mitten is a master. He's going to go all out for the sympathy vote, but in such a cunningly clever way, not even Maddie will know it.' Miles smiles. 'And, even though we've managed to keep her ankle out of the press until now, tomorrow it will be news. Especially the bit about keeping her crutches out of shot, so as not to get the sympathy vote.'

'And you know this because?'

'Madeline De-Muir has an excellent PR team.'

'I thought you were the only team she needed.'

'I'm flattered, but I rely on a small network of excellent contacts who deal with the nitty-gritty. I just drip feed whatever I need out there.' He taps the side of his nose with his forefinger. 'Mostly top secret, I could tell you, but then I'd have to—'

'Yeah, yeah, I get it.'

'Obviously, I'd have to wait until after filming has finished.' His eyes crinkle.

'Ha-ha, I'm so glad you know you aren't funny.'

Miles slaps his hand on his chest, and falls backwards onto the grass looking sorrowful. I bite the inside of my mouth to stop a traitorous giggle escaping, instead I let out a snort.

How ladylike, but I suppose the odd snort is better than hysteria.

Miles raises is head. 'How can you say such words, when my wit is world-renowned?' he says with feeling.

'I thought it was your modesty and charm.'

'Those too.' He nods solemnly.

'Two out of three ain't bad.'

Miles rolls over onto his front, elbows bent, propping his head on his hands. His expression serious as he looks at me.

I feel suddenly vulnerable, just from his expression I know he's reading my soul. Goosebumps creep up my neck and send shivers down my spine, at odds with the flush of my cheeks.

He raises his eyebrows. 'You think I'm charming?'

I shrug, lick my lips. 'I think you can be.'

'I've never been called charming before.' He gets slowly to his feet, and steps towards me. 'Am I being charming now?'

'Nooo! You're being too close,' I mutter, just as his lips brush over mine. My senses blast into overdrive, his hand slips around the back of my neck pulling me closer, deeper under his spell. I pull away, and rest my forehead on his shoulder. A myriad of emotions bubbling through me. 'Miles, no.'

'Don't hide from me.' He lifts my chin. 'You are so lovely, Christie.'

'Don't. Don't say things like that.' I try to shake myself away from his hold.

'But it's true, you are. And you don't even know the effect you have on everyone. On me.'

'Miles.' I close my eyes for a second. 'You and me, we can't, we can't be like this. Can't be anything more than what we are now.'

'And what are we now?'

'Friends.'

'Just friends?' He lets go of me, holds his arms stiffly by his sides. 'Okay, for now.'

'What do you mean?'

'What I mean, Christie,' he says, flinging his arm in the general direction of the house. 'When all this is done, you and I are going to have a serious talk about your future.'

'I know. I'm going to need to make some changes at school, but after a couple of weeks things will settle back—'

'I am not talking about your career, Christie!'

'Well then…' I take a deep calming breath. It doesn't work. 'I'd like to thank you for all your help and concern regarding my family.' I sound like a fraud, even to myself. I hardly dare look at his face – can't drag my gaze from it.

Miles shakes his head and lets out a snort, and then folds his arms firmly across his chest. 'Go on, I'm waiting.' An arrogant smile settles on his face, and I know he can tell he's got me rattled.

'I know it has been your job, but, I know, I'm sure we all know, how seriously you take your work.'

'My work?' Storm clouds gather in his eyes, and a deep frown splits his brow. 'This is not about work,' he growls. 'And let's just leave out the other people I love, because this is about you and me.'

It takes me a moment to process this information… Does he actually mean? 'Leave out the other people you love?'

'That's what I said.' His eyes don't leave my face.

'So, that means,' I can hardly bring myself to say it, 'it means…'

'It means I love you.'

I close my eyes, can feel my heart beat high in my chest, and those blasted unicorns are back doing their stuff. My hand automatically rises to cover my lips, to the memory of his kiss. For a moment I allow myself to dream of a lifetime with Miles.

In my mind's eye, I see us strolling through a meadow hand in hand, with two small children playing tag, a ditsy dog running ahead of us. But then, a shadow falls across the image. Madeline. I open my eyes to reality. 'No Miles.' I shake my head.

'What do you mean, no?'

'You don't know me, so how can you think you love me.'

'I don't know you!' He laughs, sarcasm spears through it. 'I have known you almost ten years.'

'How can you say that?'

'Because it's true! I know you inside out, Christie Harris. I have studied every picture you have ever sent to Maddie, been told about every letter!'

I cover my mouth. 'How could she, they were private!'

'I was jealous of you!'

'Pardon?'

'Always, you were all she ever talked about. You would have been maybe thirteen or fourteen and already so talented at art. I was a nineteen-year-old big fat nothing. A nobody, going nowhere. Okay, so she set me on the path, college then Uni. But when I came home, it was still, always, Christie this, and Christie that.'

'What has that got to do with her showing you my paintings? They were just for her.'

'She had made you sound so perfect, one day I just exploded. Not proud of it. Madeline told me some of what you'd written in the letter you'd just sent her; she'd always shown me your work. But she said your letter was full of problems you were having with your friends, your teachers, your mum and dad. She said there was a fair bit of attitude in there. Actually, you were a bit of a madam.'

'Those letters were supposed to be private.' My voice croaks.

'And you laughed at yourself too. For the first time, I could see you as a normal person, not the super perfect icon Maddie portrayed. After that, before she'd let me see what work you'd sent her, she'd tell me some of what was in the letter first.'

'Every letter?'

'Every single one. I was home from my second year at Uni when you sent *Score*, and then it wasn't you I was jealous of, it was him.'

'I got over him,' I say, and for the first time, realise it's the truth.

'And I got over you. Messed about, dated, and then just buried myself in whatever project Maddie had me working on. To be honest, you were just Maddie's obsession.' He drags his hand through his hair, and shrugs.

'So, what's changed? Aren't I still just her latest project?'

'At first, I thought you could be. But then, the first time I saw you, you just walked into your mum's kitchen and flung your arms around her and started talking to her. You didn't let go.'

'I remember, I'd had a rotten day, Mr Sloan—'

'And you hadn't noticed me sitting at the table, and when you did, you were so defiantly bashful, but you still held her hand, you didn't let go.'

'She's my mum, she's my best friend, and you looked perfectly at home at the kitchen table, like you'd been there for hours.'

'I had; I was. Everything about you, felt so right. It scared me. After that, I was even more determined to keep you at arm's length, for my own sanity.'

'You're not doing very well at it.'

'No, I'm not. And I've lost the battle trying to convince myself I don't love you. And I'm sorry, tonight is not the night to dump all this on you.'

'You're right, it's not.' As if I've slapped him, he turns his face away. 'It makes no difference, Miles. We aren't right together; it could never work.'

'You're wrong, Christie.'

'Maybe.' I shrug. 'Maybe I'm scared, or I'm just not prepared to take the risk.' I start walking back towards the house.

'That doesn't sound like something Christie Harris would ever admit.'

'I'm sorry. Sorry for not living up to your standard of who you think I am.'

I dare not look back. Continue to walk away. And darn the tears that threaten to fall. How can he make me feel like this tonight, knowing I've got to go and play happy families?

'Just for the record, this isn't over,' he says to my back.

I wish I could believe it.

I close the boot room door behind me, rest back on it, and drop my head into my hands. 'Why me? Why?'

All for One

... like an off-pisté skier ...

I edge my way into the snug. On the TV, it looks like Madeline's interview is starting to be wound up. Monty edges forward in his chair. 'I notice by your feet a package. Could that be what I think it is?'

Please no!

It is!

Madeline's coy smile lights up her eyes. 'It is; it's the last piece of work Christie has done for me. She hand-delivered it the other day, and I've been desperate to peep... but... I thought it might offer some insight to everyone, if they could see for themselves the effect her work has on me.'

'So, you haven't even had a sneaky peek?'

'No, and I'm very proud of myself for that! It's been torture.'

'Here, let me.' He reaches down and hands her the package. Madeline nods a thanks, and very slowly starts untying the string.

Why is this happening to me?

I wrap my arms tight around my stomach, I feel sick. Mum does one of her little tight smiles of excitement. Oh please, why?

Madeline opens up the paper, and looks at my portrait of Miles. She raises a hand to cover her mouth, her eyes wide with amazement. The camera zooms in, and a single tear drops to her cheek.

'Are you alright?'

Madeline shakes her head, and hugs the portrait. 'It's too precious. Oh, thank you, Christie, my angel.'

Monty looks directly into the camera. 'So, there we have it, too precious! And the way you're hugging it, Madeline, it looks like you're not going to share this one! But thank you for sharing your time with us, in this live broadcast. I give you, Madeline De-Muir! And now let's have a stroll down memory lane.'

The TV shows Madeline hugging the picture, then it cuts to one of her early appearances in *The Fallen*.

The snug door swings open.

'Okay, folks,' says a man I've never seen before. 'Time to join Madeline for the final shot.'

Dad stands up, but waits for me and Mum to leave the room first. 'I thought Miles would have come for us,' says Dad.

'Got called away,' says the man.

'Must have been important for him to miss this,' says Dad, as we're ushered into the lounge. Madeline tries to stand as we come in. She has rewrapped the portrait, but is still hugging it.

'Oh, Christie, thank you, it's lovely.'

'It's the last one,' I say with a shrug.

Mum and I perch, as directed on the chair arms, Dad at the back of Mum. The make-up girl takes Dad by surprise, managing to dust his face with powder before he flaps her away, next Mum, and then me. Madeline has a dust over too.

'Allow me.' Monty props the package by Madeline's feet.

I'm tempted to lift it out of the room.

'Places, we're back live in one minute,' says the assistant.

Monty sits down, and obliges the make-up girl by raising his chin while she attacks with the dusting powder.

'Didn't she do well?' says Monty. 'If you all give your shoulders a roll, you'll look more relaxed, it's only a camera crew.'

'Okay people, five, four…' The man holds up three fingers, two, one.

'So, there we have it. It's time for us to say goodbye, and as a special treat, I leave you with Madeline, and her family. Goodnight,' says Monty.

I pull my face into what will pass, hopefully, as a smile. Mum will probably look like a Cheshire cat, and Dad, well, I'll have to see when it's played back… He is still wearing his cardigan, though. We sit for what seems like minutes, but the man counts down from ten on his fingers.

'And cut!' he says.

'Well done, everyone,' says Monty. 'I think that went really well. And not showing Christie's picture, Madeline, was a masterstroke! Keeps everyone guessing.'

'It wasn't planned, I was going to turn it to show everyone how brilliant she is…'

'So, do I get to see it now?' asks Monty hopefully.

'Sorry,' she says. 'It really is too precious.'

'Oh well, I'll wait until next time,' he says with a chuckle.

'Girls,' Dad says, wrapping his arms around both me and Madeline. 'You were both awesome, well done.' He kisses the tops of our heads. Hers first. He wanders over and shakes Monty Mitten by the hand. Mum ruffles our hair, and then she goes over to Monty too, leaving me alone with Madeline.

She turns in the chair to face me. 'Oh, Christie, I can see.'

For a moment I scrunch my forehead bemused, of course she can see! But then I remember the portrait, and feel the now-familiar blush creeping up my neck.

'Oh.'

'You're in love with Miles.' Her voice is scarcely a whisper. She rests her hand on mine.

'Maybe.' I shrug. 'But it doesn't matter, nothing can come of it.'

'What do you mean, nothing can come of it? Doesn't he love you?' Her hushed voice takes on the tone of someone who's an authority in these things.

'He says he does,' I whisper.

'So, what's the problem?'

I look at her puzzled expression. She genuinely looks like she doesn't know.

She starts randomly patting my knee. 'Look, Christie, I know...' She rolls her eyes. 'Don't I know; he can be a complete pain in the ass sometimes. When he sets his mind to something, nothing can stop him! And sulk, he can sulk for England. But, actually, and don't tell him I said so, he is one of the kindest souls I've ever met, and I love him to pieces.'

'I can't, and that's why. You love him. He's yours.' My throat closes, as I force out the words.

'Hold on!' She stops patting my knee. 'What do you mean, he's mine?'

'Madeline, it doesn't take a rocket scientist to see what is between the two of you. He hangs on your every word.'

'That's what I pay him to do! He works for me.'

'And the rest! He told me, Madeline! He told me all about being the first *Keep-a-Key* kid. So, you see, I know what you are to each other. You saved him.'

Madeline looks down at her hands. 'We saved each other. That's supposed to be just between me and Miles.'

'Like my letters were just supposed to be between you and me?'

'He told you that?'

'He's told me everything.'

'Then he really does love you. Where is he anyway, he should have been the one who brought you in.'

'We had words,' I say.

'You argued?' she asks. 'Tonight?'

'It was more a disagreement than an argument, neither of us raised our voice.'

'Suppressed discord, that's worse than an argument. I take it neither of you were satisfied with the outcome?'

'Suppose not,' I mutter. What is she, a mind reader? 'It's complicated.'

'Take it from one who knows, get it sorted out. Don't make the same mistake I made, or you'll live to regret it.' She offers a tight smile; it doesn't quite reach her eyes. 'Anyway, something must have sent him scurrying off, it's not like Miles to back off until he's got what he wants.' She pulls out a mobile from down the side of the chair. 'Surprise, surprise, one new voicemail from Miles.'

She taps the phone and holds it to her ear, the colour drains from her face. She tucks it in her pocket. 'There's been some kind of incident at the gallery, he's gone to sort it out. Quick, get my crutches please. Dad! Can you drive us to the gallery? I think there's trouble.'

'Not again!' Dad huffs.

Again?

Dad jingles his car keys. 'He should just leave it to the police.'

'They're the ones who notified him!' says Madeline. I can hear the anxiety creeping into her voice.

Then I remember the phone calls Miles got from Mrs Price. I pass Maddie her crutches as she starts hobbling away from me. Dad rushes from the room.

'Christie, you stay here,' says Mum, gripping my hand. 'I'm sure it'll be something and nothing.'

'It doesn't sound like something and nothing to me!'

'You won't be able to do anything,' insists Mum.

'And she will?' I point towards Madeline, who's halfway out the door like an off-pisté skier, her crutches grabbing frantically at the ground ahead of her.

'Stay!' Mum runs out the door to catch up to Dad, who's already striding across the drive.

'Wait for me!' I shout. Coils of fear add a panicky edge to my voice. 'Please!'

I can hear the engine running, and the tyres screeching on the drive. I sprint to the car gulping air, my chest tight. Yanking open the back door, I launch myself onto the seat next to Madeline, and slam the door behind me. My whole body is prickling with tension. The car jolts forwards slamming me into the back of the driver seat.

'Seatbelts!' barks Dad, as he swerves the car down the drive.

'Press the fob! Press the fob!' squeals Madeline, as we head towards the closed gates. The gates arc leisurely open, and Dad revs impatiently.

'Don't drive so fast!' says Mum. Thankfully the roads are quiet for a Saturday evening, and Dad's driving steadies under Mum's watchful eyes. 'Did anyone think to lock the house?'

'The film crew and Monty are still there,' says Madeline. 'What a mess.'

'Monty might still be there, but at least one of the television vans is following us,' says Dad.

I turn to look out of the back window, and see it, three cars back.

In the distance, I hear the sounds of sirens.

Mum looks over her shoulder to me and Madeline. 'It doesn't mean anything; there are always sirens on Saturday nights.' She exchanges a look with Dad.

My stomach is churning like a witch's cauldron. My mouth tastes like eye of newt and toe of frog. None of this seems real.

A police car is parked across the entrance to the street the gallery is on. Dad stops and opens his window to speak to the officer. I can't make out what they're saying, but I can smell smoke. I strain to see what's happening, but all I can make out is the flashing red and blue lights in the distance.

The gallery is on fire!

All my work! All my work!

How could Madeline be so stupid as to put all my work together in one place?

'Miles,' I whisper. 'Oh, please God, no. Where's Miles?' I open the car door, and empty the paltry contents of my stomach into the gutter, wipe my mouth on the hem of my top.

'There's no way we can get any closer,' says Dad calmly. 'The officer says there's no way. I'll try to find a safe place to park, and take it from there.'

'Didn't you ask him about Miles?' I plead.

'He's just a traffic cop, Christie, he won't know anything. Let's just stay calm.'

'There! Go down there!' shouts Madeline, lunging forwards and pointing towards a back alley.

Dad turns sharply, and the car bumps down the cobbled road until it reaches a brick wall.

'Now what are we going to do?' I hiss. 'It's a dead end!'

'Look up,' says Madeline.

I can just make out the top of the gallery. Pale puffs of smoke drift from the far side.

Madeline taps the side window. 'The other side of that wall is the rough end of the gallery carpark.'

'So, this is as close as we can get,' says Dad.

Madeline looks at me; her face appears haunted in the semi-darkness of the car. She grips my hand. 'We need to find out where Miles is.'

'He'll be with the police, surely,' says Mum.

'But we need to know.' Madeline squeezes my hand. 'If one of us could get over that wall, and talk to the police.'

Mum spins round in her seat. 'Don't be so— No! You can't want Christie to go.'

'Mum, I need to,' I say. An eerie-calm settles over me.

'Christie, no!'

'Mum, I love him.'

Dad releases his grip on the steering wheel, and turns for the first time to look at me and Madeline. 'Christie, this is madness.'

'I need to do this, Dad.' My voice is low, weighed down by emotion.

Dad looks briefly heavenward. 'Is there anything I can say, or do, to stop you?'

I open my car door. 'No, Dad, I'm going.'

Deadly Serious

... finding a lifeless body ...

I let the car door swing shut, and get up close to the wall. It must be almost six feet high. I almost manage to clamp my fingers over the far side of the ledge, the coarse bricks dig into my palms as I try to get a grip. Attempting to scramble up the wall, dusty fragments crumble and fall as my feet struggle to find traction. I hear the others get out of the car. I rest my head on the cool brick.

I'll have to find another way in.

I feel Dad's hand on my shoulder. 'If I can get you over that wall, will you promise me solemnly, you won't do anything stupid?'

I turn and look into his worried eyes. 'I promise, Dad. I just want to make sure he's safe.'

Madeline pulls out her mobile, and starts tapping. I can hear the ring tone. 'He still isn't answering.'

'Keep trying. Anne, Christie needs to know you're supporting her decision here.'

Mum's eyes search mine. 'If you promise to keep safe… come here, be safe my angel.' She pulls me into a hug, sweeps my hair back out of my face, and looks like she's trying to memorise my every feature.

Dad nods. 'Okay, Christie, let's do this.'

Madeline pats my arm, I allow a semi-awkward embrace, and I'm taken aback at the tears I see in her eyes.

Madeline flutters delicate fingers under her eyes, expertly avoiding smudging her mascara. 'Phone us when you know for sure, and be careful. Love you.'

I offer a tight-lipped smile.

Dad pulls me close. 'Now, you've promised me you won't do anything silly.' He rests his hands on my head. 'Father, keep this child safe. Amen.'

'Amen,' I answer the shortest prayer I've ever heard him say.

I run my hand over the coarse bricks, feel a perverse pleasure at the smarting of my fingers.

Dad takes my hand in his. 'This side is not the problem, what you are going to land on at the other side, is. Hopefully, it's even ground.'

'It's probably not, but if I lower myself down, I should be okay.'

Dad nods. 'Yes, and if you can find the torch on your mobile, you'll be able to check it out first.'

'Good idea.' I pat my pocket.

Dad rests his back square against the wall, bends his knees, and makes a stirrup with his hands.

Mum steps forwards, and lifts my left foot into Dad's hands. 'I'm going to count to three, on three, I'm going to push you up by your bum, so you need to take a giant hop, okay? Then you need to straddle the wall with your right leg. Got it?'

'Okay.' I bend my right knee in preparation.

'Okay, on three… one… two… three!'

I hop up. Mum pushes me up with strength I didn't know she possessed. A split second later, while I still feel oddly weightless, Dad lifts me up by my foot resting in his hands.

'Straddle!' says Mum and Dad simultaneously.

I swing my right leg over and cling to uneven bricks on the top of the wall. I let out a breath I didn't know I was holding.

'Well done, Christie, you did it!' says Dad.

I laugh. 'We did it! If I didn't know you better, I'd think you've both done that before.'

'We did a bit of Bible smuggling in Russia during the eighties,' says Mum. 'Before Maddie came along.'

'M-u-u-u-m! And you tell me not to do anything silly. I can't believe you!'

'I didn't promise my parents I wouldn't do anything silly,' she says smugly. 'After all, why should I? I was married to a vicar.'

'Be careful,' says Dad, patting my dangling foot.

'Okay.' I get my mobile out, tap on the torch, and point it down to where I'm likely to land. Weeds, moss and clumps of grass form a border around the base of the wall. 'It looks okay.'

I look across the car park. I can make out two fire engines and a selection of police vehicles all with their lights flashing. Thankfully, I can't actually see any flames leaping from the gallery, but rather swirls of smoke from around the other side.

'Does there look to be anyone you can approach?' asks Dad.

'No, everyone looks to be at the other side of the building.'

'That's probably a good thing,' says Madeline. 'It means you can get closer before you're stopped.'

'Yep. You keep trying to ring Miles. I might hear his mobile when I'm closer,' I say, not sure who I'm trying to convince.

'I will.'

'Here goes…' I drop myself face down on the top of the wall, and then pull up both my legs, so I'm led flat across the top. The cold bricks dig into my skin through my thin clothes. Twisting, I try to balance my body weight onto my elbows with my legs dangling. Tiny stones jab into my forearms. Edging my legs down the side of the wall I try to get a foothold by prodding the wall with my feet.

'Arrrrhhh!' My foot slips down, thrusting my body against the wall as a chunk of brick crumbles. Digging my nails into the bricks, I try to hold for a second longer, take a breath and drop.

'Humph!' My feet hit the soft ground. Instinctively I bend my knees and drop backwards onto my bum, curling my arms around me. Turning, I sink my hands into soft grass, a safe landing.

'Are you okay?' shouts Mum.

'Yes, soft landing on my bum.' I stand, and dust myself down. 'I'm going to make my way over to the gallery now. Wish me luck.'

My mobile's torch gives enough light for me to make out where to walk on the uneven carpark. Everyone seems to be focusing on the other side of the building. I stride towards the gallery, each step hoping to bring me closer to finding Miles.

I'm close to the back door I first entered only a couple of weeks ago. The scrunch of gravel alerts me to someone coming. I run to the back door. Push it. Locked. Two firefighters, fully kitted out with breathing gear round the corner. I flatten myself against the door.

Stupid! Stupid! Stupid!

One of them runs towards me. My breathing quickens, as my eyes desperately dart about looking for an escape route, I'm cornered, can't get away, too close. I slide helpless to the ground, defeated. He grabs my arm, yanks me away from the door. Shouts. Two police officers run toward me, each taking one of my arms.

'What do you think you're doing? This building's on fire!' the first officer shouts. 'Come on, let's get you to safety.'

I turn to look back at the gallery as I'm hauled away. The ear-splitting thuds of a battering ram smashing into the gallery door, fills me with foreboding.

'I need to find someone!' I try to struggle free.

'Wait a minute,' says one of the officers looking at me. 'Is someone in there?'

'I don't know.' Tears well up in my eyes, as the horror of what danger Miles could be in overwhelms me.

'Have you seen someone go in?' asks the other officer.

'No, but—'

'Are you here with somebody else?' he asks.

'No, I'm on my own.'

'So, let me get this right. You haven't seen anyone going into the building.'

I shake my head; try to streak my hand under my running nose. 'No.'

He nods. 'And you are here on your own.'

'Yes.'

'Okay, that's all we need to know for now,' he says.

They both start steering me further away from where I need to be. I try to plant my heels into the ground, but they still keep walking, dragging me along.

'Stop!' I shout, and lift my feet off the ground, desperately try to wrestle my arms free. 'You don't understand!'

'You, young lady, are in enough trouble as it is, don't make it any worse.'

'I need to find Miles! Miles Hepworth!' They loosen their grip, and I slither to the floor. 'Humph.'

One of them holds out his hand, the other lifts me by the elbow. 'Do you know Mr Hepworth?'

'He's, he's a very close friend. We argued, and then he got called out here to this. I don't know where he is, and he isn't answering his mobile. Please, I need to find him! Can you please, please help me?' My stomach turns, I cover my mouth with my hand.

The officers exchange looks. 'First things first, let's get you somewhere we can have a proper chat.'

'Is Miles here?' I ask.

'This way, Miss.'

The roadside is unrecognisable. The flashing lights from three engines and police vehicles create a kaleidoscope of colour. I'm led mute, to a police car. An officer is talking on his radio, he turns and nods. A solitary white ambulance is the only vehicle without lights blaring.

'Has somebody been hurt?' I whisper.

'That's not something we can discuss.'

The new officer turns towards me. 'I'm Chief Inspector Kent. Can you tell me your name please?'

'I'm Christie Harris, and I'm looking for Miles Hepworth, he came here after someone from the police contacted him.'

'Thank you, Miss Harris. I've just had notification from the constabulary, informing me to expect you to turn up at some point... Not a wise decision under the circumstances.'

'Please, I need to know where Miles is.'

'Mr Hepworth was here earlier, speaking with me about recent disturbances at the gallery. He became agitated, and left abruptly.'

'Where did he go?' I look about, where would he go?

'We are not sure of his whereabouts at the present time, although there was an unconfirmed report of someone entering the building.'

'He's in there?' I whisper.

'We don't know, Miss Harris. Like I said, it was an unconfirmed report. I'm sure Mr Hepworth is well aware of the dangers of entering a burning building. The fire is now under control, and firefighters with breathing apparatus are making a thorough search of the building.'

He could be dead. I raise my hand to my throat, panic surges through my veins, my skin prickles with agitation. What if he is? What then?

What if I never hear him laughing again. Or watch as the tell-tale crinkles start at the corners of his eyes. I start to shake; a shiver takes hold of me. I rub my arms, hug myself. I touch my fingers to my lips, to where only a couple of hours ago he kissed me. When I rejected his love. What if the unicorns never frolic again?

The Chief Inspector clears his throat. 'He might not even be in there; we are just taking precautions at this stage. If you would like to wait in the car with one of the officers until we have any news, you can do. Otherwise, I'm afraid I'll have to ask you to remain behind the cordon.'

'I'll wait here,' I say, rubbing my arms.

The ambulance remains still.

'Officer, please stay with Miss Harris,' says Chief Inspector Kent, his tone neutral.

'Miss Harris,' the officer says, 'you'll be warmer in the car.'

I follow him to the car, and sit down on the back seat. He nudges the door to close it. I jam my foot forwards to stop the door from fully closing... Instinct demanding I'm not trapped in here. He seems not to notice, and the car heaves as he sits in the front. Holding the door slightly open with the tips of my fingers, I ease my throbbing foot inside the car and rub it with my other foot.

'You'll warm up in no time.'

'I'm okay.' I need to find Miles.

'The Chief's not best pleased. Someone's got a film crew here, they've probably got long lenses trained on us right now.'

'Oh.' I keep watching the ambulance. If he comes out, when he comes out, I want him to know, need to tell him how I really feel.

'Looks like we're in for a long night, keeping the public away until the building is safe and secure.'

'What will happen?'

'Once the fire is fully out, a specialist team will check if it's structurally sound. If it is, it will need to be boarded up to keep looters out. If not, the road here will need to remain closed, scaffolding put up, traffic diversions put in place, the—'

'Was it arson?'

'Can't say. Forensics will be in before the clean-up, probably on their way; they just love Saturday-night overtime.'

'Why would anyone do that?'

'I can't answer that one.'

And then I remember the fire I started in Dad's Church all those years ago. How Dad took charge of the situation… How he rationalised my actions to the troubled congregation. Only now, do I fully understand the horror of what could have happened that Sunday. The danger I put everyone in.

My whole body feels hypersensitive. Resting my elbows on my knees I drop my head into my hands, my body violently shaking. I feel cold and sick and frightened.

What if all this is my fault?

What if this is payback for all the stupid things I've ever done? My stomach makes involuntary jerks as I'm racked with silent sobs. Wrapping my arms round my body, I attempt to hold myself still by pushing back against the car seat.

My mobile vibrates in my pocket. It's Madeline. 'Has he answered?'

'No, no, so I take it he's not there?' she whispers.

'No. He was, earlier.' My voice sounds odd.

'Where are you?' she asks.

'Sat in the back of a police car, they found me too close to the gallery.'

'Well sit tight, and if… when you find out where he is—'

'I'll phone.'

I slot my mobile back in my pocket, and keep my eyes focused on the ambulance. If the paramedics spring into action—

My mobile vibrates again.

'He's answered!'

'Where?' My head swivels to look around outside. 'Where is he?'

'I couldn't make out it out clearly, only the word "gallery", so he's in there!'

I smash the car door open with both my feet and hit the ground running. A shout from the officer rings in my ears. Keeping my head low I sprint to the back of the building, I know the door has been rammed open. Please God, help me find him. I drown out the shouts and chaos about me. Need to find him.

I jump over the splintered door and into darkness. With no power the meagre emergency lighting offers only minimal help. The acrid smell of smoke attacks the back of my throat, my eyes smart. Blinking rapidly, I squint, trying to minimise the discomfort, cover my mouth with my hand.

'Miles! Miles!' I grope along the wall, feeling my way, trying to remember. Where would he go? Where would be safe? I click my mobile's torch on, push open a door. 'Miles, where are you?' I choke out.

I flash my torch about the room. Not here. Please God, I can't lose him. I follow my hand further into the building. Pushing open the next door, I recognise it as the room I sat in that first day. My torch flicks over the room.

'Miles! Where are you?'

Surely the firefighters will have checked out this room already, I turn to leave, a niggle stops me. I step into the room. Remember Suzi throwing up in the loos, me showering in my underwear.

This room has an annex to the side, I follow the wall round, where is it? My fingers feel along the smooth plastered wall, there! An alcove with a door! Moving forwards, I push the door open and listen.

I can hear his mobile ringing! 'Miles! Where are you?' I croak. His mobile stops ringing. 'Oh please! Miles, answer me! Where are you?'

Only the groans of the building answer. Fear roots me to the spot. I try to focus. The back of my throat feels like I've been drinking paint stripper, and my eyes and nose are streaming. The floorboards creak as I edge towards another door.

Tapping!

There it is again! I ease the door open, partly through fear of what I might find, and partly through fear of causing harm to whoever I might find.

My hand flies up to cover my mouth and I gasp at the sight of the lifeless heap in the middle of the room.

'No!' All the fight dies in me. I drop to the floor, scramble on my hands and knees to the mound. Tapping again. Turning back, I see him.

'Oh, thank you, God.' I clamber beside his crumpled body. Smother his head with kisses. 'Oh, thank God you're alive. I'm sorry.'

I feel oddly weightless as relief swamps me. Drained of all emotions other than love, and relief. I wipe my hand over my face, pushing away the tears.

'Christie,' he rasps. I feel him nod in my embrace. Taking turns at wiping smudges from his face and then the tears from my own face. I close my eyes and hold him close, not sure if I'm ever going to be able let him go again.

'Safe,' he murmurs.

'Yes, Miles, you're safe now. I'll get help.' I stroke his head, his brow furrows and he shakes his head, tries to speak. I can't make out what he's trying to say. His mobile starts to ring. He raises his hand and waves his fingers towards the heap in the middle of the room.

I shuffle across the floor on my bum, the thought of finding a lifeless body flits through my mind. It feels like an old dust sheet, I rummage in its folds to find his mobile.

'Got it!' I press to answer. 'I've got him Madeline. Get help. We're in the private annex near the back.'

'Thank God! How is he?' I look over to Miles slumped near the door.

'Alive.' I disconnect the call. I start to shuffle back to Miles; he shakes his head and points back to the dust sheet.

'Safe,' he croaks again.

I pull back the sheeting, and cover my mouth with my hand. I stare at the heap of paintings, haphazardly stacked together, my eyes and nose still streaming. I shake my head in disbelief. My pictures.

'Oh Miles, for these? You risked your life for these?'

'For you,' he rasps. 'They're all your life.'

'Oh Miles.' I scramble back to him, stroke his hair back off his forehead. 'I was wrong; they're just my journey so far. My journey before I met you.' I cover my mouth again with my hand, close my eyes trying to hold in the sobs. I nearly lost him for these…

Somewhere nearby, I can hear voices and feet clattering about.

'In here!' I shout as loud as my lungs and throat will allow. 'We're in here.' I start bashing my hands and feet on the wooden floor. The closer they sound the louder I stamp my feet.

A firefighter all but falls into the room.

Now we are safe.

Fastening breathing masks over our faces, the two firemen work steadily to secure Miles into a head and body restriction stretcher. Does he need it? Miles struggles to free his hands.

'Steady on, mate, it's for your own good.'

Miles grimaces, and rolls his eyes towards the mound of artwork he risked his life to save. As another firefighter lumbers in, light floods the room casting eerie shadows across the walls. He settles his hand round my arm, starts to lead me out towards the back of the gallery.

I turn to watch as Miles is manoeuvred through the door. The building groans in disapproval as we make our way back towards the smashed-in door. Uneven floors, and the giant dancing shadows hinder our progress.

Stepping out into the crisp night air, I let out a sigh of relief. A shiver runs through me. Again, I turn back to look at Miles, his face and clothing are streaked black. His knuckles blooded.

I could have lost him.

I wait for his stretcher to draw by my side, curl my little finger around his. A faint smile hovers over his lips. A surge of love gushes over me. Pulling off my mask, I bend forwards and brush back the flop of hair from his brow. Look into his eyes. The uncertainty hovering in their depths, almost crushes me.

Putting my mouth to his ear, I whisper, 'I love you, Miles Hepworth.' I rest my forehead gently on his. The relief of saying those words aloud, allows some of my guilt at rejecting him to ebb away. I feel an odd mixture of vulnerability and strength.

'Love you too, Christie Harris.' His broken voice spears my self-control.

Closing my eyes, I squeeze back the whimper threatening to escape. The smell and taste of embers all about, reminding me of how foolish I've been.

How could I have risked shattering our chance at happiness? Now he's safe, I allow myself to cry at my own stupidity.

I open my eyes as a flurry of green surrounds us. Paramedics take over from the firemen. A foil blanket is wrapped over my shoulders. I'm eased away from Miles and into a wheelchair, hurried towards the ambulance. From the corner of my eye I notice a commotion going on close to the police cordon.

Madeline is waving both her crutches in the air in a most un-De-Muir way. 'Christie! It's me! We'll meet you at the hospital! Okay?' she hollers.

I wave at her. Fight the urge to laugh out loud at how ridiculous she looks.

'Christie, don't worry, everything's going to work out fine!'

I bite my lip, wave back and nod.

I hope she's right.

Dawn

'What about Maddie?'

'Mum, Dad, go to him!' I look from one to the other. 'Honestly, I'm alright! And he's all on his own. Mum, please.'

Mum pats my knee, and stands up at last. 'Okay, if you're sure then.'

'Just go!'

Mum brushes a kiss on the top of my head. 'What about Maddie? She's still sat out there.'

I sigh. 'Like I've kept saying, she should have gone with Miles.'

'She won't go anywhere until she's seen you're alright.'

'I am. Okay, she can come in when you go. It's a stupid rule only letting two people in at a time anyway.'

Dad ruffles my hair. 'See you soon, munchkin. And try not to be such a grump, we've all a lot to be thankful for.' His grey pallor is at odds with his upbeat manner.

'I know.' My throat tightens. 'I just keep thinking what if?'

'Well don't, you're both safe.'

I nod, and they wave as they leave the room. The smell of disinfectant, and the blood-splattered screen do little to ease my anxieties. At least I know Miles has already been admitted, I think they've forgotten about me.

I could just leave. It's been hours.

Clunk, clunk, shuffle, clunk, clunk, shuffle. Here she comes – actually, looking wretched! 'Oh, Christie, there you are, poor thing! How are you feeling?'

I shrug. 'I just want to get out of here. I'm fine, really.'

'I'm sure it won't be long now.'

'It's been hours, and you should have stayed with Miles. He'll have been all on his own all this time.' Nastily, I want to say "again", but she already looks close to tears.

'Trudy and Suzi are in with him. I have no idea how Trudy managed to get them both past security. He isn't alone. I would never have left him alone.'

'How is he?'

'I shouldn't have let you go after him.' Madeline lowers her head, but not before I see her tear-laden eyes. She pulls a hankie from her sleeve and blows her nose noisily. Turns away from me to dab her eyes.

'You couldn't have stopped me.' I admit.

Madeline looks back to me, carefully made-up eyes attempt to mask earlier tears. Her composure, so beautifully executed for her audience, is now only a thin veil. Her eyes are drowning in sadness, longing. I can almost see the frightened teenager she once was, in their depths.

I reach across, touch her hand. 'Madeline, really, you couldn't have stopped me.'

'I could have tried.' She shrugs, sighs. 'I thought you'd tell the police that Miles was in the gallery, didn't expect you to go barging into a burning building—'

'I needed to find him. To tell him.' I bite my lip. Now it's my turn to look away, to hide the guilt in my eyes.

'Have you told him?' It's almost a whisper.

'Yeah, I have. I think deep down he knew already.'

'It's important to hear the words, Christie. To be honest enough to say them.'

'I know.' It's like talking to the ever-wise Auntie Maddie. 'It's complicated.'

'Because of me? Don't let it be.' She runs her fingers through her hair. 'Miles is a good man.'

'I know.' I bite my lip again.

At this rate I'll have no lips left.

'And you *do* love him, Christie, that's plain for me to see.'

I feel defenceless under her scrutiny. She knows all there is to know about me.

Madeline, taps her lips with her forefinger. 'I'll tell you something, something I've told no one before. I was sixteen, and thought I was *in love* with your father.'

'Really, Madeline! I don't want to hear about him. Honestly, this isn't the time.'

'Well, you need to hear it, whether you want to hear it or not. So, please. At sixteen, I was pregnant with you.' She touches her flat belly. 'I didn't have the nerve to tell my boyfriend, thought he'd tell me to…' She shrugs. 'I don't know what I thought he'd do. So, I didn't tell him, haven't. That's not the point, I really did love him, and I never told him. And now, all these years later, I've never been able to stop loving him. It's like a part of me is always missing, always longing for him. It's like a never-ending echo of loss. Pathetic, isn't it? I've loved him a lifetime. Your lifetime. And he doesn't even know!'

She holds her hands steady on her lap, her head is held high. At a glance anyone would think her in control, but her eyes plead for my understanding. The urge to sketch her makes my fingers twitch.

A sad smile lingers on her lips. 'You see, Christie, it was complicated.'

I meet her steady gaze, see the pain in her eyes. 'Must run in the family,' I say.

'Don't let it. Buck the trend. You mustn't let *our* relationship come between you and Miles. We'll sort out, it might take us time to get used to each other, but, you know, life can be very lonely, even when it's full of people.'

I nod, acknowledge her loneliness, feel sorry for her.

Almost.

She touches my hand. 'You both deserve more than that, everyone does.'

'How is he?'

'Miles? He has no broken bones, lots of minor cuts, burns, bruises. His hands are a mess. There are still some tests they want to run on his lung capacity, but on the whole, he's doing well. Oh, ranting about your pictures being left in the gallery. I cannot believe he risked his life for them.'

I can, he did it for me. 'I want to see him.'

'He'll most likely be sleeping.'

'I need to see him.'

Maddie sighs, but her eyes gleam with mischief. 'I suppose you expect me to help you break out of here, do you?'

'I think you owe me that much. Sorry. Sorry, just tell me which ward he's on. And if by any chance a doctor does happen to stray into here, tell him I've gone to the loo or something.'

'Ward 10, Men's Surgical. It was the only male ward with a free side-room.'

'I'll find it.' I slip my pumps on, tiptoe to the doorway. I peer out to make sure no one is about, not that I've actually seen any medical staff in ages.

'Christie, you and me, we are alright, aren't we?'

The catch in her voice lowers my defences. 'I think we will be. You're just like my Auntie Maddie, and I love her.' I step out into the deserted corridor, turn back. 'On second thoughts, come with me.'

Her face is transformed by a spontaneous smile. She inhales a deep breath. As she breathes out an aura of peace radiates from her. She nods her head, eyes filled with gratitude, and gets to her feet.

The rhythm of clunk, clunk, shuffle, swings back into action.

We make steady progress through a maze of short corridors, which lead to the main aisle running the length of the hospital.

Reception is practically deserted. Madeline perches on a seat to catch her breath. My skin prickles, as I control the urge to hurry her along.

A row of abandoned wheelchairs looks mighty tempting. We could just borrow one. Maddie stands up, positions her crutches, and we're off... Clunk, clunk, shuffle, clunk, clunk, shuffle. The aisle stretches out, crisscrossed with other corridors leading off in all directions.

'Christie, do you know where we're going?'

'I have absolutely no idea. I'm sure we'll find our way.'

Huge glass windows allow the first glimmers of daylight to ambush the overhead lighting.

The night is behind us, and now, is the promise of a new dawn...

Christie & Co

Kathleen Clunan

Acknowledgements

A debt of gratitude is offered to everyone who has supported me with my writing. I would like to thank specifically, my good friend, Margaret Leak, who gave me the confidence to keep on writing, many times over. Without her support, I doubt this book would have even reached the halfway mark.

Many thanks to the members of Tarleton Tale Tellers for their advice and support throughout. Very much appreciated.

Thanks also to Matt Kenyon of Fertile Frog, who has helped develop my vision for the *Christie & Co* book cover along with my follow-on book, *Maddie's Men*.

And finally, Dr Greg Hall, who has worked tirelessly in helping get this book to publication. Again, without his expertise and dedication, I would not have the pleasure of seeing my novel in print. Thank you.

Book 2: Maddie's Men

The Harris Connection saga continues in the sequel, *Maddie's Men*. As Christie's life seems to be sorted out, we join Maddie to experience the fallout from a lifetime of secrets. Maddie learns the hard way you cannot just walk away from your past without leaving behind a series of ticking time bombs. Unfortunately, one never quite knows when the next is about to explode or how far the ripples will be felt. The first blast from the past hits Maddie on page one, turn over the page and see for yourself.

Kathleen Clunan

Old Flame

Devour every single inch of your body

He shifts his weight from one foot to the other, folds his arms across his chest. 'So?' he demands.

'You found me.' My voice is hushed, breathy. I rest forward. 'Why don't you sit here, Scott? I could make us a nice cup of tea.'

'I haven't travelled five thousand miles to drink tea, Maddie, and I think you know it.'

I nod, pat the sofa. 'But you could sit, I feel ill at ease with you towering over me like—'

'You're ill at ease, Maddie! You feel ill at ease, do you?' Scott lets out a mirthless laugh, turns and walks to the window, rests his hands on the sill and drops his head. 'I can barely bring myself to look at you.'

Cowboy boots and faded jeans. Shirt sleeves rolled up showing off strong, tanned forearms. Open collar, no tie and about two days' worth of stubble.

I feel the old familiar sensations returning, gently, I stroke my clammy hands together. Hold the panic deep inside, kept in check, acknowledged. I try to control the palpitations sparring to control me.

'I know it must have been a shock—'

'A shock! I'd say so.' He turns to look at me.

There's no need for any level of pretence with this man. I can feel his scrutiny stripping away my years of carefully constructed defence. I have no defence; none that will appease him anyway. The set of his jaw and

1

steel eyes are more menacing than I could ever imagine they'd be.

A silent sigh escapes me. 'I never intended you to find out like this, it's all happened so quickly.'

His body, set like stone, except for the barest shake of his head, blocks out the light from my window. 'I don't know how you can sit there and say that, Maddie.' He continues to studies me. 'How could you do that to me?'

I look away from him, the pain is too raw. 'I was young…' I look back up at his face, still handsome after all these years. More so. The urge to cup his face in my hands and kiss away the hurt so brutally exposed in his eyes, draws me back. Precious images, protected from distortion, leap seamlessly into my mind's eye.

*

'I'm out of breath, Scott!' I pant.

'Then stop running! You know I'm going to catch you anyway.'

Sinking against the trunk of an ancient oak, I cherish the bite of its bark, sure it will last only seconds. Throwing my head back as his arms encircle my waist, scooping me off my feet, I let out a squeal of laughter. Half-heartedly try to wriggle out of his grasp, loving the strength of his arms around me.

My breath is fast and shallow, the buzz of anticipation fizzes through my body. I twist and gaze up into his sure face. 'And what do you plan to do now you've caught me?'

Laughter and passion dance in his eyes. 'The same thing I've done every day of this summer.'

The briefest of kisses tempts my lips. 'I can't remember, remind me.'

He lowers me to the ground, kneels beside me, leans close and whispers, 'I'm going to devour every single inch of your body—'

I giggle. 'You think?'

'Oh, Maddie, I know it. Starting with your... EAR.'

Shrieks of youthful abandon are lost in the centuries-old woodlands.

*

'I find out, by pure chance, Maddie, that I've got a fully-grown daughter. An artist, like myself, no less! And you sit there and tell me it happened quickly! I'd like to say I'm impressed by the face of you.' Scott draws his hands over his stubble and sets his eyes on mine.

'I'd moved away with Mum and Dad before I had time to tell—'

'Twenty-five years ago!'

Looking down at my hands resting palms up, I notice the beginnings of calluses caused by my crutches. 'I was sixteen and pregnant,' I say gently. 'I had little choice but to let my parents take care of me.' I raise my eyes back to his. 'You were full of your big plans. Finish college and off to America to seek your fortune. Not once did you say your plans involved raising a child.'

He turns and looks out of the window. 'They were our plans, plans for us.'

'No, I was just tagging on to your dream. Swept along by the romance of running away to the US of A. How could I steal that dream from you?'

'You stole my chance to raise my daughter, our daughter.' He turns back to me. 'I'd have looked after us, Maddie, somehow.'